About the Authors

Sarah Morgan is a *USA Today* and *Sunday Times* bestselling author of contemporary romance and women's fiction. She has sold more than eighteen million copies of her books and her trademark humour and warmth have gained her fans across the globe. Sarah lives with her family near London, England, where the rain frequently keeps her trapped in her office. Visit her at www.sarahmorgan.com

Melanie Milburne read her first Mills & Boon at age seventeen in between studying for her final exams. After completing a Masters Degree in Education she decided to write a novel and thus her career as a romance author was born. Melanie is an ambassador for the Australian Childhood Foundation and is a keen dog lover and trainer and enjoys long walks in the Tasmanian bush. In 2015 Melanie won the HOLT Medallion, a prestigious award honouring outstanding literary talent.

Andie Brock started inventing imaginary friends around the age of four and is still doing that today; only now the sparkly fairies have made way for spirited heroines and sexy heroes. Thankfully she now has some real friends, as well as a husband and three children, plus a grumpy but lovable cat. Andie lives in Bristol and when not actually writing, could well be plotting her next passionate romance story.

The Gorgeous Greeks

COLLECTION

May 2020
Seductive Secrets

June 2020
Playing Her Games

July 2020
A Greek Affair

August 2020
Seducing the Enemy

September 2020
A Greek Romance

October 2020
Her Greek Proposition

Seducing the Enemy

SARAH MORGAN

MELANIE MILBURNE

ANDIE BROCK

MILLS & BOON

First Published in Great Britain 2020
By Mills & Boon, an imprint of HarperCollins*Publishers*
1 London Bridge Street, London, SE1 9GF

www.harpercollins.co.uk

HarperCollins*Publishers*
1st Floor, Watermarque Building, Ringsend Road
Dublin 4, Ireland

GORGEOUS GREEKS: SEDUCING THE ENEMY © 2020
Harlequin Books S.A.

Sold to the Enemy © 2013 Sarah Morgan
Wedding Night with Her Enemy © 2017 Melanie Milburne
The Greek's Pleasurable Revenge © 2017 Andie Brock

ISBN: 978-0-263-28192-7

MIX
Paper from
responsible sources
FSC™ C007454

This book is produced from independently certified FSC™ paper to ensure responsible forest management.

For more information visit: www.harpercollins.co.uk/green

Printed and bound in Great Britain
by CPI Group (UK) Ltd, Croydon, CR0 4YY

SOLD TO
THE ENEMY

SARAH MORGAN

CHAPTER ONE

'No one will lend you money, Selene. They are all too afraid of your father.'

'Not all.' Selene sat down on the bed and stroked her mother's hair—hair tended regularly by hairdressers in order to keep up the appearance of a perfect life. 'Stop worrying. I'm going to get you away from here.'

Her mother lay still. She said 'from here' but they both knew that what she really meant was 'from him'.

'I should be the one saying that to you. I should have left years ago. When I first met your father he was so charming. Every woman in the room wanted him and he only had eyes for me. Have you any idea how that feels?'

Selene opened her mouth to say *How could I, when I've been trapped on this island for most of my life?* but realised that would only hurt her mother more. 'I can imagine it must have been very exciting. He was rich and powerful.' She wouldn't make that mistake. She would never let love blind her to the true nature of the man underneath.

'It's stupid to talk of leaving when we both know he'll never let us go. As far as the world is concerned we're the perfect family. He isn't going to let anything ruin that image.' Her mother rolled away, turning her face to the wall.

Selene felt a rush of frustration. It was like watching

someone adrift on a raft, making no effort to save themselves. 'We're not going to ask him. It's our decision. *Ours*. Maybe it's time we told the world this "family" is a lie.'

Her mother's lack of response didn't surprise her. Her father had dictated to them and controlled them for so long she'd forgotten she even had a choice.

Despite the oppressive summer heat and the fact that their fortress home had no air-conditioning, a chill spread across her skin and ran deep into her bones.

How many years did it take, she wondered, before you no longer believed your life was worth fighting for? How many years before hope turned to helplessness, before anger became acceptance and spirit was beaten to a stupor? How many years until she, too, chose to lie on her side facing the wall rather than stand up and face the day?

Beyond the closed shutters that blotted out the only window in the tiny bedroom the sun beamed its approval from a perfect blue sky onto the sparkling Mediterranean, its brightness a cruel contrast to the darkness inside the room.

To many, the Greek Islands were paradise. Perhaps some of them were. Selene didn't know. She only knew this one, and Antaxos was no paradise. Cut off from its neighbours by a stretch of dangerous sea, rocks that threatened ships like the jaws of a monster and by the fearsome reputation of the man who owned it, this island was closer to hell than heaven.

Selene tucked the covers around her mother's thin shoulders. 'Leave everything to me.'

That statement injected her mother with an energy that nothing else could. 'Don't make him angry.'

She'd heard those words more often than she could count.

She'd spent her life tiptoeing around 'angry'.

'You don't have to live like this, watching everything

you say and everything you do because of him.' Looking at her mother, Selene felt sad. Once, she'd been a beauty and it had been that blonde, Nordic beauty that had attracted the attention of the rich playboy Stavros Antaxos. Her mother had been dazzled by wealth and power and she'd melted under his charm like candle wax under a hot flame, never seeing the person beneath the smooth sophistication.

One bad choice, Selene thought. Her mother had made one bad choice and then spent years living with it, her heart and spirit crushed by a life spent with a ruthless man.

'Let's not talk about him. I had an e-mail this week from Hot Spa in Athens.' She'd been nursing the news for days, not daring to share it before now. 'Remember I told you about them? It's a really upmarket chain. And they have spa hotels on Crete, Corfu and Santorini. I sent them samples of my candles and my soap and they *love* them. They used them in their treatment rooms and three of their top clients insisted on taking them home and paid a fortune for the privilege. Now they want to talk to me and put in a large order. It's the break I've been hoping for.' She was buzzing inside and longing to share the excitement so it came as a blow when her mother's only response was to shake her head.

'He'll never let you do it.'

'I don't need his permission to live my life the way I want to live it.'

'And how are you going to live it? You need money to set up your business and he won't give you money that enables us to leave him.'

'I know. Which is why I don't intend to ask him. I have another plan.' She'd learned not to speak without first checking to see who might be listening and instinctively she turned her head to see that the door was closed, even though this was her mother's bedroom and she'd secured the door herself. Even though *he* wasn't even on the island. 'I'm leaving tonight and I'm telling you this because I won't be able to contact you for a few days and I don't want you to worry about me. As far as everyone is concerned I am at the convent for my usual week of retreat and meditation.'

'How can you leave? Even if you could slip past his security and make it off the island you will be recognised. Someone will call him and he will be furious. You know how obsessed he is about maintaining the image of the perfect family.'

'One of the advantages of being the shy, reclusive daughter of a man feared by everyone is that no one is expecting to see me. But just to cover all eventualities I have a disguise.' And she didn't intend to share the details with anyone. Not even her mother, who was now looking at her with panic in her eyes.

'And if you do manage to make it as far as the mainland, what then? Have you thought that far?'

'Yes, I've thought that far.' And further, much further, to a future that was nothing like the past. 'You don't need to know any of this. All you need to do is trust me and wait for me to return and fetch you. I'd take you now only two of us travelling together are more likely to attract attention. You have to stay here and keep up the perfect family pretence for just a little longer. Once I have the money and somewhere to stay I'm coming back for you.'

Her mother gripped her arm tightly. 'If by any chance you manage to do this, you should not come back. It's too late for me.'

'It drives me mad when you say things like that.' Selene hugged her mother. 'I will come back. And then we're leaving together and he can find someone else to control.'

'I wish I had money to give you.'

So did she. If her mother had maintained her independence then perhaps they wouldn't be in this mess now, but her father's first and cleverest move following his marriage had been to ensure his wife had no income of her own, thus making her dependent on him in every way. Her mother had confessed that at first she'd found it romantic to have a man who wanted to care for her. It had been later, much later, that she'd realised that he hadn't wanted to care for her. He'd wanted to control her. And so her mother's independence had slowly leeched away, stolen not by a swift kill but by a slow, cruel erosion of her confidence.

'I have enough to get me to Athens. Then I'm going to get a loan to start my business.' It was the only option open to her and she knew other people did it all the time. They borrowed money and they paid it back and she would pay it back, too. All of it.

'He has contacts at all the banks. None of them will loan you money, Selene.'

'I know. Which is why I'm not going to a bank.'

Her mother shook her head. 'Name one person who would be prepared to do business with you. Show me a man with the guts to stand up to your father and I'll show you a man who doesn't exist.'

'He exists.' Her heart pumped hard against her chest and she forced herself to breathe slowly. 'There is one man who isn't afraid of anyone or anything. A strong man.'

'Who?'

Selene kept her voice casual. 'I'm going to see Stefanos Ziakas.'

The name alone drained the colour from her mother's face. 'Ziakas is another version of your father. He's a ruthless, self-seeking playboy with no conscience and not one shred of gentleness in him. Don't be fooled by that handsome face and that charismatic smile. He's deadly.'

'No, he isn't. I met him once, years ago, on the yacht on one of the occasions we were forced to play "happy families" in public. He was kind to me.' Selene was annoyed to feel herself blushing.

'If he was kind, it was because he knew it would annoy your father. They hate each other.'

'He didn't know who I was when we started talking.'

'You were the only seventeen-year-old there. It was obvious who you were.' Her mother sounded weary. 'Ask yourself why a sophisticated man like him would spend his time talking to you when he came with the actress Anouk Blaire.'

'He told me she was boring. He said she only cared about how she looked and who wrote about her and that being with him enhanced her career. He said I was much more interesting. We talked all night.' About everything. She'd told him things she'd never told anyone before. Not about her family, of course—she was too well trained to let that particular truth slip—but she'd talked about her dreams and her hopes for the future and been grateful when he hadn't laughed. He'd listened with those sexy eyes fixed on her and when she'd asked him if he thought she might be able to run a business one day he'd spoken words she'd never forgotten.

You can do anything if you want it enough.

Well, she wanted it.

Her mother sighed. 'The schoolgirl and the billionaire. And because of this one conversation you think he'll help you?'

Come back in five years, Selene Antaxos, then maybe we'll talk.

She'd wanted to do a whole lot more than talk and she suspected he'd known that, just as she suspected he'd guessed the truth about the fabricated life she led. She'd felt more of a connection with him than she had with any other human being. For the first time in her life someone had listened to her and his words had stayed with her, day and night. When life had grown hard it had been a comfort to remember that she had someone to go to if things were desperate.

And things *were* desperate.

'He'll help me.'

'That man is more likely to hurt you than help you. You have no experience of men like him. I would not put you with a man like Ziakas. I would find you someone kind and gentle who deserves you.'

'I don't want him to be kind or gentle. I need him to be ruthless or this isn't going to work. If he doesn't have the guts to stand up to my father then there is no hope for my plan. I want to run my own business and Ziakas knows more about how to do that than anyone. He did it all himself. He lost his parents when he was young. No one helped him. No one gave him a helping hand. And look at him now. He was a billionaire by the time he was thirty and he did that by himself.'

She found his story inspirational. If he could do it, why couldn't she?

Her mother struggled upright, finding energy from anxiety. 'Do you honestly think you'll just be able to walk up to a man like Stefan Ziakas and ask him for money? He is protected from the outside world by layers of security, just like your father. Getting an appointment with someone like him would be almost impossible, especially at short notice. Even if you could somehow find a way to leave the island undetected while your father is away, Ziakas won't see you.'

'He'll see me. And I have found a way to leave the island.' Determined not to reveal too much, and even more determined not to let her mother batter her confidence, Selene stood up. 'I will be back tomorrow, which gives us plenty of time to get far away before my father returns from—from his trip.' 'Trip' was the word they both used to describe her father's frequent absences from the island. It disgusted Selene that he didn't even bother to keep his infidelities a secret. Disgusted her more that her mother accepted them as part of the marriage deal.

She couldn't allow herself to think about what she'd do if her mother refused to leave, as she'd refused so many times before. All she knew was that she didn't want to spend anther day on Antaxos. She'd lived here all her life, trapped within its rocky shores, thirsty for a life other than the one she'd been given. She didn't want to spend another day in this 'family' pretending that everything was perfect.

The events of the last week had shown her that she had to do it sooner rather than later.

Bending down, she kissed her mother on the cheek. 'Dream about what you're going to do on the first day of your new life. You're going to laugh without worrying that the sound is going to draw his attention. You're going to paint again and people will buy those paintings, just as they used to.'

'I haven't painted for years. I don't feel the urge any more.'

'That's because he didn't like you doing anything that took you away from him.' The anger was like an energy source, giving her a determination that felt close to power. 'You're going to get your life back.'

'And if your father returns from Crete early and finds you gone? Have you thought of that?'

It was like stepping off a cliff or missing a step on the

stairs. Her heart bumped uncomfortably and she wanted to clutch something for support. 'He won't return early. Why would he?'

Bored out of his mind, Stefan lounged with his feet on his desk.

Far beneath the glass cocoon that housed his corporate headquarters, Athens was slowly waking up. Athens, a city in trouble, licking its wounds as the world watched in wary fascination. People encouraged him to move his base to a different city. New York. London. Anywhere other than the troubled Greek capital.

Stefan ignored them.

He had no intention of abandoning the place that had allowed him to become who he was. He knew what it was like to have everything and then lose it. He knew how it felt to go from prosperity to poverty. He understood fear and uncertainty. And he knew all about the effort required to drag yourself back from the edge. It made winning all the more satisfying and he'd won in a big way. He had money and power.

People would have been surprised to learn the money didn't interest him. But power? Power was different. He'd learned at an early age that power was everything. Power opened doors that were closed. Power turned no to yes and stop to go. He'd learned that power was an aphrodisiac and, when it needed to be, it was a weapon.

It was a weapon he wasn't afraid to use.

His phone rang for the tenth time in as many minutes but he chose to ignore it.

A tap on the door disturbed his thoughts. Maria, his PA, stood in the doorway.

Irritated by the interruption, Stefan lifted an eyebrow in question and she pursed her lips.

'Don't give me that look. I know you don't want to be disturbed, but you're not answering your personal line.' When he still didn't answer, she sighed. 'Sonya's PA has been ringing and when you didn't answer Sonya herself called. She isn't in a good mood.'

'She is phoning to give me an update on her moods? I have marginally more interest in the weather forecast.'

'She wanted me to give you a message. She said to tell you she's not playing hostess at your party tonight until you make a decision about your relationship. Her exact words were…' Maria cleared her throat. '"Tell him it's either on or off."'

'It's off. I already told her that in words that even she should have been able to understand.' Exasperated, Stefan picked up his phone and deleted all his messages without listening to them. Even without looking he could feel Maria's censorship and he smiled. 'You've worked for me for twelve years. Why the long face?'

'Doesn't the end of a relationship *ever* bother you?'

'Never.'

'That says something about you, Stefan.'

'Yes. It says I'm good at handling break-ups. Go, me.'

'It says you don't care about the women you date!'

'I care as much as they do.'

With a despairing shake of her head, Maria cleared two empty coffee cups from his desk. 'You have your pick of women and you can't find *one* you want to settle down with? You are a success in every aspect of your life except one. Your personal life is a disaster.'

'I happen to consider my personal life an unqualified success.'

'You must want more than this from a relationship.'

'I want hot, frequent, uncomplicated sex.' He smiled

at her disapproving expression. 'I pick women who want the same thing.'

'Love would be the making of you.'

Love?

Stefan felt something slam shut inside him. He swung his legs off his desk. 'Did your job description change when I wasn't looking? Has there been some EU employment law that requires you to take charge of my private life?'

'Fine. I can take the hint. It's none of my business. I don't know why I even bother.' The cups rattled in her hand as she stalked through the door but she was back moments later. 'There's someone here to see you. Perhaps she'll be able to persuade you to get in touch with your human side.'

'She? I thought my first appointment wasn't until ten o'clock?'

'This person doesn't have an appointment, but I didn't feel comfortable turning her away.'

'Why not? I employ you to be the dragon at my door.'

'I can be dragon-like when I have to be but not when the person wanting to see you is a nun.'

'A *nun*? You have to be kidding me.'

'She says she has something urgent to discuss with you.'

Stefan gave a sardonic smile. 'If she's here to save my soul, tell her she's too late.'

'I will not. To be honest I have no idea what to say to her.'

'Any combination of words would have sufficed, providing "no" and "get out" were included.'

Maria squared her shoulders. 'I can't turn a nun away. I don't want that on my conscience.'

Stefan, who hadn't made the acquaintance of his conscience for several decades, was exasperated. 'I never saw you as gullible. Has it occurred to you she's probably a stripper?'

'I know a genuine nun's habit when I see one. And your cynicism does you no credit.'

'On the contrary, my cynicism has protected me nicely for years and will continue to do so—which is just as well given that you're turning into a soft touch.'

'I'm sorry, but there's no way I can tell a nun you won't see her. And she has a really sweet smile.' Maria's face softened momentarily and then she glared at him. 'If you want it done, you'll have to do it yourself.'

'Fine. Send her in. And then take a trip to the nearest fancy dress store and see for yourself how easy it is to hire a nun's costume.'

Clearly relieved to have offloaded that responsibility, Maria retreated, and Stefan felt a rush of irritation at the thought of an interruption that would bring him no benefit.

His irritation intensified at the sight of a nun in a black habit standing in the doorway to his office. Under the robes he could see that she was slightly built but she kept her head bowed, allowing him a single glimpse of a pale face under flowing black and white.

Unmoved by her pious attitude, Stefan leaned back in his chair and scrutinised his unwanted visitor. 'If you're expecting me to confess my sins then I should probably tell you that my next appointment is in an hour and that is nowhere near long enough for me to tell you all the bad things I've done in my life. On the other hand if you're about to beg for cash then you should know that all my charitable donations are handled through my lawyers, via a separate part of my company. I just make the money. I leave other people to spend it.'

The tone he used would have had most people backing towards the door but she simply closed it so that they were alone.

'There is no need to close the door,' he said coldly, 'because you're going to be going back through it in approximately five seconds. I have no idea what you're expecting to gain by…' The words died in his throat as the nun removed her hood and hair the colour of a pale moonbeam tumbled in shiny waves over her black habit.

'I'm not a nun, Mr Ziakas.' Her voice was soft, breathy and perfect for the bedroom, a thought that clashed uncomfortably with the vision of her in a nun's outfit.

'Of course you're not,' Stefan drawled, his eyes fixed on her glorious hair, 'but you managed to convince my hardened PA so I suppose you should get points for that.' Suddenly he was annoyed with Maria for allowing herself to be so easily manipulated. 'I'm used to women using all sorts of devices in order to meet me, but I've never yet had one stoop so low as to impersonate a nun. It smacks of desperate behaviour.'

'I'm not impersonating anyone. But it was essential that I keep a low profile.'

'I hate to break this to you, but in the business district of Athens a nun's habit is *not* considered camouflage. You stand out like a penguin in the Sahara. If you want to blend, next time dress in a suit.'

'I couldn't risk being recognised.' Her eyes flickered to the huge glass windows of his office and after a moment she sidled across and peered down at the city while he watched in mounting exasperation.

Who would recognise her? Who was she? Someone's wife?

There *was* something vaguely familiar about her face. His mind coming up blank, he tried to imagine her without her clothes to see if he could place her, but mentally stripping a nun proved a stretch even for him. 'I don't sleep with married women so that can't be the reason for the elaborate subterfuge. Do we know each other? If so, you're going to have to remind me.' He raised an eyebrow as a prompt. 'Where? When? I admit to being hopeless with names.'

She dragged her gaze from the view, those green eyes direct. 'When and where what?'

Stefan, who hated mysteries and considered tact a quality devoid of reward, was blunt. 'Where and when did we have sex? I'm sure it was amazing but you're going to have to remind me of the details.'

She made a sound in her throat. 'I haven't had sex with you!'

'Are you sure?'

Green eyes stared back at him. 'If rumour is correct, Mr Ziakas, sex with you is a memorable experience. Is it something I'm likely to have forgotten?'

More intrigued than he would have been willing to admit, Stefan sat back in his chair. 'You clearly know a great deal more about me than I do about you. Which brings me to the obvious question—what are you doing here?'

'You told me to come and see you in five years. Five years is up. It was up last week, actually. You were kind to me. The only person who was.'

There was a wistful note in her voice that sparked all the alarm bells in his head. Trained to detect vulnerability from a hundred paces so that he could give it a wide berth, Stefan cooled his voice.

'Then this is clearly a case of mistaken identity because I'm never kind to women. I work really hard *not* to be or they start to expect it and the next thing you know they're dropping hints about rings, wedding planners and a house in the country. *Not* my style.'

She smiled at that. 'You were definitely kind to me. Without you I think I would have thrown myself overboard at that party. You talked to me for the whole night. You gave me hope.'

Stefan, all too aware that he was widely regarded as the executioner of women's hopes, raised his eyebrows. He stared at that glorious hair and filed through his memory bank. 'Definitely a case of mistaken identity. If I'd met you, we definitely wouldn't have wasted a night talking. I would have taken you to bed.'

'You told me to come back in five years.'

That news caught his attention and Stefan narrowed his eyes. 'I'm impressed by my own restraint.'

'My father would have killed you.'

My father would have killed you.

Stefan stared at her, his eyes sweeping her face for clues, and suddenly he stilled. Those beautiful washed-green eyes were a rare colour he'd only seen once before, hidden behind a pair of unflattering glasses. 'Selene? Selene Antaxos.'

'You *do* recognise me.'

'Barely. *Theé mou*—' His eyes swept her frame. 'You've—grown.' He remembered her as a gangly blonde who still had to grow into her lean body. An awkward teenager completely dominated by her overprotective father. A pampered princess never allowed out of her heavily guarded palace.

Stay away from my daughter, Ziakas.

It was the unspoken threat that had made him determined to talk to her.

Just thinking of the name Antaxos was enough to ruin his day and now here was the daughter, standing in his office.

Dark emotion rippled through him, unwelcome and unwanted.

He reminded himself that the daughter wasn't responsible for the sins of the father.

'Why are you dressed as a nun?'

'I had to sneak past my father's security.'

'I can't imagine that was easy. Of course if your father didn't make so many enemies he wouldn't need an entire army to protect him.' Blocking the feelings that rose inside him, he stood up and strolled round his desk. 'What are you doing here?'

The one thing he did remember from that night was feeling sorry for her and the reason he remembered it was because he so rarely felt sorry for anyone. He believed that people made their own choices in life, but he'd taken one look at her in all her leggy, uncomfortable misery and decided that being the daughter of Stavros Antaxos must be the shortest straw anyone could ever draw.

'I'll get to that in a minute.' She bent down and caught hold of the hem of her habit. 'Do you mind if I take this off? It's really hot.'

'Where did you get it? The local dressing-up shop?'

'I was educated by the nuns on Poulos, the island next to ours, and they've always been very supportive. They lent it to me but there's no point in keeping it on now I'm safe with you.'

Knowing that most women considered him anything but 'safe', Stefan watched in stunned disbelief as she wriggled and struggled until finally she freed herself and emerged with her hair in tangled disarray. Underneath she was wearing a white silk shirt teamed with a smart black pencil skirt that hugged legs designed to turn a man's mind to pulp.

'I almost boiled to death on the ferry. You have no idea. That's why I couldn't wear the jacket.'

'Jacket?'

'The jacket from my suit. It's designed to be worn in an air-conditioned office, not a floating tin can which is how the ferry feels.'

Stefan wrenched his gaze from those bare legs, feeling as if he'd been hit round the head with a brick. Staring into those green eyes, he looked for some sign of the awkward teenage girl he'd met years before. 'You look different.'

'I should hope so. I hope I look like a businesswoman because that's what I am.' She slid her arms into a jacket that matched the skirt, scooped up her hair and pinned it with brisk efficiency. 'When you met me five years ago I had spots and braces. I was hideous.'

She wasn't hideous now. 'Does your father know you're here?'

'What do you think?'

The corner of her mouth dimpled into a naughty smile and Stefan stared at that smile, hypnotised by her lips, trying to clear his mind of wicked thoughts.

'I think your father must be having a few sleepless nights.' The wicked thoughts still very much in play, he tried desperately to see her as she'd been that night on the boat. Young and vulnerable. 'I should offer you a drink. Would you like a—' he groped for something suitable '—a glass of milk or something?'

She pushed some loose strands of her hair away from her face in a gesture that somehow managed to be both self-conscious and seductive. 'I'm not six. Do you often offer your visitors milk?'

'No, but I don't usually entertain minors in my office.'

'I'm not a minor. I'm all grown up.'

'Yes. I can see that.' Stefan loosened his collar and discovered it was already undone. He wondered if the air-conditioning in his office was failing. 'So—why don't you tell me why you're here?'

If she wanted him to ruin her father, they might yet find themselves with a common goal.

'I'm here about business, of course. I have a business proposition.'

Huge eyes were fixed hopefully on his face and Stefan felt an instant pull of lust. The explosion of attraction was instant, unmistakable—and entirely inappropriate given the circumstances.

Apart from the obvious physical changes she still looked as innocent as she had that night on the boat. It would be asking for trouble. Even he wasn't going to stoop that low.

'I'm not known for doing favours for people.'

'I know. And I'm not expecting a favour. I know a lot about you. I know you date different women all the time because you don't want a relationship. I know that in business they call you all sorts of things, including ruthless and uncaring.'

'Those are generally good traits to have in business.'

'And you never deny any of those awful things they write about you. You're happy to be portrayed as the big bad wolf.'

'And yet still you're here.'

'I'm not afraid of you. You sat with me for seven hours and talked to me when no one else could be bothered.' Folding the nun's habit carefully, she leaned forward to stuff it into her bag, oblivious to the fact that the movement gave him a perfect view of the curve of her breasts above a hint of lacy bra.

Stefan made a valiant attempt to avert his eyes and failed. 'You were sweet.'

He emphasised the word for his own benefit. If there

was one thing designed to kill his libido it was 'sweet', so why the hell was he painfully aroused? And why was she looking at him with big trusting eyes when what he should have been seeing was an appropriate degree of caution?

Come into my house, Little Red Riding Hood, and close the door behind you.

Caution nowhere in sight, she gave him a warm smile. 'It's a bit embarrassing to remember it, to be honest. I was so upset I would have done anything just to make my father mad, but you refused to take advantage of me even though you hate him. You didn't laugh at me when I told you I wanted to set up my own business and you didn't laugh when I flirted with you. You told me to come and find you in five years, which I thought was very tactful.'

She spoke quickly, almost breathless as she got the words out, and Stefan stared at her for a long moment, all his instincts telling him that something wasn't quite right.

Was he seeing desperation or enthusiasm?

Stefan bought himself some time. 'Are you sure you wouldn't like something cold to drink?'

'I'd *love* some champagne.'

'It's ten in the morning.'

'I know. It's just that I've never tasted it and I thought this would be the perfect opportunity. According to the internet you live a champagne lifestyle.' There was a wistful note in her tone that didn't make sense. He'd assumed the Antaxos family bathed in champagne. They were certainly rich enough.

'Believe it or not I try and restrict my champagne consumption until the end of my working day.' Clenching his jaw, Stefan hit a button on his phone. 'Maria? Bring us a jug of water, or lemonade, or—' he racked his brains for a suitable soft drink '—or something soft and refreshing.

With ice,' he added as an afterthought. 'Lots of ice. And some pastries.'

'That's thoughtful of you. I'm starving.'

Stefan leaned against his desk, maintaining a safe distance. 'So—you say you have a business proposition. Tell me about it and I'll tell you if I can help.' Those words felt alien on his tongue. When did he ever help anyone but himself? He'd learned at an early age to take care of himself and he'd been doing it ever since.

'I want to set up my own business just like you did. That night on the yacht, you inspired me. You talked about how you'd done it all yourself and about how great it felt to be independent and not rely on anyone. I want that.' She dug her hand into her bag again and pulled out a file. 'This is my business plan. I've worked hard on it. I think you'll be impressed.'

Stefan, who was rarely impressed by other people's business plans, gingerly took the pink file from her outstretched hand. 'Is there an electronic version?'

'I didn't want to save it on the computer in case my father found it. It's the figures that count, not the presentation.'

So her father knew nothing about it. Perhaps that explained the hint of nerves he detected beneath all that bounce and optimism.

No doubt this was her summer project, designed to fill the long boring hours that came with being an overprotected heiress, and he was the lucky recipient of her endeavours.

Shaking off the feeling that something wasn't quite right about the whole situation, Stefan flipped open the file and scanned the first page. It was surprisingly professional. 'Candles? That's your business idea?'

'Not just candles. Scented candles.' Her voice vibrated

with enthusiasm. 'I went to school in a convent. I started making candles in craft lessons and I experimented with different scents. I have three different ones.'

Candles, Stefan thought. The most boring, pointless product on planet earth.

How the hell was he going to let her down gently? He had no experience of letting people down gently. He just dropped them from a great height and stepped over their broken remains.

Clearing his throat, he cultivated what he hoped was an interested expression. 'Why don't you tell me a bit more about what makes them special? Top line? I don't need detail.' Please, God, no detail. As far as he was concerned talking about candles would be one step down from talking about the weather.

'I've called one Relax, one Energise and one—' her cheeks turned a deeper shade of pink '—Seduction.'

Something in the way she hesitated over the word made him glance up from the file. She was trembling with anticipation, and all it took was one glance to know that his first assumption had been correct.

She was a bored heiress, playing at business.

And now she'd prompted him he could clearly remember the night they'd met.

She'd been a teenager—miserable, confused and self-conscious. An ugly duckling dumped in the middle of a flock of elite swans with a doting father who barely took his eyes off her. None of the other men had dared talk to her, none of the women had wanted to, so she'd stood alone, her awkwardness almost painful to witness.

But she was no longer that teenager. She was all woman, and she knew it.

Stavros Antaxos must be having *lots* of sleepless nights.

And now she was looking at him with those big eyes filled with unwavering trust.

Stefan knew she couldn't have found a man less worthy of that trust.

He wondered just how much she knew about his relationship with her father.

The atmosphere in the room shifted.

When he was sure he had his reactions under control, he closed the file slowly and looked at her. 'So your candles are called, Relax, Energise and Seduction?'

'That's right.'

'And just how much,' he asked slowly, 'do you know about seduction?'

CHAPTER TWO

GREAT. Of all the questions to ask, he had to ask that one.

Not market share or growth forecasts—seduction.

Selene maintained the smile she'd been practising—her business smile—while her brain raced around in crazy circles getting nowhere.

What did she know about seduction? Nothing. Nor was it a skill she was ever likely to need unless her life changed radically. What she did know was that without his help she'd never get her mother away from the island. It was up to her to prove she had a viable business. 'What do I know about seduction? Not a lot. But you know what they say— you don't have to travel the world to teach geography.'

She didn't add that she had her imagination and that was already working overtime.

She'd often wondered if her teenage brain had exaggerated his appeal or whether her own misery that night, together with his kindness, had somehow mingled together to create a god from a man. But he was as gorgeous as she remembered—power, strength and raw virility merged together in a muscle-packed masculine frame that made her feel dizzy with thoughts she couldn't seem to control.

Physically he was imposing, but it wasn't his impressive height or the width of those shoulders that shook her. It was something less easily defined. A hint of danger—

the sense that underneath that beautifully cut suit and the external trappings of success lurked a man who wielded more power than even her father.

Flustered, Selene tried to remember the way he'd been on that night five years earlier, but it was almost impossible to equate that kind stranger with this cool, sophisticated businessman standing in front of her.

And the fact that he was flicking through her amateurish document so quickly left her squirming with embarrassment. He barely took any time as he glanced at each page, nothing in his face giving a hint as to his thoughts. Clearly he thought it was rubbish.

Her mother was right. He was never going to help her.

He was right at the top of his game, a busy man with huge demands on his time. According to her research, thousands of people approached his company every year for business advice and he helped less than a handful of people.

While she waited for him to comment she sipped the lemonade but after a couple of minutes of squirming in her seat restraint left her. 'So tell me honestly—' *Is it a crappy idea?* God, no, she couldn't say that. 'Er—do you see this as an investment opportunity?' She felt like such a fraud. A total impostor, just waiting for him to laugh her out of his office. It must have been obvious to him that she'd never had a business meeting with anyone except her own reflection.

He closed the file, then turned to put it on his desk. His tailored shirt pulled across his wide shoulders, emphasising hard muscle, and her heart started to thud.

She dreamed about him all the time. Had thought about him almost every hour since that night.

'Selene?'

His voice was gentle and she looked at him, startled and embarrassed to have let her concentration lapse.

'Yes. I'm listening.'

The look in his eyes told her he was skilled at reading minds and hers was probably the easiest he'd ever read.

Suddenly her mouth felt as if she hadn't touched liquid for a week.

If he guessed how she felt about him she'd die on the spot.

Her trawl of the internet had revealed a lot about his relationship with women and every scandalous story had made her heart beat just a little bit faster because they spoke of a life so far removed from hers that it was like listening to a fairy story. Glittering parties. Opening nights. Opera. Ballet. Film premieres. The list was endless, as were the names of the beautiful women he'd paraded on his arm at one time or another, and it was all she could think about now as she stared at him, waiting for his answer.

'These candles—do you have a sample?'

'Yes.' She fumbled in her bag, trying to ignore the nerves fluttering low in her belly. It was as if just being in the same room as him had somehow triggered all the alarms in her body. The attraction was so shockingly powerful it knocked her off-balance. She definitely needed to get out more. This was what happened when a father locked a daughter away. She'd turned into a raging nymphomaniac. Stefan Ziakas was going to be lucky to escape with his clothes still on.

Disconcerted, she glanced at him but that turned out to be a bigger mistake. Thick, inky lashes highlighted eyes of molten gold and his mouth was a slim, sensual line in a face sculpted by the devil to tempt women to the dark side.

Selene was unsettled by just how desperately she wanted to be taken to the dark side.

'I know this business idea has potential.' She was brisk and businesslike and hoped he wouldn't guess that she'd practised this a hundred times in the mirror. 'I have some packaging samples, but they might need to be adapted. We live in a fast-paced, stressful world. Scented candles are an affordable luxury and I'm not the only one who thinks so. The market is currently growing at forty percent.'

His mouth was such a perfect shape, she thought. She'd noticed the same thing that night on the boat as she'd stared and stared at him, willing him to kiss her. There had been a few breathless moments when she'd thought he might do just that but he hadn't, so clearly it had just been wishful thinking on her part.

Leaning forward, he extracted the candle from her grip and turned it in his fingers. 'You're expecting me to believe that this is the next big thing?'

'Why not? Don't you like candles?'

A smile played around that sexy mouth. 'You want an honest answer?'

She remembered that this was a business meeting. That she was a businesswoman. 'Yes,' she said firmly. 'Yes, I do.'

'I'm a man. The only reason a man is ever going to like candles is if there is a power cut and the generator fails, or if he finds himself dining with a woman who is ugly.'

And she was willing to bet he never found himself in that position. 'But candles are about so much more than romantic lighting in a restaurant.' She tried not to think about him dining with a beautiful woman. 'The one I've named Seduction is scented with lotus blossom and it creates the perfect atmosphere for—for—'

'For?'

His eyes gleamed and she had a strong suspicion he

was laughing at her. 'Seduction,' she said lamely, suddenly wishing she'd called it something else.

'And you know that because…?'

His voice was disturbingly soft and the laughter had gone from his eyes. Now his gaze was intense—*serious*—and Selene felt as if she'd been seared by the flame of a blowtorch.

'Because people have told me that's the case.'

'But you've never tried it yourself.' It was a statement, not a question, and she felt her face burn along with her body.

She wished he'd stuck to a conversation about market share and forecasts. 'I've tried Relax and Energise.'

'So no market research on Seduction?'

'Yes, just not—personal research.'

There was a long, pulsing silence and then he put the candle down and leaned his hips on the desk, the movement of his trousers revealing expensive polished shoes. 'Let me tell you something about seduction, Selene.' His voice was more seductive than a thousand scented candles. 'To you it's just a word, but it's so much more than that. Seduction is about tempting, enticing and persuading until you've driven someone mad with need. Yes, scent is important, but not the artificial scent of a candle—it's the individual scent of the person you're with, and it's not just scent but scent combined with touch and sound.'

Selene couldn't breathe. 'Sound?'

'When I'm with a woman I want to hear the sounds she makes. I want to hear her pleasure as well as feel it under my lips and fingers. And then there's taste…' His voice was softer now, those dangerous eyes velvety dark as he held her gaze, 'I want to taste every part of her and encourage her to taste every part of me.'

'Y-you do?'

'Scent, touch, hearing, sound, taste—seduction uses all the senses, not just one. It's about taking over someone's mind and body until they're no longer capable of rational thought—until they want just one thing and one thing only—until they're reduced to an elemental state where nothing matters but the moment.'

Selene felt dizzy. 'I think I might need to rename my candle.'

'I'm sure there are men out there who would be only too happy to use a scented candle as a prop. I'm just not one of them.'

He wouldn't need any external props to seduce a woman. Those hands would be sure and skilled. And as for his mouth—

Realising her own hands were shaking, she tucked them firmly into her lap. 'Just because you're not my target audience, it doesn't mean I don't have a viable product.' Proud of that response, she carried on. 'Will you teach me what I need to know?' As his brows rose she continued, flustered. 'I mean about marketing. Running a business.'

'I have a question.'

'Yes, of course you do. Ask me anything.' He was so cool and sophisticated and she was no more interesting than her seventeen-year-old self. 'You want to know more about the product? It's a really good-quality candle. It's made of beeswax and it's smokeless and virtually drip-free.'

'I can hardly contain my excitement.' But he was smiling as he picked up the candle again and she had a feeling his mind was still on seduction rather than the product in his hand. 'That wasn't my question.'

'Oh. I expect you want to ask me about my revenue projections. I've had an order for five thousand from Hot Spa. They're the most exclusive chain of spa hotels in

Greece. But of course you know that...' Her voice tailed
off. 'You own them.'

Stefan handed the candle back to her. 'That wasn't my
question, either.'

She gulped. Licked her lips. 'Sorry—I'm talking too
much. I do that when I'm—' *desperate* '—excited.'

'My first question,' he said slowly, 'is why someone like
you would even want to set up a business. Are you bored?'

Bored? She bit back a bubble of hysterical laughter.
'No.'

'You're an heiress. You don't need to run a business.'

He had no idea. 'I want to prove myself.'

He stared at her for a long moment. 'Which brings me
to my second question—why come to me? If you're serious
about this then your father could put up the investment.'

Selene made sure her smile didn't slip. 'I don't want
my father's name on it. This is my project. I want to own
it. I don't want anyone doing me favours.' It was a lie, of
course. She needed all the favours she could grab. 'I can't
approach the banks because they won't help me without
asking my father's permission. I tried to think of someone
who isn't under his thumb and I came up with you. You
told me to look you up in five years—'

The silence stretched between them.

Looking at his hard, handsome face she felt the confidence drain out of her. In an appalling flash of clarity she
realised she'd made a monumental mistake. Losing her
nerve, horribly embarrassed, she rose to her feet. 'Thank
you for listening.'

He stirred, uncrossed those long, lean legs and stood
up, dominating the room. 'You came to me for a business
loan. Don't you want to hear my answer?'

'I—I thought you might need time to think about it.'

'I've had all the time I need.'

So the answer was no. Her shoulders sagged. Misery seeped into her veins.

'Right. Well—'

'My answer is yes.'

Because it wasn't what she was expecting to hear, it took a moment for his words to sink in.

'Seriously? You're not just saying that because I've made it hard for you to say no?'

'No is my favourite word. I don't find it hard to say.'

But he wasn't saying it to her. 'I just thought you might be agreeing to help me beçause you don't want me to feel bad.'

A strange expression crossed his face. 'That isn't the reason.'

His eyes were on her mouth and she saw something in his face that made her heart pound just a little harder in her chest.

I lie awake at night thinking about you.

He was silent for a long moment and then strolled to the window and stared across the city. 'It is going to drive your father crazy. Does that bother you?'

Yes, it bothered her. Her safety and the safety of her mother rested on a knife-edge, which was why she had to get away.

She had a sudden urge to tell him the truth, but years of keeping her secret and loyalty to her mother prevented her from doing it. And she knew enough about Stefan Ziakas to know that he wasn't going to be interested in the details of her personal life. He avoided all that, didn't he? He would never let anything personal interfere with business. 'He has to understand that this is my life and I want to make my own mistakes. I want to be independent.'

'So this is delayed teenage rebellion?'

Let him think that if he wanted to. 'I know you're not

afraid of going up against him. I read that article recently—the headline was "Clash of the Titans". And the mere mention of your name is enough to put my father in a bad mood for days.' She stared at his broad shoulders, wondering if the sudden tension she saw there was a product of her imagination.

'And has he ever told you why?'

'Of course not. My father would never discuss business with a woman. He won't be pleased with me but he'll have to get used to the idea.' The ache in her arm reminded her just how displeased he was likely to be. 'I hadn't thought about the implications for you. If it bothers you that he'll be angry…'

'That's not a problem for me.' There was the briefest pause and then he turned back to his desk in a smooth, confident movement and pressed a button on the phone. Without any further discussion or questions he instructed someone in his legal department to start making all the necessary arrangements to loan her whatever money she needed.

Having braced herself for rejection, or at least a load of awkward questions, Selene stared at him, unable to believe what she was hearing.

He was going to lend her the money. Just like that.

It couldn't be this easy, could it? Nothing in life was this easy.

The knot of tension that had been lodged in her stomach for as long as she could remember started to ease. Anxiety was replaced by a rush of euphoria that made her feel like dancing round the room.

Apparently unaware of the impact of his decision, Stefan ended the phone call, supremely relaxed. 'It's done. My only stipulation is that you work with one of my business development managers who will give you access to all the in-house resources of the Ziakas Corporation. That way you won't be ripped off by suppliers or customers, and basically you can draw on whatever funds you need.'

He was watching her from under those thick, dark lashes and her stomach flipped.

He was *gorgeous*.

People had him *so* wrong. It wasn't right that everyone should talk about him in hushed voices as some sort of cold, conscienceless machine when he was obviously capable of all the normal human emotions. Maybe he was hard and ruthless in some aspects of his life, but to her he'd been nothing but kind.

'I—' She was dizzy with euphoria, hardly able to get her head around what had just happened. She was going to be able to start her own business, rent a small apartment and help her mother leave her father. She wanted to fling her arms round him and then remembered that this was a business meeting and she was pretty sure people didn't do things like that in business meetings. 'That's an excellent outcome. Thank you. You won't be sorry.' She should shake his hand. Yes, that was what she should do. Shake his hand to seal the deal.

Standing up, she walked towards him and held out her hand.

His hand closed over hers, warm and strong, and suddenly what had begun as a simple handshake became something else entirely. He smelt good. She had no idea whether it was shampoo or something different but it made her want to bury her face in his neck and inhale deeply. All she had to do was lean forward and she'd be kissing him. Horrified by how tempted she was, she looked down at her hand instead and saw the expensive watch on his wrist and his lean, bronzed fingers linked intimately with hers.

Her stomach clenched.

Power and masculinity throbbed from him and suddenly all she could think about was sex—which was crazy because she knew nothing about sex.

But he did.

'So now that's out of the way,' he drawled softly, 'the question is how far are you willing to take this quest for independence?'

Busy imagining those strong, confident hands on her body, she felt her heart thud. 'Why are you asking?'

'Because I'm hosting a party tonight and I find myself minus a date. How do you feel about celebrating your new-found independence in style?'

Her eyes lifted to his and she saw amusement there. Amusement and something a little bit dangerous.

The excitement came in a whoosh that drove the air from her lungs.

Her head spun. The hungry look in his eyes was interfering with the normally smooth rhythm of her breathing. 'You're inviting me to a party?' She never went to parties unless her father decided it was time to play Happy Families in public. They were the most painful moments of her life. And the loneliest, all of them fake.

She'd never been to a party for the sheer fun of it. Never been to a party where she was allowed to be herself.

She wondered why he was asking her.

'If I say no does that mean—?'

'You have my agreement on the loan. Your answer has no effect on our deal.'

In that case she should walk away. There would be time to party once she was safely away from the island. Selene licked her lips. 'What sort of party is it?'

'A strictly grown-up event. No jelly or ice cream in sight.'

A party. *With him.*

'You're asking me to come as your date?'

'That's right.'

The excitement was sharper than when he'd agreed to lend her the money. A date. A party. With this man. She'd never done anything like that in her life.

She should say no. Now that he'd agreed to help her she should get back to Antaxos, persuade her mother to leave and be long gone before her father returned. She couldn't possibly say yes even though she wanted to more than she'd ever wanted anything in her life.

On the other hand, why not?

For the first time in her life she was free to make her own decision about something. For once her father wasn't dictating her actions, no one was watching her and her mother was safe. She had no one to think about but herself. If she wanted to go to a party, she could. And wasn't that the point of all this? To be able to live her life the way she wanted to live it?

Feeling liberated, she opened her mouth. 'I don't have anything to wear.'

'That's easily solved.'

'I have this fantasy about wearing a wicked red dress and drinking champagne from a tall, slim glass with a handsome man in a dinner jacket. Would we drink champagne?'

His mouth curved into a smile so sexy it should have been illegal. 'All night.'

'And would we—?'

The devil danced in his eyes and his mouth moved fractionally closer to hers. 'If you're asking what I think you're asking then the answer is yes, we definitely would.'

CHAPTER THREE

'How did he arrange for these dresses to be delivered so fast? And how did he guess my size? On second thoughts, don't answer that.' Confronted with a rail of the most beautiful dresses she'd ever seen, Selene felt as if she'd stepped onto a Hollywood movie set. Part of her felt anxious about her decision to stay, but another part felt wildly excited. She listened to the excited part and ignored the anxiety. That, she reasoned, came from too many years of not being allowed to make her own decisions. It was natural that it felt strange.

Maria pulled an elegant clutch bag from tissue paper. 'When Stefan picks up the phone, people respond at supersonic speed. The benefits of being a man of power.'

'Except that you were the one who did the phoning.'

'True.' Maria smiled. 'Power by proxy. Why don't you start by choosing a dress?'

'Is Stefan joining us?'

'He sends his apologies. He has one more important meeting he has to take before you leave.'

'I don't mind. I'd be too self-conscious to strip in front of him anyway and it's more fun with a woman. It was thoughtful of him to arrange for you to help me.' She saw Maria's expression change. 'You don't think he's thoughtful?'

The other woman removed a beautiful pair of shoes from a bag. 'That's certainly an adjective I've not heard applied to him before.'

'He's running a business. Of course he has to be tough. But on the two occasions I've met him he's been kind to me.'

Maria put the shoes down in front of her. 'You have no idea how pleased I am to hear that. Why don't you pick a dress and try it on? Because once he's finished his meeting he won't want to hang around. Is there anything in particular that grabs your attention?'

'The red one.' There was no other choice for her and the colour matched her mood. *Bold.* 'I've never worn anything like that in my life.' She reached for a shimmering sheath of scarlet with jewels on the strapless bodice. 'This is *gorgeous.* Will it be over the top?'

'No. It's a very glamorous party. That dress is very sophisticated.' Maria stared at it for a long moment. 'Are you sure you don't want to pick a different one? Maybe the blue?'

'You don't think Stefan will like the red one?'

'I think he might like it a little too much.'

'How can he possibly like it too much?'

'Selene…' The other woman hesitated. 'Are you sure you want to go to this party?'

'*Want* to go? I'm *desperate* to go. You have no idea how boring my life has been up to now. I'm going to dress up, drink champagne and have the most amazing night with Stefan.'

'Just as long as you know that's all it will be.' Maria cleared her throat gently. 'Stefan is the stuff of female dreams, but he quickly turns into a nightmare for most women. He isn't the happy-ever-after type—you do know that, don't you? Because you seem like a really nice girl and I'd hate to see you hurt.'

Selene paused with her hand on the dress.

She knew all about hurt and this wasn't it. 'I won't be hurt. I'm excited. It will be fun to just enjoy myself for one night.' Fun to be able to make a decision to go to a party. Fun to decide what to wear. For once, her life felt almost normal.

'You don't usually enjoy yourself?'

'I have an overprotective father.' Realising that she'd said more than she intended to, Selene draped the dress over her arm. 'Is there somewhere I can try it on?'

'You'll need underwear.' Maria handed her several boxes. 'Go and change and if you need help, call me.'

An hour later Selene was the proud owner of the most beautiful dress she'd ever seen, along with a small emergency wardrobe suitable for an overnight stay at a luxury villa on a Greek island. Ahead of her lay the most exciting night of her life, and if lurking underneath her happiness was a fear that her father might return early she dismissed it.

That wasn't going to happen.

She'd have plenty of time to get home, persuade her mother to leave and be long gone before he returned.

'You can't do this. You can't take that girl to the party. It's immoral.'

Stefan glanced up from the papers he was signing to find Maria standing in front of his desk like a general facing down an enemy army.

'Now, *that's* the look you're supposed to give unwanted visitors.' He flung down his pen. 'Do I need to remind you that *you* were the one who showed her into the lion's den?'

'I'm serious, Stefan. Take someone else. Someone more your type.'

'Just this morning you were lecturing me on picking the wrong type. Make up your mind.'

'I wasn't telling you to prey on innocent girls.'

'She's an adult. She knows what she's doing.' He picked up his pen and flicked through the papers on his desk.

'She's an idealist. She thinks you're thoughtful and kind.'

'I know.' Smiling, Stefan signed the back page. 'For once, I'm the good guy. An unfamiliar role, I admit, but I'm surprised by how much I'm enjoying the novelty.'

'You're treating her like a shiny new toy that you can play with.' Maria's mouth set in a firm line. 'Send her home to her father.'

Stefan was careful not to let the sudden flare of emotion show on his face. Slowly, he put his pen down. 'Do you know who her father is?'

'No. Although she mentioned something about him being overprotective.'

'Is that a useful synonym for "tyrant", I wonder? Her father, Maria, is Stavros Antaxos.' He watched as Maria's face lost some of its colour. 'Yes. Exactly.' He heard his voice harden and it irritated him that just saying the name was enough to do that to him. He'd had over two decades to learn how to control his response.

'How on earth can a man like that produce someone as charming as Selene?'

He'd been asking himself the same question.

'I assume she takes after her mother.'

Maria looked troubled. 'But why would someone as wealthy as her, from such a close family, come to you?'

He'd been asking himself the same question. Repeatedly. 'I'm a hero, didn't you know? I'm the first man women think of when they're in trouble.'

'You're the man who causes the trouble.'

'Ouch, that's harsh.' Stefan leaned back and stretched out his legs. 'Here I am, sword at the ready, eager to chop the head off a dragon to save the maiden, and all you can do is knock my confidence.'

She didn't smile. 'Is that really what's going on here? Because it occurred to me that maybe you're using the maiden to taunt the dragon.'

Stefan's smile didn't slip. 'When we were dishing out roles in this company I picked cynic, not you.'

'We're all cynical here. It's contagious. Does she know how much her father hates you? Does she know the story?'

No one knew the story. Not even Maria, whom he allowed more liberties than most. Oh, she *thought* she knew—thought it was all about business rivalry and two alpha males acting out their deeply competitive natures. She had no idea how far back it went, or how deep the scars. And why would she? They weren't visible. He didn't allow them to be visible.

'It's because of my relationship with her father that she chose me.'

Maria's mouth flattened with disapproval.

'Are you sure this isn't a case of out of the frying pan and into the fire?'

'You're suggesting I'm worse than Antaxos? That is hardly a complimentary view of one's boss.'

'We're not talking about work right now. My admiration for your intellect and business skills is boundless but when it comes to women you're bad news. What are your plans for her, Stefan?'

'When it comes to women I never make plans. You should know that by now. "Plan" implies a future and we

both know I don't think like that. I've agreed to help her
with her business—which, by the way, looks remarkably
interesting on paper, particularly when you consider the
product. And I'm taking her to a party. I intend to provide
more fun than she's had in the rest of her life. She can
make her own decisions about how she spends her time.
She's twenty-two and on a quest for independence.' Stefan
battled a disturbingly vivid image of her breasts revealed
through a cloud of lace. 'All grown up.'

'She's very inexperienced.'

'Yes. I'm finding that unusually appealing.'

'And does that appeal have anything to do with the fact
you are the *last* man her father would want her to be with?
Thinking of her with you will drive him demented.'

Stefan smiled. 'I consider that an added bonus.'

'I'm worried about her, Stefan.'

'She came to me. She asked for my help. I'm giving it.'
It was obvious that there was something going on beneath
the surface and it intrigued him. She was playing a game,
but he wasn't sure which game. 'I don't recall you ever
being this protective of the women I date before.'

'That's because you normally date women who don't
need protecting from anything.'

'So maybe it's time for a change.' Cutting off the conversation, he rose to his feet. 'How long until she's ready?
No doubt she's still pulling clothes on and off, trying to
decide what to wear.'

'She decided what to wear in less than five seconds and
it took her barely more than that to try it on.'

Used to women who could waste the best part of a day
selecting one outfit, he was impressed. 'I like her more
and more.'

'She has a very high opinion of you.'

'I know.' He walked past her to the door and Maria made a frustrated sound.

'Where is your conscience?'

Stefan picked up his jacket. 'I don't have a conscience.'

When he'd mentioned his villa she'd imagined somewhere small. She hadn't for one moment expected this spacious, airy mansion with high ceilings and acres of glass. Here, in this testament to innovative architecture, there were no dark corners or contagious gloom, just dazzling light exploding across marble floors and picking out the warm Mediterranean colours that turned the deceptively simple interior into a luxurious sanctuary.

Outside, a vine-shaded terrace led to gardens that created a blur of extravagant colour as they tumbled down a gentle slope that led to a crescent beach. And even there the idyll didn't end. Unlike Antaxos, there were no killer rocks or dark, fathomless depths that threatened to swallow a person and leave no trace. Just sand of the softest, creamiest yellow and tiny silver fish dancing in the clear shallow water. The whole scene was so tempting that she, who avoided water, just wanted to rip off her shoes and plunge into the safe, cool shallows.

'So this is why people see the Greek Islands as a tourist destination.' She spoke without thinking and her unguarded comment earned her a questioning look.

'Was the reason for that choice in doubt?'

Staring out of huge windows across the garden to the turquoise sea, she felt something stir inside her. It was like living a life in black and white and suddenly seeing it in colour. 'Antaxos isn't anything like this. No soft sand, just nasty rocks—' She just stopped herself mentioning the rumour that a woman who'd been madly in love with her father had once fallen from those rocks and drowned.

'My father's house—our house—is built of stone with small windows.' She managed to say it without shuddering. 'The design supposedly keeps the heat out.' And it kept everything and everyone else out, too. The bleak, dark atmosphere inside the place had somehow permeated the stone so that even the building felt unfriendly. 'It's stuffy in the summer and dark and cheerless in the winter. I like the light here. You have a very happy home.'

'Happy?' He glanced up at the villa, a faint frown between his eyes. 'You think a building has moods?'

'Definitely. Don't you?'

'I think a building is a building.'

'Oh, no, that isn't true. A building can make a person feel different. Here, the sunshine makes you want to smile. And all this *space*—it feels like being free.' She spread her arms. 'I've always wanted to be a bird so I can fly.' *Fly away from the island that had held her trapped for so long.*

But she'd finally escaped. She'd done it.

This was the start of her new life.

Excited, she did a twirl. Stefan shot out a hand and steadied her before she lost her balance. 'Probably best if you don't fly here. I've seen pictures of your home on Antaxos. You live in a building the size of a castle.'

Selene was conscious of the strength of his fingers on her arm. 'It isn't anything like this. My father doesn't like spending money on material things.'

'Is there anything that your father *does* like?'

Hurting people.

She stood, searching for an appropriate response to his question, her heart a ball of pain in her chest. 'Winning,' she said finally. 'He likes winning.'

'Yes.' His hand dropped abruptly from her arm. 'Yes, he does.'

And he'd know, of course, because he was her father's

biggest business rival. She sensed the anger in him and she also sensed something more. Something dark lurked behind those sexy eyes. 'You really hate my father, don't you?'

'It's true to say he's not my favourite person in the world.' The deceptively light banter and that attractive slanting smile didn't fool her.

This man was every bit as tough as her father.

She felt a twinge of unease, but already he was strolling ahead of her. She tried to ignore the little voice in her head telling her this might not have been such a good idea after all.

It was her first party. Her first 'date' with a man. It was natural to be a little apprehensive.

She followed him through a beautiful living space with white walls and uninterrupted views of the sea into the most beautiful bedroom she'd ever seen.

Forgetting her unease, Selene stared around her in delight. 'It's gorgeous. There's a pool outside the doors and you can see the sea from the bed. It's stunning. Is this my room?'

He turned to her with a slow, deliberate smile. 'It's *my* room,' he said, his tone soft and intimate as he lifted his hand and gently pushed a strand of hair out of her eyes, 'but you're sharing it, *koukla mou.*'

She didn't know whether it was the endearment that made her heart bump harder, the seductive brush of his fingers against her cheek or the anticipation of what was to come. 'The bed looks comfortable.'

'It is. Unfortunately proving that will have to wait until later.'

'I didn't mean that.'

'I know. I'm finding your tendency to speak before you think surprisingly endearing.'

The crazy thing was she wasn't normally like that. At home she had to guard every word. She wondered why she'd suddenly lost that built-in inhibition and decided it was just because her father wasn't present. It was liberating not to have to watch what she said. 'I'm going to zip my mouth.'

That dark gaze dropped to her mouth. 'Don't. I like it.'

Heart thudding, she looked at his lips. Noticed that they were firm and slightly curved.

'No,' he said gently.

Her eyes lifted to his. 'No?'

'No, I'm not going to kiss you. At least, not yet. Tempted though I am to snatch a few moments, there are some things that shouldn't be rushed and your first time is one of them.'

The fact that he knew it was her first time should have embarrassed her but it didn't, and she didn't waste time denying something that would be obvious to a man like him.

There was an almost electric connection between them that she felt right through her body. Warmth spread through her pelvis and she felt shaky with need. She wanted him to kiss her so badly she couldn't imagine how she was going to last a whole evening without just grabbing him. 'Maybe I don't mind being rushed.'

Frowning slightly, he brushed this thumb over her lower lip, the movement slow and lingering. 'You need to be more cautious around men.'

And normally she *was* cautious, of course, not least because all the men she knew worked for her father in some capacity. But Stefan was different. He wasn't afraid of her father. And he'd got her through that horrible night when she was a teenager. 'I don't feel a need to be cautious around you. Does that sound crazy?'

'Yes.'

'I trust you.'

'Don't.'

'Why not? You're not being paid by my father.'

Silence stretched between them.

His eyes glittering, he lowered his head a fraction until his forehead was against hers and their mouths were a breath apart. The brush of his fingers against her cheek was gentle and seductive at the same time. 'You've come here with me but I want you to know it's not too late for you to change your mind.'

'I'm not going to change my mind.'

His gaze darkened. 'Maybe I should just cancel the party and we can have our own party here, just the two of us.'

Awareness twisted in her stomach. The tension was stifling. She felt as if she were standing on the edge of a deep, dark pool about to jump, with no idea whether she'd be able to save herself from drowning. 'If we have our own party here, I couldn't wear my new dress.'

'You could wear it for me.' His mouth slanted into that sexy smile. 'And I could remove it.'

Her hand was resting on his arm and she could feel the hardness of his biceps under her fingers. 'Isn't that rather a waste of an expensive dress?'

'The dress is just packaging. It's the product underneath that interests me.' His fingers stroked her neck gently and then his phone rang. He stepped back with a regretful smile. 'Probably a good thing. I need enough time to do justice to the moment. Our guests will be arriving in a few hours and in true Cinderella style *you* need to get ready.'

A few *hours*? 'How long do you think it will take me?'

'In my experience most women take a lifetime to get ready. In the hope of speeding up that process, I've arranged for you to have some help. Not only am I a knight in shining armour, I'm also a fairy godmother. In fact the extent of my benevolence is starting to astonish me.' His phone continued to ring and he dragged it out of his pocket. 'Excuse me. I need to take this.'

As the door closed behind him Selene stood still. Her cheek tingled from the touch of his fingers and the only thing in her head was the memory of hard, male muscle under her fingers.

With a shiver, she wrapped her arms around herself and turned to look at the bed. It was enormous, draped in white linen and facing the sea. Indulgent, luxurious and like nothing she'd ever seen before. Experimenting, she slid off her shoes and jumped into the middle of it, moaning with delight as she felt the soft mound of pillows give beneath her. It was like being hugged by a cloud.

She rolled onto her back and stared up at the ceiling, smiling.

She felt free.

Right this moment no one knew where she was. No one was watching her. No one was reporting her every move to her father. No one had told her where she had to be. She was here because *she* had decided she wanted to be here.

Going to Stefan for help had been her first good decision and agreeing to come to the party had been her second.

Feeling light-headed, she sprang off the bed and explored the rest of the bedroom suite.

There was a ridiculously luxurious bathroom with a wall of glass that made it possible to lie in the bath and look at the sea.

Determined to indulge herself, Selene unpacked her own candles and soap. Then she ran herself a deep bath and lay in it, enjoying the scent of the candle.

She wasn't so naïve she didn't know what was going to

happen and she wanted it to happen. She'd dreamed about Stefan for years. Had had years to think about it. *Imagine it.* It was perfect that he should be the first.

Soon, she thought. *Soon she'd know everything there was to know about seduction.*

She washed her hair and was wrapped in a soft towel, wondering why getting ready was supposed to take hours, when there was a tap on the door and two young women entered, clutching several cases.

'Selene? I'm Dana. I'm a genius with hair.' Dana pushed the door shut with the toe of her shoe. 'This is Helena—she's the make-up fairy.'

'I don't own make-up.' It was embarrassing to admit it but her father had never allowed make-up or anything that he described as 'vanity'. He'd only paid for her to have a brace because the dentist had told him it would cost him more in the long run if she didn't have one.

Dana flipped open her case. 'No problem. We have everything you'll need.'

'Do you think you can do something about my freckles and my non-existent eyelashes?'

'You're kidding, right?' Helena peered at her. 'Your eyelashes are incredible. Thick and long. What's wrong with them?'

Selene had assumed it was obvious. 'Don't you think I look a bit freakish? They're so fair they barely show up.'

'Freakish? No, I don't think you look freakish. As for being fair—that's why mascara was invented, sweetie.' With a dazzling smile, she flipped open another case to reveal an array of different make-up. 'I have everything we'll need right here.'

'Hair first.' Dana pulled a chair into the middle of the room. 'Sit. And don't look in the mirror or you'll ruin the "wow" moment and that's our favourite part. Just trust me.'

'Will I recognise myself?'

'You'll be the best version of you.'

Selene, intrigued by what the best version of herself was going to look like, sat still as the girl trimmed her hair, trying not to flinch as blonde curls floated onto her lap. 'You're cutting it short?'

'All I'm doing is taking off the ends to improve the condition and cutting in a few layers to soften it. Stefan threatened never to use me again if I ruin your beautiful hair, although if you want my personal opinion—' Dana squinted at her '—I think it would suit you short.'

He liked her hair. The thought went round and round in her head.

He liked her hair.

It was her first compliment—not actually spoken, of course, but a compliment none the less—and with it came the discovery that the feeling of flying was something that could happen inside you. Her spirits lifted and a smile touched her lips, and as well as the smile and the happiness there was something else. A lump in her throat that caught her by surprise.

'It's in great condition.' Dana's fingers moved through her hair as she snipped and combed.

He liked her hair.

The girl worked speedily and skilfully, dodging Helena, who was doing Selene's nails.

Once Selene's hair was dry Dana swept it up, twisted and pinned until finally she was satisfied. 'You're ready for make-up.'

'Can your magic make-up box get rid of my freckles?'

'Why would you want to? They're charming. Part of you. We want to keep you looking like you. That's one thing he insisted on. This is just primer I'm using, by the way.' Helena smoothed her fingers over Selene's face. 'You

have beautiful skin.' The girl opened a series of pots, po-
tions, colours, concealers, the sight of which made Selene's
head spin. 'What cleanser do you use?'

'Soap I make myself.' Selene delved into her bag and
pulled out a bar. 'Try it. I make candles, too, but Stefan
isn't convinced there's a market for those.'

'He's a man. What does he know?'

Selene smiled and her heart pounded because finally,
finally, she believed this might actually happen. Her new
life was almost visible, shining like a star in the distance.

The girl sniffed the soap. Her brows rose. 'Smells good.
And your skin is wonderful so that's a good advert.' She
dropped it into her bag. 'I'll try it, thanks.' She turned
back to Selene. 'I'm not going to use too much make-up
on you because you have a wonderfully fresh look and I
don't want to spoil that.'

It took ages, and Selene was just starting to fidget and
wonder how much longer it was going to take when Helena stepped back.

'God, I'm good at my job. You look spectacular. Don't
look in the mirror yet. Get dressed first so that you can
see the full effect all at once.' She grinned. 'I almost feel
sorry for Stefan.'

CHAPTER FOUR

STEFAN moved slowly among his guests, stirring up expectation.

'So who is she, Stefan?' A Hollywood actress who had been flirting with him for months didn't hide her annoyance at his hints that he'd brought a special guest. 'Not Sonya, I assume?'

'Not Sonya.'

'Why so mysterious? And why is she still in the bedroom and not out here, or is that a question one shouldn't ask?'

'Worn out from too much sex,' someone murmured. Stefan simply smiled and accepted a glass of champagne from one of his hovering staff.

'She leads a very quiet, very private life and this is all very new to her.' He'd discovered early in life that it was best to sail as close to the truth as possible and he stuck to that now as he carefully conjured suspense and interest among his guests.

Carys Bergen, a model who had been flirting with him for several months, strolled up to him. 'You're a wicked man. Who is this reclusive woman that you're about to produce like a rabbit from a magician's hat?'

He left his guests simmering in an atmosphere of expectation and strolled through the villa to the master bedroom suite, scooping another glass of champagne on the way.

At first he thought she wasn't in the room and he gave an impatient frown and glanced around him. 'Selene?'

'I'm here.'

He turned his head.

There was no sign of the awkward schoolgirl. The person standing in front of him in a sheath of shimmering scarlet was all woman.

'That dress was designed for the express purpose of tempting some poor defenceless man to rip it off.' His eyes weren't on the dress, but on the delicious curve of her narrow waist and the swell of her breasts above the tight jewelled bodice.

She smiled, clearly delighted by the effect she was having on him. '"Defenceless" is not a word anyone would use to describe you. And I know you spend your life escorting women who wear stunning dresses so what makes this one special?'

'The person wearing it.'

'Oh, *smooth*, Mr Ziakas.'

Unused to women whose response to compliments was laughter, Stefan handed her a glass. 'Champagne in a tall, slim glass, a red dress and a guy in a dinner jacket. This could be the first time in my life I've made a woman's dreams come true.'

'Mmm, thank you.' She took a mouthful of champagne, her eyes closing as if she wanted to savour the moment. 'It tastes like celebration.' Immediately she took another sip, and then another larger gulp.

Stefan raised his brows. 'If you want to remember the evening, drink slowly.'

'It tastes delicious. I love the feel of the bubbles on my tongue. And one of the best things about my new independence is being able to decide what I drink and what I don't drink.'

'That's fine. But, delighted though I am that you're clearly capable of enjoying the sensual potential of champagne, I'd rather my date wasn't unconscious. From now on take tiny sips and count to a hundred in between.' He held out his arm and she immediately put her empty glass down, took his arm and smiled up at him.

'Thank you.'

That wide, genuine smile knocked him off-balance. He was used to coy, flirtatious and manipulative. 'Friendly' was new to him and he had no idea how to respond.

She appeared to have no sense of caution. No layers of protection between her and the world. How the hell was she going to manage when she was no longer protected by her father's security machine?

'What are you thanking me for?'

'For agreeing to help me, for inviting me to this party and for arranging all these wonderful clothes. It's the perfect way to start my new life. You're my hero.' She stood back slightly, her eyes on his shoulders. 'You look smoking hot in a dinner jacket, by the way. Very macho. I bet all the dragons in Greece are trembling in their caves, or wherever it is dragons live when they're not munching on innocent maidens.'

'Heroes don't exist in real life and you've definitely drunk that too fast.' Stefan made a mental note to brief the staff to make her next drink non-alcoholic, otherwise she'd be lying face-down in a coma before the party had even begun.

'You're too modest.' Her eyes drifted from his shoulders to his mouth. 'People are so wrong about you.'

'You are *far* too trusting. What if they're right?'

Apparently undaunted by that suggestion, she closed

her other hand round his lapel and pulled him towards her. 'Do you know what I think? I think you've created this bad-boy image to keep people—women especially—at a distance. I think you're afraid of intimacy.'

Stefan felt darkness press in on him.

She'd found the one tiny chink in his armour and thrust her sword into it.

How? How had she done that? Was it a lucky guess?

It had to be a lucky guess. She didn't know anything about his past. No one did.

'I'm not afraid of intimacy and later I'm going to prove that to you, so don't drink any more or you'll fall asleep before we reach the interesting part of the evening.' Ignoring her puzzled expression, he guided her towards the door.

'I've upset you. Did I say something wrong?'

'What makes you think you've upset me?'

'Because your voice changed.'

Stefan, who prided himself on being inscrutable, started to sweat. Did she pick up on *everything*? 'You haven't upset me but I have guests, and I've already kept them waiting long enough. Are you ready?'

'Yes. Although I'm bracing myself to be hated.'

'Why would you be hated?'

'Because I'm with the hottest guy on the planet. All the women are going to hate me, but don't worry about it. When you're Stavros Antaxos's daughter you get used to not having friends.'

Her tone was light but he instantly thought of the night on the boat, when she'd found a hidden corner to sit, away from all the other guests. She'd worn her loneliness with a brave smile but she'd been almost pathetically grateful when he'd sat down and talked to her.

'Friendship is idealised and overrated. If someone wants

to be friends with you, it's usually because they want something.'

'I don't believe that.'

'You mean you don't want to believe it. You are hopelessly idealistic.' He held the door open for her and the brightness of her expression dimmed slightly.

'So you're saying that true friendship is impossible?'

'I'm saying that the temptation of money is too strong for most people. It changes things.' The scar inside him ached, reminding him of the truth of that. 'Just something to bear in mind for the future if you don't want to be hurt.'

'Is that what you do? Do you live your life protecting yourself from being hurt?'

Stefan, who was used to keeping his conversations satisfyingly superficial, wondered why every exchange with her dived far beneath the surface. 'I live my life the way I want to live it. Right now I'd like to attend my own party. Shall we go?'

Everyone was staring, some discreetly over the top of their champagne glasses and some more openly. But all the glances revealed the same emotion.

Shock.

Feeling like a caged bird suddenly released to freedom, Selene took another glass of champagne just because she could.

Stefan frowned. 'Are you sure you should drink that?'

'Do you know one of the best things about tonight? The fact that all of it is my decision. I decided to come to the party, I decided what dress I'd wear and now I'm deciding to drink champagne.'

'Just as long as you realise you're also choosing to have a crushing headache in the morning.'

'It will be worth it.' She drank half the glass and smiled

up at him. 'Champagne makes everything feel more exciting, doesn't it?'

'The second glass does that. After the third I doubt you'll remember enough about what happened to be excited. I advise you to switch to orange juice.'

'If it's going to give me a headache then I'll find that out for myself.'

'I'll remind you of that when you're moaning in the bathroom.'

She laughed up at him, forgetting the people around them. 'How many glasses of champagne do you have to drink before you'll kiss me in public?'

His eyes gleamed. 'I don't need to be intoxicated for that, *koukla mou*.'

'In that case—' her voice husky, Selene closed her fingers around the lapel of his jacket and closed her eyes '—kiss me.' *Just in case it never happened again. Just in case tonight was the only chance she was going to get to kiss a man like him.*

Anticipation washed over her skin and she waited to feel the brush of his mouth over hers, barely aware of the hum of conversation or the music around her as her imagination took over her mind. But he didn't kiss her. It was a moment of elongated suspense designed to torture her, and just when she'd started to think she was going to remember this moment as the most humiliating of her life she felt the tips of his fingers slide over her jaw.

She opened her eyes and met his, her heart pounding a crazy rhythm.

There was a brief silence and then he slid his hand behind her head and drew her face to his. 'What is it about you? I should walk away, but I can't.'

Desire was an ache low in her belly. 'I'm hanging onto your jacket. That could be the reason.'

He didn't smile. He didn't say a word.

For a breathless moment Selene saw something flicker in those dark eyes and then he lowered his head slowly, his eyes locked on hers. Until that moment she'd never known that a look could have a physical effect, but she felt that look all the way through her body in a rush of heat that spread right through her.

The anticipation was so acute it was almost painful—and he knew it because that sensual mouth curved slightly as he prolonged expectation.

And then the warmth of his breath brushed against her lips and she felt his free hand slide down her back and settle low on her waist as he drew her into contact with him.

She felt hardness and heat and suddenly doing this didn't feel like light-hearted fun any more. In his eyes she saw no trace of humour. Just raw, untamed male sexuality. She realised in a flash that he was controlling every second of this encounter. The pace. The intensity. Even her response. He was in charge of all of it.

And suddenly she knew that exploring her own sexuality with this man was like deciding to buy a pet and choosing a tiger. He was everything that wasn't tame or safe. Everything dangerous. Everything she'd dreamed of during those long nights when she'd imagined her life looking different.

Her mind in fast rewind, she tried to pull away. But his hand was hard and warm on her back and he held her exactly as she'd dreamed of being held.

'Close your eyes, champagne girl.' His soft command slid into her bones and she felt as if she'd just jumped off a high diving board with no opportunity to change her mind before she hit deep water.

And then his mouth touched hers and she forgot all of it as she melted under the skill of his kiss. He kissed her with erotic expertise, teasing her lips with his tongue, driving her wild with each movement of his mouth until her head was spinning and her thoughts were an incoherent blur.

It was, without doubt, the most perfect, exciting moment of her life and she wrapped her arms around his neck, her body quivering as she felt the evidence of his arousal pressing against her.

The fact that he wanted her was as intoxicating as the feelings he whipped up inside her with nothing but the skill of his mouth.

'Maybe you should get a room. I know the man who owns this villa. I could put in a good word for you if you like?'

A light female voice cut through her dreams and Selene would have jumped away from him had it not been for the fact that Stefan kept her locked firmly against him.

'Your timing is less than perfect, Carys.'

'I thought it was absolutely perfect.'

Bitterly disappointed by the interruption, Selene stole a glance at the other woman, wondering who she was.

The woman was stunning, her smile cool as she extended a hand to Selene. 'I'm Carys. And you're Selene.'

It gave her a jolt that someone recognised her. Stupidly, she hadn't even thought of that. 'You know me?'

'Of course. It's just unusual not to see you with your parents. You're such a close-knit family.'

Selene kept her smile in place. This was the part she was used to playing and she played it well. 'It's nice to meet you.'

'Mmm. And you.' Carys raised her glass to her lips, admiration in her eyes as she looked at Stefan. 'I have to hand it to you, occasionally you display a Machiavellian genius beyond anything I've ever encountered. Game, set and match, Stefan.'

Selene, who assumed that this coded exchange related to their relationship, stayed silent as Carys scooped two glasses of champagne from a passing waitress and handed one to her.

'Let's drink to your existence.'

She saw Stefan frown slightly and remembered what he'd said about not drinking any more champagne, but she couldn't bring herself to ask for orange juice in front of this sophisticated woman so she tapped her glass against hers and drank.

The alcohol fizzed into her veins and boosted her confidence. She wanted to dance but no one else seemed to be and when she asked why, Carys looked amused.

'Dancing makes one—hot.'

'Does that matter?' She started to sway on the spot and the other woman smiled.

'That's for you to decide, but if you can tempt Stefan onto the dance floor then you'll have succeeded where others have failed.'

Realising that she desperately wanted to succeed where others had failed, Selene watched as she walked away. 'She hates me. Not because of my father, but because of you. She's crazy about you.'

He gave her a sharp look. 'Not so innocent, are you?'

'I'm good at reading people.' She'd had to be. She'd learned to recognise everything that wasn't said, every emotion hidden beneath the surface, so that she could anticipate and deflect. It was how she lived her life and it was going to take more than one evening of freedom to undo that.

Thoughtful, she finished her champagne. He removed the empty glass from her hand and replaced it with orange juice.

'Here's a hint—alcohol makes you feel good for five

minutes, then you crash and you'll be crying on my shoulder.'

'I only cry when I'm happy. Although you should know I'm very happy tonight so you probably ought to stock up on tissues.' Laughing at the look on his face, she tugged her hand from his and spun onto the dance floor. Emerging from a pirouette, she smacked into Stefan who closed his hands around her arms to steady her.

'No more champagne.'

'Killjoy.'

'I'm preserving my sanity and your brain cells.'

'I just want to start living my life.' The thumping rhythm of the music made it impossible not to dance.

Stefan clamped his arm around her to restrict her movements. 'But you don't have to live it all in one night.'

The music slowed and he drew her against him. She sighed and slid her arms around his neck. 'You know when you have a dream and the reality turns out even better?'

He covered her lips with his fingers. 'I don't know what is coming out of your mouth next, but I suggest this would be a good moment to clamp it shut.'

'It's no wonder all the women chase after you because you are *seriously* hot.'

He shook his head in disbelief. 'Whatever happened to the shy, withdrawn nun who walked into my office?'

'I think this might be the real me, and the real me has never been let out before.'

Amusement mingled with exasperation. 'Should I be afraid?'

'You're not afraid of anything. That's why I came to you. I know it's not politically correct to admit it but I think I might be very turned on by strong men.' Dizzy from the atmosphere and the champagne circulating in her system, Selene leaned her forehead against his chest. 'And it doesn't hurt that you smell amazing.'

'Selene—'

'And you kiss like a god. You must have had hours of practice to be able to kiss like that. It's brilliant to have ticked the first thing on my wish list.'

'You have a wish list?'

'I have a list of ten things I want to experience the moment I leave the island and start my new life. Being kissed is one of them and I have to say you aced that one. I'm so glad it was you and not some slobbery amateur. Another is waking up next to a really hot guy.' She sneaked a look at him and he shook his head in disbelief.

'So this is what happens when an overprotected daughter suddenly cuts loose. Until a few hours ago you were a shy girl who had never been near a city. What else is on this list of yours?'

Selene discovered that her head was too fuzzy to remember in detail. 'Being able to make my own decisions about everything. Sex is on my list, too, obviously. Wild, abandoned sex.'

'With anyone in particular?' His mocking tone made her smile.

'Yes, you. I always wanted the first time to be you.' She saw no reason not to be honest. 'I hope I'm not giving you performance anxiety? No pressure or anything.'

His eyes glittered down into hers but he was no longer smiling. Somewhere during the course of their conversation the atmosphere had shifted subtly. 'I think the champagne is talking.'

'No, I'm pretty sure it was me, although the champagne might have prompted it. It's good at removing inhibitions.'

'I'd noticed.' With a driven sigh, he drew her off the dance floor and down a narrow path that led to the beach.

'Where are we going? You're walking too fast.'

'I'm removing you from public before you tip over the edge and do something you're going to regret.' He cursed under his breath as she stumbled and fell against him. '*Cristos*, I should have taken that third glass of champagne out of your hand.' His voice harsh, he swept her into his arms as if she weighed nothing and continued down the steps. 'Here's another tip. Next time stop drinking while you can still walk in a straight line.'

'There might not be a next time. That's why I'm making the most of this time. You have to live for the moment and I'm living for the moment. At least, I'm *trying* to live for the moment but it's hard to do that unless the other person is doing it too.'

'*Theé mou—*' Jaw tense, he lowered her to her feet and Selene collapsed onto the sand in a dizzy heap.

Shaking her head to try and dispel the swimmy feeling, she pulled her shoes off her feet. 'The world is spinning. Next time I won't drink quite as much quite as fast. And if you even mouth the words "I told you so" I will punch you.'

He swore softly under his breath. 'Do you even realise what could happen to you in this state? You virtually offered yourself to me.'

'I did offer myself to you, but obviously that was too forward of me because now you're frowning. Is it because you don't think a woman has as much right to enjoy sex as a man?'

He sucked air through his teeth. 'I don't think that.'

'Then why are you looking so disapproving? I was relying on you being as bad as everyone says you are.' She flopped back onto the soft sand and he gave a growl low in his throat.

'One of my few life rules is never to have sex with a drunk woman. You should be grateful for that. Stand up!

I can't have a conversation with you when you're lying at my feet like a starfish.'

'Why do men always compare me to animals? First my father says I'm a giraffe and now you say I'm a starfish. The day a man tells me I'm a whale, I'm killing myself.'

With an exasperated sigh he bent and lifted her and she tumbled against him, her body pressed hard against his. There was a tense, throbbing silence broken only by the soft sound of the sea on the sand and his harsh breathing in her ear.

'This,' he breathed, 'is *not* turning out the way I planned it.'

'Tell me about it. I thought amazing things would happen to a girl wearing a dress like this but all I got was lots of anticipation, an incredible kiss and a lecture.'

His grip on her tightened. 'You should be grateful I'm showing restraint.'

'Well, I'm not. I hate the fact you're so controlled. I'd do anything for you to just lose it for a moment and follow your deepest male instincts.'

He muttered something under his breath and then cupped her face in his hands and slanted his mouth over hers. Excitement flashed through her, slid through her limbs and deep into her bones until she felt the strength leaving her. As his tongue traced the seam of her lips and dipped inside Selene felt her tummy tighten and the world spin. His mouth moved slowly, expertly, over hers and she lost track of time and place, *of herself.*

Just when she'd decided that all her dreams about kissing were still intact, he released her.

The sense of loss was searing.

She stared up at him in the semi-darkness, acutely aware of the contrast between them. He was all raw power and masculinity. Despite her height, in her bare feet she barely reached his shoulder.

Without thinking she stretched out her hand and touched his face and instantly heard his sharp intake of breath.

'I'm taking you back to the room.'

'Yes. Take me back to your room so that we can try out your big, beautiful bed. Strip me naked and do unspeakable things to me,' she murmured, running her fingers over his biceps. 'You're very strong.'

'Strong enough to stop you doing something you'll regret tomorrow.'

'You see? You pretend to be bad, but then you're good. I hate to say I told you so, but I was right all along. Secretly you're a nice person, although right now...' Selene suppressed a yawn. 'Right now, I wish you weren't.'

'Stop talking, Selene. Whenever a thought comes into your head, just trap it there. Don't let it out.'

'That's what I've been doing all my life. If my brain is a computer then my hard drive is definitely full.' She gave a gasp as he scooped her off her feet and strode across the sand.

Mouth tight with disapproval, he carried her up a flight of illuminated steps to a private part of the villa. Brightly coloured bougainvillaea tumbled over whitewashed walls and he strode past the small pool she'd noticed earlier outside the doors of the master suite.

'This place is so romantic. Just in case you don't have the energy to make it to the beach, you can leap in here on the way.' Selene gazed at the smooth, floodlit surface of the water, thinking it was the most tranquil place she'd ever seen. Lush exotic plants clustered around the edge of a beautiful pool and the tantalising sound of water came from two elaborate water features. 'How long have you owned this place?'

'A long time.' His voice was terse. 'Can you walk or do you want me to carry you?'

'I definitely want you to carry me. I really like it.' Selene tightened her arms around his neck. 'I want you to carry me straight to bed, and teach me everything I don't know about seduction. We can call it market research.'

'The state you're in, you won't remember any of it in the morning.'

'If it makes you feel better, I'll make notes. I promise to concentrate and learn quickly. You won't have to tell me anything twice.'

'The first thing you should learn is that you should never, ever drink again. The next time you are given a choice of drink or no drink, choose no drink.' Casting her a look of undiluted exasperation, Stefan deposited her in the centre of the huge bed and turned to the woman who had just entered the room. He spoke in rapid Greek as Selene flopped onto her side.

'You're always giving out orders. Does anyone ever say no to you?'

'They work for me. They're paid to say yes. I ordered you a pot of coffee.'

'I can't drink coffee this late. It will keep me awake. Do you give orders in the bedroom?' She sat up and rested her chin on her knees as she watched him. 'Remove your clothes—lie like this—' Her voice was sultry and she saw that his powerful body was simmering with barely suppressed tension.

'*Stop* talking,' Stefan advised in a thickened tone.

Selene watched him hungrily, admiring the sleek, powerful lines of his body. 'Can I ask you something?'

'No.'

'Have you ever been in love?'

'*Stop* talking, Selene. Snap that pretty mouth of yours

shut and keep it shut.' He wrenched off his jacket and slung it on the nearest chair.

'I'll take that as a no.' Her head spinning, Selene flopped back against the soft pile of pillows that adorned the bed. 'I want to be in love. I really, really want to be in love. As long as he loves me back. I would never, ever be with someone who doesn't care for me. That's one of my rules.'

'Does this conversation have a point?'

'I'm just telling you more about me.'

'I don't need to know more about you. I already know all I need to know.'

'So you're a man who doesn't believe in love? I bet as far as you're concerned it's a myth right up there with the Minotaur and the legend of Atlantis.'

'You should definitely stop talking.' Stefan removed his bow tie with an impatient flick of his long fingers. 'Go into the bathroom and turn the shower to cold. It might help you. It would definitely help me.'

She rolled onto her stomach and leaned her chin in her palm. 'Do you know what this room needs? Scented candles. Studies have shown that nine out of ten men are more likely to get laid if there is a scented candle in the room.'

His mouth tightened. 'You know nothing about getting laid.'

'I'm doing my best but you're not being very accommodating.' Trying to distract herself from the spinning, Selene beckoned to him. 'Kiss me. And this time don't stop.'

He stilled, his eyes a dark, dangerous black. 'You are playing with fire.'

'I'd so much rather be playing with you…' Registering the exasperation on his face, she giggled. 'For a sophisticated man of the world with a shocking reputation, you're very restrained.'

'A drunk woman telling me she wants love tends to

do that to me.' Unbelievably tense, Stefan dropped his tie onto a vacant chair and undid the top button of his shirt, his eyes never leaving her face.

'I am definitely not drunk and I absolutely don't want love from you. I just want sex,' Selene said firmly. 'Really steamy sex. There's nothing to be afraid of. I won't hurt you. And you can walk away afterwards and neither of us will mention it again. It will be our little secret.'

The atmosphere shifted in an instant. For a moment she thought he was going to walk out of the room but instead he stared at her for a long time, as if he were making a decision about something.

Just when she'd given up on him taking it any further, he walked towards her with a purposeful stride.

As he approached her tummy tumbled and she felt a wild flicker of delicious, terrifying anticipation.

Her eyes collided with his and she struggled to sit up. 'Say something—'

'You've said more than enough already. It's time to stop talking.' His tone raw, he undid the buttons on his shirt with sure, strong fingers and her mouth dried.

Her stunned gaze rested on his wide shoulders and slid slowly down to his flat abdomen.

'I—I—'

'You issued an invitation, Selene. I'm here to take it up.'

As her eyes fixed on his he shrugged the shirt off his shoulders revealing a bare, bronzed torso that would have been the pride of any gladiator.

'That's what you want, isn't it?'

Still looking at her, he reached for the button at the top of his trousers…

CHAPTER FIVE

STEFAN lay with his hands hooked behind his head, watching as dawn sent beams of light across the bedroom. He could see a tiny bird dipping itself in the pool, playing innocently, blissfully unaware of the possibility of danger.

It reminded him of Selene.

Next to him, she stirred. With a moan, she flung her arm over her eyes. 'Turn the light off. Ugh—how can you be so thoughtless? It's giving me a headache.'

He turned his head to look at her, remembering how frank and open she'd been. He was starting to understand why her father was so overprotective. She was a sitting duck for any unscrupulous individual that happened to come along.

And now she was lying in his bed.

His bed. In his house, where no woman had stayed the night before. The house he'd built from nothing after Stavros Antaxos had ripped everything from his family.

Now he lay in silk sheets, but he never forgot how it had felt to lie on the cold, hard ground with the smell of rotting food in his nostrils. He never forgot the pain of seeing someone he loved laughing with someone he hated.

Stefan reached out and pushed her tangled blonde hair away from her face, remembering how open she'd been with him. It was the champagne, of course. 'It's called the sun. It's morning and your headache has nothing to do with the light.'

She peeled her eyelids open gingerly. For a moment she stared at him, as if trying to work something out. Those eyes slid from his bare shoulders to his abdomen and lower to—

'You're naked?' She shot up in bed and then groaned and immediately flopped back down again. 'Oh, my God, that hurts.'

There was something hopelessly endearing about her lack of sophistication. 'Yes, I'm naked. And so are you. That generally happens when two people spend the night together.' He waited for his words to sink in. Watched as her eyes widened and a faint colour touched her pale cheeks.

There would be regret, he knew. She would shoot out of his bed, accuse him of taking advantage of her and that would be the end of that. Except he would have taught her a lesson life hadn't yet taught her. To be cautious of people.

Next time she'd be more careful.

Next time she wouldn't drink so much with a man she didn't know—especially a man with his reputation.

Next time she'd know better than to trust someone like him.

'You undressed me and I don't even remember it.' Her voice was muffled by the pillow. 'I bet that was fun for you. I don't feel too good. Could I have a drink, please?'

'More champagne? That was your favourite drink last night.'

The sound from her throat was a whimper. 'No, *not* champagne. I'm never drinking again. It hurts so much. Why didn't anyone tell me it hurts afterwards? Water. Is there any water? A glass from the pool will do. I don't care. Anything as long as it isn't champagne.'

Stefan reached out a hand for the phone and spoke to someone in the kitchen, all the time aware of Selene burrowed into the pillow next to him like a very vulnerable, very sleepy kitten. She was adorable.

He frowned slightly, realising it wasn't an adjective he'd had cause to use before.

The sheet had slipped. He stared at the smooth skin of her shoulder, knowing that no other man had enjoyed the view he was enjoying now. Unable to help himself, he reached out and ran his hand down the length of her arm, feeling her tremble. But still she stayed in his bed. Even though the alcohol had to have worked its way out of her system, she wasn't showing any more caution than she had the night before.

Tenser than he could ever remember being, Stefan sprang from the bed and grabbed boxer shorts and jeans. 'My advice would be to go and take a long, cold shower.'

'That sounds like a truly horrible idea.' Selene winced as he pulled up his zip. 'Could you try and be a bit quieter? The noise is killing my head.'

And still she lay there. In his bed. In his home. Trusting him.

His fury with her father growing with every passing minute, Stefan dragged open the door of his bedroom suite, removed the tray from his staff with a nod of thanks and kicked the door shut.

Unaccustomed to playing the role of nurse, he poured iced water into a glass and handed it to her.

Run, part of him screamed. *Get out of here while you can.*

Still half under the covers, Selene eyed it doubtfully. 'I'm not sure if I'm thirsty after all. My stomach isn't happy.'

'You're dehydrated. You need fluid. And then you need food.'

'How can you mention food at a time like this?'

After a moment's hesitation, he sat down on the bed next to her and scooped her up, keeping his arm around her bare shoulders. Trying to ignore the softness of her flesh beneath his fingers, he lifted the glass to her lips. 'Drink. You'll feel better.' At least one of them would. He should never have brought her back here. It had been an appalling error of judgement on his part.

'I feel hideous. And I hate you for being so full of energy first thing in the morning.' Instead of taking the glass from him, she curled her fingers over his and took a few sips. 'Thank you. You're so kind.'

Kind.

The word jarred against his thoughts.

He felt a rush of exasperation. Somehow he had to kill this impression she had of him as some sort of god. 'You're naked in my bed and you remember nothing of last night.'

'I know. I'm *furious*.'

Stefan relaxed slightly. This was better. 'Good. You *should* be furious with me for taking advantage of you.'

'Oh, I'm not furious with *you*. I'm furious with myself. You kept telling me not to drink. I drank. My fault. How could I be furious with you? You've been amazing.'

'I was the one who stripped you naked.'

'It would have been horribly uncomfortable sleeping in that dress, so I'm grateful to you.'

He'd spent his life shattering women's illusions without trying and now, when he wanted to, he didn't seem able to manage it. Stefan shifted tack. 'It was a *very* exciting night. I am now familiar with every delicious inch of your body, and you,' he murmured, 'are familiar with every inch of mine.'

Still with her hands locked around his, Selene took a tiny sip of water. 'Really?'

'Really. You were so responsive. Unbelievably bold for someone with so little experience. When you suggested I tie you up, I admit I was surprised. I didn't think someone as innocent as you would be prepared to give a man that much power.' He'd expected shock. He hadn't expected a smile.

'I trust you. Whatever you want to do will always be fine with me.' Her simple declaration raised his tension levels several notches. Heat exploded through his body.

'*Theé mou*, I thought you were so trusting because you were drunk, but apparently not. What does it take to get you to show caution?'

'I can be cautious when I have to be. I just don't feel the need when I'm with you.'

'You should be angry.'

'I am angry. Angry with myself for ruining a really special night. You warned me to stop drinking and I didn't listen. You could have left me in a heap on the beach for anyone to take advantage of.'

Stefan couldn't believe what he was hearing. '*I* took advantage of you.'

'No, you didn't. And I'm the one who should be apologising to you for flirting and then collapsing unconscious. Hardly responsible behaviour. You were thoughtful and protective and you lay in bed all night wide awake, frustrated and determined not to touch me because that would have gone against your moral code.'

Why was it that her response was never what he expected? 'Selene, I don't have a moral code.'

'If that's true then why didn't we have sex?'

'What makes you so sure that we didn't?'

'I may be inexperienced but I'm not stupid. I'd know

if I'd had sex. And you wouldn't have done that. Not like that. Not with me. You protected me.'

Her voice husky, she turned her head to look at him and that look contained everything he'd avoided all his life. Depth. He'd always run from it because it led to something he absolutely didn't want. Not ever. He'd seen what that did. Seen lives ripped apart because of it.

'Stop turning me into a hero.'

'You could have taken advantage of me, but you didn't. You could have left me on the beach, but you didn't. You put me safely to bed where no harm could come to me.'

'*My* bed.'

'Where you didn't touch me.'

The rawness of the attraction was shocking. It pulled at the edges of his control, dragging him downwards. He no longer knew who he was protecting—himself or her.

'I was doing you a favour.'

'But you never do people favours, so that makes me feel even more special.' There was a brief pause and then she gave him a soft look that almost finished him. 'You're right. I should take that shower. It will wake me up and make me feel more human.' Her fingers uncurled from his and she slid from the bed, stood for a moment as if she were getting her balance and then walked towards the bathroom.

Naked.

Deciding that selflessness was definitely an overrated quality, Stefan was torn between a desire to flatten her back to the bed or throw a sheet over her. 'You should cover up.'

'What would be the point of that? You were the one who undressed me. You've already seen everything there is to see.'

* * *

She stood under the shower, feeling the cool water wash over her.

The drink and the tablets had cleared her head and reduced the pain to a dull ache. What couldn't be so easily erased was the knowledge she'd messed up what should have been the best night of her life so far. She almost wished he'd lived up to his reputation because then she wouldn't have been standing here bathed in regret.

Switching off the shower, she groped for the towel she'd put out for herself and instead encountered hard male muscle.

Swiping water from her eyes, she opened them. What she saw made her breath catch.

There was nothing tame there. Nothing gentle. Just raw male sexuality.

And he was naked, too.

'Maybe you should have locked the door, Selene.'

His silky voice made her stomach flip. 'Maybe I didn't see the need.'

'No?' He slid his hand behind her neck, his eyes locked on hers as he drew her head towards him. 'You need to develop a keener sense of self-preservation.'

'I can protect myself when I have to.' And she'd had to on so many occasions she didn't want to think about it. That had been her old life, and this was her new one. And because she didn't intend to screw her new life up a second time, she placed her hands on his chest.

His skin was warm. His muscles hard and smooth. The difference between her body and his fascinated her, and she explored him with her fingers and then pressed her mouth to his chest and heard his sharply indrawn breath.

'Are you afraid?' His voice was rough and she lifted her head.

'Excited, maybe a little nervous, but never afraid. Not of you.'

'And if I say that you should be?'

'I wouldn't listen. I make up my own mind. I trust myself.'

He smoothed her wet hair away from her face. 'Your hair is spectacular. You remind me of a mermaid.'

'You've met a lot of mermaids?'

'You're the first.' He lowered his head slowly, his mouth hovering just above hers. 'And I'll be *your* first so if you don't want this you'd better speak now.'

Her heart was pounding. 'I've never been more sure of anything in my life.'

'I do not come with a happy ending attached.' He spoke the words against her mouth, his fingers locked in her hair. 'There's a strong chance I'll make you cry.'

'I only cry when I'm happy. Don't worry, you're off the hook. I take full responsibility. This is my decision.' She felt the warmth of his hand at the base of her bare back as he drew her against him. Felt the hardness of his body against hers and closed her eyes, because she'd imagined it for so long in so many different ways but even her dreams had never felt as perfect as this.

'I might hurt you.'

'You could never hurt me.'

The hand on her back was now resting on the curve of her hip. 'I'm terrible at relationships.'

'I know. I don't want a relationship.' But she wanted *him* and the fact that he was still protecting her made her want him even more. 'I have a whole new exciting life ahead of me and nothing is going to get in the way.'

'You're crazy to do this—you know that, don't you? You should be slapping my face.'

'Stefan, *please*.' She gripped his biceps. 'I want this.

I want *you*. I always have.' He'd been her dream for so long, her lifeline, the one thing that had kept her going when she'd lain awake at night thinking how much she hated her life.

Something in her voice must have convinced him because he scooped her off her feet and carried her back to the bedroom.

The early morning sun beamed approval as he lowered her onto the bed.

Selene didn't care that it was daylight. Daylight meant that she could see him. All of him. Trembling with anticipation, she slid her arms around his neck, drawing him down to her. His hand locked in her hair.

'We're taking this slowly.'

'I don't want slowly.'

'I'll tie you up if I have to.'

'Then tie me up. Do it.'

His eyes darkened. 'You shouldn't say things like that.'

'Only to you.'

'You're far, far too trusting.' Something flickered in his eyes, the suggestion of a frown mingling with the blaze of raw desire.

If he changed his mind she'd die.

'Stefan—' Her hands slid down his body and she heard the sharp intake of his breath as she closed her hand around that part of him that was new to her. She felt silk over steel, experimented with the lightest of touches and heard him groan deep in his throat. The sudden switch of power was as intoxicating as the feel of him. The heady, extravagant excitement triggered by the fact that this man, this gorgeous indecently sexy man, wanted her as much as she wanted him was enough to wipe everything from her head except the moment.

Later she'd think of the future but not now, because right now her dream was finally reality.

'You have to slow down,' Stefan said in a thickened tone, closing his hand over hers to stop her. 'You've never done this before.'

'But I'm learning fast.'

'*Too* fast—' He rolled her under him and brought his mouth down on hers. She felt the erotic slide of his tongue and there was a whoosh of heat through her body that settled itself in her pelvis. The feeling was so maddeningly good that she shifted her hips against him.

He cursed softly and flattened her to the bed. 'You're beautiful.'

Without giving her a chance to answer, he continued his intimate exploration of her body, the wickedly sensual stroke of his tongue driving her wild. Pleasure arced through her as he toyed lazily with the tip of each breast and she wriggled and arched, trying to ease the growing ache low in her pelvis.

No one had told her she was beautiful before but he did so now, again and again, in English, in Greek, and with his lips and hands until she was a writhing mass of sensation.

She hadn't known it was possible to feel this good about herself.

'Stop moving,' Stefan groaned. 'You have no idea how hard you're making this for me.'

It was hard for him? For her it was torture, and when she felt him shift his weight and slide his hand over her quivering abdomen she thought she was going to explode.

'Please, now,' she begged.

He gave a ragged laugh and trailed his mouth lower. 'No way. I'm just getting started, *koukla mou*.'

'But I *really* want you to—'

'I know you do,' he growled, sheer overload of desire

lending an edge to his voice, 'but I want it to be good for you. Trust me.'

She wanted to tell him that it couldn't possibly be anything but good, but the smooth slide of his hand to the top of her thighs robbed her of the power of speech. His clever fingers lingered for a moment, tormenting her and magnifying the ache until she was no longer aware of anything except her own physical need. He touched her *there* and she sobbed with pleasure because he knew everything she didn't and wasn't afraid to show her.

She rocked her pelvis against him and instantly he moved his hand.

'Not yet. Stop moving.'

'I can't.'

'You will. Just lie there. Just—don't move.' He locked his hand round her wrists and lifted her arms above her head. 'Hold on and don't let go until I give you permission.'

Her hands touched the cool metal of the pretty iron bedframe and she curved her fingers around it, holding on as he'd ordered, out of her mind with sheer overload of sensation. She wanted it all. The scent of his skin. The feel of his hands, his mouth, his body— 'Please, Stefan—'

'I don't want to hurt you. I *won't* hurt you.'

'Please—'

'*Don't* speak.' His voice thickened with raw need, Stefan parted her thighs.

She was surprised she didn't feel embarrassed because it was full daylight, but she knew nothing she ever did with him would embarrass her—not even *this*.

This was his mouth on her, his tongue on her and in her, and she heard someone sobbing and realised that the sound was coming from her throat. He spread her wide, opening her to his gaze and his mouth, and his only concession to her innocence was his patience. With each skilled slide and lick of his clever tongue the warmth grew to heat, and it spread and consumed her until holding onto the bed felt like holding on for her life, because it was the only thing anchoring her. He demanded everything and she gave him what he demanded because she was no longer in control. He was.

It was almost a relief to feel the first fluttering of her body but he immediately stilled.

'No. Not yet.' His voice was rough. 'Relax. Do you hear me? Relax.'

She was almost crazy with the need and she tried to move her hips against his hand, but he withdrew his fingers from her gently.

'Not yet. I want to be inside you when you come. I want to feel it. Be part of it.'

Her eyes had closed but now they flickered open and she was treated to a close-up private view of sheer masculine power. Dressed, he was gorgeous, but undressed he was spectacular. Bronzed skin sheathed smooth curves of hard muscle and the dark hair that hazed the centre of his chest trailed down over his flat stomach and disappeared out of view. But she'd already seen and she knew, and she wanted to know more.

'Then do it,' she begged hoarsely. 'Do it now. Please. You're driving me crazy.'

'So impatient.' A sexy smile hovering on his mouth, Stefan shifted over her and curved her leg behind his back. 'I'm going to torture you with pleasure,' he murmured against her mouth, 'until you're mindless and begging—'

'I'm begging now.' Her gaze collided with his and every bone in her body melted under the fire in his eyes. 'It's you. You make me—crazy.'

His thick dark lashes lowered fractionally and he lowered his mouth to hers again, his kiss teasing and seductive. 'This is just the beginning.' The subtle stroke of his tongue and his skilled exploration of her mouth left her shaking and Selene kissed him back, her uninhibited response drawing a similar degree of reaction from him.

She was dimly aware that Stefan had pulled back slightly—that he was reaching for something from the table by the bed.

A moment later he slid one hand into her hair. Dazed and desperate, Selene's eyes collided with the fierce passion in his.

'If I hurt you, tell me,' Stefan said thickly, his other hand sliding under her writhing hips as he lifted her against him.

She could feel the male power of him but she was so wet, so ready, and she knew he'd done that for her, done everything he could to make her first time good.

His body felt hard, male and thoroughly unfamiliar. She closed her eyes and held her breath, just waiting, *waiting*, conscious of his leashed power and superior strength and wondering how this could possibly work out well despite his skill.

Braced for discomfort, she was surprised by his gentleness and care.

She'd expected him to thrust, but he entered her slowly, carefully, and she held her breath, the feeling of warmth and fullness taking her by surprise. She felt him pause and then his mouth brushed hers as he kissed her gently.

'Relax and open your eyes. I want you looking at me. If I'm hurting you, I want to know.'

She opened them.

Her heart slamming against her chest, Selene stared up at him, her gaze trapped by his. It was clear how much each slow, purposeful stroke was costing him and Selene slid her hands over his shoulders, feeling tension under hard, sleek muscle.

And then he did thrust, as if he could no longer help himself. He thrust deep and she held her breath because it felt like too much.

Buried deep inside her, Stefan sensed the change in her and paused, his breathing uneven and his eyes darkened to a dangerous shade of black. 'You feel incredible,' he said thickly. 'Tell me you're OK—say *something*.'

But she couldn't speak. Couldn't find any words to express what she was feeling. All she could do was move and when she did that the breath hissed through his teeth.

'I'll take that as an indication that I'm not hurting you.' He groaned, dropping his mouth to hers. His kiss was raw, passionate and hotly sexual, the skilled slide of his tongue winding the excitement tighter and tighter until Selene was aware of nothing except the building tension in her body.

Each controlled thrust of his body was designed to draw the maximum response from hers until the ache inside her grew agonising, her need for him a ravenous hunger that swept away sanity. Heat engulfed her as he drove her towards the peak with a smooth, expert rhythm and then her body tightened and she was launched into an entirely different world, a world that consisted of nothing but her and this man—just the two of them, blended in every way that mattered. Overwhelmed by sheer physical excitement, she was trapped in a vicious cycle of pleasure that sent spasm after spasm of pulsing ecstasy through her thoroughly over-sensitised body and drove him to the same point.

It was the most perfect moment of her life.

And when she finally emerged from that suspended state of erotic intensity, Stefan kissed her gently and rolled onto his side, taking her with him, stroking her hair away from her face with a hand that wasn't quite steady.

'That,' he said hoarsely, 'was incredible.'

Dazed, Selene kept her face against his shoulder, but he gave a low laugh and forced her to look at him.

'You're *not* hiding from me.' He stroked her flushed cheek with gentle fingers, his gaze searching. 'Are you OK?'

Lifting her head, Selene tumbled into that dark gaze. 'I feel amazing,' she mumbled. 'It's better than champagne.'

Humour in his eyes, he drew her head to his and kissed her. '*Much* better than champagne…'

Still dazed by her own shocking reaction to him, Selene closed her eyes.

She'd been worried her dream wouldn't live up to expectation, but it had.

He made her feel utterly desirable, irresistible and beautiful, and she'd never felt like that in her life before—had never imagined it was possible to feel like this. 'Thank you,' she murmured, wrapping her arms around his neck. 'Thank you for making it special.'

He muttered something inaudible in Greek and lowered his forehead to hers. 'I am now officially addicted to your body.'

Selene smiled up at him, feeling like a cross between a goddess and a seductress. 'I think I'm possibly addicted to yours, too.'

'Good. In that case I'm going to break one of my unbreakable rules and keep you here for another night.'

That statement was a reality check. A dark cloud passing in front of the sun. A reminder that this part of her life hadn't officially started yet. *Soon*. 'I can't do that. I have to go home.' Disappointment thudded through her and he lifted his head and frowned.

'Why?'

'I have to get back to Antaxos.'

'I thought you wanted to assert your independence?'

'I do. And to do that I have to go back to Antaxos.' She told herself that was her decision. She was going back for her mother, not her father. And nothing, not even the thought of going home, was going to spoil this moment. Her active mind quickly spun a scenario where she was living here with Stefan, spending her days with her body tangled with his.

She stared up at him, wondering if he was imagining the same thing, but his handsome face was inscrutable.

'Returning home isn't asserting your independence. It's regressing.'

'It's just a temporary thing.' She'd kept her plan secret, protected it as carefully as a mother would her child, desperate for it to grow, but all her defences were ripped away after the intimacies they'd shared. 'I have to get back to the island before my father returns and discovers I've gone. If he knows I came to you it will be difficult for me.'

'Returns?' There was a sudden tension in his shoulders. 'You mean he isn't there?'

'No. Once a year he spends a week on Crete. That's how I was able to get away.'

She wondered why they were spoiling the moment by talking about her father.

She wondered why he was suddenly so still. Why his expression was guarded.

'So you were hoping to return and leave again without him knowing?'

'Of course. Why do you think I came to you? Why do you think I dressed as a nun? He never would have let me leave had he been on the island. I've planned this for so long—you have no idea.'

'Why go back at all? Stay here with me.'

The invitation was so tempting. 'I can't do that. There are things I need from the island—' Years of playing a part stopped her revealing that final secret part of herself. It was how they lived. Pretending that this was normal. Keeping up the show for the outside world. 'Important things. But I don't plan to stay for any time at all. I have to be away again before he returns.'

'Because you're afraid he won't want you to leave? Stand up to him.' His tone cooler, Stefan eased himself away from her and sat up. 'Show him you're a grown-up and he might treat you that way.'

Missing the intimacy, Selene sat up, too. 'You don't know my father.'

'I know that being independent means taking responsibility for your actions and owning them. There is no reason to hide this from him. Tell him you're with me. Show him you're not afraid.'

She *was* afraid. She'd be a fool not to be and she wasn't a fool.

Selene thought about what happened when someone stood up to her father and she thought of her mother, alone and vulnerable on Antaxos.

'I can't do that. Not yet.' The magic had gone so she slid from the bed.

She felt different.

She felt beautiful.

She was aware of herself in a way that felt new. And she was aware of *him*. Of the way he watched her as she picked a dress from the clothes he'd bought her. Of the way he looked, his eyes hooded and his jaw shadowed by blue-black stubble.

'Come back to bed. I'll fly you back to Antaxos later if that's what you want. We'll pick up whatever it is you need and then you can come back to Athens with me. I'll help you with your business.'

'I have to do this by myself.'

She walked into the bathroom and turned on the shower, letting the jets of water slide over her body. Closing her eyes, she reached for the soap but he was there before her.

'This soap smells like you.'

She smiled and pushed her soaking-wet hair away from her face as he slid his hands down her body. 'It's my soap. It comes in the same three scents as the candles.'

'At least you know a bit more about seduction now.'

As he kissed her neck she closed her eyes, but this time the anxiety twisting inside her prevented her from relaxing.

Reluctantly, she pulled away from him and grabbed a towel.

'I have to go.'

It felt urgent now, to get this done so that she could start her new life. Excitement bubbled under the feeling of apprehension. She walked back into the bedroom and picked up the pretty linen dress she'd chosen from the clothes he'd provided. Her hesitation was driven by years of living with her father. He wasn't here, and yet she could hear his voice telling her to change into something more suitable. Telling her that the dress was too short, too eye-catching, too—everything.

Then she remembered her father wasn't going to see her wearing it.

From now on the only time she heard his voice would be in her head.

There would be no row because this was the last time she was going home and her father wouldn't be there.

Stefan strolled back into the bedroom, a towel knotted around his lean hips.

Determined not to be distracted, Selene let her own towel drop to the floor and reached for the dress.

Behind her she heard the sharp intake of his breath. Assuming his response was because she was naked, she lifted her head and smiled at him. He was looking at her body.

'*Theé mou*, did I do that? I hurt you?' He was across the room in three strides, his hands gentle on her arms as he turned her and took a closer look at her back and then her arms. 'You have bruises. Finger-marks.'

Selene twisted away from him and pulled the dress over her head quickly. 'It's fine. It's nothing.' It wasn't nothing, of course, but it wasn't anything she wanted him to know about. It was her past and she wanted it to stay in her past.

His face was suddenly pale. 'I thought I'd been gentle.'

'You were gentle. You were brilliant. Honestly, Stefan, it's nothing—' She stumbled over the words, feeling guilty that she had to let him think that but unable to give him an alternative explanation. 'And now I really need to go.'

'You should have told me I was hurting you. I would have stopped.'

'You didn't hurt me.' No way could she tell him, or anyone, the truth—and she didn't need to because she was fixing it. 'I just bruise easily, OK? It's nothing to do with you.' Not looking at him, she scooped her damp hair into a ponytail.

Now that the moment had come, she just wanted it over with. She wanted to get it done. 'I'll take the ferry to Poulos and the nuns will take me back by boat.'

'I'll take you back to Antaxos.'

'No! Someone might see you and call my father. I can't risk him knowing I've left the island. I need a head start on him.'

'Selene—' His tone raw, Stefan dragged his hand through his hair and shot her a look she couldn't interpret. 'He probably already knows.'

In the process of sliding her feet into her shoes, she assumed she'd misheard him. 'How can he possibly know?

He's with one of his women. He won't be home for another six days.'

'He knows because he will have seen the photographs.'

'Photographs?' Selene stared at him, her brain infuriatingly slow as she tried to make sense of what he was saying. 'What photographs?'

'The photographs of us together. You and me.'

'Someone took photographs?' Selene felt physically nauseated. The bag slipped from her hand. 'How could they? This is your home. There were no journalists. Please tell me you're joking.'

'I'm not joking.'

'No—' She felt the colour drain from her face, felt her fingers grow cold and her body sway. She saw the sudden narrowing of his eyes as he saw the change in her.

'I don't see why it would bother you. Nothing else has bothered you. Drinking too much champagne, waking up in my bed, having sex—'

'That's different. My father doesn't know about any of that.' Or at least she hadn't thought he did.

'So this new life of yours only works if your father doesn't know about it? The first step to independence is standing up for yourself. Just tell your father what you told me. That you want to start living your life. You're not asking him for money. You're just telling him how it is.' There was a tightness around his mouth and a coldness in his eyes. 'What can he do?'

Selene knew exactly what he could do. And she knew he wouldn't hesitate to do it.

'How do you even know there are photographs?' *Please let him be wrong.* 'Show them to me.'

Unsmiling, Stefan reached for his phone and accessed the internet. A few taps of his fingers later he was showing her photographs that snapped the leash on her panic.

'Oh, no...' Her voice was a whisper. 'It's you and I. Kissing. And it's a close-up. He's going to go wild. Who took that photo? *Who?*'

'Carys, I suppose.' The question didn't appear to interest him much. 'She writes a gossip column for a glossy magazine and for other places if the story is juicy enough.'

Selene processed that information. 'But if you know she writes a gossip column then you must have known there was a risk she'd take a photograph—that she'd tell the world about me. You must have known—you...' Her voice tailed off as her brain finally caught up. 'Wait a minute. She said something about you being a Machiavellian genius and I had no idea what she meant, but you *did* know. You did it on purpose. You invited me to the party with the express purpose of upsetting my father.'

'I invited you to the party because I needed a date and there you were, all vulnerable and sexy mixed in together—it seemed like the perfect solution.'

'And because you knew it would really upset my father?'

His eyes were cool. 'Yes, I knew it would upset your father. But presumably so did you. If he'd approved of what you were doing you wouldn't have had to come to me in the first place.'

'But I didn't want him to find out yet. It was so important that he didn't find out—why do you think I came to you in disguise?' Realising how naïve she'd been to trust him, Selene took a step backwards, stumbling over his shoes discarded on the floor. 'You warned me—everyone warned me about you—even Maria—and I didn't listen.' Because she hadn't wanted to. Because she'd spun a fantasy in her head and she'd lived with that fantasy for five years and she wasn't going to let anyone destroy it because it had been her lifeline. Her hope. Her dream. 'I thought you were being kind and thoughtful but all the time you were just making sure I came with you so that you could score a point against a business rival.'

His expression was blank. 'This is not about business. I separate the two.'

But she didn't believe him. No longer believed in anyone but herself. 'What sort of a man are you?'

'A man who isn't afraid to confront your father—which is why you came to me in the first place. I am *exactly* the person you knew I was when you walked into my office on that first day.' He snapped the words. 'It isn't my fault if you turned me into some sort of god in your head.'

'Well, don't worry. I don't think that any more.' She choked on the words. 'I can't believe you've done this. This is worse than anything.' Because now she was alone. She was on her own. There was no one out there who would help her. No one who cared. Certainly not this man.

'I've done you a favour. Your father will realise you're serious about wanting your independence. And before you get all sanctimonious can I remind you again that you came to me?' he said flatly. 'I didn't kidnap you, force you into a dress and thrust a glass of champagne in your hand. You were the one who begged me for money and you were pretty much willing to do anything to get it, I might add. If you cast your mind back to your drunken episode my behaviour was impeccable. You did everything you could to seduce me and I said no.'

Humiliation piled onto anger and misery. 'You're just a saint.'

'I never claimed to be a saint. You were the one who came to me in a nun's outfit with ridiculous expectations.'

She stared at him, mute, seeing the uncomfortable truth in everything he was saying. It had been her decision to come. Her decision to drink champagne. Her decision to kiss him and go to bed with him.

She'd wanted so badly to be able to make her own decisions and all she'd done was make bad ones. Lonely and desperate, she'd built him up in her mind as some sort of perfect being and the truth was a horrible blow.

He'd used her to score points against her father and she was the one who would pay the price. *And her mother.*

Thinking of it made her limbs shake. 'You're right, of course. From now on I'll be making more careful decisions. And the first will be to stay away from men like you. That's what you wanted, wasn't it? You wanted me to be more cynical. Well, now I am. I'm officially cynical.'

His features taut, he stepped towards her. 'Selene—'

'Don't touch me. You only invited me to the party because you knew it would upset him.'

'That isn't true. I invited you to the party because you're sexy as hell and your innocence was—refreshing.'

'Well, I'm not innocent any more.'

'You are overreacting. This will be to your advantage. Once he realises you're serious about being independent and making your business a success he'll let you go.' Those wide shoulders lifted in a dismissive shrug. 'I've done you a favour. There's no point in rebelling if no one knows you're rebelling.'

'I've told you this isn't about rebellion. It was never about rebellion.' Selene could hardly breathe as her mind ran swiftly through the possible consequences.

'If you allow your father to bully you, he will always bully you.'

'You have no idea. No idea what you've done. No idea of the consequences that this will have.' Galvanised into action, she stumbled around the room, gathering her things and stuffing them frantically into her bag. 'I have to leave, right now. Is there a ferry from here?' How long did she have? *How long?* She was panicking too much to make the calculation and truthfully it was impossible to know because she didn't know what time her father would have seen the photographs.

He swore under his breath. 'You need to calm down—'

'When would these photos have come out? What time?' Someone, somewhere would have seen them. She was sure of that. Her father was so paranoid and self-absorbed that he had whole teams of people scouring the media for mentions of himself. The moment the images had appeared on the internet someone would have seen them and would have told him. She had no doubt that he already knew everything. Nothing escaped him—especially something as catastrophic as this.

'I don't understand why you're so concerned. I've already told you I'm giving you the money. You'll be able to have the lifestyle you want. Buy what you like without your father's approval.'

All the money in the world would be useless if she couldn't get her mother away from the island. *'What time?'*

Stefan flicked his gaze back to the screen of his phone. 'This one was posted around midnight.'

'Midnight?' Hours ago. And she'd been lying in his bed, basking in the ability to make her own choices, unaware that she'd made nothing but bad ones. Fear gripped her like a nasty virus. She felt dizzy with it. Sick. 'If my father saw these at midnight then that means—' He might already be on his way back to the island and her mother was alone and unprotected. 'I have to leave now.'

Stefan swore under his breath and reached out his hand but she flinched away from him, flattening herself against the wall.

'Get away from me. Don't pretend you care about me,'

she mumbled. 'I know you don't. I don't *ever* want you to touch me again.'

'Fine. I won't touch you.' He spoke through clenched teeth. 'But at least stand still and look at me. The way to handle this is not to sprint home like a good, obedient girl.'

'You have no idea. You have no idea what you've done.'

'At worst I've annoyed your father and reinforced the message that you want to be independent.'

'You might have taken that opportunity away from me—' Her throat was thick with tears. If her father returned home before her, her mother would be too afraid to leave. She'd lose her nerve as she'd lost it so many times before. 'I want to leave. Now.'

'Fine, if that's what you want. Run home. That's clearly where you belong. You're a child, not a woman.' Stefan's face was a frozen mask as he strode across the room and opened a safe concealed in the wall. 'I promised you money. I always keep my promises.'

'Because you're such a good guy?'

'No.' His mouth twisted. 'Not because of that. Call my office any time you need business help.' He dropped the money into her bag and strode towards the door. 'I'll arrange for your transport home.'

CHAPTER SIX

'STEFAN, are you even listening to me?'

Stefan turned his gaze from the window of his Athens office to his lawyer, Kostas. 'Pardon?'

'Have you heard a word I've been saying? I've been telling you that Baxter has agreed to all our terms. We've been working on this deal for over a year. We should celebrate.'

Stefan didn't feel like celebrating. He listened to his friend offer profuse congratulations, his mind preoccupied with Selene.

What the hell had possessed him to sleep with someone as inexperienced as her?

Her overreaction to the news of the photographs had made him realise how young she was. She'd said she wanted independence, but then freaked out at the thought of her father finding out.

Clearly surprised by the lack of response, Kostas paused. 'Don't you want to hear the details?'

'No. I pay you an exorbitant amount to handle details for me.'

Was it the sex that had made her panic? Remembering the bruises made him shift in his seat but nothing relieved the guilt. He'd never bruised a woman before. A love-bite maybe, but not bruises like those. They were finger-marks, caused by someone grabbing her too roughly, and the worst thing was he had no recollection of doing it.

Kostas closed the file. 'Do you want to meet him in person?'

'Meet who in person?'

Stefan went through their encounter in minute detail, trying to identify when exactly he'd hurt her. He'd been gentle with her. Careful. At no point had he been rough and yet somehow he'd caused those sick-looking yellow bruises.

Yellow bruises. He frowned. 'How old is a bruise when it turns yellow?'

His lawyer stared at him. 'What?'

'Bruises,' Stefan snapped. 'Is a fresh bruise ever yellow?'

'I'm no doctor, but doesn't it take about a week for a bruise to turn yellow? Longer than a week?'

'Theé mou.' How could he have been so dense?

Driven by a sense of urgency that was new to him, Stefan pulled out his phone and called his pilot—only to be told that he'd already delivered Selene safely to Poulos, the closest island to Antaxos. From there she'd planned to catch a boat home.

Home, where presumably her father would now be waiting.

Stefan was in no doubt as to who was responsible for those bruises.

That was why she wanted to escape from the island. Not just because she wanted her independence, but because she was afraid for her life. Afraid of her father.

The memories came from nowhere, thudding into his gut like a vicious blow.

Why doesn't she come home, Papa?

Because she can't. He won't let her. He doesn't like to lose.

The emotion inside him was primal and dangerous.

How could he have been so blind? He was probably one of the few people who knew just what Stavros Antaxos was capable of and yet he'd let his own emotions about the past blind him to the truth of the present.

'He's not going to let her go. He's never going to let her go.' He growled the words and his lawyer looked at him, startled.

'Who—?'

'I'm going to get her out of there.' Driven by emotions he hadn't allowed himself to feel for over two decades, Stefan was on his feet and at the door before his lawyer had even finished his question. 'I'm going to Antaxos.'

'There is no safe landing spot on the island of Antaxos. It's renowned for its inhospitable coastline.'

'I'll fly to the yacht and take the speedboat.' He delivered instructions to his pilot while Kostas caught up with him, following him as he took the stairs up to the helipad.

'What's going on? Is this to do with Selene Antaxos?' When Stefan looked at him, he shrugged. 'The pictures are all over the internet. Why all the questions about bruises?'

His lawyer tone was several shades cooler than usual and Stefan shot him a look. 'I don't pretend to be perfect, but I don't hurt women.' Except that he had. Not with his hands, but with his actions. And by his actions he'd made it possible for someone else to hurt her physically. A cold feeling spread down his spine.

You have no idea what you've done.

Her final words still rang in his brain and alongside was a picture of Selene stuffing her new possessions randomly into her battered bag. He'd caught a glimpse of the nun's habit and samples of her soap and candles. But it wasn't the contents of her bag that stuck in his mind as much as the look on her face.

She was a woman who wore her emotions openly and over the past two days he'd witnessed her entire repertoire. He'd seen hope, mischief, flirtation, shyness, wonder, excitement and laughter. This morning he'd seen something new. Something he hadn't understood until now.

He'd seen terror.

Suddenly his collar felt too tight and he called Takis, his head of security, and instructed him to meet him at the helicopter pad.

Kostas caught his arm. 'I have no idea what you're planning, but I advise caution where Stavros Antaxos is concerned.'

Stefan shrugged him off. 'Your advice is duly noted and ignored.'

'You have brought shame upon me and upon yourself and you did it with a man I hate more than any other.'

Selene stood stubbornly to the spot, clutching her bag like a life raft as her father vented his fury. She knew better than to answer back. Better than to try and reason because his anger was never driven by reason. And she was angry with herself, too. Angry for deviating from her original plan. If she hadn't flown to the villa with Stefan she wouldn't be in this position now.

'Why him?' Her father's eyes blazed with every emotion but love. 'Why?'

'Because he's a businessman.' Because he'd talked to her when no one else had. Because he'd paid her attention and flattered her and her stupid brain had built him up into a hero so when he'd invited her to the party it had seemed all her dreams had come true. Instead of questioning what a man like him would see in a girl like her, she'd been blinded by his stunning looks and masculine charisma.

She'd lived in the moment without thinking about tomorrow and now tomorrow had come.

'A businessman? And what is your "business"?' The derision hurt more than any blow.

'I have an idea. A good idea.'

'Then why didn't you come to me?'

'Because—' *Because you'd kill it, the way you kill everything that threatens to break up our 'family'.* 'Because I want to do this by myself.'

And she almost had.

It made her sick to think how close she'd come to a new life.

All of this could have been avoided had she simply shaken hands at the point where Stefan had agreed to give her a business loan, but she'd mixed business with pleasure and even she knew you weren't supposed to do that.

'He used you. You know that, don't you? He used you to get to me and you have no one to blame but yourself. I hope you feel cheap.'

Selene closed her eyes, remembering the way she had felt. Not cheap. Special. Beautiful. But it hadn't been real. He'd done it so that he could get juicy fodder for the photographers. All those things he'd said. All those things he'd done. It hadn't been about her—it had been about scoring points against her father. He'd sacrificed her on the altar of personal ambition. 'I made a mistake.'

'We'll say he forced you. Physically he's much bigger than you, and you're so obviously innocent no one will have any trouble believing it.'

'No!' Horrified, her eyes flew open. 'That isn't what happened.'

'It doesn't matter what happened. What matters is what

people *think* happened. I don't want our family image tarnished with this. I have my reputation to protect.'

Image. It was all about image, not reality. 'He has his reputation, too. And he'll deny it because it isn't true.' Just thinking of that story in the papers made her feel faint because simmering beneath the layers of pain that he'd deceived her was guilt that she'd let him think he was responsible for the bruises.

Her father's expression was cold and calculating. 'Who cares what's true? Mud sticks. By the time he's proved it wasn't the case no one will remember your part in it, just his. People will always wonder. You'll be the innocent girl he used.'

'No.' Selene lifted her chin. 'I won't do that to him. I won't lie.'

There was a deadly silence. 'Are you saying no to me?'

Her stomach cramped. 'I can't do that to him.'

She had money in her bag. If she could just calm the situation there might still be a way to get away. She'd persuade her mother to leave. They could slip away at night. She'd—

He stopped in front of her, too close, his hands clenched into fists that he was getting ready to use. 'So if you liked being with him so much, why bother coming back?'

She knew better than to mention her mother. 'I left because I wanted to have some fun. Freedom. Rebellion.' She made free use of Stefan's misconception. 'I've been trapped here so long with no life and I wanted to get away. But I don't actually want to leave my home. Or my family.' She almost choked on the word because she knew that no family should be like hers. A family was supposed to be a unit knitted together by blood and love. All they had was blood, and too much of that had been shed.

'So you admit you behaved badly?' He flexed his fingers. 'You admit you need discipline?'

The thought of the money in the bag gave her renewed strength. 'I'm sorry my actions upset you.'

'What's in that bag?'

Her knees turned to water. 'Clothes.'

He grabbed it. Wrenched it from her fingers so hard that he tore the skin.

Selene put her hand to her mouth and tasted blood. Inside that bag were her hopes for the future and she held her breath as he wrenched open the zip and dragged out the contents without care or respect, forcing her to watch as every one of her dreams was slaughtered in front of her.

First to fall was the red dress. That beautiful red dress she'd stuffed into her bag in a gesture of defiance against Stefan. She wished she'd left it. If ever she'd needed proof that hope was ephemeral she had it now as her father took that dress and wrenched it from neck to hem. She couldn't even pretend that he didn't know what it meant to her because he watched her face the whole time, and with every rip as she flinched a little more his mouth grew more grim. When the dress was nothing more than torn strips at her feet he kicked the pile of belongings and found her candles.

Selene didn't realise she'd made a sound but she must have done because he glanced towards her swiftly, eyes narrowed, assessing the significance of what was in his hand.

'This is it? This is your business idea? Did he laugh at you?'

'No.' Her lips felt numb. 'He thought it was a good idea.'

'Because he thought he could make a fool of me, not because your business venture has any merit. Is that it? Candles? I'm almost embarrassed a daughter of mine couldn't have been more creative.'

He picked up the apparently empty bag and her heart stopped because she knew it wasn't an empty bag and that if he looked there...if he found...

'That's it,' she muttered. 'There's nothing else there.' And of course by saying that she pronounced herself guilty.

He stared at her for a long moment and then took another look at the bag. With those fat, muscular hands that had turned her mother from vivacious to victim he patted it down and unzipped pockets. And she wished she'd worked harder to hide what was hidden there. Because he found it, of course, under the false bottom she'd created—the thick wedge of money tied with a thong because she hadn't been able to think how else to keep so much cash together.

Her father untied the sexy thong and dropped it to the floor with revulsion. 'You wore that and he paid you in cash?'

'No. I mean...' She floundered. 'The cash was just an advance to—to—'

'To pay for sex.' He put the bag down slowly, his eyes glassy with rage. 'You disgust me.'

'I'll leave. I'll leave and you'll never have to see me again.'

'Leave?' His smile was ugly. 'Oh, no. You don't get to leave. You're part of this family, Selene, and that isn't going to change. This is where you belong and you're lucky I'm prepared to have you back under my roof when you've been with *him*.'

'I don't—'

The blow was unexpected. Because she wasn't prepared, the force of it banged her head against the wall and pain exploded through her skull.

Selene crumpled to the floor, tasting blood. She was so shocked she couldn't move and she fought waves of sickness as his words pelted her like stones.

'Your mother must have known about this.'

Your wife, Selene thought dizzily. *She's your wife.* 'She
didn't know. I didn't tell her.' Touching her mouth with
the tips of her fingers, she realised she'd bitten her lip.
She tried to stumble back to her feet but her legs wouldn't
hold her and she stayed on all fours like an animal, wishing she'd made different decisions, trying not to feel because feeling was agony.

'When I've finished with you I'll talk to her and she
will tell me the truth.'

The implied threat brought her up onto her knees. 'You
stay away from her! You touch her again and I'll—' she
swayed '—I'll call the police.'

He laughed. 'We both remember what happened the
last time you did that.'

Numb, Selene stared at the floor, knowing it was hopeless.

They hadn't believed her. Or if they'd believed her
they'd refused to act. Her father was charming, powerful
and able to buy his way out of trouble. At first her sense
of justice had been shaken. She'd realised that she had no
one until one night, lying in the darkness, she'd realised
that she didn't need anyone. Maybe no one else could solve
this for her, but she could solve it for herself. Which made
it doubly frustrating that she'd blown her chance.

He prowled around her and she knew from the look in
his eyes that the moment he'd finished with her he would
start on her mother.

Something sharp pressed into her hand and she looked
down and saw that she'd fallen onto one of the jagged rem-
nants of all that was left of a glass candle-holder.

She closed her hand over it, careful to avoid cutting
herself on the sharp edge. And this time when her father came in swinging she closed her eyes and plunged

the glass into his wrist. He gave a howl of pain and staggered backwards. It wasn't enough to stop him but it was enough to slow him down and Selene didn't waste a moment of her advantage. She forced herself to her feet and stumbled from the room, slamming the door behind her as she ran from the villa. He would chase her, of course, and that was what she wanted. Because if he chased her then he wouldn't be going for her mother.

She just had to hope that his temper burned itself out before he killed them both.

Stefan manoeuvred the sleek speedboat as close to the rocks as he dared. He'd picked the north side of the island, judging the currents to be less savage. His yacht was moored further out to sea where the waters were deeper and he'd launched the tender and indulged himself in a few minutes of speed and spray as he'd skimmed the surface of the sparkling ocean towards the towering cliffs of Antaxos. But that spurt of adrenaline had been brief. Negotiating the rocky approach to the island had taken all his skill and concentration.

He let the engine idle as he assessed the distance between boat and rock, judging the rise and fall of the sea. Between both lay fathoms of swirling water, ready to swallow up victims, but Stefan had no intention of being anyone's victim. Judging it perfectly he sprang, lithe as a panther, landing safely and gesturing for his team to take the boat back out.

Takis followed him. His movements were clumsier and Stefan shot out a hand to steady him as he veered dangerously close to the water.

'Didn't sign up for this. You could have picked a nice girl from the centre of Athens, boss,' Takis muttered, his face scarlet as he found his balance. 'But, no, you had to go for the pampered princess guarded by the dragon. Working for you is never boring.'

Pampered princess.

Stefan felt a stab of guilt. Hadn't he made the same mistake?

Like everyone he'd been fooled by the image the tycoon had spun for the world. The adored wife. The much loved, overprotected daughter. The happy family.

He suspected the truth was much bleaker. Almost as bleak as this island.

Antaxos.

He stared at the narrow path that led up the cliffs to the grey, fortress-like building at the top.

As a child, he'd spent hours thinking about this place. Powerless, he'd conjured up images of the almost mythical island and imagined himself storming its rocky shores. Something had burned inside him and it burned still, confusing the past with the present.

He wasn't powerless now. He'd made sure of it. From the day his father had brought him the sickening news, through choking tears he'd promised himself—*promised her*—that one day he was going to be a man of power. His quest for that had become the driving force in his life, and when he'd lost his father, too, his drive had simply increased.

A sound made him look up.

Four men dressed in black approached down the path. Bulky men, built like gorillas, whose sole purpose in life was to stop people getting close to their reclusive billionaire boss. If the rocks hadn't killed you, these men probably would.

'This is a private island. You are not allowed to land here.'

Stefan stood his ground, legs spread, using that power

he'd sweated blood to gain. 'You might want to rethink the warmth of your welcome.'

They drew closer. 'There is nothing here for tourists. You need to leave right now.'

'I'm not a tourist and I'll leave when I'm ready.' Timing it perfectly, Stefan removed his sunglasses and the man stepped back. Recognition was followed by alarm.

'Mr Ziakas!' Thrown, the gorilla exchanged a dubious glance with his two colleagues. 'Mr Antaxos doesn't receive visitors here.' But the tone had changed. There was caution now. Respect for the reputation of the man facing them. Respect and just a touch of fear because there were so many rumours about the past life of Stefanos Ziakas. 'You should leave.'

'I'll leave when I have the girl. Where is she?'

They exchanged nervous glances. 'You can't—'

Judging that they were too scared of their boss to be of use to him, Stefan strode past them towards the ugly stone building perched on the hill. His insides churned.

Images blurred in his head and he paused, reminding himself that this was about Selene and no one else.

There was a commotion behind him but he didn't turn his head, knowing that Takis could handle all four of them with his eyes closed. Providing he didn't slip on the rocks and fall in the water.

A faint smile on his mouth, Stefan swiftly climbed the steep path. He was just calculating the most likely place for an overprotective father to lock away his daughter when Selene came flying down a set of steps that led to the path. There was blood on her face, on her hands and streaked through that beautiful pale hair. She was running so fast she almost crashed into him and he closed his hands round her arms to catch her, using all his strength to stop her propelling both of them off the cliff and onto the rocks below.

Her eyes were dazed, almost blank, and he could see now that the blood came from a cut on her head.

Swearing under his breath, Stefan turned his head and ordered Takis to bring the first-aid kit from the speedboat. Then he turned back to her, touching that blonde hair with gentle fingers as he assessed the damage.

Her eyes finally focused on him. 'What are you doing here?'

If he'd been expecting a warm welcome he was disappointed because she twisted in his grip, but he was so afraid she was going to go over the edge of the cliff he kept hold of her.

'Keep still. You'll fall.'

'I know this path. I've lived here all my life.'

And he couldn't bear to think of what that life had been like. 'Did he do this?' The anger roared like a beast but he kept his emotions hidden, not trusting his ability to contain what was inside him.

'You shouldn't be here. I don't want you here. This is *all* your fault.'

'*What* is all my fault?' Stefan tried to ignore the scent of her hair and the feel of her body against his. The hot sun beat down on them but everything else was dark. The rocks, the buildings, *the mood...*

'He saw the photographs. That's what you wanted, isn't it? He was waiting here when I arrived, so if you've come here to do more damage you're wasting your time because there is nothing more you can do than hasn't already been done.'

He didn't correct her assumption that he was somehow behind the photographs. Time enough for that later. His priority was to get her away from here.

Ignoring her attempts to free herself, he examined her

head. A blue bruise darkened the skin around her eye. Looking at it made him feel sick. 'He did that?'

'I fell. I was clumsy.'

She mumbled the words and Stefan bit back his instinctive response to that lie.

'We're leaving, Selene. I'm taking you away from here.'

There was a brief silence and then she started to laugh. 'I came to you for help and doing that made things a thousand times worse. I thought you were a hero—' Her voice broke on the word. 'And just when I find out how far from a hero you really are you turn up here to make things worse. I won't be part of your stupid business rivalry.'

She was so innocent, he thought. Like a child, with a talk of heroes.

She'd stood in front of him in her business suit, spouting numbers and pretending to know what she was talking about, and he hadn't looked deeper. He'd ignored all the instincts that had told him something wasn't quite right. Because he preferred all his interactions to be superficial, he hadn't probed. Like everyone, he hadn't questioned the happy-family image. Even he, who should have known better, had believed it.

'I never claimed to be a hero but I'm going to get you away from here. I promise you that.'

'Forget it, Stefan. If there's one thing I've learned over the past few days it's that the only person I can rely on is myself.'

Before Stefan could respond someone came striding out of the villa and down the path towards them. He recognised the bulky figure of her father.

Stavros Antaxos. Rich, reclusive and rotten. His features were set in a scowl that made closer to bulldog than man and his body groaned from an excess of good food and a shortage of physical exertion.

Stefan topped him by a foot but the other man didn't appear to notice him. His attention was fixed on his daughter.

'You're hurt, Selene—you shouldn't have run. You know how clumsy you are.' His concerned tone caught Stefan off-balance and he realised in those few seconds why no one had questioned the happy-family image so carefully created by this man. He was a master.

His expression was warm and caring as he stepped closer and it was only because Stefan was still holding her that Stefan felt her flinch.

Acting instinctively, he stepped in front of her, shielding her with the muscular power of his body while inside him the anger snapped at its leash. *'Kalimera.'* His voice was silky-smooth and deadly and the older man stopped and looked at him, apparently seeing him for the first time.

His expression altered. Something flickered in those eyes. Something deeply unpleasant. *'Ziakas!'* The other man's face grew ugly. 'You dare show up on my island after what you've done? You made a whore of my daughter. And you did it publicly to humiliate me. You took her innocence.'

Emotion almost blinding him, Stefan was about to answer that accusation with a few of his own when Selene pushed in front of him.

'He didn't take my innocence. *You* did that a long time ago when you became everything no father should ever be.'

Shock crossed her father's face. 'If I've been strict it's because I was trying to protect you from unscrupulous men who would use you to get to me.' His eyes bored into Stefan but Selene shook her head.

'No. You wanted to control me, not protect me. I know what you are, even if no one else will believe it. I won't do it any more. I won't pretend to be this perfect family. It's over.'

Stavros's expression changed slightly. 'You're very emotional, and I'm not surprised. You must be feeling very hurt. Used.'

Stefan saw the confusion on Selene's face and presumably so did her father because he carried on. 'I don't know what this man said to you, but I'm sure it has confused you. He used you to get at me so don't make the mistake of thinking that he cares for you.'

'I know that.' Selene lifted her chin. 'And I used him to get away from you, so that probably makes us equally manipulative. It was my choice to have sex with him.'

Her father moved quickly for a man carrying such excess bulk but Stefan was faster, blocking the blow and delivering two of his own, one low and one straight to the jaw that gave a satisfying crack and sent the other man sprawling on the path.

The Antaxos security team moved forward but Stefan turned his head and sent them a single fulminating glance because now he had evidence of why she'd been so desperate to leave home.

'You really want to defend a man who hits women? Is that in your job description?' When they hesitated, he transferred his gaze to the man now crumpled at his feet.

The man who was responsible for so much pain.

His knuckles throbbed. 'Get up.' Stefan barely recognised his own voice. It was thickened with anger and rage and suddenly he knew he wasn't safe around this man. 'This is what you do to women, isn't it? You live in this place so they can't escape and then you treat them like this. And they don't all get away, do they?'

'Stefan—'

Selene's voice penetrated that mist of fury but he ignored her, all his attention focused on her father.

'I'm taking her away from you. You've lost her. And

I'll be contacting lawyers and the police. The real police, by the way—not the ones you've bribed.'

He watched with a complete lack of sympathy as the tycoon dragged his overweight frame upright, staggering slightly as he stood. Without the support of his security team he appeared to shrink in size.

Stefan turned briefly to Selene. 'Go. Get in my boat. Takis will help you.'

He knew that, wounded and publicly humiliated, Stavros Antaxos was perhaps even more dangerous now than he'd been a few moments ago but to Stefan's surprise instead of denouncing his intention to take his daughter the man appeared to crumple, the fight draining from him.

'If she wants to go she can go, of course. I just want the best for her like any father would. But if she goes then she must live with the consequences.'

Stefan frowned. 'The only consequences will be positive ones. Get in my boat, Selene.'

But she didn't move. Her eyes were fixed on her father. 'I can't.'

He glanced at her impatiently, thinking that he must have misheard. 'What?'

'If I leave, he'll hurt her. That's what he means by living with the consequences. He'll hurt her and it will be my fault.'

'Who?'

'My mother. He'll hurt my mother.' It was a desperate whisper. 'It's what he always does when I don't do what he wants.'

'Your *mother*?'

And then it fell into place, all of it, and he wondered why on earth it had taken him so long to work it out. *This* was why she'd wanted the cash. To get her mother away from the island. And she'd wanted to do it while her father was away in Crete. This was the plan. No rebellion. No business plan. Just an escape plan.

An escape plan he'd wrecked.

She had no other source of income. No place to go. All her resources cut off by this brutal tyrant.

Exasperation that she hadn't told him the truth mixed in with another, unfamiliar emotion. *Guilt?* 'Where is your mother now?'

'In her room.'

With a simple movement of his head Stefan indicated that his head of security should deal with it. Reluctantly, he let go of Selene. 'Do you feel well enough to show Takis the way? If so, go and bring her here.'

Face pale, she glanced at her father and then back at him. It was obvious she didn't know whom to trust and the uncertainty in her face almost killed him.

'Just fetch her.' Unnerved by the blood still oozing from her head, Stefan took a dressing pad from one of the security team and quickly bound her head. 'Stay close to Takis and if you feel dizzy, tell him. I'd go with you but I have some business to finish here.'

Switching from intimidating hulk to pussycat, Takis smiled at Selene and took her hand. 'Which way?'

When they were a safe distance away and out of earshot, Stefan turned his attention back to her father. Turned to have a conversation that was long overdue. Finally he had the power he'd wished he'd had as a child and he used it now, feeling a rush of grim satisfaction as Antaxos's security team melted into the background, not wanting to get between the two men. 'You and I have things to discuss.'

CHAPTER SEVEN

Numb with shock, Selene sat in the stateroom of Stefan's luxury yacht, watching over her mother.

She knew she had to move but she ached from head to foot after her fall onto the hard floor. Every time she tried to boost her spirits panic descended, squashing her flat. She had nothing. No money, no home, no job, no means to support herself. And the craziest thing of all was that none of that depressed her as much as the knowledge that Stefan had set her up. That nothing about that night had been real.

It was humiliating to admit that she'd been so naïve it hadn't even occurred to her to be suspicious when he'd invited her to attend the party. She'd seen him as heroic instead of as he really was—a ruthless businessman who would stop at nothing to get what he wanted.

He was no better than her father.

She was going to have to try and find someone else to give her a business loan but she already knew her father would block every avenue.

In the midst of her lowest moment ever, the door to the stateroom opened.

Stefan stood there, casually dressed in dark jeans and a shirt that did little to disguise the muscular frame that even her father had found intimidating.

Ignoring the tug of lust deep in her belly, Selene started to boil inside. Misery turned to anger.

How *dared* he stand there, so cool, controlled and *sleek*, when her life was falling apart because of him? Yes, some of it was her fault, but if she'd known what he was going to do she would never have made that decision.

Anger simmering, she stalked through the door and closed it behind her, anxious not to wake her mother and determined to maintain her dignity no matter what.

Determined not to be trapped in a room with him, she chose the steps that led to the luxurious deck, relieved to find that Antaxos was no longer even on the horizon. It was gone and she hoped she'd never see it again.

Stefan strode after her. 'You and I have things to discuss.' He spoke through his teeth, as if he were hanging onto control by a thread. 'But first I want to know why you refused to see the doctor.'

'I don't need a doctor.' She was so shaken by what he'd done she could hardly bring herself to speak to him. 'But you should definitely see one because there has to be something *seriously* wrong with you to even contemplate doing what you did to me.'

The flare of shock in those fierce dark eyes revealed that her response wasn't the one he'd been expecting. 'I rescued you.'

'You rescued me from a situation of *your* making. That doesn't score you any points.' Her voice rose. 'Before St George killed the dragon did he first poke it in the eye with a burning stick and drive it mad so that he'd look good when he killed it? I don't think so.'

Stefan eyed her with the same astonishment he would have shown had the dragon in question just landed on his polished deck. '*You* are angry with *me*?'

'Furious. Livid.'

'Then that makes two of us.' He snapped out the words. 'But before we have this conversation I want the doctor to check you over. You had a nasty blow to the head. Do you have a headache? Blurred vision?'

'I'm seeing you perfectly clearly, Stefanos, and believe me you are *not* looking good.'

His jaw clenched. 'I would appreciate a professional opinion on your health.'

'You need a professional to tell you I'm steaming mad? You can't see that for yourself? If that's the case then you're even more insensitive than I thought.'

His only response to that was a slight tightening of his firm, sensual mouth. 'You received a significant blow to your head. I want him to check that you're all right.'

'Why? Because you care so deeply about my welfare? Or maybe because your master plan isn't finished yet? What am I supposed to do next? Dance naked on national TV?' It gave her some satisfaction to see the streaks of colour tracing the lines of his cheekbones. 'You used me. The whole thing was a set-up—the champagne, the dress, the... the sex.' Why on earth had she mentioned the sex? It was the last thing she wanted to think about. She wouldn't *let* herself think about it. She didn't dare. 'It was all planned so that someone could take the most incriminating photos possible.'

'That is *not* true.'

'That's why you rescued me, isn't it? To score another blow against my father.'

He threw her a simmering glance of raw emotion. 'Stop looking for conspiracy theories. None of this would have happened if you'd told someone your father was abusive.'

'I tried. No one would believe me. We are a happy family, remember? My father is a pillar of society. A philanthropist. He is ruthless, but part of his appeal has always been that he is a family man. People believe that.' She saw from the expression on his face that he'd believed it, too. 'Do you know that he even supports a charity for abused women?' The irony of it almost made her choke. 'I called the police once.'

'And?'

'He told them I was going through a difficult teenage phase. They believed him. Or maybe they didn't—' she shrugged '—maybe they were just afraid of what would happen if they arrested him. Either way, it just made it worse for me and for my mother.'

He turned away and closed his hands over the rail of the yacht. His knuckles were white.

'You let me think I caused those bruises.' The rawness of his tone caught her off-balance. 'You let me think I'd hurt you.'

A sharp stab of guilt punctured her anger. Thrown by the sudden shift in the conversation, she stared at his rigid shoulders and suddenly she was right back in his bed, naked and vulnerable. 'I—I didn't know what to say—'

'The truth would have been good. I blamed myself for being rough with you but I couldn't work out how or when. I went over and over it in my mind.'

'I didn't think it would bother you that much.'

'Why? You think all men like to bruise their women?' He turned, his voice a dangerous growl. 'Is that what you think?'

She shook her head. 'No. I just—I wasn't thinking about you. I was thinking about my mother. If I'd told you the truth you either wouldn't have believed me or you would have tried to stop me.'

'Or perhaps I would have helped you. If you'd mentioned just once when you were presenting your business plan that this was all about escaping from your father we

wouldn't be here now. If you'd told me the truth instead
of letting me think I'd hurt you—'

'You did hurt me.' Selene felt her insides wobble and
reminded herself that everything that had happened between them had been fake. 'I thought you were such a hero.
You talked to me that night on the boat. You were kind to
me when no one else was. When things were terrible at
home, I lay there and dreamed about you. I planned how it
was going to be when I finally met you again. How I was
going to look. What I was going to say. And every time I
imagined it you were the hero.'

His breathing was shallow. 'Selene—'

'And when I finally planned our escape you were part
of it. I'd worked through every scenario, making sure that
even if it didn't work it wouldn't make things worse. I had
a market for my candles, a way of earning money. I was
prepared for everything. Everything except a man who lied
to me. A man who used me as a pawn in his stupid business rivalry.' Dizziness washed over her like a giant wave
and she swayed slightly, resisting her body's attempts to
persuade her to lie down.

Dark brows brought together in a frown of concern,
Stefan reached for her.

She stepped away from him. 'Do not touch me,' she said
thickly. 'Do not touch me ever again, do you hear? You
might not have bruised me physically but you hurt me more
than my father ever did.' Because she'd cared. Oh, God,
she'd really cared. But there was no way she was admitting that now. He'd already had too much of her.

Eyes wary, he watched her. 'You're bleeding.'

'Good. I hope it stains your deck.'

'*Theé mou*, you are the most stubborn woman I have
ever met. Will you at least let me change the dressing on
your head before we continue this conversation?'

'No. And this conversation is over.' She fixed her gaze somewhere past his broad shoulders so that she wasn't distracted by those killer good looks which could lull a woman into thinking he was a good person. 'All I want from you is to stop at the nearest port. Then you can get back to trampling the innocent as you build your empire. You and my father are each as bad as the other.'

'I'm not dropping you anywhere. Your father is being arrested as we speak. He'll be charged but we can't be sure he won't be released. As you rightly say, he has powerful friends. You're staying with me and that's non-negotiable. Now, sit down before you fall down.'

Yesterday she would have taken his words to mean he wanted her with him but she knew better now.

'If you're planning on keeping me for leverage against my father I can assure you he won't care what you do.'

'That is *not* what I was thinking.'

'Of course it wasn't. You'd never use a person like that, would you, Stefan?'

'Selene—'

'Just so that we're clear about who we're dealing with, he isn't going to care if you throw my dead body over the side of your boat even if you've packaged me in red sequins and a bow.' She was horrified to discover a lump in her throat. 'My father doesn't love me and never has.'

What was it about her that was so unlovable?

Knowing that this wasn't the time to dwell on that, she blinked and cleared her vision. But it was too late because he'd seen and instead of backing away, which was what she would have preferred, he moved closer.

His hands were gentle on her face, tilting it as he urged her to look at him. 'If that is the truth then you are better off building your life without him. I will help you do that.' The softness in his voice almost finished her.

'No, thanks. I've already experienced your idea of "help". From now on I help myself. I don't want anything to do with either of you.'

'You're not thinking the situation through. You have nowhere to go.'

The fact that it was true did nothing to improve her mood. Panic squeezed her insides. 'I wouldn't stay on this boat with you if it were the only piece of dry land in the Mediterranean. I'd rather be eaten by sharks.'

'That's extremely unlikely in these waters.'

'Are you mocking me?'

Her voice rose and he went unnaturally still.

'No. I'm merely trying to stop you making a rash, emotional decision that will harm no one but yourself.'

'So now you're saying I'm rash and over-emotional?'

'*Cristos*, stop twisting everything I say! If you had told me the truth I would have ensured your safety. And that is enough of the past. You need to think about the future. I'm willing to offer you and your mother a home—on a temporary basis, of course,' he added swiftly, 'until you can find somewhere suitable.'

Selene heard that hastily added qualifier and burst out laughing. 'I'm almost tempted to say yes. It would serve you right to find yourself living with a woman *and* her mother. That would really cramp your style. Relax, Stefan. I can't think of anything worse than living under the same roof as you.'

His jaw was clenched. 'It's probably wise to stop talking while you're this upset because you're going to say things you don't mean.'

'I mean every word.'

'I'm trying to help you.'

'You're the one who taught me to be cautious.' Her gaze lifted to his shoulders, travelled over the bronzed skin at the base of his throat and finally met those dark eyes that could seduce a woman with a single glance. 'I don't want your help. I never want to see you again.'

Below deck in the owner's suite, Stefan poured himself a large drink, but when he lifted it to his mouth his hand was shaking so badly the liquid sloshed over the side.

Cursing softly, he put the glass down and closed his eyes, but that didn't help because his mind was tortured by images. Images of her stepping back onto the island not knowing whether her father was waiting. Images of his anger spilling over. Images of that beautiful hair streaked with blood.

Gripping the glass, he drank, feeling the fire burn his stomach.

While he'd been on the island he hadn't dared let himself feel, but he was feeling now and the emotion hit him so hard he couldn't breathe. He'd never let it out before and because he'd never let it out he had no idea how to haul it back inside again.

Business rivalry. She thought this was about *business*?

He had no idea how much time had passed but eventually he heard a voice behind him.

'Boss?'

It was Takis.

Not willing to reveal even a sliver of weakness, Stefan kept his back to him. 'Problems?'

There was a brief pause. 'Possibly. The girl and her mother have gone.'

'Gone?' He was surprised how normal he sounded. Surprised by the strength of his voice given the turmoil inside him. 'Gone where?'

'Left the boat, boss.'

'How can they have left the boat? Did they swim?'

'Er—the boat docked twenty minutes ago, boss.'

Docked?

Stefan turned his head, saw the port, and realised with a stab of shock just how long he'd been down here. While he'd been trying to get himself under control they'd arrived in Athens.

'How can they have gone?'

'No one was looking, boss.'

Stefan rolled his shoulders to ease the tension. 'You are telling me that two women, at least one of whom was in a weakened state, managed to leave my boat unobserved by any of my so-called security team within two minutes of arriving at Athens?'

'It would seem so. I take all the blame.' Takis sounded sheepish. 'Fire me. Truth is, I wasn't expecting them to leave. Selene is a very determined young woman. I underestimated her.'

'You're not the only one guilty of that.' Stefan stared blindly out of the window, knowing that the blame was his.

Instead of listening, instead of proving he was someone she could trust, he'd been angry—and she had no way of knowing that the root of that anger had nothing to do with her.

No wonder she'd walked.

She'd had enough of male anger to last her a lifetime.

Takis cleared his throat. 'I'm worried he might go after her, so I've already got a team on it and I've briefed a few people. Called in a few favours. We'll find her.'

Stefan knew that the Ziakas name had influence. He had links with everyone from the government to the Athens police. But he also knew better than to underestimate his enemy, and in this case his enemy was formidable and motivated.

Stavros Antaxos wanted his wife and daughter back

and he had a web of contacts every bit as impressive as Stefan's.

Takis was watching him. 'Have you any idea where she might go? Any clues?'

Where could she go? How did she plan to support herself?

She'd left the island with nothing. Not even the battered old bag holding her candles and soap and the money he'd given her.

Tension rushed into his shoulders. She had no one to defend her. No way of earning money.

He imagined some unscrupulous man handing her a drink. Imagined him being on the receiving end of that sweet smile and quirky sense of humour. Imagined her naked with another man—

Sweat broke out on the back of his neck and he uttered just two words.

'Find her.'

CHAPTER EIGHT

THREE weeks later Selene was balancing plates in a small *taverna* tucked away in the labyrinth of backstreets near the famous Acropolis when she heard a commotion behind her.

'Hey, Lena, take a look at *him*,' breathed Mariana, the waitress who had persuaded the owner to give Selene a job when she'd appeared out of nowhere only hours after she'd slipped away from the luxurious confines of Stefan's yacht. 'That man is smoking hot. He should come fitted with air-conditioning.'

Terrified of losing concentration and dropping the plates, Selene focused on her task until the meals were safely delivered to the table. 'Two *moussaka*, one *sofrito* and one *kleftiko*.' She was so nervous of doing something wrong and losing her job she didn't even look to see who was attracting everyone's attention and anyway, she'd had enough of 'smoking hot' men. 'Can I fetch you anything else?'

'Just that indecently sexy Greek man who has just taken the table behind you, honey,' the woman murmured, her eyes fixed in the same direction as Mariana's. 'Do they all look like that around here? If so, I'm moving here. No question.'

'That would be great for the economy.' Selene added

fresh cutlery to the table and removed empty glasses. On
her first day she'd dropped a tray. It had only happened
once. She'd learned to balance, concentrate and not overload. 'How are you enjoying your holiday? Did you make
it to Delphi yesterday?' This was the part of the job she
loved most of all—talking and getting to know people,
especially when they returned to the *taverna* again and
again. She'd used her mother's maiden name and no one
knew who she was. The anonymity was blissful, but nowhere near as blissful as being able to live her life the way
she wanted to live it. 'I'm going there on my next day off.'

'We followed your advice and went early in the morning. It was perfect. It's always good to have local knowledge.'

Knowing that her 'local knowledge' had been rapidly
acquired over a three-week period, Selene smiled. 'I'm
glad you had a good time.'

'We did. And talking of good times—' the woman
peeped over the top of her sunglasses '—that guy makes
me want to forget I'm married. If he's looking for company, send him my way.'

A nasty suspicion pricking the back of her neck, Selene
turned and glanced towards the man who was attracting
so much attention.

Stefan lounged at a table in the far corner of the *taverna*. Even without the expensive suit there was an unmistakable air of wealth and power about him, and yet
she knew women stared not because of the promise of
riches but because his raw masculine appeal promised
sex as they'd never had it before. He attracted women like
iron filings to a magnet with no apparent effort on his behalf. Perhaps that was why, she thought numbly. Perhaps
it was his supreme indifference that provided part of his
appeal. Every woman wanted to be the one to catch the

attention of a man whose attention wasn't easily caught. There wasn't a woman alive, even those happily married, who could look at this man and not wonder what a night with him would be like.

And *she* knew.

His gaze locked on hers and she knew her changed appearance hadn't fooled him for a moment. In that single look she was hit with the full force of his masculinity. Her body burned under his steady appraisal but even though she wanted to she couldn't look away.

Something passed between them. Something raw and primal that made it impossible to think of anything but those intense, unforgettable hours she'd spent in his bed.

Desperately, she tried to remind herself that none of it had been real. At least, not for him.

'Kalimera.'

He spoke softly and Selene almost stumbled, tightening her grip on the tray to stop it from crashing to the ground.

It wasn't fair that she should feel like this.

By rights she should be able to look at him and want to slap his face. Instead all she wanted to do was grab the front of his exquisitely tailored shirt with both hands and rip it open, exposing the man underneath. On the surface he seemed so urbane and sophisticated—*civilised*—and yet beneath the trappings of success was a man who had fought his way to the top with his bare hands. He had no scruples about doing what needed to be done to get what he wanted. Of course he didn't. He ran his business according to his own agenda with no thought for anyone else. He'd used her to score points against her father. Knowing that, she wanted to look away, but those dark, dangerous eyes wouldn't release her from that invisible bond that held her trapped.

Her brain appeared to have shut down and she was

breathing so fast she started to feel light-headed. 'What are you doing here?'

'Pausing for a drink in a local *taverna* after a long, stressful day at work.' He stretched out his legs, as relaxed as she was tense, those dark eyes watchful.

'Why pick this one?'

'You already know the answer to that.'

Why would he have tracked her down? Why go to that trouble?

She could feel everyone watching them, straining to hear the conversation. Saw her boss watching her with a frown and remembered just how precious this job was. 'What can I get you?'

'Just coffee.' Somehow he managed to make that instruction sound intimate. 'I like your hair. The cut shows off your face.'

The compliment threw her and she lifted her hand to her newly cropped hair.

She'd cut it herself, with blunt scissors and nothing but a chipped mirror in which to view the results. With a few hacks of those scissors she'd become Lena. And when she'd finished hacking she'd scooped up the mounds of soft golden hair and added them to the rubbish where no one would find it. It was the first thing she'd done in her new life. The second was to get a job, and she knew she'd been lucky to get this one when so many were struggling.

'What do you want, Stefan?'

'You didn't have to cut it. You don't have to hide.'

Panic gripped her and she glanced over her shoulder to check no one was listening. 'I'm not hiding. I'm working in a restaurant in full daylight. And I'd like to take your order.'

'You're trying not to draw attention to yourself. You've cut your hair. You're nervous. I can protect you.'

There was a strange fluttering low in her belly. 'Too late. I don't believe in heroes any more.'

'How about man's ability to make a mistake. Do you believe in that?'

She didn't dare listen. He was smooth, persuasive and a master negotiator. She knew he would probably be capable of convincing her of anything.

'I'll fetch your coffee.'

'What time do you finish?'

'It doesn't matter. I don't want you to come here again. You *mustn't* come here again. You're too—conspicuous.' Her heart thudded hard against her ribs. The thought that her father might find her made her feel sick. She'd contemplated hiding away but that would have made it impossible for her to work, and if she couldn't earn money she couldn't be independent. And that wasn't all, of course. She refused to live her life in hiding.

He read her mind and his gaze darkened. 'I won't let him hurt you.'

'You were the reason he hurt me last time. If you come here, you'll attract attention. I don't want you here again.'

He reached out, those long, strong fingers trapping hers. 'I repeat—he won't hurt you.'

'And how do you plan to stop him? I'd rather rely on myself, thank you.'

'The police questioned him and then released him. You haven't been out of our sight for the past three weeks.'

The shock was physical. She snatched her hand away from his. '*Our* sight?'

'I had to ensure your safety. As you pointed out when we last met, my actions put you in danger. The least I could do was fix that. He won't touch you again.'

'You've had me followed?'

'For your safety.'

The thought made her grow cold. He'd had her followed and she hadn't noticed. She'd been alert, on the look-out, but she hadn't noticed. How could that have happened?

She looked around but no one stood out. There were tourists. A group of Americans. An English couple. A bunch of local men. Two giggling teenage girls. 'How? Who has been watching me?'

'You wouldn't have seen them so stop beating yourself up for being unobservant.'

'I've been looking.'

'Takis only employs the best in his team. If you'd spotted them they would have been out of a job.'

Takis. Selene remembered how kind he'd been to her mother that day. How kind he'd been to her. 'He's…' She sighed. 'I liked him.'

'I only employ the best, too. As I said—you don't need to be afraid.'

'I'm not afraid. And I don't appreciate you interfering.'

'You accused me of putting you in danger. You have to allow me to put that right.' His tone was conversational. Casual. No one watching them would have guessed they were talking about anything more significant than the menu.

'If you don't want to put me in danger the best thing you can do is stay away.'

'We'll talk about it over dinner, Selene.'

'No way.'

'Last time we spent an evening together we had fun.' He hesitated. 'I want to see you again.'

The air left her lungs in a rush and she was so shocked she simply stared at him. Terrified that someone might have overheard, she didn't dare look at anyone. 'The last time we spent an evening together you ruined my life. And my name is Lena. I'll fetch your coffee.' She backed away from him, knocking into the table behind her.

The last time we spent an evening together we had fun.

Those words sent images rushing back into her head. Images she'd been trying to delete for the past three weeks.

She walked briskly back inside the *taverna*, shaking so badly she was convinced everyone would notice.

Fortunately they all seemed too overawed by the identity of their illustrious visitor to pay any attention to her pale face.

'Everything OK?' Mariana walked up to her, her cheeks pink from the heat. 'It's a hot one today, that's for sure.'

A rowdy group of young men took a table near to them and Selene took a step towards them, but Mariana stepped in front of her in a smooth move.

'I'll take them. They look as though they've had a bit too much to drink already. Just my type.'

Selene frowned. 'I can handle it.'

'You serve Ziakas. He's more important. Plenty of people round here wish he'd give up running his company and run Greece. He'd soon sort out our problems. You only have to look at him to know there is nothing that man doesn't do well.'

Selene stared at her for a moment, wondering how she could have been so obtuse. 'You work for him. *You're* the one who has been watching me.'

Mariana hesitated and then shrugged. 'One of them. I don't see why it has to be a secret. If a man was going to all this trouble for me, I'd want to know. I mean, the guy has done everything except call in air support. He obviously adores you.'

'I thought we were friends?'

'We are friends. Just because I'm an expert in hand-to-hand combat doesn't mean I can't have female friendships.'

Selene's head was reeling. 'So you're—?'

'Ex-military. But fortunately I also make a mean cappuccino. It's a useful skill.'

Mouth tight, Selene picked up the coffee order from the counter and thrust the cup to Mariana. 'In that case you can serve him. He's your boss.'

'A few layers above me. Technically I work for Takis. I don't understand why you're upset.' Mariana's expression was curious. 'The guy has virtually enlisted the Marines to keep you safe. And he is so tough. If a guy like him were that keen on me I wouldn't be complaining. Unfortunately I only attract losers and once they discover I can break their arm with one twist they run away terrified. No idea why.'

'He's not keen.'

'Right. So he's going to all this trouble just for his entertainment? I don't think so.' Marianna added a spoon to the saucer. 'Why not just go out with him a few times? Have some fun with his bank account?'

'The problem with rich guys,' Selene said tightly, 'is that they think all that money gives them the right to trample all over you.'

Mariana's gaze slid to Stefan. 'He can trample on me any time he likes. Sadly he hasn't looked once in my direction and that's because he can't stop looking at you. Are you seriously not going to do anything about that?'

'No, I'm not. Tell me one other thing—did he arrange for me to have this job?'

Mariana pulled a face. 'I—'

'Great. So I didn't even get this on my own merits.' Furious, confused, she walked over to the group of men. 'What can I get you?'

They were rowdy but good-natured, and this was their third trip to the *taverna* in the same week so she recognised them immediately.

'Hey, Lena—' one of them winked at her '—what are the specials tonight?'

She told them, handing out menus and taking their drinks order, shifting slightly to one side when the man's hand covered her bottom.

'I recommend the lamb.'

'We're going clubbing later. Will you come?'

'I'll be too tired after working here all day, but thanks for the invitation.' She was used to deflecting invitations and she kept it light and friendly, kept the smile on her face, all the while aware of Stefan seated two tables away, listening to every word.

She felt him watching her. Felt those sinfully sexy eyes following her every move as she moved between tables serving tourists and locals.

He sat still as Mariana delivered his coffee, and continued to watch Selene until her nerves were shredded and she hardly dared hold a plate in case it slipped from her sweaty fingers.

The fact that they'd been watching her without her knowledge freaked her out.

Who else was watching her?

Suddenly she made a decision.

Walking through to the bar area, which couldn't be seen from the restaurant, she smiled sickly at the owner and told him she was feeling unwell. The job wasn't real anyway. He'd only given her the job because the Ziakas machine had swung into action.

She went to the bathroom, pushed open the window, climbed through it and dropped onto the street outside.

Brushing off the dust, she derived some small satisfaction from the knowledge that she wasn't making it easy for him. No doubt he'd track her down again in no time if he wanted to, but that didn't mean she had to hand herself over.

Heart pounding, she sprinted along the maze of streets that led back to the tiny room she was renting, all the time expecting to hear the heavy tread of masculine footsteps behind her.

She was just congratulating herself on successfully slipping away when a male hand curved over her shoulder.

Terrified that it might be her father or one of his men, Selene turned round swinging but it was Stefan who caught her arm.

'It's all right. It's just me.' His voice was roughened with concern. 'But it might not have been. Why are you doing this to yourself? Why are you making it hard for us to protect you?'

'I've been followed and watched over for the whole of my life. I am trying to escape from that.'

'I offered you my help but instead you choose to spend your day working in a *taverna* being propositioned by sleazy men in Hawaiian shorts.'

'And what are you, Stefan? A sleazy man in an expensive suit? At least they're honest about what they want.' Still shaken by the panic that had gripped her when he'd touched her shoulder, she pressed herself against the wall. 'I really have no idea why you're even here. I've served my purpose and we both know you're not interested in anything or anyone unless it serves a purpose.'

'Since when did you become so cynical?'

'Since I accepted that you're a cold, emotionless megalomaniac with no redeeming qualities. Now, if you'll excuse me, I'll—'

'No.'

He planted his arms either side of her, caging her, and she gasped, shoving him hard.

'Don't *ever* trap me like that.'

'Then don't run.' But he lowered one of his arms. It made virtually no difference because he was standing so close to her there was no way she could move. 'I did *not* invite you to that party because of your father. I invited you because you were sweet and sexy and because I wanted to spend time with you.'

'I don't want to talk about this. It's too late, Stefan.'

'Journalists take photographs of me all the time. It's part of my life. So much a part of it I didn't think of it. Had you explained to me the importance of your father not knowing, it might have occurred to me.'

'I arrived in your office in disguise. Didn't that give you a clue?'

'You told me he disapproved of what you were doing and I had no reason not to question that. You were dressed in a nun's outfit—' his eyes gleamed with self-mockery, '—I assumed that what came out of your mouth was the truth.'

'But you knew I wanted to keep my visit to you a secret.'

'I didn't even think about it. There is a world of difference between a disapproving father and an abusive father. I thought you wanted to make your mark on the world. I didn't know he was leaving marks on you.' There was a brief pause. His mouth tightened. 'You should have shared that with me.'

'Apart from that one abortive attempt to tell the authorities, I've never shared it with anyone.'

'But you shared something else with me you've never shared with anyone.' His fingers brushed her cheek, surprisingly gentle. 'You could have trusted me, Selene.'

She felt her body respond instantly and knew that the biggest danger to herself came from him.

'So you're saying what happened is my fault?'

'No, it was mine.' His hand dropped. 'And I apologise because the possibility of photographs should have occurred to me and it didn't. But the reason it didn't was because I've lived with it for so long I don't notice it any more.' His leg brushed against hers. Her mind blurred.

Melting inside, Selene pressed herself hard against the wall in an attempt not to touch him. 'It really doesn't matter. I've moved on.'

'But you've moved on without me,' he said softly, 'and that isn't what I want. Your mother seems well.'

'She's very well. She's been staying in the same artists' community she lived in when she first arrived in Athens as a teenager. She's painting again and her confidence is returning. It's wonderful to see that after—' She broke off, eyes wide. 'Wait a minute, how do you know she's well? You've followed her, too?'

'Naturally we are concerned. Unlike you, she welcomes the protection. It has allowed her to relax and enjoy her new life and her old friends.'

Selene thought about how frightened her mother had been. 'All right—' her voice sounded stiff '—maybe I'm grateful to you for helping my mother, but don't think it's going to change the way I feel about you.'

'You're very cynical all of a sudden, *koukla mou*. It doesn't suit you. It isn't who you are.'

'It is now. And it was being with you that made me this way.'

'So you've changed personality in a matter of weeks? I don't believe that. You are the most open, trusting person I've met.'

'You mean I'm stupid.'

A frown touched his brows. 'No. I do not mean that.' He took a deep breath. 'I realise we have some obstacles to overcome, but it would be much easier to overcome them if I wasn't worrying about your safety all the time. I want you to come and stay at my villa, at least for a while.'

The temptation was so great it horrified her. 'No, thanks.'

'I don't want you living on your own.'

'Well, I want it. I've lived under my father's rules for so long I want the freedom to come and go as I please. I can wear what I like. See whoever I like. Be who I want to be.'

'And who do you want to be?'

She'd thought about nothing else.

'Myself,' she said simply. 'I want to be myself. Not someone else's version of who they think I should be.'

'So if I ask you—the real you—out to dinner, will you say yes?'

Selene swallowed, unsettled by how much being this close to him affected her. What scared her most in all this was how badly she lost her judgement around him. She didn't want to be the sort of woman who lost her mind around a man. 'Why are you bothering? Why are you so persistent?'

'When there is something I want, I go for it. That's who I am.'

'And you're pretending that's me? Come on, Stefan, we had one night. A whole night. I'm already the longest relationship you ever had.'

'And I'm the only relationship *you've* ever had.' His eyes were dark and not once did they shift from hers. 'Are you telling me you don't want to explore that? Are you telling me you don't think about it?'

The heat went right through her body. 'I try not to because when I remember I also remember how you used me to score points with my father.'

A muscle flickered in his jaw. 'You don't believe that it was not intentional?'

'No, I don't.' She didn't dare. She was *not* going to be gullible. 'I think you're trying to talk your way out of trouble.'

He stared down at her for a long moment. 'Even if you don't want to eat with me you're working yourself to the bone trying to afford to live. Let me help you.'

'I don't need or want your help. I'm doing fine by myself.'

'Working in a *taverna*?' He lifted his hand and touched her cropped hair. 'What about your scented candles? What happened to the dream?'

'The dream is still there. I'm working to get the money I need to set up in business.'

'You're determined to do things the hard way?'

'I'm determined to do things myself.'

'I said I'd give you a business loan. That offer still stands.'

'I no longer want anything from you.'

His gaze was suddenly thoughtful. 'You're worried you can't control your feelings around me?'

'You're right about that. There's a possibility I could punch you. I can't be sure it won't happen.'

For some reason that made him smile. He stepped back and glanced up at the run-down building. 'This is where you're living?'

'Where I'm living is none of your business. Neither is where I'm working or who I'm seeing. This is my life now and I'm not sharing the details with anyone.'

His mouth tightened as he took in the paint blistering on the woodwork. 'I want to help you and that help is not linked to what happens between us.'

'Nothing is going to happen between us. Next time I get involved with someone it will be with a man who has strong family values and who doesn't treat commitment as a contagious disease to be avoided at all costs.'

'Family. You still believe in family after what he did to you?' Lifting his hand, he traced her lower lip with his thumb, a brooding look in his eyes. 'Love just makes you vulnerable, *koukla mou*. You are hurting because you loved.'

'I'm not hurting.'

'I saw your face that day on the island. I saw the way you looked at him.'

'He's my father. You can't just undo that.' How did they come to be talking about this? It was something she'd never talked about, not even to her mother. It felt wrong to want love from someone for whom you had no respect. 'But it's—complicated.'

'Emotions are always complicated. Why do you think I avoid them?'

Despite herself, she found herself wondering about him. She saw the shadow flicker across those moody eyes and the sudden tension in his shoulders as he let his hand drop.

'My advice? Forget your father. He isn't worth a single tear from you. And as for family—' he eased away from her '—travel through life alone and no one can hurt you.'

His words shocked her. 'Thanks to my father I've been alone for the best part of twenty-two years and that sucks, too. He alienated everyone. My life was a lie. For the first time ever I'm making friends and I'm loving it. No one knows that my surname is Antaxos. No one cares. I'm Lena.'

A noisy group of tourists surged down the narrow street and she flinched.

He noticed her reaction instantly. 'And you're looking over your shoulder all the time. Come with me and you won't have to look over your shoulder.' He stepped closer to her, protecting her from the sudden crush of people. His thighs brushed against hers and her stomach clenched. 'I can protect you from your father.'

But who would protect her from Stefan?

Suffocated by the feelings inside her, Selene lifted her head and their eyes met.

The noise of the crowd faded into the background and all she could think was that he was the most insanely good-looking man she'd ever seen. And then he was kissing her, his mouth possessive, skilled, explicit as he coaxed her lips apart in echoes of what they'd shared that night at his villa.

When he finally lifted his head she had to put her hand on his chest to steady herself.

'I want to start again,' he said roughly, cupping her face in his hands and lowering his forehead to hers. 'I've never felt this way about a woman before. Everything that happened between us was real. All of it. And deep down you know it. Give me a chance to prove it to you.'

His body was pressed up against hers, and it was an incredible body. Hard muscle, height, width—he was exquisitely proportioned. Even though the night was oppressively warm, she shivered.

He lifted a hand to her short hair, toying with the ends. 'I'm attending a charity ball tomorrow on Corfu. It's going to be glamorous. Men in dinner jackets, champagne in tall, slim glasses. Your kind of evening.'

Once again temptation pulled at her but this time she pulled back. 'No, thank you.'

His eyes gleamed with exasperation. 'What happened to the sweet, trusting girl who drank too much champagne and tried to seduce me? She would never have said no to a good night out.'

'She grew up the night you used her to score points over a business rival.' Terrified by her own feelings, she pushed past him but he caught her arm, his fingers holding her still.

'What if my feelings for your father have nothing to do with our conflicting business interests?' He spoke in a tone she'd never heard him use before and it made her pause.

'Of course they do. You're just two alpha males who have to win, and because two people can't both win it's never going to end.'

'Your father ruined my father.' His voice was hoarse and not entirely steady. 'He took everything from him, starting with my mother.'

When Selene simply stared at him, he carried on. 'I was eight years old when Stavros Antaxos landed in his flashy yacht and tempted her away with the promise of a lifestyle beyond her imagination. And just in case she ever changed her mind and considered returning to her husband and son he made sure there was nothing to return to. He destroyed my father's fledgling business, his self-respect and his dignity, and the irony was he didn't need to. The day my mother walked out my father lost everything that mattered to him. He loved her so much that his life had no meaning once she'd gone. So before you judge me remember I have more reason than most for knowing just how low your father will stoop.'

Selene was welded to the spot—and not just by the shock of that unexpected revelation and by the pain she saw in his face. It was the first time she'd seen him display any real human emotion. 'I—I didn't know.'

'Well, now you do.' His tone was flat. His expression blank.

'There have always been women, of course. Before his marriage and afterwards.' She said the words to herself as much as him. 'It was one of the things I hated most— that my mother just accepted it as part of her marriage. I wanted her to have more self-respect, but she was dazzled by him to begin with and then ground down by him. He sucked the personality from her.'

'Yes. That's how he operates.'

'It's driven by insecurity.' She saw it clearly now and wondered why she hadn't before. 'He doesn't believe someone will stay with him if they can leave, so he stops them leaving. He makes them feel weak. As if they can't survive without him.' And suddenly she knew and the realisation made her feel sick. 'There was a woman—a woman who was in love with him years before my mother ever came on the scene—and she drowned on the rocks off Antaxos.'

He released her suddenly. 'We never knew if it was an accident or if she jumped.'

Without waiting for her to respond he strode away from her, leaving Selene staring after him in appalled silence.

Your father ruined my father.

The woman who had drowned was his mother.

'Stefan, wait—*Stefan*.' But her voice was lost in the crowd and he was already out of sight, his long, powerful stride eating up the ground as he walked out of her life, leaving her with nothing but the knowledge she'd been terribly, horribly wrong about him.

CHAPTER NINE

STEFAN sat sprawled in his chair at the head of the table, his features stony as he listened to his executives discussing a business issue that should have interested him but didn't. His mind was preoccupied with memories he himself had unlocked. It was like ripping open an old wound, tearing through healing tissue and exposing raw flesh. It wasn't just pain, it was screaming agony. But worse than that was the thought of Selene struggling on her own, looking over her shoulder all the time, never able to relax and just enjoy her new life.

Despite the efficient air-conditioning, sweat beaded on his brow.

As well as watching Selene they'd been watching Antaxos but her father hadn't shown his face since their encounter on that day.

What the hell had possessed him to get involved with Stavros Antaxos's daughter? It was a decision that had 'trouble' written all over it.

'Stefan—?'

Hearing his name, he glanced up and saw Maria in the doorway.

It was unheard of for her to interrupt him in a meeting and Stefan rose to his feet in a cold panic. He told himself that Takis would not have let anything happen to Selene, but still his limbs shook as he walked to the door.

'What's wrong? Have you heard from her?' His voice trailed off as he saw Selene standing in his office, the sun sending silver lights shimmering through her newly shorn hair. She wore a simple cotton strap top and a pair of shorts that revealed endless length of tanned leg.

Tears streaked her pretty face.

His world tilted. '*Theé mou*, what has happened?' He was across the room in two strides, his hands on her arms. 'Has he found you? If he's threatened you in some way then I'll—'

'He hasn't threatened me. I haven't seen him.' She choked out the words. Sniffed. 'Nothing like that.'

'Then what the hell is wrong? Tell me.'

The quiet click of the door told him that Maria had left the room, which meant that he was alone with someone who repeatedly made him feel as if he were poised on the top of a slippery slope about to plunge to his doom.

'I was so wrong about you and I'm sorry.' Her eyes lifted to his. 'I— This is *all* my fault. After I met you that night and you were so nice to me I built you up in my head as some sort of hero. I thought about you all the time, I dreamed about you, and then I met you and you were this amazing guy—' Her voice cracked. 'And we had that night, and it was fun, and you were so incredibly sexy, and being in your bed was—well, I just—I never thought anything could feel like that—'

'You need to breathe, *koukla mou*.'

'No, I need to tell you this because I feel *horrible* and I'm not going to stop feeling horrible until I've said what I have to say and you have to listen.'

'I'm listening,' Stefan assured her, 'but I need you

to calm down. I thought you only cried when you were happy?'

'Turns out that's another thing I was wrong about. But mostly I was wrong about you. I was so panicked when I saw those photos, and you were so unconcerned about it I assumed you were responsible. I didn't even think about it from your point of view. Of course you didn't know about my father. Why would you? And I was so used to playing my part in this so-called happy family that I didn't even know how to tell someone that it was all fake.'

'None of this matters now. It's fine.'

'No, it isn't fine. Because you came to that island to rescue me and all I did was yell at you, and then I found out you'd got me the job and had people watching me so that I was safe, but did I thank you?' Her voice rose. 'No! I yelled at you again.'

'You wanted to be independent. I understand that.'

'I was embarrassingly unrealistic. I have no experience, no credentials, nothing that would make an employer take me on, and yet I thought I'd be able to just walk into a job and when I did I didn't even question it. If it hadn't been for you I probably would have been sleeping rough—'

'I've done that and I didn't want it for you.' He wiped that image from his mind.

'You've been so kind to me,' she mumbled, 'and I didn't deserve it. I was mean and I'm not a mean person. But I can see it all more clearly now.'

'You have been through more than anyone should have to. Why would you trust me? I was your father's enemy— that's why you came to me in the first place.'

'But I never saw you as that. I knew you weren't. I knew you were good. You *are* good.' She was standing so close to him he could smell the scent of her hair and see the flecks of black in her green eyes.

'*Don't* start that again.'

'I'm not. I know you're not a hero, but you are good. I also understand now that your mother walking off like that when you were so young must have put you off relationships for life.'

'I have had plenty of relationships.'

'I mean real ones, not just sex. You don't let anyone close because of it and that breaks my heart, because you deserve to have a lovely family.'

Stefan felt a flash of panic. 'Believe me that is *not* what I want. You are far more sensitive about this than I am. It was a long time ago and my mother was just another of your father's many conquests. It happened long, long before he met and married your mother.'

'But you're still hurting. Of course you're hurting. You brush it away like dust on your sleeve but we both know you haven't left it behind. You're carrying it with you into everything you do—your business and your relationships. It's the reason you work so hard and it's the reason you don't get involved with women. It's the reason you don't have a family. You're afraid of losing what you love.'

Her insight shocked him. 'I really don't—'

'I was the one who opened the wound. I pushed you and pushed you and suggested it was just because you were fighting over business—as if you could be that superficial.'

Stefan, who had spent his life being exactly that superficial was floored. 'Selene—'

'I'm sorry.' She flung her arms round him and hugged him tightly.

He stood immobile, the feel of her softness against him driving the breath from his body. And there was that smell again. The smell of her soap that always drove him wild. He closed his eyes and clenched his teeth to try and hold back the rush of feeling.

He couldn't remember being hugged by a woman except as part of foreplay. He stood rigid, unsure what to do next. 'I should probably get back to my meeting.'

'Couldn't they have the meeting without you? We could go somewhere private.' Her voice was muffled in his chest. 'We could have fun and do a few more things on my list.' She was still hugging him, her body warm against his, her arms wrapped around him.

'If we're doing things on your list why do we need to be private?'

'Because most of them involved getting naked with you.'

Stefan gave an incredulous laugh. 'You are the most confusing woman I've ever met.'

'I'm the least confusing woman you've ever met. I'm honest about what I want.'

'And what *do* you want?' He forced himself to ask the question even though he wasn't sure he wanted to hear the answer.

'I want quite a lot. First I'd like you to help me with my business.'

'I thought you didn't want my help?'

'It was incredibly stupid and childish of me to say that. Of course I want your help. I'd be mad to turn it down, wouldn't I? You know more about business than anyone and although candles make you wince I know I have a viable business. But I have no idea how to make it reality. If you're still prepared to help me, I'd be grateful.'

Stefan relaxed slightly. Business was the easy part. 'I'll help you.'

'I'm prepared to work as hard as I have to. I'm excited about it.' Her eyes sparkled. 'I've given up the job in the *taverna*—they only took me on because of you so I felt bad taking a job from someone else. I want to concentrate on my business and if you could loan me enough to live on while I get everything off the ground I'd consider myself fortunate. But I will pay you back. It's a loan, not a gift. No more money tied in a thong.'

Stefan lifted his brows. 'That is a creative way of keeping money in one place.'

'With hindsight it wasn't such a clever idea. My father found it.'

The thought horrified him. 'It's a good job you ran from him when you did.'

'It's a good job you turned up when you did. Thank you for that, too. And I was very impressed that you managed to land a boat on that side of the island without sinking it. That will go down in Antaxos legend, I can tell you.'

'I don't understand how you could have lived with that man all your life and escaped unscathed.'

'I'm not unscathed. I dreamed of heroes. It made me unrealistic. I created a mythical person who could defeat my father and leave him grovelling with apology—' She frowned. 'Come to think of it, you did leave him grovelling.'

'But there was no apology.'

'That would have been asking for a miracle.' Her hand was resting on his chest. 'Aren't you going to ask me what else I want apart from help with my business?'

'Go on.'

'I want to be with you. I want to go on dates like normal people. I want to have lots of sex.'

Stefan breathed deeply. 'You shouldn't say things like that—'

'I'm just saying it to you. I know I'm asking a lot because you don't normally date women. This is the part where you tell me you'll break my heart, you don't want happy-ever-after and that the longest relationship you've ever had lasted three courses over dinner.' Her arms slid round his neck. 'And this is the part where I tell you I just want to have fun with someone I trust. I want to explore the chemistry with someone I feel safe with. I want to make love with you the way we did that night at the villa and this time I don't want to have to rush off in the morning.'

Heat spread through his body. 'Selene—'

'But if you'd rather go back to your meeting...' Her finger trailed down his neck. 'Or if being hugged is making you uncomfortable and you'd rather go back to living your life in an isolated bubble, that's fine with me. Actually it's not fine with me, and if that's what you decide you'll probably find I'm just as persistent as you are when I want something.'

He caught her hand in his. 'You're driving me crazy.'

'Good. Because I haven't slept since that night at your villa. I've turned into a sex maniac. If you could do something about that, I'd appreciate it.' Her fingers tangled with his. 'Look at it this way—if it doesn't work out you can just dump me and move on. Isn't that what you always do? It's never caused you a problem before. What's different this time?'

His collar was constricting his throat and he extracted himself from her arms, yanked at his tie and flipped open the top button of his shirt. 'Your first instinct was probably the right one. You should stay away from me. I'm not good for you.'

'Maybe you are. And maybe I'm good for you. But if we don't do this we'll never find out.'

'I know that this product is special. It's a luxury. A treat. Something to make a woman feel pampered. If we sell it in supermarkets as an everyday item, it loses its appeal. It's a high-end product. I thought maybe if we made it exclusive to your spa hotels to begin with it might add to the feel that this is a superior product.'

Selene stopped talking, aware of the twelve people in the room all watching her. It should have felt daunting, but only one person interested her and that was the man who lounged at the head of the table. Stefan hadn't spoken a word since the meeting began and yet it was obvious from the body language of everyone in the room that his opinion was the one that mattered.

He'd removed his jacket. On the surface he was no different from anyone else, and yet he throbbed with authority and power. Even without speaking he commanded the room and Selene felt something stir inside her.

He was shockingly handsome, those dark lashes framing eyes that looked at her with raw sexual promise.

Imagining that mouth on hers, she lost the thread of her speech.

He smiled, and the fact that he so clearly knew what she was thinking infuriated her and at the same time made her insides turn to jelly.

She didn't want to be that predictable, but she loved the fact he could read her. She didn't want him to be so sure of her, but she wanted him to know her. She wanted that intimacy.

'Exclusive,' she said firmly. 'That's the approach I think we should take. By making it hard to get, people might want it more.'

His eyes held hers. Amusement danced there, along with something infinitely darker and more dangerous.

There was an expectant silence. Heads turned to Stefan and finally he stirred.

'It's a high-risk strategy but I like it. Put it into five of our hotels to test it and if it's successful we'll roll it out across the whole group.'

Selene felt the tension ooze out of her. She'd presented her ideas to a commercial task force put together by Stefan and they'd discussed everything from packaging options and advertising to demographics and market forces until her brain was a blur.

'Start exclusive.' Adam, head of Ziakas Business Development, picked up one of the candles and nodded. 'I can work with that. Jenny?'

Jenny was head of public relations for the Ziakas Corporation. 'Yes, our campaign should focus on the luxury element. We'll invite a few journalists for pamper days—they can share their experiences. Spread the word. Create demand. I'll have some companies pitch ideas.'

By the time the meeting eventually finished Selene had been on her feet for almost four hours, but she'd learned so much and her head was buzzing.

'We're done here.' Stefan rose to his feet, dismissing everyone, but as Selene closed her laptop—her brand-new laptop—he stopped her. 'Not you.'

Finally the room cleared and it was just the two of them left alone.

'So...' Stefan strolled round the table, his attention focused on her. 'By making it hard to get, people might want more? I can confirm that's the case. Do you have any idea how much control I had to exercise today?'

Shaken by the look in his eyes, she swallowed. 'Did you?'

'Yes. Normally I like to pace during a meeting. Sitting still drives me mad.'

'So why did you?'

'Because you look disturbingly hot in your suit and I've been aroused for the entire meeting. *Not* comfortable.' He slid his hand behind her neck and drew her face to him. 'Are you wearing stockings under that skirt?'

'Maybe. Possibly.' Her heart was pounding. 'So you would have said yes to anything? Does that mean you thought my ideas were rubbish?'

'No. It means I thought your ideas were excellent but you talk too much.' His eyes were on her mouth. 'You had me sold in the first ten minutes. You could have stopped then and I could have taken you to bed and avoided this prolonged torture.'

'I needed to convince the rest of your team.'

'You only needed to convince me. I'm the one who counts. And now I've had enough of talking about candles.' His eyes gleamed. 'I'm all burnt out.'

'Very funny. Are you laughing at me?'

'I never laugh at business. You have a good product. A product you believe in. You should be proud, *koukla mou*.'

'You shouldn't call me that when we're working. I don't want people to think this is favouritism.'

'I don't care what people think, but just for the record I can tell you that everyone who works for me knows I'm incapable of favouritism.' He slid his fingers into her cropped hair. 'I like it like this.'

'So do I. It was a bit of an impulse but now I've got used to it I think it suits the new me.' She was so aware of him, her body stirring at the memories of how it felt to be with him, and her heart went crazy as he curved his hand around her face and kissed her gently.

'Pack up your things. We're leaving on a market research trip.'

'What sort of market research?'

'You want to sell your product in my exclusive hotels. You've never even stayed in one. So we're going to take your Seduction candle to a hotel and see how it performs in a field test.'

She gave a gurgle of laughter. 'Where?'

'Santorini. You once told me you didn't know Greek Islands could be beautiful. I'm going to broaden your education. It's time you experienced sex against a backdrop of dramatic views and spectacular sunsets.'

'What? Right now?'

'Yes, now. We're going to spend time alone together. Just me, you—' he kissed the top of her nose '—and your candle.'

'And my soap. Don't forget the soap. It's a useful addition to the range.'

'How can I forget the soap?' His hands slid into her hair and his mouth hovered close to hers. 'I smell it on you and it drives me crazy because it makes me think of you naked in my shower.'

'You have a focused mind, Mr Ziakas.'

'I do indeed. And right now it's focused on you.'

They flew to Santorini in his private jet and Selene was dazzled by her first views of the stunning volcanic island with its pretty whitewashed houses and blue-domed churches overlooking the sparkling Aegean Sea.

'It's stunning. I didn't even know places like this existed.'

'Did you never travel anywhere with your father?'

'No. He liked to give the impression of being loving and protective, keeping us out of the media glare, but in reality he just didn't want us to cramp his style. I think he probably stayed in places like this all his life, but without us.'

'This' was the Ziakas Hot Spa, an exclusive hotel consisting of individual private suites nestling into the hillside overlooking the Caldera.

'I never imagined anywhere as romantic as this existed,' Selene murmured as she walked onto their private terrace and stared across the sea.

'You surprise me. Your brain appears to have infinite capacity for dreaming.'

'I know. It's what kept me sane. But this…' She sighed happily and picked up a card from the table placed in a strategic position overlooking the sea. 'This place even has…' She read the card and looked at him in astonishment. 'A pillow menu?'

'Duck as the starter, goose as the main, hypo-allergenic for dessert.' Smiling, he stripped off and dived into their private pool, soaking Selene in the process.

She stood there, gasping, showered in droplets. 'Thank you. Now I'm wet.'

'Good. Join me.'

'We're in public.'

'We are not in public. This is their best suite and it isn't overlooked. And I am the boss.' He gave her a slow, wicked smile. 'No one will dare disturb us, and if they do you have a choice of over seven different pillow types with which to assault them. Are you going to join me voluntarily or do I have to fetch you?'

She put down the pillow menu. 'This is my work suit. It's wet.'

'I'll buy you another. You have to the count of three to get naked. One—'

'But—'

'Two—'

Selene toed off her shoes and wriggled out of her skirt and jacket.

Stefan groaned as he saw her stockings. 'You're killing me.'

'Good.' She slid the stockings down her legs slowly, enjoying his reaction. 'By the way, I'm keeping my underwear on.' As she held her breath and jumped in she thought she heard him mutter 'Not for long…' but the cool water closed over her head and felt blissful on her heated skin.

She surfaced to find him right next to her.

His hand was on her hip and then her waist, and a fierce stab of excitement shot through her body and pooled in her pelvis.

I love you.

The words flew into her brain but for once she managed to stop her thoughts popping out through her mouth because she knew this one would send him running.

Instead she stayed still and savoured the contrast between the cool of the water and the heat of his mouth.

She was here. She had now.

That was enough.

Behind them, the setting sun was dipping down to the sea, but neither of them noticed the spectacle that drew tourists from all over the world. Their focus was on each other.

Her mouth was as urgent as his, her hands as desperate to touch and explore, and this time it was all the more exciting because she used the knowledge he'd given her. When she ran her tongue along the seam of his sensual mouth he groaned and tried to take possession, but she held back just a little bit, enjoying the feeling of power that came from knowing she was driving him crazy. But holding back only worked as long as he allowed it, and when he clamped his hand on the back of her head and held her for his kiss it was her turn to moan. His kiss was deliberate and unashamedly erotic, each skilled slide of his tongue a tantalising promise of things to come.

When he closed his hands over her bottom and lifted her she instinctively wrapped her legs around him. Her sensitive skin brushed against his solid, muscular thighs and she realised she was naked—that somehow in the heat of that kiss he'd removed the last of her clothing and she hadn't even noticed. But she noticed now, felt the heat of him brush against her, and the contrast drove her crazy. She dug her fingers into his shoulders, felt resistance and hard muscle beneath sleek bronzed skin.

'I want you.' His eyes were so dark they were almost black, his voice a low growl. 'Here. Now.'

Maybe had she been more coherent she would have worried about the danger of being spotted, but she was beyond caring and simply moved her hips against him in a desperate attempt to relieve the ache between her thighs.

When his hand slid between her legs she gasped against his mouth. The gasp turned to a moan as his fingers explored her with all the intimate knowledge that had driven her wild the first time. His breathing was harsh and shallow, tension etched in his features as he turned her mindless.

And then he shifted her slightly and surged into her. He was hot, so hot in contrast to the cool water, and it felt so impossibly good that she sucked in air and stopped breathing.

'Cristos—' His voice was hoarse, his mouth warm on her neck as he struggled to breathe, too. 'You feel—'

'Don't stop. Please, Stefan—' The need in her was so primal she could do nothing but move her hips.

With a soft curse his fingers tightened on her, his grip almost painful. 'Just—wait—'

'Can't—' Eyes closed, she arched into him, took him deeper if that were possible, and he groaned and gave in to it.

He felt smooth, hard, powerful, and the excitement spread through her until there wasn't a single part of her body that couldn't feel him. She tried to rock her hips but his hands were clamped on her, holding her, limiting her movements, so that he was the one who controlled the rhythm. He was merciless with each stroke until the orgasm ripped through her and she sucked in gasping breaths, only dimly aware that he was gripped in his own fierce climax. And then his mouth was on hers and he kissed her through the whole wild experience, swallowing her cries, her gasps, words she wanted to speak but couldn't until the whole thing was nothing but a blur of sexual pleasure.

And when it was over, when her body finally stopped shuddering, he cupped her face in his hands, staring down at her with a stunned look in his eyes.

'That was—'

'Incredible,' she muttered and he lowered his head and kissed her. But it was a gentle, lingering kiss designed to soothe not seduce.

'I don't know what you do to me—'

'You were the one doing it to me—you wouldn't let me move.'

'I didn't dare.' He caught her lower lip gently between his teeth, his eyes fixed on hers. 'You are the sexiest woman I've ever met.'

'You better not have lied about the fact we're not over-looked or I just might turn into the most self-conscious woman you've ever met.'

He closed his hands around her waist and lifted her easily onto the side of the pool. 'Let's take a shower. I think it's time to put in an order from the pillow menu.' He vaulted out of the pool after her, water streaming from his bronzed, powerful shoulders.

It was impossible not to stare and of course he caught her staring. *'Don't* do that.' Snatching a towel from the nearest sun lounger, he pulled her to her feet and wrapped it around her. 'I have to— I can't think when you're naked—'

She was about to ask why he wanted or needed to think but his hand was in his hair and he was clearly striving for some semblance of control.

'You're incredible.' She could say that, surely, without freaking him out? It wasn't what was in her heart but it was all she dared say at this stage. Apparently it was the right thing because he scooped her off her feet and carried her through to the bedroom.

'I'll demonstrate just how incredible—'

She giggled and tightened her grip on him. 'You're going to do your back in.'

'It's not my back I'm worried about. It's other parts of me.'

'Really? Because I might be able to help you with that.' She slid her arms round his neck and pressed her lips to the damp skin of his throat. Then she lifted her head and looked around the bedroom, with its glorious views over the sea. 'I love it here. I could stay forever.'

She felt the change in him. Felt it ripple through him as he lowered her to the ground.

'Why don't you take the first shower? While you're doing that I'll check my e-mails.'

His tone was a shade cooler. Another person probably wouldn't have noticed but she was so tuned in to every subtle shift in her father's moods that she sensed the change instantly.

Confused, she stood for a moment clutching the towel, watching as he strolled to the bed and pulled his phone out of his abandoned trousers.

A moment ago he'd been focused on her and now his focus was on his phone. His business. His world. He'd shut her out as clearly as if he'd closed a door between them.

And she didn't understand it.

Selene cast her mind back to try and work out what

she'd said. 'I love you' had stayed firmly in her head, so it definitely hadn't been that.

All she'd said was that she loved it here so much she could stay forever. And that couldn't possibly—

Forever.

Her head snapped up and she stared at the ceiling, wondering how she could have been so stupid. She'd used the word 'forever' and it had to be his least favourite word in the English language.

The fact that it had been a throwaway comment didn't make a difference. It had triggered alarm bells and he'd backed off—withdrawn as quickly as if she'd booked the church. And now his attention was focused on his e-mails as if their steamy, erotic encounter in the pool had never happened.

Selene took a step towards him, then changed her mind and instead walked quietly into the shower and closed the door.

If she brought it up, tried to talk about it, she would just make it worse.

She understood that he was running from attachment. She understood that he kept his relationships short and superficial. She knew all that so it wasn't fair of her to feel this sick disappointment, was it? She knew *him*.

Reminding herself of that, she hit the buttons on the shower. There was an assortment of expensive, exclusive bath products but she ignored them and reached for a bar of her own soap from the bag she'd packed. *Relax*, she thought numbly, letting the scent of it flow over her and into her. It was what she needed.

And tomorrow she'd give him some space.

Show him she wasn't going to crowd him.

CHAPTER TEN

STEFAN lay in the dark, wide awake as she slept. She'd fallen asleep snuggled next to him and now one slender arm was wrapped around his waist and her head was buried in his shoulder as she breathed softly.

The scent of her soap—*that smell that he associated only with her*—slid into his brain and blurred his thinking.

He wanted to extract himself from her grip but he didn't want to risk waking her.

The night was warm but he was cold with panic.

He shouldn't have brought her here. He'd sent out all the wrong messages and then compounded it by not even waiting for her to undress before having sex with her in the pool.

The intensity of it made him uncomfortable. He was used to being in control, not losing control. He was used to walking away. Used to keeping himself separate. And yet here he was, his limbs tangled with hers, anything but separate.

Tomorrow, he promised himself as he stared into the darkness, when she woke he'd make some excuse. Take her back to Athens and explain he couldn't mix business with pleasure.

Having decided on that approach, he fell asleep—and

woke hours later to find the sun blazing into the room and the bed empty.

'Selene?' Assuming she was in the bathroom, he called her name, but there was no response. He sprang from the bed, prowled out to the terrace area and found no sign of her.

Alarm flashed through him and he reached for his phone and called hotel security, who told him that Selene had been in the hotel spa since it had opened.

Slightly unsettled by just how relieved he felt hearing that, Stefan relaxed and decided to take the opportunity to work. No doubt she was enjoying a massage or something similar and would be back shortly. Then they'd have the conversation he'd been planning. He'd emphasise that this was just fun, not anything serious, and they'd go from there.

Hours later he started to worry that she still hadn't returned.

He was about to call the spa when the door opened and Selene walked back into the suite, wearing a pristine white uniform presumably supplied by the staff of the spa.

His eyes slid to her wonderful curves. 'Where have you been? You've been gone all day.'

'I've been working. Wasn't that why we came here? Market research?' She put her bag down on the sun lounger and slid off her shoes—white pumps that had obviously been provided along with the uniform. 'I've spent the day in the spa, talking to the staff and the customers. It's been so useful. They loved the candles, by the way, and the whole approach of exclusive seems to work for them.' She ran her hands through her hair. 'It's so hot. I'm going to change out of my uniform and then take a dip in the pool.'

'Selene—'

'And I wanted to talk to you.' Her hands were on the buttons of her dress and he felt heat whoosh through him.

This was it.

This was the moment when she talked about the future. Where she tried to turn today into tomorrow and the day after.

'Selene—'

'I felt really strange talking to them about business when they know I'm sharing your suite. It doesn't feel professional. So I propose we end the personal side of our relationship right now. It's been fun, but we don't want to ruin everything.' She poured herself a glass of iced water from the jug on the table. 'Do you want water? I'll pour you some. It's important to drink in this heat and, knowing you, you've been working so hard you've forgotten to drink.'

'End our relationship?' Having planned to suggest exactly the same thing, Stefan was thrown by how badly he didn't want to do that. 'Why would you want to end our relationship?'

'Because I want to be taken seriously in business and that isn't going to happen if I'm having sex with the boss.'

'I don't like hearing you describe it in those terms.'

'Why not? I'm just describing exactly the way it is.'

She drained her glass and he found himself staring at her throat. And lower.

'It isn't awkward and I'm not your boss. You don't work for me. I'm simply investing in your business. It's different.' He wondered why he wasn't just jumping through the escape hatch she'd opened and perhaps she did, too, because she looked surprised.

'It's not that different. I just don't want things to be awkward.'

'I don't have that word in my vocabulary. I do what

suits me and if people don't like it that's their choice.' He watched as she lowered the glass.

'I wasn't talking about things being awkward with other people. I was talking about being awkward between us.' She put the empty glass down on the table. 'It was fun, but I think we should call it a day. Move on.'

'Well, I don't.' Furious, almost depositing his laptop on the terrace, Stefan rose to his feet, dragged her into his arms and kissed her. Her mouth was soft and sweet and the more he tasted, the more he wanted. Desire clawed at him, brutal and intense, driving out every thought he'd had about cutting the threads of this relationship. Usually he was wary of anything that threatened his sense of purpose, but in this case she'd *become* his purpose. He lifted his head. 'You're not moving on. *We're* not moving on.'

She looked dazed. Dizzy. 'I—I assumed that was what you wanted.'

So had he. 'Well, it isn't.'

He wondered if 'moving on' meant seeing other men. The thought had him scooping her up and taking her back to bed.

He was a mass of contradictions, she thought days later as she sat across from him in the pretty restaurant that overlooked the bay and the sunset. She'd been so sure that he'd been freaked out when she'd said the word 'forever' and she'd intentionally stayed out of his way, giving him space, only to return and have him behave as possessively as if their relationship were serious.

She wondered if she'd overreacted. If she'd imagined it.

Candles flickered in the faint breeze and sounds of Greek music played in the background.

It felt so far from her old life. 'Has anyone heard anything of my father?'

Stefan frowned. 'You don't need to be worried about your father.'

'I just wondered. I know you're in constant touch with Takis.'

'Of course. He's my head of security.'

'And you briefed him to tell you where my father is at all times.'

'He told you that?'

'He didn't want me to keep looking over my shoulder and worrying.'

Stefan hesitated and then reached for his wine. 'Your father hasn't left Antaxos since that night, although he did have a visit from the police.'

'He will have seen more photographs of us together.'

'But he hasn't acted. He knows he can't touch you. I won't let him touch you.'

The savage edge to his tone shocked her. 'You're so angry with him. Is it because of your mother?'

'No. My mother was an adult. She made a choice and left of her own free will.' He frowned into his glass. 'It took me years to see that.'

'That must have been painful.'

'Because I had to come to terms with the fact she chose him over my father and me? Yes, it was painful. I'd spent years planning how I could become more powerful so that I could storm the island and free her. It took me too long to realise she wouldn't have wanted to be freed.'

That was what had driven him, she realised. He'd wanted power. He'd wanted to be able to wield whatever power he needed.

'But you're still angry—'

'I'm angry because of the way he treated you.' Slowly, he put the glass down on the table. 'My mother had a choice. You didn't. You were trapped there.'

His words warmed her and confused her.

They suggested he cared and yet she knew he avoided that degree of emotional attachment to anyone. She wondered if he was driven by guilt. If he was still blaming himself for exposing her to danger.

She didn't dare hope it was anything else and she certainly didn't dare ask him.

She was just enjoying the moment, and if a part of her wanted it to be more than a moment—well, she ignored it.

She had now. She had him.

'But you rescued me.' Ignoring the envious glances of the other women in the restaurant, Selene lifted her glass. 'I can't believe you're giving me champagne after last time. You swore you'd never do it again.'

'You can drink it as long as you're with me.' His fingertips slowly caressed her wrist and she felt his touch right through her body.

It terrified her that she felt like this. It made her vulnerable, she realised. For her, this had moved beyond fun. It was the most intense experience of her life and the thought of losing it was terrifying.

'It seems ages ago,' she murmured, 'that night at your villa.'

'A lot has happened since then.' His eyes were on hers and then on her mouth and she knew he wanted exactly what she wanted.

'Stefan—'

'Let's go.' Without releasing her hand, he flung money down on the table and propelled her out of the restaurant, either oblivious or indifferent to the interested looks of the other diners.

He released her hand just long enough to ease his car out of its parking space and then slid his fingers into hers again and pressed her hand to his knee, driving one handed through the narrow streets. She probably should have been worried, but the only thing she could focus on was the hardness of his thigh under her hand and the firm grip of his fingers as they held hers.

Her breathing grew shallow. She tried not to look at him but lost the battle and turned her head briefly at the exact time he turned to look at her. Their eyes clashed. Their gazes burned and he cursed softly and brought the car to a ragged halt outside the hotel.

Throwing the keys to the parking attendant, Stefan strode directly to their suite.

They were barely through the door before his hand came behind her neck and he was kissing her.

Mouths fused, they stumbled back and the door slammed shut.

He braced one hand against the door, his other hand holding her face for his kiss, and she wanted it so badly, was so desperate for his touch, his kiss, his body, that her fingers fumbled on the buttons of his shirt. She tore it, sent buttons flying, slid her hands down hard, male muscle and then dragged her mouth from his and kissed her way down his bronzed chest.

She heard the breath hiss through his teeth as she moved lower. Heard him swear softly as she flipped open the button of his trousers, slid the zip and freed him.

She ran her hands over him, loving his body, savouring each moment as she took him in her mouth, first the tip and then as much of him as she could. He gave a harsh groan, both hands braced against the doorframe, as she explored him with the same intimacy with which he'd explored her.

'Selene—' His voice was ragged, his hands unsteady as he lifted her, kissed her hard and backed her towards the bed.

They fell, rolled, and rolled again until she was straddling him. He slid her skirt up her thighs, his hands urgent, his eyes dark with raw need as he wrenched her panties aside. She lowered herself fractionally, held his gaze as she paused and then took him in, took him deep, felt her body accommodate the silken power of him and saw the effort it took him not to thrust, to stay in control.

His eyes closed. His jaw tensed. His throat was damp with sweat, his struggle visible in every gorgeous angle of his sexy face, but she didn't want him to struggle against it. She wanted him to let go of that control and she wanted to be the one who made him do it.

'Stefan…' She murmured his name, leaned forward and licked at his mouth, her body hot and tight around his until he moaned and caught her hips in his hands, trying to slow her down.

She grabbed his hands and pushed them upwards, locking them above his head. He could have stopped her, of course. He was infinitely stronger. But either he was past defending himself or he realised how badly she wanted to take charge because he didn't fight her, just let her hold him there as she slid deeper onto his hard shaft.

'Wait—you have to—'

'Can't wait—' She was past waiting, or slowing down, or stopping or anything else, and so was he. When he thrust hard and deep she felt the power of it right through her body, felt the first fluttering of her own release and then his.

They exploded together, the ripple of her orgasm stroking the length of his hard shaft and taking him with her, on and on, until she collapsed on top of him, spent and stunned.

Weak and disorientated, she tried to roll away from him but he curled his arms around her and pulled the covers over them both.

'Where do you think you're going?'

It was the first time he'd held her like this.

The first time their intimacy had continued after sex.

Drugged with happiness, Selene smiled but didn't say anything. She wondered if he even realised what he'd just done. If not, then she didn't want to risk spoiling it by pointing it out.

He cared for her. She was sure of it.

It was true he hadn't actually said that in as many words, but he'd shown it in a million ways. He'd come after her and rescued her from the island. Then, when she'd escaped from him, he'd made sure she was all right. He'd got her a job and had people watching her so that her father couldn't get to her. And when she'd suggested they end their personal relationship and just focus on the business side of things he'd dismissed the idea instantly.

'I think you might just have killed me,' he murmured, turning his head to look at her.

His eyes were a dark, velvety black and she stared at him and felt something shift inside her.

'I love you.' She said it softly, without thinking, and immediately wanted to snatch the words back because he tensed for a second and then lifted his hand and stroked her hair gently.

'Don't say that.'

'Even if I mean it?'

'You don't mean it. You just feel that way because I'm your first lover. And because you had five years to build me up as a hero in your head.'

'That isn't—' She was going to say that wasn't why she loved him, but she didn't want to risk ruining the moment, so she simply smiled and closed her eyes, keeping her thoughts to herself. 'Let's go to sleep.'

But she was awake long after he was, staring into the

darkness, telling herself that if she kept saying it maybe a time would come when he wanted to hear it. When he might even say it back.

After a blissful week at the spa on Santorini they flew back to Athens and Stefan was sucked back into work, spending long hours in the office and travelling while Selene focused all her attention on the launch of her business.

She missed the intimacy of their suite on Santorini, missed the time when they'd been able to focus only on each other. She wondered if he'd suggest going again, but he was buried under work and the next time she flew to one of his hotels she did it alone.

Of course 'alone' never really was alone, because if he couldn't be with her himself then Stefan made sure Takis was with her. Her protection was something he wouldn't delegate to anyone else and she was touched by the evidence of how much he cared for her. It was there in everything. From the way he held her, confided small details of his life growing up, and from the way he made love to her.

But he never said he loved her and had made it clear he didn't want her to say it either.

Two weeks after they'd arrived back from Santorini they were both due to attend a charity ball and she dressed carefully, excited at the prospect of spending a whole evening with him even if it was in the company of other people.

'I've missed you,' she said cheerfully, taking his arm as they walked to the car.

'I've been hideously busy.'

'I know. I've been worried about you.' She saw him frown briefly as he slid into the car after her.

'Why would you be worried?'

'Because you work too hard,' she said softly. 'Because I care about you.'

'You don't have to worry about me.'

'Why not? Presumably you worry about me or you wouldn't arrange for someone to be with me all the time—and not just someone: Takis. It's all part of caring.'

His eyes were fixed straight ahead, his profile rigid and inflexible. 'I put you in danger. It's up to me to make sure you don't suffer for that.'

'That's all it is? Guilt?' Suddenly it upset her that he couldn't at least admit to caring just a little bit. 'You care about me, Stefan, I know you do.'

'We've arrived.' His tone cool, he unsnapped his seat belt and opened the door even though the car had barely come to a halt.

Exasperated, Selene started to speak, but he was already out of the car and standing on the red carpet waiting for her while the paparazzi crowded together to take photographs.

More photographs, she thought dully. More photographs of another fake life. Another evening where she had to pretend that what was on the surface reflected reality. Another evening of lies and never saying what she really felt. Fortunately this was her particular area of expertise, so she smiled dutifully, held his hand, posed for photographers, ate a reasonable quantity of her meal, listened attentively to speeches and did everything she was expected to do—just as she had for her father.

And all the time she felt numb inside.

'Do you want to dance?' Stefan rose to his feet and frowned when she didn't respond. 'Selene?'

She rose automatically. 'Yes, of course.'

His eyes narrowed on her face but she ignored him and walked onto the dance floor, then stopped dead. 'Actually, no.'

'No?' He drew her into his arms but she stayed rigid.

'I can't do this.'

'I thought you'd enjoy it, but if you don't want to dance you just have to say so.'

'Not the dancing. All of it.' She lifted her eyes to his. 'I can't be fake any more. I won't live a false life. I've done it for as long as I can remember and it stops now. This is who I am. This is what I feel. I'm not going to hide any more.'

His expression was guarded. 'Hide what?'

'The way I feel about you.' The look in his eyes should have silenced her instantly but she was beyond being silenced. 'I tiptoed round a man for twenty-two years of my life, Stefan, watching every word I said, trying not to upset him. I won't live like that again. I want to be able to express how I feel without worrying that I'm upsetting the person I'm with.'

His eyes darkened. 'Are you suggesting I'd hurt you?'

His interpretation shocked her. 'No, of course not. But the fact that you don't want me to tell you how I feel is making me miserable.'

'You're miserable?'

'Yes,' she whispered. 'Yes, I am. Because I love you and you don't want to hear it. I have to bite my tongue and squash everything I'm feeling down inside and I hate that.'

He didn't answer her. Just stared at her in silence while the couples around them moved slowly on the dance floor.

And suddenly she realised she'd done it again. She'd created something in her head out of nothing. When was she going to realise that just because she wanted something to happen it didn't mean she could think it into happening?

She could want him to open up, but that didn't mean he ever would.

And she could live with that or she could make a different choice.

A choice that didn't need her to compromise everything that mattered to her.

Music flowed around her but all she was aware of was him and the huge pain pressing down on her chest. 'I can't do this…' Her words were barely audible but clearly he heard her because his face seemed set in stone. 'I can't be with a man who is afraid to feel. And I can't be with a man who doesn't want to hear how I feel. I thought I could, but I can't. I'm sorry.' Mumbling the words, she pulled away from him. 'I hope you find someone. I really do. I want that for you.'

Heart breaking, knowing she had to get away before she made a terrible fool of herself, she forged her way through the crowded dance floor, slipped through a side door into a carpeted corridor and walked slap into her father.

'Hello, Selene.'

Her legs turned to water. Seeing him here was the last thing she'd expected. Since she'd been with Stefan she'd stopped looking over her shoulder. Behind her she could hear music from the dance floor, but this part of the corridor was empty and he was between her and the only exit. 'I didn't know you were here.'

'So you're still trying to make a fool of me?'

'I'm not trying to make a fool of you. I'm just living my life.'

'You came here in public with that man. He is setting you up in business. How do you think that looks to people? My biggest competitor sponsoring my daughter in her pathetic business venture.'

It was always about him, she thought dully. Always about his public image. Never about anyone else.

'It has nothing to do with you and the only reason I had to ask him is because you wouldn't help me. This is my business and it isn't pathetic. It's real. That's why he's helping me. He's sees the potential.'

'Potential?'

His laughter made Selene flinch.

This was what had drained her mother's confidence. The consistent drip of derision that eroded like acid.

For the past month she'd lived in a protected bubble. She'd forgotten what it felt like to be put down all the time. She'd forgotten how it felt to watch every word she spoke and feel her way through every conversation. 'He's helping me because I have a really good business idea that is going to make him money.'

'You're still as naïve as ever. His only interest in you is as a weapon to strike me.'

'Why do you always think everything is about you?' The words flew from her mouth and she immediately clamped it shut, cursing herself for not thinking before she spoke. Once it had been second nature to do that but with Stefan she spoke freely about everything. Well, everything except one thing. The most important thing. And she couldn't think about that now.

As always her father pounced on weakness. 'Has he ever said he loves you?'

As always he picked the words designed to do maximum damage. To inflict maximum pain.

His timing was so perfect this time she even wondered if he'd somehow overheard their exchange on the dance floor. No. He couldn't have done. If he'd been anywhere near the dance floor she would have seen him.

Or would she?

She'd been so wrapped up in her own misery she hadn't been paying attention to anyone around her.

'What Stefan says or doesn't say to me is none of your business.'

'In other words he *hasn't* told you he loves you. And now you're fooling yourself that he will say it given time.'

'I won't talk about this with you.'

'He's using you. And when he's got what he wants he'll dump you just as he's dumped every woman before you. Women are a short-term distraction, nothing more.'

She had no intention of telling him she'd just ended it.

'Don't you even care?' Horrified, she heard her voice crack. 'You're supposed to be my father. You're supposed to love me and want me to be happy. Instead you only ever smile when my life is falling apart. It pleases you that I'm unhappy.'

'If you're unhappy then it's your own fault.' There was no sympathy in his face. 'If you'd stayed at home with your family instead of destroying it, your life wouldn't be falling apart.'

'I did *not* destroy our family! You did that.'

'You are a hopeless dreamer. You always have been. You're a sitting duck for the first guy who comes along and shows you some attention.'

'That is enough.' A cold, hard voice came from behind her and Selene turned to see Stefan standing there in all his powerful fury, that angry gaze fixed on her father. 'You don't speak to her again—ever.'

'And why would you care, Ziakas? You used her.'

'No. It was you who used her. You used her to project the image of a happy family but you've never been a father to her. And I care because I love her and I won't let you upset someone I love.'

Selene couldn't breathe.

She'd wanted so badly to hear him say those words. Even though she knew he'd only said it to protect her from her father, she felt something twist inside her.

There was a long silence and then her father laughed. 'You don't believe in love any more than I do.'

'Don't bracket us together.' Stefan's voice was pure ice. 'I am nothing like you.' He took her hand, his touch firm and protective as he drew her against him. 'Let's go. There's nothing for you here.'

Stefan steered her through the crowd and down into the gardens. She was pale and unresponsive, walking where he led her but not paying any attention. Only when he was sure they were in private did he stop walking and that was when he saw the tears.

Her face was streaked with them, her eyes filled with a misery so huge that it hurt him to look at it.

'He's not worth it.' He cupped her face in his hands, desperate to wipe away those tears while everything inside him twisted and ached just to see her so unhappy. 'He isn't worth a single tear. Tell me you know that. *Theé mou*, I wish I'd punched him again just for having the nerve to approach you.'

'He waited until I was alone.'

'Like the coward he is.' Seriously concerned, he gathered her close, hugged her tightly. 'I had no idea he was even here or there is no way I would have let you walk away from me. Takis is here, but because you were with me—'

'I can protect myself. I've done it my whole life.'

'And the thought of you alone with him, growing up with him, horrifies me. I can't bear to think of it.'

'You grew up alone. That's worse.'

'No. It was easier. All I had to do was move forward. You had to escape before you could do that. Every time I think about how I messed that up I go cold.'

'It was my fault for not telling you. Don't let's go over that again.' She eased out of his grasp and brushed the heel of her hand over her cheeks. 'Sorry for the crying. I know you hate it.'

'Yes, I hate it—I hate seeing you unhappy. I never want

to see you unhappy.' He realised that he'd do anything, *anything*, to take those tears away.

'Thank you for what you said in there. For standing up for me when he said all those awful things about you just being with me to get back at him.'

When he thought of the contempt in her father's eyes he felt savage. Shocked by the extreme assault of emotion, he pushed aside his own feelings and concentrated on hers. 'What he said wasn't true. You do know that, don't you? Tell me you're not, even for a moment, thinking to yourself that he might have been right.'

'I'm not thinking that. I know what we had was real.'

The fact that she put it in the past tense sent a flash of panic burning through him. 'It *is* real.'

But she wasn't listening. 'He called my business pathetic.'

'He will eat those words when he sees the success of your business, *koukla mou*. And he *will* see it.'

'Thank you for believing in me. You're the first person to ever do that. Even my mother didn't think I could do it.'

'But you believed in yourself. You came to me with your candles and your soap and the beautiful packaging you'd made yourself. You are *so* talented. Your business idea is clever and you work harder than anyone on my team. If you weren't already making a success of being an entrepreneur, I'd employ you straight away.'

Her hand rested on his chest, as if she couldn't quite bear to let him go. 'But you probably wouldn't have offered to help me if I hadn't been who I was.'

'I probably would.' He gave a half-smile. 'I'm a sucker for a woman dressed in a nun's costume.'

There was no answering smile and he was shaken by how badly he missed that ready smile. He'd taken it for granted. She was always so bouncy and optimistic and yet now she just stood there, shivering like a wounded animal.

'Selene—'

'I should go. Someone might see me and take a photograph.' Finally she smiled, but it was strained. 'See? I'm learning. I don't want my father knowing he made me cry. That's one act I'm prepared to keep up until the day I die.' She rubbed her hand over her face again. 'It was kind of you to come to my defence. Kind of you to tell him our relationship meant something.'

'It wasn't kindness.' He'd realised it the moment she'd walked away from him. 'I do love you.'

'Yes, I know.' There was no pleasure in that statement. Her face didn't light up. She just looked incredibly sad. 'I know you do, Stefan. But you don't want to. It scares you.'

'Yes, it does.' He didn't deny it because he knew only honesty would save him now. 'I didn't want it to happen. I've done my best not to let it happen by picking women I couldn't possibly fall in love with. I controlled that.'

'I know that, too. I know *you*.' She eased out of his arms. 'I really do have to go. I don't want anyone taking a photograph of me like this.'

'I'll take you home. Then we'll fly to my villa.' He saw her hesitate and then shake her head.

'No, not this time. I'll see you in the office on Monday. We have the ad agency pitch.'

'I'm not talking about business. I'm talking about us.' It was a word he'd never used before. 'I've just told you that I love you.'

'But you don't want to. You don't want to feel that way and I can't be with a man who always holds part of himself back. Even though I understand all your reasons and I'm sympathetic, I want more. I know love makes a person vulnerable but I want a man who is prepared to risk everything because the love is more important than protecting himself. And I want him to value my love and allow me to express it.'

'Selene—'

'Please don't follow me. Not this time. I'll see you in the office on Monday.' Mumbling the words, she hurried away from him, walking so fast she almost stumbled.

She applied layers of make-up, added blusher, but still she looked pale when she walked into the Ziakas building.

The glamorous receptionist smiled at her. '*Kalimera.* They're all waiting for you in the conference room.'

But when she walked in the room was empty apart from Stefan, who was pacing from one end of the room to the other.

When he saw her, his face paled. 'I was afraid you wouldn't turn up.'

'Why? Today is important.' Horrified by how hard it was to see him, she glanced around the room. 'Where is everyone?'

'I sent them to get breakfast. They're coming back in an hour. I need to talk to you. I need you to hear what I have to say.'

Her heart clenched at the thought of going over it again. 'There really isn't—'

'You were right—I do love you.' Tension was stamped in every line of his handsome face. 'I think I've loved you from the day you walked into my office dressed as a nun, determined to find a way through my security cordon. Or maybe it was before that—maybe a part of me fell in love with the seventeen-year-old you—I don't know.'

She'd never seen him look like this. Never seen him so unsure of himself. 'Stefan—'

'You were so open about your feelings. I'd never met

anyone like you. It frightened me and it fascinated me at the same time. I liked the fact that you spoke openly without guarding every word. It made me realise the other people in my life were—' he frowned as he searched for the word '—fake.'

'So was I.'

'No. I saw *you* that night. The real you. And when you walked into my office that day and pulled out your candles and asked for a loan I was so cynical, so sure I knew everything there was to know about women and had it all under control. I didn't look deeper. I judged you based on everything that had gone before. But the truth was I knew nothing about you. You shook every preconceived idea I had about women. That night when you had too much champagne—'

'You were so kind to me.'

'You have no idea how much self-control it took to keep my hands off you.' He groaned, dragging his fingers through his hair. 'You were sweet and sexy rolled into one and so unbelievably curious—'

'Why was it unbelievable? You're the most gorgeous man I'm ever going to meet. I wanted to make the most of it.'

'When I worked out your reasons for wanting to leave the island I couldn't believe I'd been so blind. I couldn't believe I hadn't worked it out.'

'Why would you? My father can be very persuasive.'

'And I have more reason to know that than most.'

'None of this matters now.'

'No, it doesn't, because you're mine now and I'm never letting you go.' His voice hoarse, he crossed the room in three strides and took her face in his hands. 'Until I met you all I knew about love was how much damage it could do. I didn't want that. I spent my life avoiding that.

I couldn't understand why anyone would take that risk and I certainly didn't want to, so I kept my relationships short and superficial—and then I met you and suddenly I didn't want to do either of those things. For the first time ever I cared whether I saw a woman again. I wanted to see you again.'

'And you were scared.'

'Yes, and you knew that. You knew I was scared. You knew I loved you.'

'I thought you did. I hoped you did. But I never thought you'd admit it. Or want it.'

'I do want it. I want you.'

He kissed her gently, his mouth lingering on hers, and her head reeled and her thoughts tumbled as she tried to unravel the one situation she hadn't prepared for.

'I— It's too complicated. You hate my father.'

'It's not complicated. I'm not marrying your father and I'm hoping you won't want to invite him to our wedding.'

Her heart thudded and skipped. 'Is that a proposal?'

'No. I haven't reached that part yet but I'm getting there. I have something for you.'

He reached for a box on the table and her brows rose because she recognised the packaging.

'That's one of my candles.'

'Close. It's one I had developed just for you. You already have Relax, Energise and Seduction. This one is called Love.'

Love?

He wanted to marry her?

Hands shaking, Selene opened the box and saw a diamond ring nestling in a glass candle-holder. 'I don't know what I'm more shocked about—the fact that you're asking me to marry you or the fact that you've actually given me a candle. Does this mean I'm actually allowed to light it in the bedroom?'

'You can do anything you want with me in the bedroom,' he said huskily, sliding the ring onto her finger and then kissing her again. 'Just don't tell me it's too late. Don't tell me you've given up on me for taking so long to discover what you knew all along.'

'I'm not telling you that. It's not too late. It's never too late.' She stared down at the ring on her finger, hypnotised not just by the diamond but by what it symbolised.

'How did you end up such an optimist with a father like yours?'

'I refused to believe that all men were like my father. I knew they couldn't be—especially after I met you. I believed in something better and I wanted that. Why would someone want to repeat the past when the future can be so much better?'

His lips were on hers. 'You are an inspiration, *koukla mou.*'

'Not really.' She melted under his touch. 'I'm just trying to have the life I want. Which probably makes me horribly selfish.'

'Then we're a perfect match, because you know I don't think of anyone but myself.'

But he was smiling as he said the words and so was she, because the happiness was too big to keep inside.

'You kept shutting me out.'

'You were so affectionate. So open. I kept shutting you out and when you said those words I panicked.'

'I know.'

'I'm not panicking now.' He trailed his fingers down her cheek. 'So any time you want to say them again, that would be good.'

She smiled again. 'What words?'

'Now you're torturing me, but I suppose I deserve it.'

'I'm not torturing you—' she wrapped her arms round his neck '—I just don't know which words you mean.'

'You're a wicked tease.' His mouth was hot on hers and she gasped as he lifted her onto the table.

'Any moment now thirty people are going to walk into this room.'

'Then you'd better say those words fast—unless you want to say them in front of an audience.'

'Which words?'

He cupped her face. 'The ones where you tell me how you feel about me.'

'Oh, *those* words.' She loved teasing him. 'I've forgotten how to say them because you didn't want to hear them. They've vanished from my brain.'

'Selene—'

'I love you.' For the first time she said it freely, and she smiled as she did so because it felt so good to be truly honest about her feelings. No more hiding. No more pretending. 'I really love you and I'll always love you.'

They kissed, lost in each other, until they heard applause and both turned to see a crowd in the doorway led by Maria, who was smiling. Behind her stood Takis, Kostas and all the other members of Stefan's senior team.

Blushing, Selene slid off the table and Stefan muttered under his breath.

'What does a guy have to do to ensure privacy round here?'

'We came to congratulate you.' Maria produced two bottles of champagne which she put on the table and then turned to hug Selene. 'I'm so delighted. I know it's a little early in the day, but we thought it was appropriate to celebrate the occasion with champagne.'

Stefan eyed the bottles with incredulity. 'You shouldn't

even have been aware of the occasion. Were you listening at the door?'

'Yes.' Maria was unapologetic.

Takis eyed his boss cautiously and then slid into the room, put a tray of glasses on the table and hugged Selene, too.

Choked, Selene hugged them both back. 'Thank you for watching over me and being so kind.'

'If everyone could stop hugging my future wife,' Stefan drawled, 'I'd quite like to hug her myself. But it appears I no longer have any influence in my own office.'

'This is a special occasion, boss,' Takis muttered, releasing Selene. 'Some of us had given up on ever seeing this day.'

Unbelievably touched, Selene slid her hand into Stefan's as his executive team piled into the room. 'This is so great! Can we open the champagne? I always wanted to live a champagne lifestyle—although preferably without the headache.'

Takis reached for the nearest bottle. 'Champagne in a breakfast meeting. A typical working day in the Ziakas Corporation.'

Stefan rolled his eyes. 'Clearly you've never seen what happens to Selene when she drinks champagne.'

'I'm lovely when I drink champagne—and anyway I have Takis to extract me from danger.'

'That's *my* job now. I'm signing on full-time.' Stefan pulled her back into his arms and kissed her, ignoring their audience. 'Which is just as well if you intend to go through life with a glass of champagne in your hand.'

She smiled up at him. 'Good things happen when I drink champagne. You know that.'

'Yes.' His eyes glittered into hers. 'I do.'

There was a thud as the champagne cork hit the ceiling,

and Selene beamed as Takis handed her a glass of champagne. 'We have four advertising agencies sitting in the lobby, waiting to pitch to us. They're going to think we're very unprofessional.'

'They can think what they like.' Stefan tapped his glass against hers and bent his head to gently kiss her mouth. 'Just this once I'm mixing business with pleasure.'

* * * * *

To Laura Melania Kacsinta Berna

Thanks for being such a lovely

This one is for you! Xy

CHAPTER ONE

ALLEGRA KALLAS WASN'T expecting a fatted calf or a rolled-out red carpet and a brass band. She was used to coming home to Santorini with little or no fanfare. What she expected was her father's usual indifference. His polite but feigned interest in her work in London as a family lawyer and his pained expression when she informed him that, yes, currently she was still single. A situation for a Greek father of a daughter aged thirty-one that was akin to having a noxious disease for which there was no known cure.

Which made her wonder why there was a bottle of champagne waiting on a bed of ice in an ice-bucket with the Kallas coat of arms engraved on it and a silver tray with three crystal glasses standing nearby, and why he was gushing about how wonderful it was to have her home.

Wonderful?

Nothing about Allegra was wonderful to her father. Nothing. What was wonderful to him now was his young wife Elena—only two years older than Allegra—and their new baby Nico, who apparently weren't expected back from Athens until later that evening as Elena was visiting her parents. And since little Nico's christening wasn't until tomorrow…

Who was the third glass for?

Allegra slipped her tote bag off her shoulder and let it drop to the leather sofa next to her, the fine hairs on the back of her neck standing up. 'What's going on?'

Her father smiled. Admittedly it didn't go all the way to his eyes, but then the smiles he turned her way rarely did. He had a habit of grimacing instead of smiling at her. As though he was suffering some sort of gastric upset. 'Can't a father be pleased to see his own flesh and blood?'

When had he ever been pleased to see her? And when had she ever felt like a valued member of the family? But she didn't want to stir up old hurts. Not this weekend. She was home for the christening and then she would fly back to her life in London first thing Monday morning. A weekend was all she was staying. She found it too suffocating, staying any longer than that, and even that was a stretch. She glanced at the champagne flutes on the tray. 'So who's the third glass for? Is someone joining us?'

Her father's expression never faltered but Allegra couldn't help feeling he was uneasy about something. His manner was odd. It wasn't just his overly effusive greeting but the way he kept checking his watch and fidgeting with the cuff of his sleeve, as if it was too tight against his wrist. 'As a matter of fact, yes. He'll be here any moment.'

Something inside Allegra's heart kicked against her chest wall like a small cloven hoof. 'He?'

Her father's mouth lost its smile and a frown brought his heavy salt-and-pepper eyebrows into an intimidating bridge. 'I hope you're not going to be difficult. Draco Papandreou is—'

'*Draco* is coming here?' Allegra's heart kicked again but this time the hoof was wearing steel caps. 'But why?'

'Elena and I have asked him to be Nico's godfather.'

Allegra double blinked. She had thought it a huge compliment when her father and his wife had asked her to be their little son's godmother. She'd assumed it was Elena's idea, not her father's. But she hadn't realised Draco was to be Nico's godfather. She'd thought one of her father's older friends would have been granted the honour. She hadn't realised he considered Draco a close friend these days, only a business associate—or rival, which seemed more appropriate. The Papandreou and Kallas names represented two powerful corporations that had once been close associates, but over the years the increasingly competitive market had caused some fault lines in the relationship.

But Allegra had her own issues with Draco. Issues that meant any meeting with him would be fraught with amusement on his part and mortification on hers. Every time she saw him she was reminded of her clumsy attempt as a gauche teenager to attract his attention by flirting with and simpering over him and, even more embarrassingly, the humiliating way in which he had put a stop to it. 'Why on earth did you ask *him*?'

Her father released a rough-sounding sigh and reached for the shot of ouzo he'd poured earlier. He tipped his head back, swallowed the drink and then placed the glass down with an ominous thud. 'The business is in a bad way. The economic crisis in Greece has hit me hard. Harder than I expected—much harder.

I stand to lose everything if I don't accept a generous bailout merger from him.'

'Draco Papandreou is…is *helping* you?' Every time Allegra said his name a sensation scuttled down her spine like a small sticky-footed creature. She hadn't seen Draco since she'd run into him at a popular London nightspot six months ago where she'd been meeting a date—a date who had stood her up. A fact Draco had showed great mirth in witnessing. *Grr.*

She loathed the man for being so…so *right* about everything. It seemed every time she made one of her stupid mistakes he was there to witness it. After that embarrassing flirtation on her part when she'd been sixteen, she had quickly transferred her attention to another young man in her circle. Draco had warned her about the boy and what had she done? She'd ignored his warning and got her heart broken. Well, not broken, exactly, but certainly her ego had got knocked around a bit.

Then, when she'd been eighteen, Draco had found her helping herself to the notoriously potent punch at one of her father's business parties she was supposed to have been helping him host and had lectured her about drinking too much. Another lecture she'd wilfully ignored…and, yes, he'd been there to see her coughing up her lungs a short time later. Double *grr.* Admittedly, he'd been rather handy with a cool face cloth and had gently held her hair back from her face…

But it hadn't stopped her hating him.

Not one little bit.

Even in all the years since, when she ran into him he had an annoying habit of treating her as if she was still that gauche teenager and not a grown woman with a high-flying legal career in London.

'Draco has offered me a deal,' her father said. 'A business merger that will solve all my financial problems.'

Allegra gave a disdainful snort. 'It sounds too good to be true, which usually means it is. What does *he* want out of it?'

Her father didn't meet her gaze and turned slightly to pour another drink instead. She knew her dad well enough to know he only drank to excess in one of two states: relaxed or stressed. Stressed seemed to be the ticket this time. 'He has some conditions attached,' he said. 'But I have no choice but to accept. I have to think of my new family—Nico and Elena don't deserve to be punished for my misfortune. I've done all I can to hold off the creditors, but it's at crisis point. Draco is my only lifeline…or at least the only one I'm prepared to take.'

His new family. Those words hurt her more than she wanted to admit. When had she ever felt part of his *old* family? She'd been a 'spare part' child. A rescue plan, not a person. Her older brother Dion had contracted leukaemia as a toddler, and back in those days parents had been encouraged to have another child in case the new baby was a bone-marrow match. Needless to say, Allegra hadn't come up with the goods. She had failed on both counts. Not a match. Not male. Dion had died before Allegra was two years old. She didn't even remember him. All she remembered was she had been brought up by a series of nannies because her mother had been stricken with unrelenting grief. A grief that had morphed into depression so crippling, Allegra had been sent to boarding school to 'give her mother a break'.

Her mother had 'accidentally' taken an overdose of sleeping tablets the day before Allegra was to have come home for the summer the year she turned twelve. No one had said the word 'suicide' but she had always believed her mother had intended to end her life that day. The hardest part for Allegra was the sad realisation she hadn't been enough for her mother. Her father hadn't even bothered to hide his disappointment in having a female heir instead of the son he had worshipped. Hardly a day had gone by during her childhood and adolescence when Allegra hadn't felt the sting of that disappointment.

But now her father had moved on with a new wife and a new baby.

Allegra had never belonged and now even less so.

'Draco will tell you about our agreement himself,' her father said. 'Ah, here he is now.'

Allegra whipped around to see Draco's tall figure enter the room. Her eyes met his onyx gaze and a strange sensation spurted and then pooled deep and low in her belly. Every time she looked at him she had exactly the same reaction. Her senses jumped to attention. Her pulse raced. Her heart flip-flopped. Her breath hitched as though it were attached to strings and someone was jerking them. Hard.

He was wearing casual clothes: sandstone-coloured chinos and a white shirt rolled past his strong, tanned forearms, which took nothing away from his aura of commanding authority. When Draco Papandreou walked into a room every head turned. Every female heart fluttered…as hers was doing right now, as though there were manic moths trapped in her heart valves. He oozed sex appeal from every cell of his six-foot-three frame. She could feel it calling out to her feminine hormones like an alpha wolf calling a mate. No other man had ever made her more aware of her body than him. Her body seemed to have a mind of its own when he came anywhere near.

A wicked mind.

A mind that conjured up images of him naked and his long, hair-roughened legs entwined with hers. The only way she could disguise the way he made her feel was to hide behind a screen of sniping sarcasm. He thought her a shrew, but so what? Better that than let him think she was secretly lusting after him. That the embarrassing crush she had foolishly acted on when she'd been sixteen had completely and utterly disappeared. That her dreams didn't feature him in various erotic poses doing all sorts of X-rated things with her. She would rather be hanged and quartered and her body parts posted to the four corners of the earth than admit the only sex she'd had in the last year or so had been by herself, with him as her fantasy.

That—God help her—the last time she'd had sex with a partner it had been Draco she had thought of the whole time.

'Draco, how nice of you to gate crash a private family celebration. No hot date tonight with one of your bottle-blonde bimbos?'

His mouth lifted at one corner in his signature half-cynical, half-amused smile. 'You're my date, *agape mou*. Hasn't your father told you?'

Allegra gave him a look that would have snap-frozen a gas flame. 'Dream on, Papandreou.'

His dark eyes glinted as if the thought of her saying no to him secretly turned him on. That was the trouble with having had a crush on a man since you'd been a pimple-spotted teenager. They *never* let you forget it. 'I have a proposal to put to you,' he said. 'Would you like your father present or shall I do it in private?'

'It's immaterial to me where you do it because nothing you propose to me would ever in a thousand, million, squillion years evoke the word "yes" from me,' Allegra said.

'Er… I think I can hear one of the servants calling me,' her father said and left the room with such haste it looked as though he were running from an explosion. But then, whenever she and Draco were left alone together the prospect of an explosion was a very real possibility.

Draco's gaze held hers in a tether that made the base of her spine shiver. 'Alone at last.'

Allegra broke the eye contact, walked over to the drinks tray and casually poured a glass of champagne. Or at least she hoped it looked casual. She wasn't a big drinker but right now she wanted to suck on that bottle of champagne until it was empty. Then she wanted to throw the bottle at the nearest wall. Then the glasses, one by one, until they shattered into thousands of shards. Then every stick of furniture in the room.

Smash. Bash. Crash.

Why was he here? Why was he helping her father? What could it possibly have to do with her? The questions tumbled through her brain like the champagne tumbling into her glass. Her father's business was hanging in the balance? How could that be? It was one of the most well-established businesses in Greece, and had operated for several generations. Other business people looked up to him, in awe of all he had achieved.

Her father had always brandished his wealth like it was a ten-thousand-strong flock of golden-egg-laying geese. How had it come to this?

Allegra turned and gave Draco a sugar-sweet smile. "Can I offer you a drink? Weed killer? Liquid nitrogen? Cyanide?"

He gave a deep rumble of a laugh that did strange things to her insides. Things they had no business doing. Not for him. 'Under the circumstances, champagne would be perfect.'

She poured a glass and handed it to him, annoyed her hand wasn't quite steady. He took the glass but in doing so his fingers brushed against hers. It was like being touched with a live current. The shock of it sent a jolt through her entire body, making her hormones sit up and beg for more. She snatched her hand back and then wished she hadn't. He had an uncanny ability to read her body language like a cryptographer reading code.

Everything about him unsettled her. Made her feel things she didn't want to feel. But no matter how hard she fought it she couldn't take her eyes off him. It was as though magnets were attached to her eyeballs and he was true north. She had seen a lot of beautiful men over the years but no one came close to having Draco's pulse-tripping features. Ink-black hair with just enough curl to make her want to run her fingers through it and straighten out those sexy kinks. A mouth that was not just sensual but sinfully sculpted. A mouth that made her think of long, drugging kisses. The mere thought of his hard male mouth crushing hers was enough to make her get all hot and bothered and breathless.

She had felt that mouth on hers. Once. Had felt it and

had responded to it, only to have him push her away with an ego-crushing comment about how a silly little girl like her could never satisfy a man like him. For years that cruel put-down had savaged her self-esteem. It had ruined her sexual confidence—not that she'd had much to begin with. Damn him for being so darned attractive. Why couldn't she stop gawping at him as if she were still that stupid, star-struck kid with a crush?

He had shaved but the potent male hormones surging around his body would be enough to defeat any decent razorblade. Dark stubble was peppered along his lean jaw and around his mouth.

Dear God, she had to stop looking at his mouth.

She picked up her glass of champagne but before she could take a sip he held his glass within reach of hers. 'To us.'

Allegra pulled her glass back before it could touch his, sloshing the champagne down the front of her blouse. Of course, she was wearing silk. The saturating liquid made her right breast stand out even though it was inside a lace bra. Why was she so ridiculously clumsy around him? It was mortifying. She brushed off the excess liquid with her hand but it only made the dampness worse, making the upper curve of her breast cling to the fabric as though she were in a wet T-shirt competition.

Draco handed her a clean white handkerchief. Of course he would be carrying a clean white handkerchief. 'Would you like me to—?'

Allegra snatched the square of cloth off him before he could finish the sentence. No way was she letting him touch her breast even if it was through four folds of cotton. She couldn't guarantee a suit of armour and

Kevlar vest would keep her from responding to his touch. She dabbed at her wet breast and never had such a task seemed so erotic. Even her breast thought so. It was tingling and her nipple peaking…but maybe that was because Draco's dark obsidian gaze was following her every movement over it. She screwed the handkerchief into a tight ball and tossed it to the coffee table. 'I'll have it laundered and returned to you.'

'Keep it as a souvenir.'

'The only souvenir I want from you is the word "goodbye".'

His eyes held hers again in a spine-shuddering, resolve-melting lock. 'The only way that's going to happen is if I pull out of this business merger.'

'I don't care about the merger.'

'Maybe not, but you should. It rests solely on your compliance with the terms of the deal.'

Terms? What terms?

Allegra disguised her unease by shaking her loose hair back behind her shoulders in a gesture of indifference. But she was far from indifferent. Something about his unwavering gaze made her feel he was toying with her, like a cat with a mouse it had cleverly cornered. What on earth could he want her compliance over?

Since *that kiss* years before, there had always been a climate of tension between them. A tug of war of wills. A power struggle that crackled the air when they were in the same room together. He was her enemy and she didn't care who knew it. Hating him made it easier for her to forget how much she'd wanted him. Hating him kept her safe from her own traitorous hormones that were annoyingly, persistently, immune to every other man but him. 'My father's business affairs are of no concern to me. I am completely independent of him and have been for the last ten or so years.'

'Independent financially, maybe, but you're his only daughter. His only child. He paid for your stellar education. He gave you everything money could buy. Don't you care he's about to lose everything without my help?' His deeply carved frown added to the grave delivery of his words.

Allegra wished she didn't care. But the trouble was, she did. It was her Achilles' heel—her weak spot, the raw, vulnerable part of her personality—the need to feel loved and valued by her only living parent. She had sought it all her life to no avail. In spite of her father's shortcomings, inside she was still that small child looking for his approval. Pathetic, but true. 'I fail to see what any of this has to do with me. I simply don't care what state my father's business is in.' She knew she sounded cold and unfeeling but why should she care what Draco thought of her?

He studied her for a long moment. 'I don't believe you. You do care. Which is why you'll agree to marry me to keep the business afloat.'

Shock hit her in the chest like a punch. *Marry him?* Allegra widened her eyes. Not saucer-wide. Not dinner-dish-wide. Platter-dish-wide. Surely he hadn't just said that? The M word? Him and her? Married? To each other? She blinked and then laughed but even to her ears it sounded on the verge of hysterical. 'If you think for one second I would marry anyone, let alone you, then you are even more of an egomaniac than I thought.'

Draco's gaze continued to hold hers in an intractable

lock that was a tantalising tickle to her girly bits. 'You will do it, Allegra, or see your father's business die a slow and painful death. It's on life support as it is. I've been drip-feeding your father money for the last year. He hasn't got the funds to repay me even if I waive the interest. No one will lend him anything now, not after the way things have panned out in our economy. I came up with this solution instead. This way everyone wins…in particular, you.'

Allegra couldn't believe his arrogance. Did he really think she would agree to such a preposterous deal? She hated him with a passion. She couldn't think of a single person she would *less* like to marry. Well, she could, given her line of work, but that wasn't the point. He was a playboy. A fast-living Lothario who churned through women like a speed-reader churned through cheap paperbacks. Marriage to Draco would be emotional suicide, even if she didn't hate him. 'You're unbelievable. What planet are you on that you would think I would see this as a win for me? Marriage isn't a win for any woman. It's a one-way ticket to serfdom, that's what it is, and I won't have a bar of it.'

'You've been hanging around divorce courts way too long,' he said. 'Plenty of marriages work well for both parties. It could work for us. We have a lot in common.'

'The only thing we have in common is we both breathe oxygen,' Allegra said. 'I dislike everything about you. Even if I were on the hunt for a husband, I would never consider someone like you. You're the sort of man who would expect his pipe and slippers brought to him when he gets home. You don't want a wife, you want a servant.'

His half-smile was back, making his impossibly black eyes twinkle. 'I love you too, *glykia mou.*'

Allegra thinned her gaze to hairpin slits. 'Read my lips. I am not marrying you. Not to save my father's business. Not for any reason. No. No. No. No.'

Draco took a leisurely sip of his champagne and put the glass down on the coffee table with exacting precision. 'Of course, you'll have to commute between London and my home for work, but you can use my private jet—that is, if I'm not using it myself.'

Allegra clenched her hands into fists. 'Are you listening to me? I said I am *not* marrying you.'

He sat on the sofa and leaned back with his hands behind his head, one ankle crossed over the other with indolent grace. 'You haven't got a choice. If you don't marry me then your father will blame you for the collapse of his company. It's a good company but it's been badly run of late. That business manager your father appointed a couple of years ago when he had that health scare didn't do him any favours. I can undo that damage and turn the business around so it's profitable again. Your father will stay on the board and have a share of the profits I guarantee will be more than he has received in decades.'

Allegra bit down on her lip. It had been a worrying time when her father had had a cancer scare. She had flown back and forth as much as she could to help him through his bout of chemo and radiation. Not that he'd shown any great appreciation, of course. But to marry Draco to save her father from financial ruin? It was as if she had suddenly stepped into the pages of a Regency novel.

But her father needed her. *Really* needed her. There

could have been worse men than Draco to offer for her, she had to admit. The sort of men she faced down in court. Mean men. Dangerous men. Men who had no respect for women and who used their children as weapons and pay-backs. Men who stalked, bullied, threatened and even killed to get their own way.

Draco might be arrogant but he wasn't mean. Dangerous? Well, maybe to her senses, yes. Her senses went into a dazzled and dizzying frenzy when he came close. Which was a very good reason why she couldn't marry him.

Wouldn't marry him.

'Why me?' Allegra said. 'Why would you possibly want me for a wife when you can have any woman you want?'

His eyes did a lazy sweep of her from head to foot and back again, sending a frisson through every cell in her body. 'I want you.'

Those sexily drawled words should not have made her feminine core do a happy dance. She wasn't vain but knew she was considered attractive in a classical sort of way. She had her mother's English peaches-and-cream complexion, her dark blue eyes and slim build, but she had her father's jet-black hair and drive to achieve.

But Draco dated super-models, starlets and nubile nymphets. Why would he want to shackle himself to a hard-nosed career woman like her, especially when they fought at every chance they got?

Over the years she had done her level best to hide her attraction to him. The Embarrassing Incident when she'd been sixteen was filed away in her mind in the drawer marked 'Do Not Open'. These days she sneered instead of simpered. She derided instead of drooled. She flayed instead of flirted.

Falling in love with Draco Papandreou would be asking for the sort of trouble she helped other women extricate themselves from on a daily basis. Love did weird things to women. They got blindsided, hoodwinked, charmed into looking at their men through rosy love-tinted glasses that failed to show up their faults until it was too late.

Allegra wasn't going to be one of those women—a victim of some man's power game, leaving her as vulnerable as a rain-soaked kitten. 'Listen, I appreciate the compliment, such as it is, but I'm not in the marriage market. Now, if you'll excuse me, I'm going to—'

'The offer is for today and today only. After that I start asking for my money back. With interest.'

She sent her tongue over her lips but they felt as dry as the cardboard cover on one of her expert reports. The economic crisis in Greece was serious. So serious that many well-established companies had hit the wall like over-ripe peaches. She might have some issues with her father but not to the point where she wanted to see him ruined and publicly humiliated. Not now he had a wife and young baby to provide for. Allegra liked Elena. She hadn't expected to, with Elena only being two years older than her, but she did. It some ways Elena reminded her of herself—trying too hard to please everyone in an effort to be loved and accepted.

But if she married Draco to save her father from financial destruction she would be exposing herself to the sort of sensual danger she could well do without. For years she'd kept her distance from him. After that mortifying encounter when she was sixteen, it was her only way of protecting herself. But how would she keep her distance if she were married to him? 'This marriage you're…erm…proposing…' It was lowering to find her voice sounding so scratchy. 'What do you get out of it?'

His eyes shone with a devilish gleam that made her inner thighs tingle as if he had stroked her intimately. No one else could do that to her. Turn her on with a look. Make her so hungry for him she had trouble keeping her hands off him. She would like nothing more than to run her hands all over that strong male body to see if it was as deliciously hard and virile as it looked. When had she not burned with lust for him? Ever since she'd been a teenager with newly awakened hormones he'd been her go-to fantasy guy. No one else came close. He had all but ruined her for anyone else and he hadn't so much as touched her, other than incidentally, since that kiss. 'I get a wife who's hot for me. What more could a man want?'

Allegra kept her expression under tight control. 'If you want a trophy wife then why not select one from your crowd of sexy little sycophants?'

'I want a wife with a brain between her ears.'

'Any woman with half a brain would steer clear of a man like you.'

Her insult only made his smile tilt further, as if he was enjoying himself at her expense. 'And if you were to provide me with an heir…'

'A…what?' Allegra's voice came out like a mouse's squeak. 'You're expecting me to have…?'

'Now that I think about it…' He rose from the sofa with leonine agility. 'An heir and a spare might be a good thing, *ne*?'

Was he teasing or was he serious? It was so hard to

tell behind the sardonic screen of his gaze. 'Aren't you forgetting something? I don't want children. I have a career I'm not prepared to sacrifice for a family.'

'Lots of women say that but in most cases it's not true. They say it as an insurance policy in case no one asks them to marry them.'

Allegra's mouth dropped open so far, she thought her toenails would be bruised. 'Are you for real? What jungle vine did you just swing down from? Women are not breeding machines. Nor are we waiting around with bated breath for some man to stick a ring on our finger and carry us off to be their domestic slave. We have just as much ambition and drive as men, sometimes even more so.'

'I'm all for your drive.' His eyes did that glinting thing again. 'That's another thing we have in common, *ne*?'

The less she thought about his sex drive, the better. No one oozed it more potently than him. He was the poster boy for pick-up sex. He moved from relationship to relationship faster than a driver late for an important appointment changed lanes. What had brought about this sudden desire to play family man? He was only thirty-four—three years older than her. Or was it his way of twisting her arm? The arm that was attached to her hormone-charged body that strangely—since that night six months ago in London—kept reminding her every time she had a period she was over thirty and childless. 'I don't know where you got the idea I would agree to this farcical plan. Did my father suggest it?'

'No, it was entirely my idea.'

His idea? Allegra frowned. 'But you don't even like me.'

He came and stood in front of her, his superior height making her feel like a child's rocking horse standing up to a Clydesdale stallion. He didn't touch her but she could feel the magnetic pull of his body making every cell in hers gravitate towards him. She raised her eyes to his, momentarily losing herself in those bottomless pools of black with their fringe of thick lashes.

Why did he have to be so wickedly attractive? Why did her hormones jump up and down in ecstatic glee when he was close? Her gaze went to his mouth, drinking in the way his lips were both firm yet sensually supple, the lower one generous, the top one slimmer, but not enough to be considered cruel. It was a mouth always on the verge of a smile, as if he found life amusing rather than sad. Had she ever seen a more kissable male mouth?

'We could be good together, *agape mou*. Very good.'

Allegra suppressed the shiver his provocative words evoked. His voice was deep and mellifluous and his Greek accent—so much stronger than the faint trace of it in her voice—never failed to make her skin prickle in delight.

He always spoke English to her because she had let her Greek slip after living so long in England. She understood it more than she could speak it but she could hardly describe herself as fluent. She had always spoken English to her Yorkshire-born mother and she suspected her neglect of her father's language was a subconscious way to punish him for not being the father she longed for. 'Look, Draco, this has to stop. All this talk of a marriage between us is pointless. I'm not—'

He took one of her hands and enfolded it in the cage of his. His fingers were warm and dry, the tensile strength in them making something in her stomach drop like a book falling from a shelf. Make that a dozen legal textbooks. Who knew her hand was so sensitive? It was as if every nerve was on the outside of her skin, tingling, making her aware of every pore of his. 'Why are you so frightened of getting close to me?'

Allegra had to swallow a couple of times to find her voice. 'I—I'm not frightened of you.' *I'm frightened of me. Of how you make me feel.*

His thumb began a slow stroke of the fleshy base of hers. It was as light as a sable brush on a priceless canvas but it triggered an explosion of sensations that ricocheted through her body. Her heart picked up its pace as though she'd been given a shot of adrenalin with a crack chaser. Her brain was scrambled by his closeness, her resolve to keep her distance gone missing without leave.

His eyes searched hers for a long, pulsing moment. It was if he was committing every one of her features to memory: the shape of her eyes, her nose, her cheeks, her mouth and the tiny beauty spot just above the right side of her top lip.

Allegra licked her lips, then realised what a blatant giveaway that was—the primary signal of attraction. It was as if her body was acting of its own accord. Her will, her determination to resist him, was overridden by a primal need to touch him, to have him touch her. To have him kiss her until she forgot about everything but how those firm, male lips felt on hers.

What are you doing?

The alarm bell of her conscience shattered the moment and she pushed against his chest and stepped back to create some distance between them. 'Don't even think about it, buddy.'

His mouth tilted in a knowing smile. 'I'm a patient man. The longer I wait, the better the satisfaction.'

Allegra had a feeling there would be a heck of a lot of satisfaction going on if she were to submit to his passion. The sort of satisfaction that had mostly eluded her in her previous encounters. She wasn't good at sex, or at least not with a partner. She could get things working fairly well on her own, but with a partner she found it too distracting to orgasm. Dead embarrassing, but at least she had been able to fudge her way through it. So far.

But she suspected Draco wouldn't be fooled.

Not for a minute.

Allegra refilled her glass for something to do with her hands. She was conscious of him watching her every move, his dark gaze resting on her like a caress. Her skin tingled, her pulse raced, her insides coiled tight with need. A need awakened by him. 'I think it's best if we forget we had this conversation. I don't want anything to spoil Nico's christening tomorrow.'

'What will spoil it will be you refusing to marry me to save your father's skin,' Draco said. 'You haven't got a choice, Allegra. He needs you like he's never needed you before.'

It was far more tempting than she wanted to admit. Not just because of how it would make her father finally appreciate her, but because she couldn't stop thinking about what it would be like to be Draco's wife. Sharing his life with him, sharing his luxury villa on his own private island. Sharing his body. Being pleasured by him, experiencing the full gamut of human passion. It was a dream come true for the gauche teenager she had once been.

However, she wasn't that girl any more.

But then a thought dropped into her head. Had her father and Elena only asked her to be godmother to Nico because of Draco and his offer? Would they have asked her without the merger and the marriage condition? Wasn't she good enough on her own to be Nico's godmother? Why did she have to partner with her enemy? A man she loathed with the same passion she desired him.

Allegra twirled her glass and placed it back down on the tray next to the champagne bottle. 'Here's a hypothetical question for you. If I were to marry you then how long would you expect the marriage to last?'

'For as long as I want it to.'

And how long would that be? Allegra turned to look at the view from the window to give herself more time to think. The sunlight was so bright it was almost violent. The intense blue of the Aegean Sea, and the equally vivid blue domes in contrast to the stark white of the houses, never failed to snatch her breath. It was picture-postcard perfect, especially from her father's luxury villa in Oia, where the best sunsets in the world were occurred.

It was home and yet it wasn't.

She'd always felt like she had a foot in both countries and it added to her sense of not really belonging anywhere.

If she married Draco to save her father from financial disgrace, where would that leave her when it was time to call an end to their marriage? Few marriages ended with a mutual agreement to part. There was nearly always one party who wasn't happy about the break-up. Would that be her? And—if he wasn't joking about the heir he said he wanted—there was no way she would have a child under such circumstances, with the knowledge that the marriage had no guarantee, no promise of full and lasting commitment.

Allegra turned back to look at Draco. 'Still speaking hypothetically here. What about my career? Or do you expect me to give that up?'

'No, of course not,' he said. 'But there will have to be compromises occasionally. I have business interests in London, as you know, but most of my time is spent in Greece. I think the fact you have your own career will enhance our marriage rather than complicate it.'

'And you would expect me to be with you most of the time?' Allegra said it as though it was the most unreasonable request in the world. As though she'd be committing to daily root-canal treatment.

His expression flickered with amusement. 'Isn't that what husbands and wives do?'

Allegra sent him a speaking look. 'Ones that are in love with each other, maybe. But that hardly applies in our case.'

One side of his smile went a little higher. 'You've been in love with me since you were a teenager. Go on—admit it. That's why you haven't got married yet or dated with any regularity. You can't find anyone that does it for you like I do it for you.'

Allegra affected a laugh. '*Seriously?* That's what you think?' What signals had she been giving off to make him think she was still that clumsy teenage girl?

She wasn't that infatuated fool any more. She was all grown up and she hated him. Hated. Hated. Hated him.

His eyes gleamed like wet paint. 'When was the last time you slept with a man?'

She folded her arms across her body and pursed her lips like she was a schoolmistress staring down an impertinent child. 'I'm not going to give you details of my sex life. It's none of your damn business who I sleep with.'

'It will be my business once we're married. I expect you to be faithful.'

Allegra unfolded her arms and planted her hands on her hips instead. 'And what about you? Will you be faithful or will I have to turn a blind eye to your little dalliances like my mother did for my father?'

Something hardened around his mouth, making it appear flatter, less mobile. 'I am not your father, Allegra. I take the institution of marriage very seriously.'

'So seriously you're prepared to marry a woman you don't love, for a short period of time, just so you can acquire a flagging business?' She made a scoffing noise. 'Don't make me laugh. I know why you want to marry me, Draco. You want a trophy wife. A wife who knows which knife and fork to use. A wife you can take anywhere without worrying she might embarrass you. Then, when you've got me to pop out an heir, you'll get bored, send me on my way and keep the kid. I'm not doing it. No way. Find some other puppet.'

She pushed past him to leave the room but he snagged her wrist on her way past, bringing her around to face him. Her skin burned where his fingers gripped her, but not a painful burn, more of a sizzling, tingling burn that sent heat rushing through her body and pooling in her core. He had rarely touched her since that kiss other than by accident. The contact of his flesh on hers was like being zapped with a lightning bolt. It made every nerve beneath her skin pirouette. His thumb found her thrumming pulse and soothed it with slow, measured strokes while his eyes held hers prisoner.

'I was only teasing about the heir,' he told her. 'But think carefully, Allegra. Yes, I am in the market for a suitable wife, and you fit the bill. But this is also your chance to get your father to finally notice you. You won't just be helping him, but Elena and little Nico, by providing them with security. If the business goes under, it will take them down with it.'

He had found another weak spot. Elena and Nico. They were the innocents in this situation and their future would be compromised if she didn't do something. Allegra could offer her father a loan but the sort of money Draco was talking about was in the millions. Many millions. She was wealthy, but not wealthy enough to float a multi-million-euro corporation. She let out a rattling breath and looked down at their joined hands. How could she turn her back on her father's financial plight when she was the only person who could do something? If her father went down, Elena and darling little Nico would be collateral damage. She couldn't stand back and let that happen. Not when she could help it. She would have to marry Draco. *Gulp.* 'It seems I don't have any choice.'

Draco brought her chin up so her gaze meshed with his. 'You won't regret it. I can guarantee it.'

You think? Allegra brushed his hand away from her chin and took a step backwards. 'I'm not agreeing to this for any other reason than to save my family. Are you absolutely clear on that?'

His eyes shone with a triumphant gleam that made the backs of her knees tingle. 'But of course.'

She disguised a swallow, trying not to notice the way his eyes kept glancing at her mouth. 'When are you thinking of…doing it? I mean, getting married?'

'I have already taken the liberty to make all the arrangements. We'll be married next weekend. I would have done it this one but I didn't want to steal little Nico's limelight.'

Allegra's eyes bulged in alarm. 'So soon?'

'It is a little rushed, but it will be a relatively simple affair. Just a handful of close friends and family.'

'But what if I want the whole shebang?'

'Do you?'

She blew out another breath and averted her gaze. 'No…'

'You'd be surprised at what can be done in a short period of time when you have money. If you want a white wedding, then that's what you will have.'

Allegra had never been the sort of girl to hanker after the fairy-tale wedding. She had rarely even thought of getting married. Her career had always been her top priority. She normally avoided bridal shops and didn't drool at jewellers' windows. But ever since she'd been a bridesmaid at a friend's wedding a couple of months ago she had started to think about what it would be like to be a bride. To be loved by someone so much they would promise to spend the rest of their life with her. It was indeed a fairy tale, one she saw turn to ashes and heartache every day of her working life.

'We'll be married on my island retreat,' Draco said. 'It will be easier to keep the press away.'

Allegra had never been to Draco's private retreat but she had seen photos. He had a villa in Oia, an apartment in Athens and other homes on Kefalonia and Mykonos. But his secluded retreat on his private island had the most amazing gardens and an infinity pool that was perched on the edge of a vertiginous cliff. It would make a stunning wedding location.

And a perfect spot for a honeymoon.

Do not even think about the honeymoon.

'Aren't you worried what the press will make of us?' Allegra asked.

He gave a loose-shouldered shrug. 'Not particularly. I've grown accustomed to them speculating on my private life. Most of the time they make stuff up.'

Not everything was fiction. She had seen enough photos of him surrounded by beautiful women to know he wasn't living the life of a Tibetan monk. Far from it. He was considered one of Greece's most eligible bachelors. Women were elbowing each other out of the way to score a date with him. What would everyone say when they heard *she* was to be his wife? A single-minded career woman like her, marrying a fast-living playboy like him.

It was laughable.

'You'll have to take a week off work, of course,' he said. 'We'll take a short honeymoon on my yacht.'

Her heart flapped like a goldfish trapped in the neck of a funnel. 'Hang on a minute—why do we need to have a honeymoon?'

There was a spark of something at the back of his gaze. Something dark and sensual and spine-tinglingly wicked. 'If you need me to spell that out for you, *agape mou*, then you've been living an even more cloistered life than I thought.'

Allegra crossed her arms, holding them tightly against her stomach. *A honeymoon? On his yacht?* His yacht was no cheap little fishing dingy, but it could never be large enough for her to feel safe. Safe from her own wicked, traitorous desires. She would need a cruise liner or an aircraft carrier for that and even that would be no guarantee. 'Look, I'm prepared to marry you for the sake of my father, but I'm not going to sleep with you. It will be an on-paper marriage. A marriage in name only.'

Draco came back to where she was standing but she had moved back against the wall, which gave her nowhere to escape. And with her hands crossed over her body she didn't have room to unwind them to push him away. She breathed in the scent of him—lime and cedar with a hint of something that was unique to him. It unfurled around her nostrils, making them flare to take more of him in. She felt drunk on him. Dazzled by the pheromones that swirled and heated and mated with hers.

He slipped a hand to the side of her head, his fingers splaying through her hair until every root on her scalp shivered in delight. His eyes had that dark, twinkling spark of amusement that did so much damage to her resolve. Lethal damage. Irreparable damage. 'And how long do you think an on-paper marriage between us would last, hmm?' His voice was a deep burr that grazed the length of her spine like a caress from one of his work-callused hands. 'I want you and I intend to have you.'

Allegra couldn't stop staring at his mouth—the way his lips shaped around every word; the way his stubble made her want to press her mouth to his skin to feel the sexy rasp of his regrowth. *Kiss me. Kiss me. Kiss me.* The chant was pounding an echo in her blood. She didn't want to be the one to make the first move. Not like she had done all those years ago, when she'd thrown herself at him only to be brutally rejected. She wasn't that girl any more. Making the first move would give him too much power. She could resist him. She could. She could. She could.

As if he could read her mind, he brought a fingertip to her mouth and traced a slow outline of her lips, setting off a round of miniature fireworks under her skin. 'Such a beautiful mouth. But I'm not sure if you're going to kiss me back or bite me.'

She inched up her chin. 'Try it and see.'

His smile was lazy and lopsided and sent her belly into free fall. But then he tapped her lower lip with his index finger and stepped back. 'Maybe some other time.'

CHAPTER TWO

Draco picked up his champagne glass because, unless he gave his hands something to do, he knew they would be tempted to jump ahead a few spaces. He could wait. Sure he could. Allegra was all for keeping things on paper but he knew she would crack before the ink was dry on their marriage certificate.

He knew she was attracted to him. She'd had a teenage crush on him, which had amused and annoyed him in equal measure back in the day. He'd been a little ruthless in handling her back then, but he hadn't been interested in messing with a teenager, especially so soon after his break-up with the ex he'd thought he was going to marry. Back then, Allegra had been young and starry-eyed, fancying herself in love, and had needed to be put firmly in her place.

But she was a woman now—a beautiful woman in the prime of her life.

And he wanted her.

Ever since London, Draco had realised Allegra was exactly what he was looking for in a wife. And when her father, Cosimo Kallas, had come to him for help, he had seized his opportunity and made his financial support conditional on marrying her. Besides, there were other men who were circling like sharks for the money her father owed them, men who he knew wouldn't hesitate to go after Allegra next. He couldn't stand by and let one of them force her into their bed to settle the debts he could pay without flinching. Who knew what might happen to her? Her father had angered a lot of his business associates. Draco wasn't going to let anything happen to her because her father was a fool.

Allegra was classy. She was well-educated, she was well-spoken and she was half-Greek. And, with her untouchable air, she was jaw-droppingly gorgeous. She could have graced a catwalk or been found starring on an old-world Hollywood movie set. She walked like a dancer, her slim figure moving effortlessly across the floor. Her glossy black hair was straight and hung almost to her waist. When she moved, it moved with her in a silk curtain that held his gaze like a super-powerful magnet. He couldn't stop himself from imagining that silky black skein draped over his chest, her long, slender legs entwined with his.

Draco suppressed a shudder of anticipation. He was hot for her. Seriously hot. So hot he only had to look at her and his blood would thunder. He couldn't seem to keep his eyes off her. When she'd spilled her champagne, the silk of her blouse clinging wetly to the perfect globe of her breast had made his blood shoot south in a torrent. He had rarely touched her in the past. Since that kiss when she was a teenager, he had respectfully kept his distance because he hadn't wanted any boundaries to be crossed. He had made it clear he wasn't interested back then and he hadn't wanted to give her mixed messages.

Now was different.

Their marriage wouldn't be for ever, just long enough to secure the business and get Allegra out of his system. Draco had nothing against long-term marriage, but he couldn't see himself doing the time.

He had teased Allegra with that talk of an heir to suss out her feelings on the issue of children. It wouldn't be fair to lock her into marriage—even a short-term one—if she was desperate to have kids. Thankfully, she wasn't, and it was the last thing he wanted from this marriage. Given his childhood, he wasn't sure he could ever see himself having a family.

When his mother had died from a gangrenous appendix when Draco was six, he and his father had been a team intent on survival in a world that didn't notice, let alone help, the desperately poor. Draco had a clear memory of walking with his fisherman father past the Kallas corporation headquarters one day only a month before his father's death. His dad had looked up at the building with its shining brass sign and expressed how he wanted Draco to aim high, to dream big and bountiful, to make something of himself so he wouldn't have to struggle the way he had done. When his father had been killed in a boating accident four weeks later, Draco had been left to fend for himself.

But his father's words had stayed with him, motivating him, fuelling his drive and determination. He'd clawed his way out of poverty, working several menial jobs while trying to get an education. At nineteen, he'd part-owned a business, and had gone on to own it fully when the partner had retired. He had gone from strength to strength after that, building and expanding each company he acquired. He was a self-made man and he was proud of it.

No one could say he wasn't a prize catch.

Not now.

And who could be a better wife for him than Allegra Kallas—the daughter of the businessman who owned the corporation his father had singled out that day with such aspiration? Acquiring the company would be a symbol of Draco's success. A token of the dreams and hopes his father had had for him and that he had now fulfilled in his father's honour.

Draco watched her sipping her champagne, sitting there on one of the plush leather sofas. Her long legs were crossed, one racehorse-slim ankle moving up and down in a kicking motion—the only clue she was feeling agitated. Her expression had gone back to her signature cool mask of indifference, which was another thing that secretly turned him on. He was amused how she took that schoolmistress tone with him. When she tried to stare him down with those flashing, unusually dark blue eyes, it made him hard as stone. Harder. He could feel the throb of it even now.

He'd wanted to kiss her. Of course he had. What man with even a trace of testosterone wouldn't want to feel that lusciously soft mouth? He'd tasted those sweet, hot lips once and couldn't wait to do it again. But he knew if he moved too soon it could shift the balance of power. He wanted his ring on her finger. He wanted her hungry. He wanted her begging. He wanted her to be honest about her lust for him. For lust after him she did. He should know the signs because he was experiencing them himself. He couldn't take his eyes off her generous and supple mouth. Couldn't stop thinking about that mouth opening over him, drawing on him, sucking him till he blew like the volcano Santorini was famous for.

Draco met her eyes across the space that separated them. She raised a perfectly groomed eyebrow at him, that starchy, English aristocratic, 'I'm too good for the likes of you' spark in her eyes making him want to carry her off fireman-style and show her just how good he could be for her. 'Another drink to celebrate our engagement, *agape mou*?' he said.

Her mouth was puckered like the drawstrings of an old-fashioned purse. 'Don't call me that. You know you don't mean it.'

He pushed away from the window where he had been leaning. 'Here's the thing—we have to act like a happy couple, even if in private you want to play pistols at dawn.'

Her chin came up to a defiant height. 'No one's going to believe it, you know. Not us. We're known to positively loathe each other.' Her cheeks went a shade darker. 'Especially after that night in London in December.'

He smiled at the memory. It wasn't the first time he'd felt that tingle of attraction. More than a tingle. A shockwave that had left him buzzing for hours afterwards. 'Ah, yes. It wasn't one of your best moments, was it? I was only trying to help and what did I get? A glass of red wine poured in my lap. Hardly the behaviour of a grown woman.'

Her jaw looked as though she were biting down on a metal rod. 'You provoked me. And it was either have that wine in your lap or splashed in your face, and your throat cut with the glass.'

He tut-tutted and shook his head at her as if she were a wilfully disobedient child who consistently disappointed him. 'It seems I may have to teach you how to behave. That will be fun: *Wife Behaviour for Beginners*.'

She sprang off the sofa as if something had bitten her on the behind, throwing him a look that would have stripped tarmac off a road. 'You think you're so smart, manipulating me into this farce of a marriage, but I've got news for you. I will not be a doormat. I will not be treated like a child. I will not sleep with you. Do? You? Understand?'

Draco loved it when she got angry with him. She was always so buttoned up, cool and controlled. But with him she showed the depth of passion in her personality others didn't see. She was feisty, a firebrand with a flaying tongue and a whip-quick wit. He enjoyed their verbal sparring. It was a big turn-on for him. Few women stood up to him or challenged him the way she did. He liked that she had spirit. That she wasn't afraid to lock horns with him.

He would much rather she locked those gorgeous lips on his, but all in good time.

'I understand you're a little apprehensive about sex, but I can assure you, I'm excellent at it.'

Twin pools of bright pink flared on her cheeks. 'I am not apprehensive about sex. I have sex—I have it all the time. I just don't care to have it with you.'

How he wanted to make her eat every one of those words and lick them away with that hot little tongue of hers. He wanted that tongue all over his body. *He wanted. He wanted. He wanted.* It pulsed through him like an ache. He'd been too long between relationships. It had been weeks—no, months—since he'd had sex. He'd been too busy, distracted by work and the dire financial situation Cosimo Kallas was in, to bother about hooking up with anyone.

But now he was ready.

He was so ready he could barely keep his hands off those slim hips, from pulling her against him so she could feel how ready. 'You will share my bed even if you don't share my body to begin with. I won't have my household staff snickering behind my back at my inability to consummate my marriage.'

She glared at him so hotly he thought the champagne in his glass was going to boil. 'If you so much as lay one finger on me, I'll scream loud enough for them to hear me in Albania.'

Draco gave an indolent smile. 'I can guarantee you'll scream, *glykia mou*. You certainly won't be the first. Most women in my bed do.'

Her mouth went into a flat line and her hands clenched into tight little white-knuckled balls. Her whole body seem to vibrate like a child's battery-operated toy. 'I'm surprised you want to wait until we're married. Why don't you throw me to the floor and have your way with me now?'

'Tempting, but alas, I'm a civilised man.' He swept a hand behind him where he'd entered the room earlier. 'See? No knuckle marks along the carpet.'

Her caustic look showed just how uncivilised she thought him. She swung away and put herself behind one of the sofas, as if she needed to barricade herself. 'I suppose you're only making me wait to ramp up the torture quotient.'

'The sort of torture I have in mind will be mutually pleasurable.'

She shook her hair back behind her shoulders in a

haughty manner. The silky swing of it always fascinated him. It was like the swish of a curtain. 'I find it hard to understand how you could want to bed a woman who hates you. It seems a little kinky to me.'

'You don't hate me, Allegra. What you hate is how you can't get your way with me. You need a strong man. Someone who will allow you to express that passionate nature you keep under wraps all the time. I'm that man.'

She gave one of her derisory laughs. 'Hello? We've actually had a women's movement during the last century. Didn't you hear about that or were you too busy clubbing mammoths and dragging them back to your cave?'

Draco's groin tightened at her witty come-back. She always gave as good as she got, which was another reason he thought her perfect wife material. He didn't want a doormat. He didn't want someone who didn't have the spirit to spar with him.

He wanted her.

It was as simple as that. Since he'd seen her in London he had lost interest in other women. He had found the dating scene increasingly boring and predictable. But every encounter, every conversation, with Allegra was full of surprises. She stimulated him physically and intellectually.

He reached into his top pocket and handed her the ring box he'd brought with him. 'That reminds me—I have something for you. If it doesn't fit, I'll have it adjusted.'

She took the box and cautiously opened it, as if whatever was in there might leap out and bite. But then she let out a breath and picked up the diamond solitaire with almost worshipful fingers. 'It's beautiful.' She looked up at him, her blue eyes showing a hint of uncertainty he found strangely touching. 'It looks frightfully expensive...'

Draco shrugged. 'It's just a ring. I threw a dart at the counter. This was the one it hit.'

She slipped the ring over her knuckle. 'It fits.'

'Must be an omen.'

Her gaze flicked to his. 'I'll give it back when we divorce.'

Draco didn't want her thinking there was any hint of romance in his choice of a ring. He'd done that once and it had been the worst mistake of his life. 'Keep it. I'm not sure any future bride of mine would want to wear a second-hand ring.'

She opened and closed her mouth, as if she couldn't find what to say. Then she looked down at the ring winking on her hand. It was a moment before she looked up at him again. 'How can I be sure you won't play around while we're married? You've played around all your adult life. Men like you get bored with one lover.'

Right now, Draco couldn't imagine ever being bored by her, but it didn't mean he would propose anything long-term. Long-term was for the in love, and that hardly described him in this case. He wasn't going to go down that path ever again. In lust? Yes. Big time. 'When I get bored, I'll let you know. We can end the marriage before anyone gets hurt.'

'Perhaps I'll get bored first,' Allegra said. 'Women have the right to choose their own husband, not have one thrust upon them. If I wanted to choose one, then you'd be the last man I'd consider. The very last.'

Draco smiled at the insult and moved across to

the door. 'We'd better let your father know the happy news. But, let me remind you, apart from your father no one—and I mean no one—must know this isn't a love match. I'm not interested in the press attention it would receive otherwise.'

Later, Allegra didn't know how she got through the rest of the evening, with Draco and her father chatting away over dinner like two good mates who'd just nailed a successful business deal. Damn it. *She* was the business deal. How could this be happening? Married to her worst enemy! And it was happening so quickly. Her phone hadn't stopped buzzing with incoming messages because Draco had taken the liberty of announcing their engagement on social media. Every platform of social media. *Grr.* It annoyed her because she'd been left looking like an idiot for not saying anything to her friends and colleagues about her 'secret relationship' with Greece's most eligible bachelor.

But when her secretary and best friend Emily Seymour texted, WTF? Is this a joke? Allegra couldn't quite bring herself to lie to her.

No joke but it's not what you think. Will explain later. Can't talk now.

Emily's text came back.

Can't wait! Knew you had a thing for him since that guy was a no-show. He's so HOT!!!'

She'd followed the word 'hot' with an emoticon of flames burning.

Allegra texted back.

MOC. No sex.

Emily sent an emoticon of a person laughing and holding their sides.

Allegra rolled her eyes and typed back.

I mean it!

She put away her phone before she was subjected to any more teasing. She wasn't sure how Emily had picked up on her attraction to Draco. But then, Emily was a bit of a romantic. What signals had Allegra given off? Or was she protesting *too* much?

'Well, I think I'll leave you two to chat while I head off to bed,' Allegra's father said, rising from the table. He paused by Allegra's chair and placed a hand on her shoulder. 'I know you'll be happy with Draco. He's exactly what you need.'

There were a hundred retorts she wanted to throw back but in the end she stayed silent. Her father gave her shoulder a quick pat, as if he were patting a dog he didn't quite trust, before he left the room and quietly closed the door behind him.

Draco twirled the amber contents of his brandy glass, his gaze steady on hers sparkling with amusement. 'Nice to know I've got the father-in-law's big tick of approval.'

Allegra picked up her wine glass and surveyed him over the top of the rim. 'What a pity you don't have mine. But that doesn't seem to matter to you—I wonder why? Maybe you've engineered this because you're secretly in love with me. Is that it?'

His expression became shuttered and he put down his own glass with a soft little thud. 'I'm not sure I'm capable of romantic love. I'm a little too practical for that. But I care about you, if that's any consolation.'

She gave a laugh. 'People *care* about their pot plants. How nice to know you'll offer me water and fertiliser occasionally.'

His crooked smile came back and sparked a sardonic glint in his gaze. 'Whenever you want fertilising, you just let me know.'

Allegra sent him a gimlet glare even though her ovaries were packing their bags and heading to the exits. And it was not just her ovaries that were getting excited. Her feminine core was contracting with a pulsation of lust that made it difficult to sit still in her chair. She had never really thought about having a baby before now. She was a career girl, not an earth mother. An image popped into her head of her belly swollen with his child. His DNA and hers getting it on and producing a baby with dark eyes and dark hair. She saw another image of him holding that baby, his strong arms cradling the tiny bundle while his eyes met hers in a tender look…

She gave herself a mental shake. 'So, you've never been in love? Apart from with yourself, I mean.'

He gave a soft chuckle and draped one arm along the back of the neighbouring chair. 'I'm not averse to a bit of self-love now and again. How about you?'

Allegra wasn't going to give him an account of her sex life even if these days it was mostly with herself. 'I thought I was in love with my first boyfriend but we both know how that ended.' And it had been Draco's fault. Damn him.

'Did you sleep with him?'

'Yes,' she answered in spite of herself.

'And?'

Allegra gave him a 'wouldn't you like to know?' look. 'You think I'm going to swap bedroom tales with you? It was your fault it was such a dis—' She clamped her mouth shut, furious she'd given away more than she'd intended.

'It was consensual…wasn't it?' There was a note of concern in his tone and he moved forward in his chair with a frown pulling at his brow.

'Yes.'

He was still frowning, his posture tense, on edge. 'What happened to make it such a disaster? Is that the word you were going to say?'

Allegra looked at the rim of her glass rather than meet his probing gaze. 'I wanted to get rid of my V card and he seemed the right one to do it with.' She twisted her mouth. 'Obviously these things are easier for you guys. You seem to have fun no matter what.'

'Biology isn't always fair,' Draco said. 'To women especially.'

There was a little silence.

'You were right about him, though,' Allegra said. 'He was such a loser in the end. He told all his mates what a disappointment I'd been in bed. Needless to say, I was completely and utterly mortified.' Why she was telling him that excruciating detail escaped her. Emily was the only other person she had told, because it was too painful to think about, let alone recount to someone else. And too skin-crawlingly embarrassing.

'Yes, well, I reckon he only said that to take the attention off his own inadequacies,' Draco said. 'He should've made your pleasure a priority. That's the golden rule of decent manhood.'

She was pretty certain none of Draco's lovers had ever complained about his lack of prowess in bed. Just the thought of him pleasuring her with that virile body of his was enough to make her get all excited downstairs. But why was she talking about this stuff with him? If she told him much more, he would realise she was practically a nun.

'Fancy an evening stroll out on the terrace?' he asked after a moment, as if he sensed she was uncomfortable with the subject.

'I miss all this when I'm in London,' Allegra said once they were outside and looking at the dark blue, wrinkled silk of the ocean below with its silver band of moonlight shimmering on the surface. 'But then, when I'm here I miss lots of things about London.'

His shoulder brushed against the skin of her bare arm, his left hand within a couple of millimetres of her right one where it was resting on the railing. 'It's a problem when you love two places. That's why I move between the two, so I get the best out of each of them by commuting between seasons. But, of course, not everyone has the financial flexibility to do that.'

The early summer evening air was scented with the salt spray of the sea and the faint but familiar fragrance of the vigorously blooming bougainvillea hanging in a swathe of crimson over the side of the terrace. The far off braying of a donkey and the clanging of the rigging of the yachts in the marina lower down carried in the light, warm breeze.

Allegra stole a covert glance at Draco. The moonlight put his impossibly handsome features into relief, making him look all the more like he had stepped off a marble plinth in an antiquities museum. The high, intelligent forehead with the prominent jet-black eyebrows, the strong nose and sculpted mouth were etched on her brain like a tattoo. What other man had ever compared to him?

It was a cliché, but tall, dark and handsome—and Greek—was her poison. She was lethally attracted to him. She knew it. He knew it. It swirled in the air when they were alone together like a potent but forbidden drug. One taste and Allegra knew she would be addicted. Which was why she had to keep her distance, even though every cell in her body was trembling with the need for contact. It didn't matter how much she fantasised about Draco in secret. No way could she afford to indulge in a physical relationship with him. He had rejected her once. She wasn't going to let him do it again.

But it would be kind of exciting to kiss him...

He turned and saw her looking at him, and before she could put any distance between them he lifted a finger to her face and tucked a breeze-teased tendril of her hair back behind her ear. His face was mostly in shadow, but she could see the moonlight reflected in his gaze like a glint of quartz in black marble.

Allegra knew she should step away, knew too she should brush his hand aside, frown at him and tell him to back off in her sharp, schoolmistress-y tone. But it seemed her mind and body had other ideas. Wicked ideas. Dangerous ideas. Ideas that made her picture her body crushed beneath his, his mouth clamped to hers, their bodies writhing in mutual, skin-shivering ecstasy. She drew closer to him as if someone had a hand in the small of her back, her hips brushing against his. The shock of the erotic contact made her insides twist and coil with lust, her breath hitch and her heart race. She saw her hands slide up to lie flat on his chest, the hard muscles flinching as if her touch electrified him.

Draco's hands went to her waist, his fingers gentle but as hot as a brand. His muscle-dense thighs were so close she could feel their heat and sense their latent strength. His head came down but his mouth hovered rather than landed, his warm, brandy-scented breath mingling with hers.

Allegra sent her tongue out over her lips to moisten them, her whole body poised in that infinitesimal moment before final touchdown.

Go on. Do it. Kiss me and prove that you want me as much as I want you. 'Are you going to kiss me?'

'Thinking about it.' His voice was two parts gravel, one part honey, making her insides quiver.

'What's to think about?' She moved even closer, her breasts, bumping against his chest, making her flesh tingle. 'You know you want to.'

If she was wrong, this was going to be mortifying.

Draco's breath moved in a sexy waft along the side of her mouth, the rasp of his stubble grazing her cheek like fine-grade sandpaper. 'You've had way too much to drink,' he said.

'I'm not drunk—not even tipsy.' *Not on alcohol, that is.*

His tongue glided over her beauty spot, then circled it as if he were circling one of her nipples. A savage jab of lust assailed her, pooling in a liquid heat between her thighs. Then he moved his mouth to her jawbone, his lips working their way up in nibbles and nudge-like movements to the sensitive space below her ear. Her whole body shivered when Draco's teeth gently caught her earlobe, the tender tug sending a riot of sensations in a quick-silver streak down to the base of her spine. Her legs were without bones, without ligaments, trembling to stay upright and only doing so because his hands on her waist were keeping her there.

His mouth kept up its disarming of her senses, taking her on a journey of heady arousal unlike anything she had experienced before. Who knew her jawbone was an erogenous zone? Her jawbone! His lips nibbled their way down to the space between her lower lip and her chin. He was so close to her lips. *So* close… Close enough for them to buzz, tingle and ache for him to cover them with his mouth. But, still, he kept his lips away from hers as if he had made a private vow of kissing celibacy.

Draco's hands moved from her waist to cradle both sides of her head, his fingers splaying under the weight of her hair in a sensual glide that made something at the base of her spine heat, sizzle and melt. 'You are so damn beautiful,' he said in that same deep, gravelly burr.

'So kiss me, then.' Allegra slid her hands around his neck, which brought her lower body flush against his. She could feel the battle going on in his body where it was touching hers—the urge of the primal in combat with his iron will and steely self-control. Her own self-control was nowhere to be seen and she couldn't be bothered to send out a search party.

She wanted him to kiss her.

She needed him to kiss her.

She would *make* him kiss her.

She needed it like she needed her next breath. She would die if Draco didn't give in to the desire she could feel throbbing in his flesh where it was pressed against her. Mutual desire. Dark, wicked desire that refused to go back into its cage now it was released from its prison of denial. If he kissed her it would prove she wasn't the only one who was vulnerable. It would prove he had his weak spot—*her*. This time he wouldn't push her away with a cutting comment. This time she would kiss him as a woman kissed a man, not as a fumbling teenager. She would show him he wasn't as immune to her as he wanted her to think. 'Kiss me, Draco. What are you scared of?'

His hands came back down to settle against her hips, his fingers harder now—possessive, almost. His eyes were sexily hooded, his gaze honed in on her mouth. 'Are you sure you know what you're doing?'

Allegra moved like a sinuous cat against the hard frame of his body, her arms winding around Draco's neck, her fingers tugging, stretching and releasing his black curls. His erection was hot and heavy against her belly, the pounding of his blood echoing the deep, urgent thrumming of her own. She could feel her own moisture gathering, her body preparing itself for the pleasure it craved. Never had she felt desire like it. It was a raging fever, a torrent of need that refused to be ignored. Allegra wasn't going to sleep with him, but one kiss would be enough to take the edge off it, surely? What harm would one kiss do?

'You want me so bad,' she said.

His body pressed harder against her as if he hadn't

the strength of will power to do otherwise. His hands tightened their grip on her hips, his fingers digging into her flesh as if he never wanted to release her. 'Yes. I want you.'

Draco didn't say it out loud, but she could hear the word 'but' somewhere in that statement. Allegra brought her hand around to trace the outline of his mouth, her stomach pitching when the soft pad of her fingertip caught on his stubble. 'I bet you've kissed a lot of women in your time.'

'A few.'

She sent her fingertip down the shallow stubble-covered dip between his lower lip and his chin. Her eyes came back to his intensely dark gaze. 'Did you know you were my first kiss?'

'Not until you kissed me.'

Did he have to remind her how inexpert she had been?

'I've learnt since then. Don't you want to see how much I've improved?'

Allegra sensed he was wavering. He kept silent but his body spoke for him, his desire for her pulsing invisibly in the air like sound waves. His breath mingled with hers. His body was hot and urgent against hers, increasing her hunger for skin-on-skin contact. She slipped her arms back around his neck and rose on tiptoe, bringing her mouth to his in a soft touchdown. When she lifted off, his lips clung to hers like a rough surface to satin. Allegra touched down again, moving her lips against the warm, firm heat of his in an experimental fashion, discovering their texture, their shape. Their danger.

Draco drew in a breath and took control of the kiss,

crushing her lips beneath the fervent pressure of his. His hands went from bracketing her hips to cradling her head, angling it so he could deepen the kiss with a spine-wobbling glide of his tongue through her already parted lips. She welcomed him with a breathless sigh, his tongue tangling with hers in an erotic duel that had unmistakably sexual overtones. Her inner core recognised them, contracting in a fireball of lust that threatened to overwhelm her. Allegra kissed him back with feverish intensity, as if his mouth was her only succour and without it she would cease to exist.

He made a low, growling sound in the back of his throat and explored every inch of her mouth, his tongue sweeping, swirling, diving, darting until her senses were spinning like a top set off by a slingshot. Need ricocheted through her, clamouring to be assuaged. Begging, pleading, to be satisfied with every breath she snatched in while his mouth worked its fiery magic on hers.

One of Draco's hands went to her breast, cupping it in a possessive hold that sent another wave of sensation coursing through her body like sheet lightning. His thumb found her nipple, rolling over it through the fabric of her dress and bra, but she might as well have been naked. The thrill of his touch, even through two layers of fabric, was enough to make Allegra whimper for more. He moved to her other breast, cupping and caressing her through her clothes as if they were star-crossed teenage lovers on a clandestine date. His mouth left hers to blaze a blistering trail of fire down her neck and décolletage, his stubble ticking and tantalising her, his lips and tongue ramping up her desire until she felt like a pressure cooker about to blow.

But, while her self-control was shot to pieces, it seemed his was not.

Draco slowly drew back from her, still holding her in the circle of his arms but without chest-to-chest contact. She felt the loss keenly—her breasts were still tingling from his touch, from being crushed so tightly against his body. She searched his face for a moment but his expression was largely unreadable...all except for that glint of triumph lurking in the depths of his gaze.

Allegra slipped out of his hold and straightened the front of her dress. Time to rein things in. She couldn't allow him to think she was his for the asking. She had proved her point...sort of. But she had a disquieting feeling Draco had proved his own. 'Just to remind you. Kissing is fine, but that's as far as it goes.'

One side of his mouth came up in a slanted smile. 'You seriously think you can maintain that, even if by some remote possibility I agreed to it?'

Allegra raised her chin. 'Those are my rules.'

'Here's what I think of your rules.' He stepped back into her body space, standing close enough for her to feel the tug of attraction pulling at every one of her organs like invisible silken cords. His eyes moved back and forth between both of hers, searching, penetrating, challenging. She drew in a breath but it caught on something in her throat. Her thighs were less than a couple of centimetres from his, her breasts getting all excited about his chest being even closer.

Draco sent a fingertip idly down the slope of her cheek, then continued his tantalising pathway to the fullness of her bottom lip, his finger moving over its already sensitised surface like a mine sweeper. It took all her self-control and more not to take his finger into her mouth, to swirl her tongue around it and draw on it with her lips. The urge to do so was so primal and raw it made her insides quake with need. Allegra licked her lip instead, but her tongue came into contact with his finger on its return journey and an explosion of lust barrelled through her. She gripped the front of Draco's shirt, pressing her body against his, her mouth going to the exposed, tanned skin of his neck, sucking, nibbling, grazing him with her teeth and finally—*dear God, finally*—finding his mouth.

His lips moved with thrilling expertise on hers, his tongue delving deeply to call hers into sensual play. She made little breathless sounds of approval when his hands clasped her by the hips to hold her against his heat. She wanted more. Needed more. She sent her hands on a journey of discovery, sliding them over his hardened length, shaping him through his trousers, her own feminine muscles a frenzy of excitement.

After a moment, Draco placed a hand over hers to stop her from going any further. 'If we play by the rules, then those rules have to be fair.'

Allegra gave a shrug and stepped back, as if she didn't care either way, even though her body was crying out for release and her fingers were aching to feel the weight and heft of him. 'Can't take a little fooling around, Draco?'

His eyes glittered in the darkness. 'I would have you here and now but your father's household staff might be shocked. Don't look now, but his housekeeper Sophia's been watching from the window behind you.'

Allegra's cheeks grew so hot she was sure she was contributing to global warming. How had she let herself behave in such an abandoned way? She prided herself on always acting with poise and decorum around the staff. She wasn't the sort of person to behave recklessly or immodestly. But in Draco's arms she became a wanton woman with no thought for anything other than her body's needs. Needs that still thrummed and hummed inside her like a plucked violin string.

'Well, we are supposed to be acting like a couple in love,' she said. 'I might say you were doing a mighty fine job of it too.'

He gave a soft laugh. 'Don't confuse good old-fashioned lust with love.'

Allegra turned back to look at the ocean cast in its silver glow from the moonlight. She was conscious of Draco standing beside her, close enough for their arms to be touching. Even though his was covered in finely woven cotton, she could still feel the sensual energy of him. The potent vibrancy of him. Couldn't stop imagining how it would feel to have those strong, tanned arms wrapped around her in the grip of passion. 'What if you fall in love with me?' The question was out before she could block it. Had she sounded as if she *wanted* him to fall in love with her?

He turned and leaned his back against the balustrade, his hands resting on the railing either side of his hips. 'We've covered this, Allegra. I'm not sure I'm capable of loving you.'

Allegra flashed him a look. 'How charming of you to say.'

He gave a shrug, as if he recognised the veiled insult but was not going to apologise for it. 'Just saying.'

Of course, Draco falling in love was only a remote possibility. His heart was untouchable. He wasn't the type of man to allow himself to be vulnerable. He was the one who controlled his relationships to a set timetable. Few relationships of his had ever lasted more than a few weeks—one or two, perhaps, a couple of months.

Allegra looked down at her right hand resting next to his on the railing. His skin was so dark and hair-roughened compared to her pale, smoother hand. It was an erotic reminder of all the essential male and female differences between them. If she moved her pinkie a couple of millimetres she would touch him. The temptation to do so was a force inside her body over which she seemed to have little or no control. It was as though he were an industrial-strength magnet and she was a tiny iron filing. He had beautiful hands—broad and dusted with black hair that also lightly touched the backs of his long, strong fingers.

She couldn't stop thinking about those clever hands on her body. Not through her clothes, but on her naked skin. Draco wasn't averse to physical labour. He didn't sit behind a desk all day. He was the sort of man who didn't mind getting his hands dirty at the coalface of the businesses he ran. What would it feel like to have those hands gliding over her flesh? Touching her in places that hadn't been touched in so long she had almost forgotten what it felt like to be a woman?

She sent him a sideways glance. 'Why haven't you been in a long-term relationship before?'

'I have.'

'A month or two is not considered long-term.'

A beat or two of silence passed.

'I had a partner for close to a year once.'

He had? 'Really? I never knew. Gosh, you kept that awfully quiet. The press always—' Allegra thought it best to stop speaking before she revealed how closely she had been following his love-life in the media. It had been a bit of an obsession over the years One she wasn't too proud of, but she'd always had an unhealthy fascination with whomever he was squiring around town and for how long.

There was another long moment of silence.

'I was thinking about asking her to marry me.'

Allegra turned so she was facing him. Draco's face was backlit by the moonlight, so it was hard to make out his expression, but she could see his mouth had a rueful twist to it. 'You were?'

'I even bought the ring.'

She'd never heard even a whisper of an engagement. Why hadn't it been made public? Who wouldn't be interested in a self-made playboy like him settling down? Draco had dragged himself up from abject poverty to become one of Greece's most eligible bachelors. Who was the woman? Who had captured his attention to the degree he would offer to marry her? And, more to the point, why hadn't he gone ahead with the marriage? 'What happened?'

He pushed away from the railing and turned back to look at the moonlit view. She could only see one side of his face but it was enough to make her suspect he didn't like talking about the memory. His features had a boxed-up look about them, the line of his jaw tense, his gaze looking into the far-off distance. 'It turned out she wasn't the one after all.'

'She said no?'

He glanced at his watch and frowned. 'I'd better be on the move. I have some work to do back at my villa before I call it a day.'

Allegra placed her hand on his forearm when he turned from the railing. His muscular arm was warm and the dark, masculine hair faintly prickly under the softer skin of her hand. 'Wait. Tell me what happened.'

Draco went to brush her hand away as if it were a fly but she dug her fingers in. 'Leave it, Allegra.'

No darn way was she going to leave it. Not while she had a chance to find out who he was behind the persona of suave and ruthless businessman. 'I told you about my first time. It wasn't easy talking to you about that, let me tell you. I've only ever told my best friend, Emily. Surely you owe me this one confession?'

It was a moment before he spoke. He stood there looking down at her with her hand on his arm without seeming to move a muscle. But then his arm flexed under her touch and he let out a stream of air that sounded resigned. 'She had someone else lined up. Someone far richer than me. I ended up buying the guy's company a couple of years ago when it got into trouble. Sold it for a profit too. A handsome profit.'

As you do when you're filthy rich and want revenge.

It was a timely reminder to Allegra that the field they were playing on was tipped in his favour. He could be calculating and ruthless when he needed to be. Hadn't Draco already proved that with his non-existent marriage proposal? 'What did your ex think about that?'

He gave a breath of a laugh, a glint of cynicism entering his gaze, making it harder, darker. 'She asked to meet in private and offered herself to me.'

Allegra couldn't explain why she felt such a sharp dart of jealousy. What did she care who he slept with and why? She might care once they were married, but his past was his past, and it had nothing to do with her.

'What did you do?'

'What do you think I did?'

'Told her to get lost?'

'Wrong.' His eyes contained a gleam of malice. 'I slept with her first and *then* I told her to get lost.'

CHAPTER THREE

ALL THROUGH THE christening service the following day, Allegra couldn't stop thinking about the ex who had spurned Draco's proposal. She'd tried searching for information on the net, but there was nothing about him having been in a long-term relationship. How many years ago had it been? Had it been long before he'd risen to the top, while he'd been still making his mark on the world?

Was that why he had never fallen in love and insisted he never would? Was that why he only ever hooked up with women for short periods of time—because developing an attachment would make him too vulnerable? If he had truly loved the woman, then Allegra could understand how hurt he must have felt—especially when his ex had supposedly chosen someone because they were richer than him. It would have been a cruel slap to the ego for someone as proud as Draco Papandreou.

There were few men richer than him in Greece now. His empire was vast, not just the luxury yacht building, which was growing exponentially across the globe, but also property. He owned numerous villas, not just for his own private use, but also for lease to super-wealthy customers. He had a sharp eye for business and had rescued many from collapse, building them up over time and selling them for a massive profit. He rarely spoke in public about his humble background as the only child of a fisherman, but she guessed it was a powerful motivator to keep expanding his business empire.

But Draco was also an enigmatic man. He only allowed people so close and he never allowed anyone to manipulate or hoodwink him. He was a good judge of character, a fact she had witnessed first-hand when he'd warned her about her first boyfriend. He'd been familiar with the boy's family—this being Greece and all—and had told her she was wasting her time with someone who only wanted to date her because she came from money. *That* had stung. No sixteen-year-old girl with confidence issues and a body she hadn't quite grown into wanted to hear something like that.

But, unfortunately, Draco had been right.

The boy had crowed about how he'd bedded her and then joked about what a disappointment she'd been as a partner. The vernacular he'd used had made the insult all the more hurtful and shaming. It had taken her years to sleep with another partner. Years. And even the last time she'd had sex—which was so long ago she could barely recall what he'd looked like—she had worried he was judging her on her performance, filing away notes to laugh about with his friends in the bar later. Allegra had blamed Draco for it all because she had only gone after the boy after Draco's rejection. The boy's cruel taunts had seemed to echo Draco's ego-crushing dismissal, further shattering her self-esteem.

Allegra looked across the formal room overlooking the terrace where everyone had gathered for drinks to wet the baby's head. Her father was doing more than wetting his son's head. She had lost count of the number of glasses of champagne he had put away. Was he worried about this merger or relieved it was now all sorted? He looked happy—the happiest she had seen him in years. But then, why wouldn't he? He had his perfect little family now, and his left-on-the-shelf daughter of thirty-one was being married off to solve his business woes.

Elena caught Allegra's eye and came over, carrying Nico in her arms. 'I haven't had a moment to speak to you in private, Allegra,' she said, smiling broadly. 'I can't tell you how happy your father and I are about you and Draco. Your dad's been so stressed lately but since he heard you and Draco are getting married it's like a weight's been lifted off him. You *are* happy about it, aren't you? It's just, you've been a little quiet and...'

Allegra forced a smile. Acting had never been her thing but there was no time like the present to learn. 'Of course I'm happy. I'm just feeling a little overwhelmed. It's all been such a whirlwind.'

'Yes, but Draco never waits around for paint to dry, does he?' Elena said with a light laugh. 'I think it's so romantic he wants to marry you as soon as possible.' She glanced at Allegra's abdomen. 'I don't suppose it's because you're...?'

Allegra avoided her gaze and looked at the baby instead, stroking a gentle finger down his tiny petal-soft cheek. 'No. It's just...we both have work commitments booked in months and months ahead and there's only this small window of time available.'

Who knew she could be so good at lying?

'But you do want children, don't you?' Elena asked, handing Nico over for her to cuddle. 'I mean, when you're ready? It would be awful to miss out. I thought I was going to until I met your dad and accidentally fell pregnant. I still pinch myself, you know.' Her gaze went to Allegra's father across the room and she sighed. 'I still can't believe he married me. I didn't think I'd ever find someone to love me.'

But did Allegra's father love Elena? The question seemed to hang suspended in the air like a cobweb. Whether her father felt the same love towards his young wife as she did towards him was questionable. He'd wanted a male heir, and he'd wanted a malleable Greek woman who wouldn't question his authority and who would be content to stay at home and rear the children.

'I've not really thought much about having kids. My career has always been my baby,' Allegra said. She had never been the sort of girl to peer into prams or go gaga at the mention of a baby. Her career had been her entire focus. She had put everything before it. But holding little Nico made a cordoned-off corner of her brain wonder what it would be like to have a child of her own. Nico's tiny rosebud mouth opened on a yawn and he stretched his little body, one tiny arm with its starfish hand flailing in the air. She captured his hand and pressed a kiss to each miniscule finger, marvelling at the perfect little fingernails.

Elena leaned in to straighten the hand-embroidered christening gown that had been in the Kallas family for over a hundred years. Allegra hadn't worn it as an infant because the privilege was exclusive to sons, a tradition that had been another reason to make her feel an outsider. Draco had mentioned the possibility of a child but he'd been teasing. It made sense that he wouldn't want any permanent legacies from their short-term union. And why was she thinking about having babies with him, anyway? She was supposed to be keeping their marriage in name only.

Good luck with that.

'Will you be all right with him for a moment?' Elena asked. 'I just want to pop to the bathroom and change my breast pads.'

'Of course.' Little Nico wriggled again then opened his eyes, looked at her and smiled a gummy smile. Allegra felt a wave of love so powerful it was like an invisible fist grabbing her heart. This was her half-brother and she was melting like honey on a hotplate. What would she have felt if it had been her own flesh and blood? She tickled the baby's button-sized chin. 'Hey, little guy, who's been a beautiful boy while all this fuss is going on?'

Draco came alongside Allegra and, slipping his arm around her waist, offered the baby a finger, which little Nico grabbed with his tiny hand. 'It's hard to believe how small babies are—he's like a doll.'

'Yes,' Allegra said. 'I keep worrying I'm going to drop him. I suppose you get used to it when it's your own.'

'You're a natural. You look like you've been holding babies all your life.'

She gave a wry movement of her lips. 'Yes, well, I like the ones you can hand back. Do you want a hold?'

'No way.' He took a step back and held his hands up like stop signs, as if she were handing him a ticking bomb. 'I'm no good with babies.'

'Go on.' Allegra kept coming at him with the baby. 'You're a big macho man. You're surely not scared of a tiny, defenceless baby?'

Draco looked as though he was going to resist, but then his expression took on a resigned set. 'If I drop him, then it will be your fault.'

'You won't drop him.' Allegra came near so she could transfer the baby into his arms. The closeness of him stirred her senses into a swarm of longing. The fresh lime scent of his aftershave with its woody notes was intoxicating and alluring.

He took the infant, holding him slightly aloft, as if not wanting to get too close. But then Nico smiled and gurgled up at him, and Draco brought him against his chest and gently rocked him in his arms, looking down at the baby with a small smile. Allegra hadn't expected the sight of him with a baby in his arms to stir her so much.

'I've never been a godfather before,' he said after a moment.

'Nor me a godmother,' Allegra said. 'I'm not sure what sort of spiritual adviser I'll make. Sometimes I feel I could do with some spiritual guidance myself.'

'Don't we all?'

She angled her gaze at him. 'What? The invincible Draco Papandreou in need of advice? Wonders will never cease.'

He gave her a self-deprecating smile. 'You'd be surprised. It took me a long time to get control of my life. I almost lost my way a few times.' He looked down at the baby again, his smile dimming slightly. 'Especially after my father was killed. I suddenly found myself all alone in the world.'

'How old were you when your mother died?'

'Six.'

Allegra had been twice that age when her mother

had died and she still missed her terribly. How hard must it have been for Draco as a small child to lose his mother, only to lose his father a few years later? 'It must have been awful for you when your father died so suddenly. Who looked after you?'

'I looked after myself.'

She frowned at the cynical edge to his tone. 'But how did you survive? Didn't some relatives take you in?'

His expression reminded her of a suit of armour. She could see the outline of his face but only through a mask of steel. 'What few relatives I had were not interested in a fifteen-year-old boy with an attitude problem.'

'So what did you do?'

'I fended for myself.'

'How?'

His eyes took on a sardonic glint. 'You really want to hear some of the wicked things I got up to? I might shock you.'

'Try me and see.'

He glanced down at the baby and then gave Allegra an inscrutable smile. 'Not in front of little Nico.'

Allegra was frustrated he didn't trust her enough to tell her what his childhood and adolescence had been like. Was his tragic past one of the reasons he wanted to settle down now? It was all very well, her harbouring secret little fantasies about having a baby of her own but, even if Draco had wanted one, having a baby together would cause a whole lot of complications she could well do without.

She had acted for a number of women divorcing husbands from a different country, which made the care arrangements for children particularly complex, especially if the split was acrimonious—and of course many, if not most, were. It was a legal and personal minefield and one Allegra wanted to avoid at all costs. She knew enough about Greek men, and Draco in particular, to know he would not want to live apart from his child or children. He would want control. And he would do whatever it took to maintain it. Luckily, a baby wasn't part of the deal.

Nico began to get restless and, as if tuned in to her baby's needs by radar, Elena came back and took him from Draco. 'Time for a feed, I think,' she said. 'You two make great babysitters, by the way.'

Once Elena left, Draco led Allegra out to a shaded part of the garden near a fountain where the tinkle and splash of water cooled the warm atmosphere. 'There are some legal aspects of our marriage to deal with. Can you free up some time mid-week? I'll be in London tying up some other business. I'll set up an appointment with my London-based lawyer so we can sort everything out.'

Allegra had no problem with signing a pre-nuptial agreement. She had investments, property and other assets of her own she didn't want to jeopardise when it came time to divorce. But it was a stinging little reminder of the cynical mind-set he had about their relationship. 'Sure. Just give my secretary, Emily, a call and get her to put it in my diary.'

'I know what you're thinking. But I have shareholders to protect, and I'm sure you too have assets you don't want to see compromised. It makes things less complicated when we wrap things up.' He waited a beat before adding, 'It's not meant to be an insult to you, Allegra.'

'I didn't take it as one.'

He lifted a fingertip to the space between her eyes and smoothed away a puckered frown. 'Then why are you frowning at me like that?'

Allegra forced her facial muscles to relax. 'I always frown when I'm thinking.' She moved closer to the fountain and trailed her fingers in the cool water. 'It feels weird to think this time next week we'll be married.'

His hands came to rest on the top of her shoulders, his tall, strong frame standing just behind her. The intimacy of his proximity sent a rush of fizzing heat through her flesh. She had to fight the urge to lean back into his embrace, to feel the stirring of his body. 'Having second thoughts?' he said.

And third and fourth and every number this side of a thousand.

'It wouldn't matter what thoughts I had, though, would it? I haven't got any choice. I have to do this or watch Elena and Nico suffer.'

He turned her around and meshed his gaze with hers, his hands going to rest lightly about her waist. His gaze searched hers for a long moment, his expression containing a hint of a frown. 'I know this has been difficult for you. Your father's situation has made things far more time pressured than they could have been. Creditors are impatient people these days. But, in time, I hope you'll come to see this as a good solution all round. For you especially.'

Why for her especially?

Marriage was such an enormous step for anyone, even when the two parties loved one another. But when neither of them were in love, then how did that bode for them? Sure, some arranged marriages seemed to work well, but surely that was good luck, or maybe one or both parties became so resigned to their situation they decided it was more tolerable to love rather than hate.

Allegra had felt such intense antagonism towards Draco for so long, she didn't understand why she felt so attracted to him. Was it her frustrated female hormones playing perverse tricks on her? The more time she spent with him, the more she realised she had fashioned him in her mind as an archenemy.

Funny, but he didn't feel like an enemy when he touched her. When he looked at her with those black-as-tar eyes with their unknowable depths. He didn't feel like her opponent when he kissed her, when his tongue played with hers in an erotic mimicry of sex that made her blood sing full-throated arias through her veins. Nor when his hands cradled her breasts or held her lightly by the waist, as he was doing now.

His fingers tightened a fraction and he stepped closer—close enough for her to feel the need rising in him that mirrored the ache rising in her. His eyes went to her mouth in a sexily hooded way that never failed to get her pulse on the run. He lowered his head as if in slow motion, leaving her plenty of time to block the kiss if she wanted to.

She didn't.

His lips were dry and warm on hers, just a brush stroke at first—a light touchdown of surface rediscovery. But then he touched down again, once, twice, and on the third time something restrained in him escaped and his kiss became one of passionate heat and urgency.

The same hot-blooded urgency coursed through her

from her mouth to the very centre of her womanhood. The sexy glide of his tongue into her mouth made her whimper in approval, her arms going around his neck to bring her body even closer to the glorious hardness of his. Draco's hands came up to cradle her face, his head angled to one side so he could deepen the kiss, taking her on a journey of thrilling, pulse-thudding excitement as her need for him built to a level she would not have thought possible even a few days ago. She tangled her fingers into the thick pelt of his hair, her mouth feeding off his. His teeth nipped her lower lip and then his tongue swept over it like a salve. He did the same to her top lip, his nip and tugs so gentle, but they caused a tumult of sensations to rocket through her body and pool in a liquid, sizzling fire deep in her core.

'Hey, break it up you two,' one of Allegra's father's friends called out from some distance behind her. 'Save it for the honeymoon.'

Draco set her from him with a smile at her father's friend Spiro while keeping her by his side with an arm around her waist. 'How's it going, Spiro?'

'Not as good as things are going for you, I'll wager,' Spiro said with a wide grin. 'So, you two finally got together. He's a good catch, eh, Allegra? You must be feeling pretty pleased with yourself, landing a man like him.'

Why's that? Because I was rabid-dog ugly and left on the shelf and no one in their right mind would ever have offered for me in a thousand, million years?

Allegra ground her teeth so hard behind her smile she thought she would have to be tube fed for the rest of her life. 'Actually, Draco is the one who got the prize catch, aren't you, darling?'

Draco's smile set off a smouldering glint in his eyes. 'But of course, *kardia mou*. I'm the hands down winner in this union.'

Allegra's back teeth went down another centimetre. But thankfully Spiro moved on to chat to other guests who had come out to the garden to enjoy the shade and light breeze coming in from the ocean. 'You're really enjoying this, aren't you?' she said out of the side of her mouth.

'You know what Spiro is like,' Draco said, leading her back towards the house with a firm, warm hand in the small of her back.

'Yes, he's a man who thinks all a woman wants is a man with a big bank balance. I find it *so* insulting. A man isn't a financial plan. I know there are probably some women out there who are gold-diggers, but personally I would never marry someone because of his wealth. It's no measure of who he is as a person.'

He gave her lower back a circular stroke, making her legs feel as though someone had snipped her ligaments. 'I agree with you. But, on the other hand, the fact that someone has had the discipline and drive to work and accumulate wealth must demonstrate some admirable qualities, surely?'

Allegra gave a snort. 'I had a client a couple of years ago. She married a man who'd inherited a veritable fortune from his parents. He was the laziest, most obnoxious man I've ever met. He was abusive to his wife, both during and after their marriage, and he was so darn mean about supporting his own kids once it ended. Money does something to some people. It brings out the worst in them, and then people get hurt. I see it all the time in my job.'

Draco tucked her arm through his. 'At least we come to this marriage as equals, or close enough to being equals.'

'I would hardly call my wealth equal to yours.'

'Perhaps not, but we've both worked hard for what we've got, and neither of us would like to lose it.'

There were worse things to lose…

Like my heart, if I'm not careful.

Emily was at Allegra's office door before she'd even had time to put her tote bag away when she arrived back at work on Monday morning. She closed the door behind her and pulled out the chair opposite Allegra's desk. 'Okay, so give it to me. What the hell is going on? Do you have any idea how gobsmacked I was to hear you're getting married?'

'I told you—it's a marriage of convenience,' Allegra said. 'My father's got himself into a financial pickle and Draco is bailing him out with a merger.'

Emily's brow puckered. 'But how come he wants to marry you?'

Allegra dropped her shoulders with a 'thanks for the compliment' look. 'Apparently he wants a wife and I tick all his boxes.'

Emily made an apologetic movement of her lips. 'Sorry, didn't mean to suggest you weren't marriage-able or anything. You're gorgeous, and any man with a skerrick of testosterone would be thrilled to have you as his wife. But you've always been so against marriage—which to be frank is a bit of an occupational hazard around here. You broke out in hives before Julie's wedding, remember?'

Allegra remembered all too well. It wouldn't have

been a good look to be in the bridal party photos with
red splotches all over her face and neck—but apparently it hadn't been hives but a reaction to the facial
she'd had the day before as part of the hen's party spa
day. Just as well the make-up artist had done an excellent job of disguising it with cover-up. 'That was an
allergic reaction—'

'I rest my case.'

Allegra rolled her eyes. 'Anyway, I've agreed because…well… I've agreed, that's all. I've known him
since I was a teenager. I used to run into him at corporate functions and stuff with my father.'

*And proceed to embarrass myself with humiliat-
ing frequency.*

'But six months ago you were spitting chips about
how arrogant and up himself he was,' Emily said. 'Now
you're wearing his ring. Show me, by the way.' She
leaned across the desk to grasp Allegra's hand. 'Oh.
My. God. Isn't it gorgeous?'

'Yes, I couldn't have chosen better myself.' Which
made Allegra wonder if Draco knew her better than
she'd thought, despite his claim he'd selected the ring
at random. What else did he know about her?

Emily sat back down with a sigh. 'Gosh, I wish some
handsome billionaire would force me into a marriage
of convenience. *Is* he a billionaire?'

'Pretty close to it, I think.'

Emily leaned forward again, her toffee-brown eyes
suddenly full of concern. 'You sure you're doing the
right thing? I mean, you don't have to go through with
it, you know. You can always say no even as the priest
is asking you if you'll take this man and so on.'

Allegra couldn't say no, but explaining why to her

friend might make her look even more pathetic than she felt. She was ashamed about wanting to please her father at her age but there was no escaping it. 'I know what I'm doing, Em.'

'You said no sex, but surely you were joking?' Emily said. 'I mean, look at the guy. What's not to want?'

Allegra could feel her cheeks giving her away. 'I've told him it's a hands-off affair.'

Emily snorted. 'Like that's going to work. Did he actually agree to that?'

'Not in so many words, but he has to respect my wishes or—'

'Wishes, schmishes,' Emily said, eyes twinkling. 'You want him. That's why you were so cross about him that night in December. It was him you wanted, not that loser who didn't have the balls to show up when he'd been the one to ask you out in the first place.'

'I was cross with Draco because he seemed to be amused by the fact I was stood up by my date,' Allegra said. 'I didn't find it amusing. I found it humiliating.'

'What you found humiliating was Draco witnessing you being left high and dry,' Emily said. 'No girl wants a guy she fancies to see her rejected by someone else. It's not good for the ego. Speaking of egos—am I going to be your bridesmaid, or aren't you having one, since your wedding's so rushed and all?'

'Sorry, Em.' Allegra gave her friend a grimace. 'It's a really quiet affair with only a handful of guests on his private island.'

'His private island.' Emily grinned. *No problemo.* She slipped off the desk and straightened her skirt. 'But I expect a full report with photos when you get back from your honeymoon, okay?'

'Will do.'

'Where are you having your honeymoon?'

'On his yacht.'

Emily's eyes sparkled. 'You're toast.'

CHAPTER FOUR

ONCE THE LEGAL work had been seen to during the week, Allegra didn't see Draco again until the day before the wedding, when she arrived at his private retreat via a helicopter he had chartered to meet her at Athens airport. Her week had been a nightmare of juggling work, arranging a wedding dress and packing for their 'honeymoon'. Every time she even thought the word, much less said it, it made her pulse gallop. She knew he wasn't the sort of man to force himself on her. It was her own uncontrollable desires she was worried about.

Emily was right. How on earth was she going to resist him? Spending a week on a yacht with Draco was going to test her resolve like a chocolate addict standing in the middle of a chocolate fountain with her mouth open. She had no self-control around him. He only had to look at her with that black-as-sin gaze and her heart would skip as if it were jumping rope for England *and* Greece.

She had work commitments back home once the honeymoon was over, but apparently Draco had business meetings that week in London, so they would be travelling back together.

Just like a normal couple…

When Allegra arrived at the island it was like stepping into paradise. The eye-popping blue of the ocean with its fringe of sand on the villa side as white as powdered sugar was nothing short of stunning. The island was part of the Cyclades group and the andesite rocks, lava domes and prismatic columns of its cliffs and hills were geologists' eye candy. They were relics of the intense hydrothermal activity of millions of years ago and gave the islands, and this one in particular, a sense of timeless beauty.

But it was the villa itself that made her breath come to a slamming halt. It was eye-squinting white, built on four levels with an infinity pool that overlooked the pristine beach below. Gardens that looked like something out of a fairy tale surrounded the villa, and there were cypress pines everywhere, including a thick forest of them on the hills at the back of the island.

Allegra had expected Draco to meet her, as he'd arranged the day before. But only that morning he'd sent a brief text to say he couldn't make it. *Couldn't* or didn't want to? When she'd pressed the pilot for more information, he'd informed her Draco was tied up with something on the island which, considering a wedding was taking place the following day, wasn't such an unreasonable excuse. There was certainly a lot of activity going on for all that it was to be a small ceremony.

But when a woman in her late fifties came bustling out of the front door of the villa, welcoming Allegra in broken English, to her surprise she found herself feeling disappointed Draco hadn't welcomed her himself. What about his insistence they act like a normal couple in front of his staff?

'Kyria Kallas,' the housekeeper said. 'Kyrios Papandreou will be here soon. He is…how I say?…too busy?'

Allegra hoped it wasn't a foreshadowing of their future. She had never been important to her father. Work had always come first. Was she to suffer the same treatment by Draco? She might not want this marriage, but the idea of being so overlooked sent a shudder down her spine.

Allegra smiled at the housekeeper and assured her she was fine without him being there when he had so much to do. She found out the woman's name was Iona, that she had been working for Draco for five years and he was the best employer in the world. Allegra had trouble getting the woman to stop gushing about him. No doubt Draco's charm had worked its magic on the widow who, from what Iona said, he had rescued off the streets of Mykonos where she'd been left to fend for herself after her husband had divorced her, leaving her with virtually nothing out of a thirty-year marriage other than the clothes on her back. Allegra knew Draco was a financially generous man, but she hadn't seen him as the type to take in a homeless person and train them up to be his housekeeper.

Iona led her inside and showed her the wing of the villa she would be staying in prior to the wedding. It was a beautifully decorated suite of rooms with a marble bathroom complete with a freestanding bath with elegant gold taps and fittings. The furnishings in both the bedroom and sitting room were a lush combination of velvet, silk and brocade, and crystal chandeliers hung overhead. Allegra was no art expert, but the works on the walls were a mix of old and new, with a few pieces that looked like they were worth millions. The views from the windows were so breath-taking, she couldn't stop staring and wondering how anyone could ever get used to being surrounded by such beauty and the grandeur of nature at its finest.

One of the staff brought in her luggage and once he had gone Iona asked if she could press the wedding dress and any other clothes that needed attending to.

'That would be lovely, thank you.'

Allegra wandered over to the window overlooking the ocean and the gorgeous stretch of sand that sloped to the sparkling water below. Even though inside the villa was beautifully air-conditioned, the thought of a swim at the beach was so tempting she was rustling through her bag to retrieve her bathing costume before Iona could get it unpacked. She decided on her one-piece because she didn't feel like parading around in a bikini that was smaller than most of her underwear—a last-minute present from Emily.

There was a pathway with steps down to the beach that went past the infinity pool. Allegra decided against using the pool because it was so exposed to the villa. She didn't fancy the household staff watching her while she swam—or her version of swimming, anyway.

The sand was hot between her toes when she took off her sandals, and the sun beat down on her back and shoulders when she slipped off her light cotton beach poncho. The water was as warm as a bath and as clear as drinking water—so clear she could see fish darting away with every step she took. She went deeper and then did a shallow dive, her whole body sighing with pleasure when the water closed over her heated sticky flesh. It was like being baptised by nature, reborn and renewed by the elemental pulse of the water that had lapped this beach for aeons.

She swam back and forth, marvelling at the fish below her, and enjoying the sensation of the sun shining down on her back and legs after a miserable summer so far back in London. It was pure bliss to feel the water move over her body with every stroke she took, the sound of it splashing and the occasional cry of a seabird the only sounds she could hear.

Maybe she could get used to this sort of life—a week or two in London working her butt off and then coming back to this. To sun, sand and sea…and a sinfully handsome, sexy husband.

Draco came back to the villa, from seeing to an issue with one of his junior staff members at the staff quarters, to find Allegra had gone down to the beach. He could see her from the terrace, moving through the water like a mermaid, her long, black silky hair floating out behind her. His hormones shuddered at the sight of her. Her navy-blue and white one-piece highlighted her neat figure in all the right places—places he couldn't wait to get his hands on again.

He had only touched her breasts through her clothes and that had been enough to make him crazy with lust. She insisted their relationship would remain unconsummated, but every time he kissed her the message from her response was the opposite. He wasn't the sort of man to push a woman into doing things she didn't want to do, but everything so far told him Allegra *did* want him. Wanted him as badly as he wanted her.

He walked down to the beach and stood with one

hand over his brow, shielding his eyes from the sun, watching her slice through the water. But, as if she sensed his gaze on her, she stopped, stood upright in the waist-deep water and swung the wet curtain of her hair behind her back. She looked like a goddess arising from the depths of the ocean. The water droplets sparkled off her like a spray of carelessly flung diamonds, her creamy skin almost as white and pure as the sand.

Draco shucked off his jeans, T-shirt and shoes and walked into the water towards her. He would have slipped off his undershorts as well, but he decided to keep things in his pants, so to speak. Making love to Allegra with his staff watching from above was something he was keen to avoid. Once they were on his yacht and away from prying eyes, well, who knew what might happen?

He came closer to her and ran his eyes over her body. His flesh tingled, wondering if her hands and mouth would be as thorough as his searching gaze in the not-too-distant future.

Her eyes met his in a flinty lock. 'Is all your terribly important business sorted now?'

Draco placed his hands on her waist but, while she didn't resist, she stood statue-firm with her eyes spearing him like dark blue darts. 'Sorry, *agape mou*. I had an issue with one of my young staff. A homeless kid I took in a few months ago. He's having some problems with the rules I've set down.'

She blinked a couple of times and her whole body sagged as it lost its rigid stance. 'Oh…'

He moved his hands to her arms, stroking her wet skin cooled by the water. It was like caressing silk. Every cell in his body pulsed and strained to get closer to her. The blood pounded to his groin, his brain filling with images of him pinning her to the sand and getting all hot and primal with her. 'You can't be seen scowling at me the day before the wedding, *ne*?'

Allegra let out a breathy little sigh and stepped closer, placing her hands flat on his chest, making his blood roar all the harder. 'I'm sorry… I was just feeling a bit overwhelmed with it all. Is he OK, this employee of yours?'

Draco held her by the hips, his need for her closing the distance between their bodies like a bridge of lust. 'I found Yanni under the influence of something back at the staff quarters. I wasn't sure if it was alcohol or something else. I had to make sure, because he's got a history of substance abuse.'

She bit into her lower lip with her teeth. 'Oh, how terribly worrying for you. Is he all right?'

'Yes, but he's going to have one hell of a hangover in a few hours,' Draco said. 'I've got someone watching him and keeping him hydrated.'

'How old is he?'

'Sixteen going on thirty.' Draco grimaced and added, 'He's seen things you and I wouldn't dream of even in a nightmare. He's been living on the streets since he was ten years old.'

Her brow was as creased as the lines the wind had made in the sand. 'How did you come by him?'

'He tried to pick-pocket me. I caught him, and he fought like a demon, but then I realised he was sick with withdrawals from something. He was shaking and sweating and not in his right mind at all. He was barely coherent. I took him to a rehab centre and got him some help, but of course he relapsed as soon as he was released. You can't be on the streets and on God knows what substances for six years without having a struggle to get clean.'

Her brow was still slightly furrowed. 'So you took him in yourself? To live with you here on your island?'

'Yes, because he's safe here—relatively,' Draco said. 'This being an island, I can keep him away from the nightclubs and bars and seedy types who want to exploit him to do their dirty work for them. He's a good kid underneath all the bluster, he's just had some bad stuff happen to him.'

Her expression was thoughtful for a beat or two of silence. 'Did you spend time on the streets?'

Draco didn't like talking about the time after his father had died and he'd been left alone in the world. He had no money other than the pittance his father had saved which hadn't even covered the funeral expenses. It was a time he would rather forget because his life could have turned out so different—or ended altogether—if he had made some of the bad choices Yanni had made. Taking care of the teenager was a way of reaching back in time to be the sort of mentor he had found in his first boss, Josef.

'A few months. It was tough. I could have gone either way. But I managed to get out of there and make something of myself to honour my father.'

'How did you go from there to where you are now?'

'Guts and determination,' Draco said. 'And some luck. I got work down at the boat yard and the owner of one of the yacht-tour fleets took me on. I went to night school to finish my education and juggled a couple of other jobs to get some money behind me. I bought my way into the business and then bought it outright from Josef when he retired. I built it up and expanded it after that. I figured Yanni needs someone like Josef was to me. Tough but fair.'

Allegra gave him a lopsided smile and her hands slid up to link around his neck, bringing her body even closer to his until he could feel the cool, wet press of her breasts and the hot swell of her mound. 'I didn't realise you were such a nice guy underneath all that arrogance.'

Draco smiled and settled his hands on the sweet curve of her bottom, his gaze briefly dipping to the shadow of her cleavage. 'If you knew what I was thinking right now, there's no way you would ever call me nice.'

Her eyes shone with the same excitement he could feel throbbing through his body. Her fingers laced through his hair, her lips parting, and the tip of her tongue snaking out to leave a glistening sheen of moisture over them. 'Are you going to kiss me for the sake of any staff who might be watching?' Allegra's voice was husky, her warm breath wafting across the surface of his lips. She smelt of sun and salt and sunscreen, and something else that made his self-control throw its hands up in defeat.

Draco gave a mock 'let's get it over with' sigh. 'All right—if you insist.' He brought his mouth to hers in a kiss that spoke of the longing in his body. He explored the interior of her mouth, his blood rushing like a torrent at her response. Her tongue tangled with his, playing cat-and-mouse and hide-and-seek and I-want-you-right-now. He brought her as hard up against him as he could, his hands cupping her bottom until he could feel the intimate seam of her body. Never had he wanted someone so desperately. It was like a fire in his system, roaring through the network of his veins, making him zing from head to foot with sexual energy and demonic drive.

Her soft little whimpers drove him wild, so too the way her hands played with his hair, pulling and tugging until every hair root on his scalp tingled. Her mouth was wet and salty and he fed off it like an addict on a drug he couldn't resist.

He brought his hands up to stroke her breasts through the wet fabric of her bathers but that wasn't good enough for him. He wanted to feel those gorgeous globes of sexy female flesh, skin on skin.

He *needed* to.

He *ached* to.

Draco turned them around so his back was to the villa, somewhat shielding her from view. He slipped the straps off her shoulders as if he were unwrapping a gift. Allegra's breasts were neither small nor large but somewhere perfectly in between—creamy white with dark pink nipples erect as he was. He palmed them first, allowing her to get used to the slight roughness of his hands from working in his boat yard. She made a mewling sound when his thumbs rolled over her nipples, her mouth giving his sexy little nips and nudges that made his spine shiver as if sand were trickling down between his vertebrae. She caught his lower lip between her teeth in a little kittenish bite that made him wonder if he was going to jump the start like a teenager on his first sexual encounter.

He pushed her breasts upwards to meet his descending mouth, stroking his tongue around and over her nipple on her right breast, and then the left one, leaving them wet and peaking. Draco moved his mouth to explore the curve of her breast—the top side, the underside and the delectable space between. Allegra tilted her head back, her long hair trailing like black seaweed in the water behind her. She offered her breasts to him like a worshipper offers something to a god. He made the most of it. Beyond caring if his staff was watching from the villa. He subjected each of her breasts to an intimate exploration with his lips and tongue and with gentle nibbles of his teeth, evoking a panting response from her that thrilled every drop of testosterone in his body.

He was so hard, it was painful. But, as if she knew the agony he was going through, one of her hands slipped down between their jammed-together bodies and freed him from his undershorts. Her fingers were cool and firm around his length, stroking and squeezing him under the cover of the water. Not such a great cover, given the water was as clear as bottled water, but he was well beyond worrying about that.

He pulled her bathers down past her hips, slipping his hand down to cup her mound, letting her body feel the subtle pressure of his touch. She moved urgently against his hand, gasping against Draco's mouth. 'Please...' The cry sounded as desperate as he felt. 'Please. Please. Please...'

He traced his finger over her, teasing her with his strokes, finally slipping a finger into her hot, moist body, stroking the swollen heart of her until she came with a rush against his hand. He felt every contraction and ripple of her inner muscles, the sexy panting of Allegra's breathing delighting him more than he could have imagined. She was so responsive to him. What full-blooded man wouldn't be pleased about that? Nothing satisfied him more than giving a partner pleasure, but somehow Allegra's pleasure meant something to him.

Something he couldn't quite explain.

Draco withdrew his finger and held her while she recovered. Her cheeks were lightly flushed and it travelled all the way down to her décolletage in a rosy tide. She sent her tongue out over her lips again, her gaze a little dazed. 'That was…'

'Good?'

She pulled at her lip with her teeth, her gaze slipping out of reach of his. 'Unexpected.'

'In what way?'

'I don't normally… I mean I've never done that with a partner…'

He inched up her chin so her gaze reconnected with his. Allegra's blue eyes swam with uncertainty…or was it shyness, or a combination of both? 'The first time you've had sex in the water?' he asked.

She took a tiny barely audible swallow. 'The first time I've come with a partner present.'

Draco frowned. 'Really?'

She gave a self-deprecating grimace, her half-mast lashes screening her eyes. 'Yes, well, I can do it by myself, but as soon as a guy is there, pressuring me to get on with it, I just…freeze.'

To say he was stunned was an understatement. How had she put up with such an imbalance in her love life for so long? Or was it because of her first sexual encounter? The shame from being humiliated by some jerk who probably hadn't known how to make love to her anyway? Draco's guts roiled with anger at how she had been treated. She was responsive to him. Incredibly responsive, which meant she trusted him. Trust was an enormous part of sex, particularly for women, whose bodies could be so easily exploited by too rough a handling. He was all for a bit of athletic sex, but there was no way he would ever hurt or humiliate a partner during it, nor would he settle for anything less than mutual pleasure.

But, right now, his pleasure could wait.

He slid his hand along the side of her face, an unexpected wave of protectiveness sweeping through him. 'Listen to me, Allegra. You can trust me to always put your pleasure first. You can take as long as you need. Women are wired differently from men. A good lover will understand that and allow his partner plenty of time.'

Her smile was shaky around the edges and her cheeks still tinged with flags of pink. 'So much for the hands-off arrangement. We're not even married yet and look how I'm behaving.'

He brushed her wet hair back from her face, looking into her dark blue eyes almost the same colour as the ocean. 'This chemistry between us isn't something to be ashamed of, *glykia mou*. It's to be celebrated. It bodes well for a healthy marriage between us.'

She moistened her lips and her gaze flicked briefly to his groin. 'But what about you? Aren't you going to…?'

Draco shook his head. 'Not that I don't want to, but

the next time we make love it's going to be to consummate our marriage. And preferably we'll be alone on my yacht without half my staff watching from the wings.'

She sank her teeth into her lower lip. 'That hardly seems fair to you... I mean, things were getting pretty heavy there, just then.'

He took her hands in both of his and held them against his chest in case Allegra went in search of him. He could only take so much, especially from those silky little hands that seemed instinctively to know how to handle him. 'It's a man's responsibility to control his desires, at all times and in all circumstances. I want you. Make no mistake about it. I can't think of a time I wanted someone more. But tomorrow will be all the better if we wait.'

Her mouth formed a twist of a smile. 'Careful, Draco, you're starting to sound like our marriage is going to be a normal one.'

He held her gaze for a beat. 'In bed, it will be.'

Allegra walked back along the sand to the pathway leading to the villa with Draco's hand holding hers. Her body was still vibrating with aftershocks from the pleasure he had evoked. It made her aware of every inch of her flesh, as if all the nerves had been given steroids and were twice their size and three times as active.

How had it happened?

Why had she allowed Draco to touch her like that? He hadn't followed through to claim his own pleasure, so didn't that make her seem a little pathetic? Like that teenage girl she used to be? Her wanton response to him demonstrated her vulnerability. She was a fool to give him more ammunition. She was supposed to be resisting him. Rejecting his advances, not encouraging such intimate contact. Not only encouraging it but responding to it like she had never responded to anyone before. Her breasts felt fuller, more sensitive, her inner core tingling with the memory of his inserted finger. If she was going to shatter into a thousand pieces with the glide of his finger then what was going to happen when he made love to her fully?

What do you mean 'when'?

Allegra ignored her conscience. Her conscience could take a running jump off the nearest cliff and drown in the Aegean Sea. Her conscience didn't realise what it was like to be thirty-one years old and so feverishly in lust with a man she couldn't sleep at night without her body writhing in frustration.

What was wrong with having a 'married' affair with Draco? It was one of the perks of the deal. The *only* perk as far as she could see. Well, there might be a few more, but she didn't want to think about them just now. Perhaps sex could be fine as long as she kept her emotions out of it, which shouldn't be too much of a problem, because her emotions had never been involved before.

No. She was ready for this. More than ready. Her body deserved some excitement after the miserable drought it had been subjected to. It would make the prospect of getting married more palatable, knowing that as soon as they were alone they would be making love… No. *Having sex.*

Better get the terminology right from the outset. She wasn't a romantic. That was Emily's territory.

Emily was the one who dreamed of being swept off her feet and carried off into the golden sunset by a handsome prince. A fantasy that had so far done Emily zero favours.

Allegra was far too practical for all that nonsense, which was part of the reason why she had got to this age without falling in love. She had ruled it out. Put a line through the notion. She had always kept herself from getting too attached to the men she occasionally dated. She was a career woman through and through, but career women needed sex too, didn't they? They couldn't be expected to do nothing but work. It wasn't healthy. Balance was what she needed. A balance of work and pleasure, and how better to get it than to be married to heart-stalling, sexy-as-sin Draco Papandreou who would allow her to come and go for work and play?

Thing was... Allegra had a feeling she might want to play a lot more than work. And to come more than go—no pun intended. The thought of flying back to London, to dismal weather, traffic-clogged streets and difficult clients when she could have all this sunshine, white sand and water as blue as lapis lazuli didn't hold any of the appeal it used to, when she'd been desperate to get away from Greece after visiting her father and get back to her normal routine.

All the paperwork, the phone calls, the emails, the lengthy court appearances and the constant tension from dealing with difficult partners of distraught, angry or bitter clients.... Here all she had to listen to was the sound of seabirds, the ocean lapping the shore and the whisper of the wind in the pines.

When they got to the top of the path, Allegra pushed

back some wisps of salt-encrusted hair out of her eyes. 'I so need a shower.'

Draco's smile had a hint of devilment. 'I'd join you but that would be asking way too much of my self-control.'

A tiny doubt peeped out from behind the curtain in her mind... What if his self-control was only that strong because she hadn't done it for him? Down in the water, she'd been sure he would lose control and be swept away on a tide of passion just as she'd been.

But he hadn't.

He had stepped away from her as if they had innocently embraced and not been in the throes of making... Strike that. *Having sex*. Did it mean she would always be the one in the relationship with less power? The one who needed most, lost most. She saw it every day at work. Women who cared too much, loved or desired too much, lost out in the end.

Was she going to end up one of those women she privately pitied?

Draco's gaze went to the frown pulling at her brow before she could iron it out. He placed his hands on her shoulders and gave them a gentle squeeze. 'I know what you're thinking.'

Allegra screened her features. 'I'm hot and sticky and have sand in places I didn't even know I had places.'

He gave a soft laugh and stroked the back of his bent knuckles down her right cheek. 'Don't doubt yourself so much, *agape mou*. You have no reason to feel insecure with me.'

Like that's going to reassure me.

Allegra had never felt more insecure, more worried she was stepping over a vertiginous cliff into the unknown…or maybe not so much the unknown as the dreaded. Within less than twenty-four hours, she would be married to Draco Papandreou. She would wear his ring and share his bed and all his gloriously luxurious villas. But there was one truth she couldn't escape from no matter how much she tried to ignore it.

She would never have his heart.

CHAPTER FIVE

ALLEGRA PREPARED FOR her wedding day like any other
bride, the only difference being that a knot of panic
had settled in her stomach and, as each second climbed
towards the time of the ceremony, the knot tightened,
drawing all her intestines into a clotted ball.

Elena had flown in from from Santorini by helicopter first thing with Allegra's father and baby Nico,
and was on hand to help her get dressed. Iona, Draco's
housekeeper, was in her element, fussing over Allegra
as if she were her own daughter. In spite of Allegra's
reservations and nerves, she couldn't help feeling re-
assured by their cheery presence. They believed this
was a romantic wedding day for the bride and groom
and she didn't want to be the one to prick their bubble
with the hatpin of honesty.

Along with Elena and Iona were a hairdresser and a
make-up artist flown in specially, apparently at Draco's
command. Allegra knew he was keen to keep up appearances, but it still touched her that he had gone to
the trouble of organising their attendance. It might not
be her choice to be married under such circumstances,
but there was no way she was going to look like a fright
show on her wedding day.

But that wasn't the only surprise.

The sound of the helicopter blades overhead announced yet another wedding guest arrival.

Not long after, Allegra was about to slip on her dress when there was a knock at the suite's door.

'That will be your bridesmaid,' Elena said, beaming.

'But I'm not having a—'

'Surprise!' The door burst open and in came Emily, carrying a garment bag folded over one arm. 'One bridesmaid arriving for active duty.'

Allegra blinked back a sudden rush of tears. 'Em, what are you doing here? I—'

'Don't cry! Your make-up will run,' the make-up girl said, dashing back over with a cotton pad, eye shadow and eyeliner brushes like an artist touching up her precious canvas.

Emily handed her garment bag to Iona, who bustled off to press the dress ready for her to put on. 'Draco called me at work a couple of days ago and asked me to come. He told me not to tell you as he wanted it to be a surprise.'

It was more than a surprise. Allegra couldn't understand why he'd gone to so much trouble, contacting her friend and workmate without telling her. But then he didn't know Emily knew their marriage was one of convenience. Had her friend blown it? Had Emily let slip she'd been let in on the secret against his express wishes?

Once the make-up artist had tidied up her face, Allegra clasped Emily by the hands. 'I'm *so* glad you're here.'

Emily grinned like a child let loose in a sweet shop with a platinum credit card. 'You should've warned me about Draco's wealth. I didn't realise you could have silver service on a helicopter. And he flew me first class from London to Athens last night and put me up in the most amazing hotel. I lost count of how many champagnes I was served on that flight. I felt like a movie star. That man has serious class.'

'Em...?' Allegra gave her a 'did you or didn't you?' look.

Emily's smile never faltered and she gave a covert wink. 'You should see the dress I've got. Actually, I've got three, so you could choose the colour you like best.' She went over to Iona who had hung the three dresses on silk-padded clothes hangers. 'Shell-pink, baby-blue or café latte?'

'The shell-pink,' Allegra said, turning to Elena, who was hovering nearby. 'What do you think, Elena? It would go best, don't you think?'

Elena nodded. 'Absolutely. It's perfect with the oyster silk white of your dress. Speaking of your dress— we'd better get you into it. We've only got a few minutes until the ceremony starts.'

Allegra felt like a royal princess when the girls and Iona helped her into her dress and veil. She had never had so much attention showered on her and she was surprised to find she was enjoying it. Having Emily there meant so much to her. Why had Draco gone to so much trouble? It made her feel that he cared for her. *Really* cared for her. Or did he just *really* care what people made of their somewhat hasty wedding?

Elena and Iona went ahead to take their positions on the velvet-covered and ribbon-festooned seats set either side of the strip of red carpet laid down in the formal garden.

Emily stayed to adjust Allegra's veil before they made their way out. 'You look amazing, sweetie. You could model for one of those bridal magazines.'

Allegra grasped her friend's hands again. 'You didn't let on that you know, did you?'

'No, but even if I took my contacts out I could see you're halfway to being in love with him, if you're not fully there already,' Emily said. 'Truly, he's something else to look at, isn't he? And that smile. Gosh, I'm halfway in love with him myself.' She winked. 'Only kidding.'

Allegra drew in a steadying breath and smoothed her palms over the satin of her figure-hugging gown. 'Are you sure I look okay? I don't look fat, do I? I bought this in my lunch hour and now I'm wondering if I should've—'

'You look a-maz-ing,' Emily said. 'That dress is perfect for you. It highlights everything I hate about you: your breasts, your hips, your bum—which is so tiny I wouldn't even classify it as a bum. Seriously, hon, you're going to pop Draco's eyeballs.'

Allegra adjusted the cleavage of her dress and grimaced. 'As long as I don't pop out of this dress.'

She stood at the top of the strip of red carpet with her father a short time later, trying to settle the hive of nerves in her stomach. While it was nice to have Emily here, and for Elena and Iona to be so kind and helpful, it didn't take away from the fact this wedding was not her choice. Not even marriage to Draco, the most attractive and sexy man she knew.

Especially because it was Draco.

He had too much power over her. Too much sensual power, which he had already demonstrated with stunning expertise. Seeing him in that sharply tailored suit and neatly aligned bow tie was enough to get her pulses racing. His dark-as-night gaze met hers and the edges of his mouth came up in a smile that spoke of triumph, rather than the emotion she hadn't realised till now she wanted to see.

But she didn't even like Draco. Of course she didn't… And marrying a guy who only wanted you to secure a much-prized business deal was a little lowering, to say the least.

'Ready to go?' her father asked.

'I could have done this on my own, you know,' Allegra said in a low tone so no one nearby could overhear. 'I don't believe in fathers giving away their daughters. It's positively feudal.'

Her father gave her arm a squeeze that was almost painful. 'Don't spoil it for me, Allegra. I've waited years for this day. I wasn't sure it was ever going to happen.'

She drew in a tight breath, stung by the partially veiled criticism in his voice. 'I'm only doing this for Elena and Nico. You do know that, don't you?'

'You should be grateful he was the one who won you,' her father said with a clipped edge to his voice. 'There were one or two other less savoury types who were interested but he outbid them with his offer of marriage. Hugely.'

A cold hand pressed on Allegra's spine. What did her father mean, Draco was the one who'd won her? *'What?'*

'Now is not the time to talk about it,' her father said. 'Ask him later.'

And then he led her inexorably towards Draco.

* * *

Draco had been prepared for Allegra looking beautiful. He had always known she would make a spectacularly gorgeous bride. And she didn't disappoint. She was a vision in an oyster silk slip of a dress that clung to all her assets like an elegant evening glove. Her simple white veil hung over her face and down her back in a floating cloud. Her hair was swept up in a coronet do that gave her the look of a princess that was nothing less than breath-snatching. He covered his reaction to seeing her with a smile that could have been termed gloating, but there was no way he was going to let her see he considered this ceremony as anything but a means to an end.

The deal was balanced firmly in his favour and he was fine with that. It was the way he did business and this was, after all, about business. He stood to gain the most out of getting her hand in marriage. Allegra didn't need his wealth or status because she had her own. He had played on her need to please her father who, in his opinion, didn't deserve it. Cosimo Kallas was a narcissist who was only happy when the attention was squarely on him. His wife Elena had been chosen because she was young and beautiful and attracted to him.

Just like you chose Allegra.

Draco shook off the jarring thought like he was shaking something off the back of his suit jacket. His marriage to Allegra was much more than that. He hadn't picked her from a line-up. He'd known her since she was a girl of sixteen. He admired her. He respected her. He *wanted* her.

And her father's business—and, more importantly,

her welfare—was a pressing issue that needed a solution, so here Draco was offering it. If he hadn't offered for her, another man would have done so with far more nefarious purposes. The business world was cutthroat and conscienceless. He knew enough about some of the rich and powerful creditors to know they wouldn't have thought twice about using her father's debts to force Allegra into their bed. If she thought being married to him was bad, he didn't like to guess what she would think about some of the alternatives.

This was his way of keeping them out of the equation.

It wasn't as if they would be living in each other's pockets. Draco liked that Allegra was independent, that she had her own career and commitments, because it would leave him free to see to his. He was prepared to be faithful because he didn't see any reason not to be during a short-term marriage. His father had instilled in him the trust needed to have a satisfying relationship. He had always admired his father for the commitment he had made to his mother that had continued long after her death.

And Draco knew the chemistry between Allegra and him was the best he'd ever experienced. He could only expect it to improve the more they explored each other. He couldn't wait for all this fuss to be over so he could get her alone and turn their marriage into a real one in every sense of the word. Allegra wanted him. Hadn't he proved that down at the beach? Their relationship would be one based on mutual lust.

The string quartet began playing 'The Bridal March'. Emily came up the red carpet first, but Draco couldn't take his eyes off Allegra, waiting at the end of the archway with her father, to begin the walk towards him. Had he ever seen a more stunningly beautiful woman? She looked like a bride from an old black-and-white movie. Her skin was luminous, her make-up emphasising the intense blue of her eyes, the aristocratic height and slope of her cheekbones and the pink perfection of her kissable mouth with that gorgeous beauty spot just above it. The silk dress moved with her body, making his hands itch and twitch to unpeel her from it and explore those delectable curves.

He drew in a breath but was more than a little shocked to find it caught on something in his throat. He'd always made a point not to be moved by weddings. They reminded him too much of his ex. Of all the hopes he had invested in that doomed relationship. Of his own calf-love foolishness. He'd been to a few over the years—friends' and colleagues' and business associates'—and he had never had his breath lock in his throat. It felt almost as if his whole life had somehow been slowly but surely heading towards this moment. That every road so far had led to this time, this place, this person walking towards him.

Allegra came to stand beside him and through the gossamer of her veil met his gaze. She gave him a trembling smile that plucked on a tight string deep in his chest. 'Hi…'

Draco had to clear his throat to speak. The uncertainty in her gaze, the slight wobble in her voice, made him wonder if she was experiencing the same unexpected groundswell of emotion. 'You look beautiful.'

The priest stepped forward with a broad smile. 'Dearly beloved, we are gathered here…'

Finally it was time to kiss his bride. Draco drew

Allegra closer and pressed his mouth to hers in a kiss that felt unlike any other kiss he had ever experienced. It wasn't because of the witnesses gathered or the solemnity of the occasion. It was a kiss that had a sacred element to it. A promise had been made and this kiss sealed it. Her lips clung to his, her hands resting against his chest, her right one over the thud of his heart.

Allegra smelt of summer flowers and her lips tasted of strawberries. He held her against him, praying his erection would cool it in time to turn to walk back through the gathered guests. He'd always considered it tacky when a wedding kiss went on too long. But now he wished he could freeze time. Stay right there and sup at her mouth until this burning ache in his flesh subsided—if it ever would.

He eased back to cradle her face in his hands. Her blue eyes shimmered as if she wasn't far off crying. '*Yia sou*, Kyria Papandreou,' he said.

She blinked a couple of times, as if to stop from tearing up any further. 'Thanks for bringing Emily here. It means such a lot to me. And for all the other… stuff.'

Was that why she was feeling emotional? The little jab of disappointment hit him under the ribs. Of course it wasn't about him. It was about her friend. He'd wanted to bring her friend here because Allegra no longer had a mother to support her and, besides, what bride didn't need a bridesmaid? He had asked his best friend to be his best man so it only seemed fair for Allegra to have someone she trusted and valued by her side. 'My pleasure,' he said. 'I thought she might hit it off with one of my friends from university, my best man—Loukas Kyprianos. He has a thing for English girls.'

'Even so, it was nice of you to go to all that trouble.'

He looped her arm through his and turned with her so they were facing the guests. 'Shall we let everyone get on with the party?'

It was a great party, Allegra had to admit, even though she spent most of it wondering about Draco's true motives in marrying her. She hadn't been able to get him alone to ask him to clarify what her father had told her. But it resonated with the sort of man he was. He might be ruthless when it suited him, but she knew him well enough to know he wouldn't stand for any sort of criminal behaviour. Who were the faceless men who might have blackmailed her into their bed if he hadn't intervened? The thought was too distressing to hold in her mind—like finding a cockroach in her glass of milk. It was revolting to picture herself with another of her father's business associates. Surely her father wouldn't have expected her to do it if Draco hadn't put his hand up and proposed marriage?

Why *had* he put his hand up? Could there be any other reason?

No. Why else had he said the marriage was temporary? Because he wanted to have her, but he needed an escape route, that was why. He'd been prepared to do the honourable thing by her, but promising to love, protect and provide for her for the rest of her life was a step too far.

Allegra looked around the party of revelling guests, her mind still in a whirling turmoil. It didn't take much for a gathering of Greeks to have fun when there was family, food and alcohol involved. Not that Draco had any family there. It struck her how alone in the world he was. He had friends and associates but no blood relatives. Weddings were times when families came together and celebrated with the couple.

She suddenly missed her mother with a pang that sat under her ribcage like a stitch pulled too tight. Not that her mother had really been there for her in the truest sense, but she ached for the mother she might have been if things had been different. But, strangely, she had a sense her mother would have approved of Draco. He was strong and disciplined, unlike her father, who had a tendency to live for himself rather than others. Draco didn't talk himself up, either. He did things in the background that one would ever hear of if he had any say in it. Would he have told her about the other men? He hadn't even told her about his commitment to Iona. His housekeeper had revealed it, not him. Iona had even told Allegra while she was helping her get dressed for the ceremony that Draco had set up a superannuation account for her with generous donations that set her up for a luxurious retirement.

Allegra stood with her arm looped through Draco's as various guests came over to chat. As if Iona could sense Allegra had been thinking about her, she came bustling over, cheeks pink from drinking champagne, and her eyes bright with happiness for her employer and his new bride. She grasped each of their hands as though she was making a pledge, her eyes going misty as they had during the service. 'Be happy. Be forgiving. Be friends.'

Draco leaned down to kiss his housekeeper on both cheeks. 'We will. I promise.'

Allegra waited until Iona had wandered off to talk to some other guests before she looked up at Draco. 'She's so lucky to have you. She told me she would've still been on the streets begging if it hadn't been for you.'

His arm went from around her waist to hold her hand, his thumb stroking the back of it in gentle movements. 'What she needed when her husband ditched her for someone younger was a lawyer like you. She had no one to stand up for her. She reminds me of my mother. She's a good woman, loyal and hard working.' He waited a beat. 'You rarely speak of your mother. Were you not close?'

Allegra grimaced. 'My mother never got over my brother's death. Losing him destroyed her. She gave up on life after that. My father would never admit it was suicide. He maintains the accidental overdose verdict the doctor put on the death certificate but I know she had given up. She simply couldn't go on.'

His hand cupped hers as if he was holding something fragile and precious. 'That must have been extremely tough on you, losing her under such awful circumstances. It's not as if your father is the nurturing type.'

'Yes, well, he wanted a son and heir, and when that son got sick he wanted another one to fix him, or—in a worst-case scenario—take his place,' she said. 'I turned up instead—female and an abject failure because I didn't have the right genetic make-up to save Dion or replace him.'

Draco's forehead creased into furrowed lines. 'But surely your father never said—?'

'He didn't have to,' Allegra said. 'I got the message loud and clear. Even my mother on a bad day would make it pretty obvious what a disappointment I was. That's why I was sent to boarding school in England so young. She didn't like being reminded of her failure to produce a healthy son and heir. I ruined her chances of falling pregnant again. She had to have a hysterectomy after my birth because I ruptured her uterus. I only found all this out when I was older but it explained a lot about my childhood. She wasn't the cuddling type, although there were plenty of photos with her cuddling my brother. She lost interest once he died and the only cuddles I got were from my nannies.'

Had she told him too much? Overloaded him with her Dickensian childhood drama? She rarely spoke of her childhood to anyone. Even Emily had only heard the cut-down version. She didn't like painting herself as a victim, but growing up without the security and comfort of parental love was something she carried like a scar. Mostly she could ignore it, but when she saw people interact with their parents, and in partic-ular their mothers, the wound opened all over again. But she and Draco were alike in that they had both lost their mothers while young. If anyone could understand, it would be him.

Draco let out a long sigh and stroked the back of her hands with his thumbs, holding her gaze in a con-cerned manner. 'I've always been amazed at how well you turned out, given the tragic circumstances you were born into. But I had no idea you felt so unloved.'

And now I've signed up for a loveless marriage. Lucky me.

'To be fair, I think my father loves me in his way. Or at least, he does now that I've saved his precious business.' She met his gaze with a 'no secrets now' directness. 'He told me there were other men who had their eye on me. Why didn't you tell me that yourself?'

Draco's frown lowered as if he was thinking deeply and was troubled by those thoughts. 'I didn't want you to worry about it. I'd solved the issue as far as I was concerned.'

'It was an honourable thing to do...'

He shrugged as if they were talking about whose turn it was to take out the trash. 'I figured, better the devil you know.'

Allegra studied his unreadable expression for a beat. 'I'm starting to wonder if I know you at all. You're full of little surprises.'

'Don't read too much into my actions,' he said, expression still inscrutable. 'Your father isn't my favourite person in the world. I've always made excuses for him because the loss of a child is such a big thing. It's not the sort of grief you can easily move on from on. Although, he seems to have done so now.'

'Yes, his little affairs were his way of handling things,' Allegra said. 'My mother didn't seem to care what he did—she accepted it as normal. Even as young as I was, that used to really bug me. I often wondered if he'd stayed faithful to her would it have helped her heal a little better?'

'Maybe, maybe not.' He gave her hands a squeeze. 'Such sad talk for a wedding day, *ne*?'

Allegra gave a rueful smile. 'It's not like it's a normal wedding day, though, is it? I felt a little guilty acting in front of Iona. I hope she doesn't end up hating me for not being madly in love with you like every other woman on the planet.'

Draco's thumbs stilled on her hands as if they'd

been set on pause. His eyes held hers in a searching
lock that made her feel that he was seeing more than
she wanted him to see. Allegra's heart stammered. Had
she given herself away? Shown how vulnerable she was
to him? Not just in terms of physical attraction, but in
terms of feelings she didn't want to feel but couldn't
seem to control.

She couldn't fall in love with him. Couldn't.
Couldn't. Couldn't. It would be unrequited if she did.
He had locked his heart away and she had better not
forget it. His reasons for marrying her were not just
physical, but it didn't mean he loved her. He'd wanted
to protect her. Any decent man would have done the
same. The best she could hope for was the desire he
had for her would last. But it was a fragile hope. A
hope on a ventilator and a timer.

But then he slipped her arm back through his and
smiled. 'Don't you have a bouquet to toss?'

CHAPTER SIX

THE SUN WAS setting by the time Draco steered his luxury boat away from the jetty on his island. Allegra stood beside him, a light wrap around her shoulders, and waved back to the guests standing on the jetty and the beach, including Emily, who was in proud possession of the bouquet.

Emily was standing a short distance from Draco's best man, Loukas Kyprianos, and Allegra could see the goggle-eyed looks Em was casting his way, as if she couldn't believe what she was seeing. On the handsome scale, Loukas was like Draco—*off* the scale. But, while Draco had a tendency to smile rather than frown, Loukas had a more brooding demeanour, hinting at a man who preferred his own company and kept his own counsel. Emily wasn't the sort of girl to get her head turned by a good-looking man, but she was a sucker for a man with secrets, given she had one or two of her own.

Draco manoeuvred the boat into the direction of the setting sun, which was now a fireball of red suspended on the smoky-blue plane of the horizon. A swathe of stratocumulus clouds reflected the burnished gold of the sun below and the grey and indigo bruise-like streaks of colour above.

A light breeze moved over the surface of the water, sped up by the passage of the boat. It played with Allegra's hair, which was already in two minds whether to stay up in her coronet do or give up and swing about her back and shoulders. She pushed the straying strands away from her face and resisted the temptation to slip her hand into Draco's outstretched one as he stood at the wheel.

He smiled down at her. 'All right? Not seasick yet?'

She shook her head. 'No. I'm pretty good on boats normally. Although, I guess I shouldn't speak too soon.'

'You'll be fine. The weather forecast is good.' He glanced back at the jetty. 'How's Emily getting on with Loukas?'

Allegra cocked her head. 'Are you trying to set them up or something?'

He gave a shrug. 'If it happens, it happens.'

'He doesn't look the type who needs a hand in that department,' she said. 'Who is he? He's seems familiar, but I'm sure I haven't met him before today.'

'He keeps a low profile—or tries to,' Draco said. 'We met at university. I was doing a business degree and he was doing computer engineering and software development. He's designed some of the most sophisticated security systems in the world. So secure, most government agencies such as MI5 and the FBI use his software.'

Good luck, Em.

'So is he on the lookout for a wife?' Allegra asked.

He gave her one of his crooked smiles. 'Not Loukas. His parents divorced when he was a young child and apparently it was one of those acrimonious, "use the kid as a weapon" ones. He doesn't talk about it and I know better than to ask. Both his parents have re-married and subsequently divorced, his father several times over. One thing I do know, he will never get married himself. It was hard enough getting him to agree to come to our wedding. You'd think I'd asked him to have a lobotomy.'

'Did you tell him it was a marriage of—?'

'No.' The tone of his voice underlined the word. 'We're close but not that close. No one is that close to Loukas. No one.'

Allegra chewed at her lip, watching the sun swal-lowed by the blue lip of the horizon. Why hadn't he told his best friend? Was it really because Loukas was a bit of a closed book himself? Why not tell his friend the truth? Or had he done it to protect her from anyone pitying her? 'I told Emily.'

'I know.'

She glanced at him in surprise. 'You do?'

Draco's expression was amused rather than an-noyed. 'I figured you would. She's a nice girl. Seems to have her head screwed on.'

'Did you let on you knew she knew?'

'No.'

'I'm sorry, but I couldn't lie to her,' Allegra said. 'Everyone else, yes, but not Em. She would've figured it out anyway. She knows I'm not the sort of person to fall in love on a whim. But don't worry, she won't tell a soul. She's fiercely loyal and completely and ut-terly trustworthy.'

'Good to know.'

There was a little silence broken only by the slap of the water hitting the sides and hull of the yacht.

'Do you want to take the wheel for a while?' Draco asked.

'I don't know… I might run into another boat or something.'

'There's no one else out here. Come on. Stand in front of me and I'll steer with you.'

Allegra moved to stand in front of the wheel and he came in behind her, his arms either side of her body, his hands resting on top of hers where she was gripping the steering wheel. Who knew steering a yacht could be such a turn-on? The warm, hard presence of his body behind her made every nerve in her core jump up ready for duty. His broad hands almost completely covered hers, his fingers long, strong and so very capable. Deliciously, dangerously capable.

She could feel him against her bottom cheeks, the rise of his flesh an erotic reminder of what was to come. She shivered when he moved closer, his stubbly jaw grazing her cheek when he leaned down to help her navigate a larger than normal wave. The rocking motion of the yacht pushed her further back against him, sending her senses into overdrive. 'I want you,' he said.

'I would never have guessed.'

He gave a soft laugh. 'Minx.' He tongued the cartilage of her ear, the sensations rippling through her like waves. 'But then, I've wanted you since that night in London.'

Allegra shuddered when his teeth tugged on her earlobe. 'Funny, but I didn't pick up that vibe.'

He moved his mouth to the sensitive spot on her neck just below her ear. 'What vibe are you picking up now?'

'I'm thinking the honeymoon is about to start.'

He turned her so she was facing him, his eyes gleaming like high-gloss black paint. 'I need to drop anchor.'

Allegra linked her arms around his neck and gave him a sultry smile. 'I can think of something more fun we can do instead.'

He smiled and pressed a brief, hard kiss to her mouth. 'Go below and I'll be with you once I've got things up here under control…'

Allegra descended to the main cabin where a bar, sofas and large-screen television were located. There was a kitchen off that with a separate dining area, which wouldn't have looked out of place in a top-end-of-town restaurant. The master bedroom—one of four bedrooms on board—was big enough to sleep a football team as well as their support staff and sponsors. Maybe even some fans.

She was no stranger to luxury accommodation, but Draco's yacht was beyond anything she had seen before. Butter-soft leather sofas and ottomans, Swarovski light fittings and lamps and knee-deep, cream-coloured carpet. Polished timber woodwork and Italian marble in the wet areas such as the bathrooms. There was even a hot tub on the upper deck and a spa bath in the main bathroom. A bottle of champagne was in a silver ice-bucket with two glasses beside it, left by Draco's staff, along with their luggage, which had been unpacked and stored in the hand-crafted built-in wardrobes in the master suite. There was a supply of gourmet food in the fridge and pantry, both cooked and fresh ingredients, as well as a wine fridge with enough wine and champagne to host a cocktail party for a hundred guests.

Allegra couldn't look at the king-sized bed without a shudder of excitement. The same shudder of excitement she'd felt when Draco had said he'd wanted her when he'd run into her in London six months ago. She'd thought he'd been mocking her for sitting there so long, trying to make her glass of wine last the hour, trying not to check her watch and chew her lip and nails until they bled. But behind that glinting black gaze he had been sizing her up for himself. What had stirred his interest? Was it that he'd seen her as a convenient bride, a single woman on the wrong side of thirty who he'd assumed would stumble over herself with gratefulness when he offered for her?

But his motives had been far more honourable than that. Why had he done that? He was effectively saving her father's business and her, too.

Allegra sat down on the cloud-soft mattress and sighed. Why was she fussing over the fact he wasn't in love with her? People had sex without being in love all the time. It wasn't a prerequisite these days, even for marriage. Lots of people enjoyed a workable marriage with companionship and mutual respect holding them together. Romantic love didn't always last, anyway. The limerence period in a new relationship at best lasted two years. After that the relationship settled into the bonding phase…if it was going to, that was. Draco surely wouldn't let theirs go on for half so long?

It wasn't as if she was in love with Draco. But what if she succumbed to that lethal charm? She had already told him more than she'd told anyone about herself. It was as if her carapace had melted away. She actually liked him. As in *really* liked him. Liked his company, his smile, his dancing eyes, his body.

Dear God, his body.

The sound of his footsteps coming down to join her was enough to set her pulses off like thoroughbreds at the starting gate. Why hadn't she thought to buy some sexy lingerie? She'd been so determined to resist him but how long had that lasted? One kiss and she'd all but begged him to take her. One kiss! What if she was hopeless in bed? What if she couldn't orgasm with him? What if she took ages and ages, and he got fed up, and she had to pretend. and then she would be embarrassed and feel under even more pressure next time and—

The door of the bedroom opened and Allegra jumped off the bed as though she'd been shot out of a cannon. 'Erm… I think I'll have a drink. Would you like champagne? I feel like some, don't you? This is a good one. Wow… I've been to the vineyard. It was amazing, so picturesque.' She fumbled with the foil around the top of the bottle, sudden nerves and shyness assailing her.

Draco came over, took the bottle from her and placed it back in the ice-bucket. He put his hands on her waist, his expression as tender as she had ever seen it. 'You're nervous.' He said it as a statement, not as a question.

Allegra pulled at one side of her lower lip with her teeth, her cheeks feeling as if someone had lit a fire under them. 'It was probably a fluke down at the beach. I might not be able to do it again.'

He lifted her chin with the tip of his finger, holding her gaze with his. 'No one's keeping time here, *agape mou*. You can take all the time you need. We don't have to even do this tonight if you don't feel up to it. It's been a long day.'

'Don't you want to…?'

Draco's thumb brushed back and forth over her cheek like a metronome. 'Of course I do, but not if you don't feel in the mood.'

I've been in the mood for you since I was sixteen.

Allegra lowered her gaze to his mouth. 'I don't have any nice lingerie…'

He smiled. 'Do you really think I'd even notice? What I want to see is you. All of you.'

She shivered at the smouldering look in his eyes. The look that said 'I want you'. The look that spoke to her female flesh like the sun does to an orchid. Ripening it, opening it. Making it bloom and swell and release its scent. She placed her arms around his neck, moving closer so her body touched his from hips to chest. 'Make love to me…please?'

His mouth came down to cover hers in a kiss that spoke of deep, primal male longings only just held in check. Draco's lips moved against hers in a soft exploration, his tongue parting her lips with a gentle glide that made her skin prickle in delight. He courted her tongue, driving her senses wild with escalating need. She whimpered her desire into the warm, minty cavern of his mouth, her hips pushing against his with the need for more stimulation. His hands went from her waist to settle on her hips, holding her against his pulsing length. The eroticism of it thrilled her, awakening every nerve in her body, every sense on high alert.

Draco deepened the kiss with a bolder thrust of his tongue, a movement that made Allegra's inner core respond with a burst of feminine moisture, that instinctive, involuntary response that signalled her readiness, her eagerness, her desperation. One of his hands peeled away her dress as though he were removing cling film. It pooled at her feet and she blindly stepped out of it, her mouth still clamped to his. Her hands moved to undo the buttons of his shirt, her fingers struggling with the task in her excitement. With every button she undid, she placed her mouth to his skin, breathing in the intoxicating scent of him with that hint of lime and leather and late-in-the-day man.

He unclipped her bra and gently cradled her breasts in both his hands, his mouth moving from hers to glide down with blistering heat to her décolletage and over the upper curves of her breasts. The graze of his stubble made her insides clench with need, the glide of his tongue over her flesh evoking a murmur of approval from her lips. Draco's mouth opened over her nipple, drawing on it with light suction, the nerve endings responding with a frenzied dance of excitement she could feel right down to her core. He kissed the outside of each breast, then the undersides, and then her cleavage, his bristly face on the soft slopes of her flesh sending shivers of reaction all through her body.

Had anyone ever paid this much attention to her breasts in the past? Had anyone touched them with such gentleness? Cradled them and worshipped them? Treated them with such respect?

Draco's mouth came back to hers, subjecting it to another pulse-tripping exploration, his tongue mating with hers in a dance that made her ache for him become unbearable. She moaned her 'rescue me' plea into his mouth, her hands fervent, desperate on his body. She set to work on his belt and trouser fastening, sliding her hands over his flat abdomen, her palms and finger pads tickled by the prickle of his masculine hair.

He took over for her, shrugged off his shirt, unzipped his trousers and stepped out of them, his shoes and socks. Allegra couldn't help feeling touched he had left her knickers on until he was completely naked first. It showed a sensitivity she hadn't experienced with other partners. Only when he was fully naked did his hands go to her hips, gently sliding her knickers down her thighs so she could step out of them.

His gaze moved over her body, the desire in them ramping up her own. She pressed herself against him, her senses thrilling at the hard jut of his erection against her belly.

Draco moved her backwards towards the bed, laying her down and coming down alongside her, one of his hands on her abdomen deliciously close to the throb of her need. 'I don't want to rush you,' he said.

Rush me! Rush me!

Allegra was beyond words; all that was coming out of her mouth were breathless gasps and moans when his hand moved lower. She sucked in a breath when he brought his mouth to her belly button, swirling his tongue into its shallow pool until her back was arching off the mattress.

He moved his mouth down to the heart of her, preparing her by kissing her folds, stroking his tongue over her labia before separating her gently with his fingers and anointing her with his tongue in tantalising strokes and flickers that triggered an explosion of sensations that shook her like a rag doll. She bucked and arched and whimpered and cried as her flesh burst into a song that reverberated throughout her body until it finally subsided, leaving her in a languid, limbless state.

Allegra reached for Draco, stroking her fingers along his length, silently urging him to enter her body. After a moment, he eased back from her touch. 'What do you want to do about condoms? Are you on the pill?'

'I take a low-dose one to regulate my cycle.'

'Maybe we should use protection for the time being.'

It touched her that he'd given her a choice, not just gone ahead without consulting her on protection. He reached for a condom in a drawer beside the bed and sheathed himself. He came back to her, angling his body over hers so she didn't have to take his full weight.

That was another thing that struck Allegra about Draco. How many times had partners climbed aboard, so to speak, with little or no consideration for her comfort?

He smoothed her hair back from her face, his eyes dark and eager but with that element of concern that spoke of a man who didn't take consent for granted at any stage of the encounter. 'It's not too late to stop if you'd rather not do this.'

Allegra fisted her hands in the thick pelt of his hair. 'If you stop now, I'll never forgive you. I want you. Want, want, *want* you.'

His slanted smile made something in her stomach swoop. His mouth came down and covered hers in a drugging kiss that escalated her desire to another level that had her panting, writhing, wriggling to get the friction she craved. Finally, Draco came to her entrance, gliding into her with a smooth, thick thrust that made her gasp in relief and excitement. Her body welcomed him, squeezing him as if it never wanted him to leave. He moved his body within hers, deeper and deeper, gradually increasing his pace but making sure she was with him all the way.

Allegra was more than with him. She was a part of him. Consumed by the sensations ricocheting through her from the top of her scalp to the tips of her toes. Each thrust created friction against her, but not quite enough. It was like being suspended on a precipice, dangling there with the abyss beckoning. She whimpered and arched her hips, trying to position herself so she could fly.

Draco slipped a hand between their bodies and caressed her intimately, stroking his clever fingers over the swollen heart of her femininity until she broke free and flew and flew and flew. Fireworks, flashes, fizzes and floods coursed through her flesh. Her mind emptied of everything. It was as if, in those frantic moments, she'd become only flesh and feelings. Feelings that swept through her, flinging her out the other side just in time to sense Draco's final plunge.

He tensed above her, his breathing ragged, his guttural groan when he spilled making the surface of her skin tinkle and tingle with goose bumps. She held him during the short but savage storm, gripping his taut buttocks, holding him to her until he finally sagged as the waves of pleasure faded away.

Allegra couldn't remember a time when she had felt so close to another person. The skin-on-skin contact wasn't new, nor was having sex. The tangled limbs, and the sweat-beaded bodies and the crinkled bed linen were not foreign to her, either.

But the sense that her body had spoken to his, responded to his as it had responded to no one else, made her realise this wasn't just sex. What they had done was make love. Draco had worshipped her body, not exploited it. He had caressed it, not coerced it. He had respected it, drawing from her a depth of passion she had never given to anyone else. She hadn't been capable of it with anyone else. Her body had never wanted anyone like it wanted him. It was as if she was programed to respond to his touch and his touch alone.

Draco leaned his weight on one elbow and used his other hand to stroke her cheek. His eyes held hers in a gentle tether that made her feel even closer to him. It was as if he had glimpsed who she really was and liked what he saw. 'You were wonderful.'

Allegra gave him a shy smile. Silly to be feeling so shy after what they'd just done, but still. 'I don't suppose you've had too many complaints from lovers.'

He idly curled a strand of her hair around one of his fingers, the slight tug on her scalp making her shiver in delight. 'It's nothing any man should take for granted. What pleases one woman might not please another. Communication is the key and, of course, respect.'

She traced her fingertip around the sculpted perfection of his mouth, her core giving a little aftershock at the thought of the ecstasy his sensual mouth and potent body had given her. Pleasure she could still feel in every cell of her flesh like the echo of a far-off bell.

A thought suddenly crept up on her. What if Draco ceased to be satisfied by her? What if he became bored and went in search of someone else? She had witnessed first-hand her mother's shame at being shunted aside for a new mistress. It had made her mother even more depressed and disengaged from life. Allegra had often wondered if her father had been partly to blame for her mother's suicide by his inability to comfort and support her emotionally. She wondered if he was capable of doing it for Elena.

Draco smoothed a fingertip over her forehead. 'You've got that frowning look again. What's troubling you?'

Allegra gusted out a sigh. 'Nothing.'

He pressed his thumb pad on her bottom lip, moving it in a slow back-and-forth stroking motion. 'Talk to me, *agape mou*. It is good to communicate verbally and physically, *ne*?'

She couldn't quite meet his coal-black gaze and aimed for his stubbly chin instead. 'I guess I'm wondering how long this will last.'

He brought her chin up so her gaze meshed with his. 'This?'

Allegra licked her lower lip, tasting the salt of his thumb pad. 'Us. Having…sex. Don't most married couples drift into a less passionate relationship over time? What will you do then? Find someone else?'

A frown formed a bridge between his eyes. 'Didn't you hear me promise to be faithful above all others earlier today? While we're officially married I will be faithful, as I expect you to be.'

While we're officially married… Allegra searched his gaze, wondering, hoping, praying he meant every word. But how could she be sure? Didn't most people mean those vows at the time they spoke them? She was surprised to find *she* had meant them. She might not love him, but she still meant to honour the commitment as far as it was possible to do so. 'But our situation is a little different… We're not starting our marriage at the same place as other couples. What if you fall in love with someone? Someone you meet at work or wherever?'

His finger captured another tendril of her hair and began toying with it. 'What if you fall in love with someone?'

Allegra had trouble holding his penetrating gaze. She pushed out of his hold, swung her legs off the bed and reached for something to cover her nakedness. His shirt was the only thing handy and she slipped it on and crossed it over her chest without doing up the buttons. How could she fall in love with someone else when Draco was all she could think about? 'I don't think that's likely to happen.'

'Then why do you think it will happen to me?'

'Because it happens,' she said. 'It happens and you can't always control it. I represent so many clients whose partner met someone's gaze across a room and that was it. End of marriage. Most never thought it would happen to them. They thought they had a good relationship and then are suddenly left with the heartache of being rejected for someone younger and more beautiful. It's still easier for men to stray, especially when kids come along. It's hard work, bringing up a family, and some men can't cope with the focus not being on them any more.

'My father is a classic example. He got tired of my mother's depression after Dion died and got someone else on the side. Lots of them over the years—both she and I lost count. She was barely cold in her grave before he parked a new mistress in the house.'

Draco got off the bed, pulled on his trousers and zipped them. 'Not all men are your father, Allegra. Your parents' situation was tragic. The loss of a child would test any solid relationship and your parents' relationship, from all accounts, wasn't solid. But don't paint me with the same brush. It's insulting, for one thing. And, for another, I'm not capable of the emotions you describe.'

Allegra frowned. 'But you're not incapable of feeling love. I saw the way you interacted with Iona. And I know you loved your father and grieved terribly when he was killed because you hate talking about it. Look at the way you put everything on hold yesterday to see to Yanni. You *care* about people, Draco. You care a lot. You might not call it love but many would.'

His tilted smile had a touch of cynicism. 'Yes, I care, and to some degree that could be called love. But as for romantic love? I did that once and it was the most foolish mistake I've ever made. I'm not going to repeat it.'

'What happened between you and your ex?'

He made a move to the door but she intercepted him and stalled him with a hand on his arm. 'Talk to me, Draco,' Allegra said. 'I've told you so much about my own stuff but you keep your stuff to yourself. I would like to know so I can understand you better.'

'There's nothing to understand,' he said, but she noted he didn't pull away. 'I was nineteen and full of the confident arrogance of youth. I thought she cared about me the way I cared about her. She didn't.'

A penny dropped inside Allegra's head. 'You were nineteen?'

Draco gave her a rueful look. 'Yes, right at the time you made that pass at me. I was still feeling a little raw. You got the rough end of it. Under other circumstances, your crush would have been a compliment, but instead it was a brutal reminder of the one who got away.'

Allegra bit her lip. 'I'm sorry. No wonder you were so…so angry.'

He brushed a finger over her lower lip as if to remove the sting of the bruising kiss he had pulled away from so long ago. 'It was wrong of me to take it out on you.' His hand drifted away. 'That was why I was so against you getting it on with that boy a couple of years later. I saw something in him that reminded me of my ex.'

And for all these years Allegra had hated him for it. 'But weren't you rather young to be thinking about marriage at nineteen?'

'For some people, yes, that would've been too young. But I'd been on my own since my father died,' he said. 'I felt ready to build a life with someone. Turned out I wasn't as ready as I thought.'

Allegra wondered if Draco would ever be ready to settle down for life after such a disappointment. His commitment to her was conditional. A two- or three-year marriage was hardly a lifetime commitment. No mention of love, just caring. How long was that going to be enough for her? 'I wish I'd listened to you about that boy. It would have saved me a lot of hurt and embarrassment.'

He gave her an on-off smile and turned away to shove his feet back into his shoes, before he reached for a T-shirt and hauled it over his head. 'I'm going up on the bridge to check on things. I'll leave you to rest or whatever. We'll have some supper once I secure us for the night in a sheltered cove not far away from here.'

Allegra's shoulders sagged when the door clicked shut on his exit. She was being silly. What did it matter if he didn't love her? Refused point blank ever to fall in love with her? They could still have a satisfying relationship. Far more satisfying than any relationship she'd had before. Sure, it wasn't the fairy-tale relationship she secretly yearned for, but how realistic were those yearnings anyway? She knew more than most about the sort of heartache that came from idealistic expectations in relationships.

This way was safer. They had a mutual desire for each other and were both intelligent and rational people with a lot more in common than most.

Besides, she wasn't in love with him.

And she would be perfectly safe as long as she stayed that way.

CHAPTER SEVEN

DRACO DROPPED ANCHOR and stood and breathed in the warm night air scented with the brine of the sea. He loved being out on the water, away from all his responsibilities, the burdens he had been carrying since he was a teenager, when life had seemed so hard and impossibly cruel. Out here he could breathe. He could reflect on the goals he had achieved instead of dwelling on the ones he hadn't.

He wasn't sure why he'd told Allegra about his ex, not in so much detail. But she had shared a lot about herself, deeply personal stuff that couldn't have been easy to share. He enjoyed being out here with her—maybe a little too much. The desire that roared between them wasn't something that was going to fade away any time soon. Not on his part, anyway. Draco didn't know what it was about her that made him so fired up. She was beautiful, but then, he had slept with many beautiful women.

No, it was more than that. She was captivating. She was smart and funny and she responded to him with such fervency it couldn't fail to delight him. Hadn't he always known that? Wasn't that why he'd been so hands-off with her for all these years?

But he wasn't hands-off with her now.

And that was something his body was thrilled about. More than thrilled. Excited, exhilarated, ecstatic. He'd had great sex before, too many times to count. But with Allegra something else happened apart from the physical act of sex. Something deeper. Her trust in him gave their intimacy a quality he hadn't experienced quite like that before. Her lack of experience was uncommon in a woman of her age and Draco couldn't help feeling pleased about it. It reeked of a big, fat Greek double standard but he was privately pleased she hadn't shared her body with lots of partners. It gave her relationship with him more significance, as if she had waited for him. What man didn't want a wife who was fiercely attracted to him? It would at least keep her from straying. If Allegra wanted him, then she would think twice about leaving the relationship before he was ready for it to end. Her desire for him was something he could rely on to keep her true to the commitment they'd made that morning.

But as for loving her...

Of course he cared for her, in his way. Care, concern, tenderness, love—weren't they much the same thing? But being *in love*, well, he wasn't going down that road again if he could help it. Draco wasn't such a cynic he couldn't see it worked for some people. People who were less guarded about their emotions. Less... disciplined. But he wasn't one of them.

Not now.

He had learned his lesson the hard way and had learned it well. Opening his heart to love had been foolish and immature and he had paid a high price for it. A price he refused to pay again. He could live a perfectly satisfying year or two with Allegra as his wife without the complication of emotions he didn't need or trust.

The word love was overused these days. People tacked it on to the end of just about every conversation like some sort of verbal talisman. But how often did they mean it? *Really* mean it? He only had to look as far as Allegra's father to see how little those words meant. Cosimo Kallas bandied those three little words around his new wife all the time, but how long before he found someone else to play with when Elena was too tired, or preoccupied with child-rearing?

At least Draco had the self-discipline to refrain from such peccadilloes. His father had set him a good example. Loyalty ran deep in Papandreou blood. Papandreou men stood by their promises even when it hurt. When they made a commitment, they saw it to completion, even if things got tough. He wouldn't have offered to marry Allegra if he hadn't thought he was capable of seeing the commitment through while they wanted each other.

It was a perfect arrangement for both of them. She was a career woman with no immediate plans to have children. He had his own work commitments that took him around the globe at a moment's notice. This way both of them could enjoy the benefits of an exclusive relationship until it was time to move on. What wasn't to like about her? She was beautiful and amusing and sexy and had a whip-quick intellect. He was tired of dating women who didn't have any conversation or little if no sense of humour. Tired of being feted like he was some sort of guru or celebrity.

Draco liked that Allegra saw him as her equal. Liked that she argued with him, debated with him, stood up to him. He had a strong personality but, rather than it intimidating her, it brought out the steely, uncompromising will in hers. He enjoyed sparring with her. Their verbal spats were as exciting as foreplay. He got hard thinking about her prim little mouth firing off another vituperative round at him. Telling him what she thought of him when he could read her body felt the exact opposite. He found it invigorating to interact with her verbally and, of course, physically.

Once he got the yacht settled for the night, Draco went back below deck to find Allegra in the kitchen sipping a glass of water. She had showered and was dressed in yoga pants and a lightweight, dove-grey boyfriend sweater that had slipped off one creamy shoulder. Her hair was still damp from her shower and was in a makeshift knot at the back of her head. She had looked traffic-stopping stunning that morning at their wedding, but his body leapt at the sight of her, even in such casual clothes and with no make-up on, her unfettered breasts outlined by the drape of her top, and his breath caught like a fish hook in his throat.

She put her glass down and raised her chin in that aristocratic manner of hers, as if they hadn't been writhing around naked and sweaty on his bed less than an hour ago. 'I hope you weren't expecting me to get supper ready?'

Draco smiled at the tiny spark of defiance in her gaze. After their little heart-to-heart she was pulling back from him, resetting the boundaries after their intimacy. Was she unsettled by the intensity of their love-making? If so, he knew the feeling. He could do with a little regrouping himself to re-establish the balance of power between them. Sex had a habit of tipping things in a relationship. Good sex, that was. And it didn't get much better than what they'd experienced together. 'Are you hungry?'

The tip of Allegra's tongue passed over her lips, her gaze slipping to his mouth for the briefest moment before her chin came back up. 'Depends what's on the menu.'

He closed the distance between them, allowing her enough room to step aside if she wanted to, but she stayed where she was, her dark blue eyes showing nothing of the tug of war her body was undergoing. But Draco could sense it. He could sense her arousal, the silent thrum of it moving back and forth like a radar signal between their locked gazes. The blood surged in his veins, his need growling and prowling through his body in response to the tempting proximity of hers. He glided a fingertip down the hinge of her jaw, stopping below her up-thrust chin, feeling the delicate quiver of her flesh at his idle touch. 'How about we start with a little appetiser?'

He brought his mouth down to the side of her mouth, the tip of his tongue circling her beauty spot, evoking a tiny whimper from her and a sway of her body towards his. He traced his tongue over her plump lower lip, following the delicate ridge of her vermillion border like an artist drawing a fine line. Allegra made another soft mewling sound, her hands going to his chest, the press of her palms inciting a rush of red-hot desire, making his legs tremble at the knees and his groin bulge and burn.

Draco moved his tongue to her top lip, sweeping it across the soft surface before taking it lightly between his teeth, a soft little 'come play with me' tug that made her press even closer, her hands fisting into his T-shirt. He cupped her bottom, drawing her hard against him, torturing himself with the feel of her soft curves against the pulsing hardness of his body. 'I want you.' Those were the only three little words he wanted to say. The only words he wanted to hear from her. The only words that mattered right now.

'I want you too.' Allegra linked her arms around his neck, opening her mouth against his, inviting him in with a flick of her tongue against his lower lip.

Heat roared through his body, his desire for her like a wildfire that had jumped containment lines. Every cell in his body throbbed with it. Vibrated with it. He kissed her deeply, exploring every corner of her mouth, breathing in the scent of her shampoo and body wash— the frangipani and freesia mix that so bewitched his senses. Her tongue tangled with his in a duel that made the base of his spine hum. Her hands tugged and re- leased his hair at the back of his head, making him even wilder for her. The intoxicating mix of part plea- sure, part pain ramped up his desire until it was a dark unknowable, uncontrollable force deep in his body.

Draco lifted her to prop her on the bench behind, stepping into the space between her parted thighs. Her legs wrapped around his hips, her mouth clamped to his in a kiss that was more combative than anything else. It was as though she resented her attraction to him, wanted to punish him for it. He took the kiss to a deeper level, thrusting his tongue into the warm, moist recesses of her mouth until she was clinging to him and making purring, breathless sounds of encourage- ment. Her hands clasped his head, her fingers digging deep into his scalp, but he enjoyed the roughness of it, the urgency of it. The thrill of having her turned on like a wild cat.

He pulled up her boyfriend sweater, accessing her breasts with his hands, holding them, cupping them, and running his thumbs over the peaked nipples. He sent his mouth on a tour of discovery, down the soft skin of her neck, the delicate framework of her collar bone and the scented valley between her breasts. He licked each one in turn, taking his time, drawing out the pleasure until Allegra was writhing, and pushing and grinding her hips against him in an unspoken plea for more.

He hauled her top over her head and tossed it to the floor, coming back to cradle her breasts in his hands, holding their silky weight, watching the waves of sensual delight pass over her features. He released them to pull off his shirt so she could access his chest, her mouth burning him, branding him with hot, damp little kisses that made the need in him tighten, tighten and tighten... He tugged at her yoga pants and she slipped down off the bench to free them from her body, leaving her in a tiny pair of black knickers with tiny hot-pink bows.

Draco picked Allegra up, carried her to the living area and laid her on one of the leather sofas. He removed the rest of his clothes and came down beside her, his mouth coming back to hers in a kiss that sent incendiary heat throughout his body. Her tongue wrestled and writhed with his, her lips soft, supple and playful. Her teeth got into the action with little kittenish bites that made the blood thunder through his veins.

It had been a long time since he'd worried about losing control but, with her mouth working its mesmerising magic on his, he seriously wondered whether he would go the distance. Need pulsed, powered and panted through him. Allegra's body beckoned to him, her legs opening, her arms around his neck as tight as a vine.

Draco put his hands to her wrists, encircling them like handcuffs, but she was so slender his fingers overlapped. 'I should get a condom.'

She pushed herself back against him, her breasts cool and soft against the wall of his chest, her eyelids lowered to half-mast like a sexy siren's. 'I'm on the pill. Make love to me. *Now.*'

That was another thing he hadn't done in a long time and then only the once: gone bareback. But in the context of their exclusive relationship he didn't have the usual list of reasons why he should halt proceedings to access protection. Allegra was taking contraception, in any case. He cradled her face in his hands, locking his gaze with hers. 'Are you sure?'

Her pupils were wide with desire, her mouth plump and pink from kissing him. 'We're married. And we're not going to sleep around, right? I'm clean, but if you need to get test—'

'Done,' Draco said. 'I was tested six months ago when I ended a fling. I haven't been with anyone since.'

Her eyes widened in surprise. 'No one? No one at all?'

He brushed an imaginary strand of hair away from her face. 'Seeing you that night reminded me of the chemistry we've always had. We have a passionate connection that's not just physical but intellectual. I decided that night I wanted you and, with your father's business worries taking centre stage, I soon came up with a plan to have you before someone else did. I had already been drip-feeding him money. What was a bit more to get what I wanted?'

Allegra rolled her lips together, her eyes shifting out of reach of his. 'It sounds a little…clinical…'

He brought up her chin with his fingertip. 'Does this feel clinical to you?' Draco kissed her softly, lingeringly, allowing her time to respond with the fervent passion he knew she couldn't contain. Her mouth flowered open, her arms going back around his neck, her soft little moan of acquiescence as sweet as any music he'd ever heard.

He moved from her mouth to kiss a pathway down between her breasts to her belly button, swirling his tongue around the tiny whorl of flesh before going lower. Allegra gave another whimper—part excitement, part nervousness.

He calmed her by placing a palm on her belly. 'Relax, *glykia mou*. I won't hurt you.'

She drew in a breath and he separated her tender folds, discovering her all over again. The secrets of her body, the scent and softness, the thrill of feeling her respond to his lips and tongue, was intoxicating to him. She arched up and shuddered as the orgasm powered through her in waves he could feel against his tongue.

She flopped back against the sofa cushions and he came over her, gliding into her with a long, deep thrust that made the hairs on his head shiver and shudder at the roots. Draco cut back a groan, but he couldn't slow down. Not now. Not now this urgent, desperate need was on the run. It broke free from his body, exploding out of him in a hot rush of relief that rained goose bumps all over his quivering flesh.

He was floating…floating…floating…all of his senses dazed into somnolence.

Draco stroked a lazy hand up and down the slim length of Allegra's thigh as if he were stroking a purring kitten. 'I hope I didn't rush you. Things got a little crazy just then.'

She shifted against him, her head tucking underneath his chin like a dormouse preparing for hibernation. 'No, it was…wonderful.' Her voice was as floaty as he felt. 'Truly wonderful.'

Draco looked down at her, pleased to see a curve of a smile on her mouth. He played with her hair, freeing it from its elastic tie, lifting it up and letting it tumble back through his fingers. 'We're good together, Allegra.'

She peeped up at him. 'The best?'

He gave her hair a teasing tug and then brought his mouth back down to hers. 'The best is yet to come.'

Allegra woke in the quietude a little while before dawn. The only sound she could hear was the gentle wash of the water against the sides of the yacht. Draco was sleeping spoon-like behind her, one of his arms over her waist, his legs entwined with hers. She had never spooned anyone before. It was such a cosy, intimate feeling to be curled up together, skin to skin. She listened to the sound of his breathing, feeling each rise and fall of his chest against the naked skin of her back. She glanced down at the band of his tanned, hair-roughened arm around her waist, the contrast of his darker toned skin against her creamy white making something tingle and shiver deep and low in her belly.

The curtains weren't drawn as they were so far away

from anyone in the private cove they'd anchored the yacht in the night before. The stars were like handfuls of diamonds flung over a dark velvet blanket, twinkling, winking, existing in a timeless and spectacular array. It struck her how long it had been since she had seen the stars in such magnificence. Her life had become so busy with work she rarely saw the night sky, other than in the city, where the light pollution all but wiped their brilliance out, apart from a stubborn handful. Allegra hadn't even taken holidays lately...not since her father had his cancer scare and she had used up all her leave, so the occasional star-gazing she did while taking a break had gone by the wayside.

Draco sighed and shifted behind her, his arm tightening around her body. 'Are you awake?'

Allegra felt the stirring of his erection against her bottom, sending a rush of physical memory through her body. 'I hope that's not your idea of foreplay.'

He chuckled and turned her so she was facing him. His dark eyes glittered as brightly as the stars outside. 'Here's the rule. You don't get to leave my bed until you've had a good time.'

Allegra traced the line of his smiling mouth with her fingertip. 'I'm having a very good time. Better than I thought possible.'

He captured her finger and kissed the tip, holding her gaze with the ink-dark steadiness of his. 'Not sore?'

She surreptitiously squeezed her legs together but wasn't quite able to disguise her wince when the overused muscles gave a faint protest. 'No...'

One black brow rose, demanding the truth. 'Not at all?'

Allegra caught her lower lip in her teeth. 'Well... maybe a little bit. That was quite a workout for me, given I'm a little out of practice and all.'

Draco stroked her forehead with such exquisite tenderness it made her chest feel strangely tight. 'I'm sorry. I should've thought and taken it more slowly.'

She lowered her gaze and went back to tracing his mouth, lingering over his lower lip and the rich coating of stubble below it. 'I guess I must seem a bit of a pariah, getting to this age without a healthy sex life.'

He inched up her chin again, his eyes lustrous and dark. 'I have enough female friends and colleagues to know how hard it is for a career woman to juggle work and relationships. Some men don't like not being the centre of a woman's world. Some careers are more demanding than others.'

'Yes, well, I had to fight hard to get where I've got,' she said. 'And, in spite of all the sacrifices I've made, I've still not made partner in the firm, nor will I be.'

'Is that what you want? To be made partner?'

For years, it was all Allegra had wanted. It had consumed her—the drive to achieve, to be recognised as competent and capable amongst her peers, especially the more senior ones. But lately her motivations had undergone a change. She still loved her job, but it didn't feel as satisfying as it once had. She found herself thinking of all the bad things about her work instead of all the positive things. 'I don't know...maybe it's time I shifted firms or something. I seem to have come to a bit of a career dead-end.'

'The glass ceiling?'

'That and other things...' Other things such as that niggling sense she was missing out on something.

Something far more important than a partnership in a law firm.

Draco threaded his fingers through hers and brought her hand to his chest. 'Ever thought of working over here in Greece? You could set up a consultancy of your own. You could help women like Iona.'

Allegra had always resisted the thought of working in her homeland. She had been so determined to be independent of her father. But she knew there were opportunities over here that would be career enhancing and personally satisfying. 'I'm still trying to figure out how I'm going to juggle my London job without taking on anything else.'

'I'm not expecting you to quit your job to cater to my needs,' Draco said. 'You have the right to work where you please. I have business commitments in England too. I'm just putting it out there in case you'd like to think about it.'

'What would be the point of setting up a legal practice I will then have to close once our marriage is over?'

His gaze suddenly seemed to be darker than normal. More intense. His brows were drawn slightly together in a small frown. 'Wouldn't you have had to leave when you wanted children, in any case?'

'Whoa there, buddy.' Allegra pulled her hand out of his and got off the bed to put some distance between them. 'How did we get from clever career moves to kids? You know my feelings on this.' Even as she was saying it she was feeling the opposite.

I want kids. I want them with you.

How had it taken her this long to recognise that niggling sense of dissatisfaction with her life was because she wanted a child? She had never seen herself as a mother, but since she'd been with Draco she couldn't get the thought out of her mind. But her pride wouldn't allow her to express it openly. How could she talk of her longing for a child when Draco had married her for all the wrong reasons? A child deserved to be born in love, not convenience. A baby was a blessing, not part of a business deal.

Draco left the bed and slipped on a bathrobe, the twin of the one Allegra had shoved her arms through and tied around her waist. 'What's the matter? I'm not insisting we have a child together. I'm just putting it out there for discussion. There's no harm in that, is there?'

'Why discuss it at all?' Allegra threw him a brittle glance. 'We're not staying married for ever. That was the deal, wasn't it? Why are you shifting the goal posts now?'

A muscle moved like a tic near his mouth. 'Let's drop the topic. It was a spur-of-the-moment thing. Forget I said it.'

'No. Let's talk about it,' Allegra said. 'It's obviously been playing on your mind. I thought you were only teasing when you first mentioned it. But you have no relatives to speak of. Most Greek men want an heir, especially men as wealthy as you. *Were* you teasing?'

He released a long, slow breath as if he were regulating his response. 'I was. But now I'm…wondering.'

Allegra wasn't sure she wanted to discuss it when she already knew what the outcome would be. They could have a child together but it didn't mean Draco would fall in love with her and stay married to her for ever. 'It's all right for you men,' she said. 'You don't have to interrupt your career to have a family. You don't have to give up your body for nine months, and longer still to breastfeed, and then spend years putting your aspirations on hold. You want the joy without the hard work.'

She was on a roll but she was spouting forth stuff she no longer believed the way she had even a few days ago. But she didn't want him to think her so willing to give up everything for him.

Not when he didn't love her.

But you don't love him, so why does it matter?

Allegra sidestepped the prod of her conscience. She didn't want to think about her feelings for him. It was dangerous to think about how he made her feel. She was confusing good sex with love, just like so many of her clients did. A couple of good orgasms and she fancied herself in love? Ridiculous. It was oxytocin—that was what it was. The bonding hormone tricking her into thinking she was falling in love with him. She was in lust with him. That was all. Lust. Lust. Lust.

'I'm aware of the commitment it is for a woman to have a child,' Draco said. 'But you're in a much better position than most women. With or without a husband, you could hire any necessary help, so your career wouldn't be compromised.'

'A nanny, you mean?' Allegra knew all about nannies. Nannies who came and went, who pretended they loved you and then moved on with barely a moment's notice after their affair with the husband of the house came to light. Nannies who made you feel wonderfully secure, only to rip that rug of security from under your feet so you were left in the inadequate care of a mentally unstable mother. 'No way would I allow a stranger to raise any child of mine.'

She turned away to straighten the bed for something to do with her hands, pulling up the sheets with a vicious tug as if she was putting the subject to sleep once and for all. She sensed him watching her and tried to relax her jerky movements, to control her body language.

But then she felt Draco come up behind her, his hands going to her shoulders and gently turning her to face him. His dark brown eyes were full of concern, not criticism, disarming her completely. 'This is a painful subject for you, *ne*? Then we will leave it alone. I don't want to upset you. I want to spend this week enjoying your company.'

Allegra was enjoying his company a little too much. How was she going to keep her heart out of this when he was so damnably attractive? She blew out a long breath. 'It is a painful subject. I hated being brought up by nannies. I would only just get used to one and then she would leave unexpectedly—mostly because her affair with my father had ended. He went through three or four that way. I'm sure that's why my mother didn't protest about me being sent to boarding school so young. She figured it would keep my father's affairs off site, so to speak.'

Draco squeezed her shoulders. 'Was boarding school tough on you?'

'It wasn't a picnic, that's for sure,' Allegra said. 'I didn't feel I belonged there. I was half-Greek with an accent that was nothing like all the upper-class English girls. I got rid of the accent as soon as I could and tried to fit in. But going home for holidays was just as hard. It was like culture shock. My mother couldn't cope with a child underfoot. I reminded her too much of Dion.'

His frown was so deep it drew his eyebrows into a single bar of black. 'Why do you think your parents didn't divorce?'

'I don't know... I guess because my father would have felt bad about leaving her after Dion died,' Allegra said, moving out of his hold to fold her arms across her middle. 'In the end she left him. I thought he'd bring home a love child well before this. But he didn't seem interested in marrying again until Elena got pregnant.'

'Elena seems happy with her situation.'

'Yes, well, she would be, wouldn't she?' Allegra said. 'She has a beautiful baby boy and she's married a man she loves. What's not to be happy about?'

His frown deepened. 'I thought you liked Elena.'

'I do—a lot,' Allegra said. 'She's sweet and caring, and has a lot of sensitivity, and heaps of integrity too. I just worry she might not be able to hold my father's interest in the long term.'

The same worries I have about you.

'Your father might finally settle down now he has his son and heir,' Draco said. 'But I see why you'd be concerned for Elena.'

Allegra rolled her lips together for a moment. 'You don't see the similarity?'

A flicker of puzzlement passed over his features. 'What similarity?'

'Between our situation and theirs.'

A muscle tightened in the lower quadrant of his jaw. 'No, quite frankly, I don't. It's a completely different situation. I've told you our marriage has a time limit. I promised to remain faithful during that time and, unlike your father, I am a man of my word. You have no reason to feel insecure with me. I might have a more colourful past than you but I have never cheated on a partner. Never.'

'But we're not in love with each other, so in a way we're worse off than Dad and Elena.'

Something shifted at the back of his gaze, as if he was reordering his thoughts. 'Perhaps we're not, in the romantic sense of the word, but in every other way that counts.' Draco held out his hand. 'Come here.'

Allegra came as if he had an invisible cord attached to her body, tugging her back into his orbit. He took her by the waist, holding her against the frame of his body, his eyes meshing with hers in a lock that made her inner core tighten in excitement. There was no way she could resist him. It didn't matter if he didn't love her. She wanted him anyway.

He cupped her cheek with one broad hand, his touch as gentle as if he were cradling priceless porcelain. He brought his mouth down in a feather-down kiss that stirred her senses into a stupor. Her lips clung to his. Need rose in her like a tide, leaving no part of her body immune. Her breasts tingled where they were pushed against the hard wall of his chest, her legs feeling as if they had seaweed for bones. Draco's mouth came back down to claim hers in a firmer kiss, his tongue entering her mouth in a sensual glide that made her insides twist and coil like kelp.

He eased back for a moment to look at her with eyes glittering with desire. 'Breakfast or back to bed?'

Allegra pulled his head back down. 'Read my lips.'

CHAPTER EIGHT

DRACO HADN'T HAD a holiday for months, so he kept telling himself that was why he was feeling so relaxed after a week sailing around the islands. He'd chosen a couple of private hideaways he was familiar with where he and Allegra had swum in quiet coves with the fish darting below them or had lain on pristine beaches.

But, if he were honest with himself, he knew it was because Allegra was proving to be the best thing that had happened to him in a long time. Maybe ever. He woke each morning with a tick of excitement in his blood. Not just because the sex they had was getting better and better, but because the companionship they'd developed had settled into friendship unlike he'd had before with anyone else. He looked forward to discussing things with her—current affairs or business things that came through on email. She had a good mind and sound common sense and he enjoyed listening to her take on current issues. They had cooked together, read together, walked, swam and snorkelled together.

And made love.

Draco couldn't quite bring himself to call it sex any more. Weird, because sex was supposed to be sex. It always had been in the past. But with Allegra it was something more. Something more cerebral…even—*dared he say it?*—emotional.

He shied away from the thought and where it was leading. It wasn't love but physical bonding. It happened when the sex was particularly good. His body craved hers. Hungered for her closeness. Got restless when she wasn't nearby.

It was his hormones going crazy.

Nothing else.

Speaking of hormones, he hadn't returned to the subject of children. He still wasn't entirely sure why he'd brought it up when he had. When proposing, he had brought it up as a test to see what her plans were on the issue. But lately, he'd started to wonder if Allegra was projecting a cover-up opinion. He'd wanted to make sure he wasn't doing the wrong thing by her by tying her to a childless marriage. But she remained adamant that having a family was not on her horizon. It hadn't been on his either, but for some strange reason he kept thinking about it. He had no living close relative. It hadn't used to bother him but now it kept niggling at him. He was getting a taste of fatherhood with Yanni and it wasn't always pretty.

Did he have what it took to be a good father? His father had been a great dad. Hard-working and committed to him no matter what life had thrown his way. But his father had been killed tragically and life had been tough without a father to guide him. Tougher than he wanted any kid of his to experience…

But if Draco suggested he and Allegra have a child it would change everything about their arrangement. Make it more permanent. The only trouble was…

He didn't do permanent.

* * *

When Allegra came up on deck the last morning of their trip, she slipped her arm around Draco's waist and smiled up at him before looking at the sun rising over the water in a golden wash of glittering light. 'So beautiful.'

He dropped a kiss to the top of her head. 'I think so.'

She looked up into his dark gaze and wondered how she had ever thought she'd hated him. The last few days had been some of the most relaxing and enjoyable of her life. She couldn't remember a time when she had felt more in tune with her body. Not just its sexual needs but in terms of general health and wellbeing. She had energy, she slept well and she woke up feeling refreshed and excited about the day and what delights Draco had planned.

But now Allegra was starting to dread the thought of going back to the real world. The world where work, long hours and difficult people sawed at her nerves, kept her awake at night and turned her stomach into a churning mess. 'Do we really have to go back today? Why can't we stay out here for ever?'

He drew her closer, his hands settling on her hips. 'That would indeed be a dream. But duty calls, I'm afraid. I've already had five calls from various staff members over urgent matters. I shouldn't have turned on my phone until after we berthed.'

Allegra toyed with the collar of his polo shirt, her hips resting in the cradle of his. Such intimacy seemed so natural now. Her body still leapt at his touch, her skin tingling and tightening when he gave her *that* look. The 'I want to make love to you and make you scream with pleasure' look that spoke to her woman-hood and made it do cartwheels, handstands and back-flips in excitement.

But, while the intimacy was fabulous, their communication could do with some work, especially over the last twenty-four hours. She had sensed a subtle with-drawing in him, as if he was only comfortable with being intimate sexually, but not emotionally. There was so much they hadn't discussed in any detail about their relationship going forward. Where would they live? Would he expect her to move in with him? He had bought a new townhouse in Hampstead a year ago. Her little house in Bloomsbury was her pride and joy. She couldn't imagine giving it up, as it was a symbol of her independence. The first place she had called home. *Her* home.

She lifted her gaze back to his. 'We haven't talked about our living arrangements when we get back to London. Will you stay with me or at your place in London?'

'Most married couples live together. But I don't expect you to move out of your home.'

Allegra wasn't sure what to make of Draco's answer. Did it mean he wanted to keep separate accommodation? Why would that be? The doubts gathered like seagulls above a fishing vessel, circling her brain, looking for a place to land. Would he keep his house in London so he could keep his distance when it suited him? 'So you plan to keep your place as well?'

'It wouldn't be a sound business move to sell just at this moment,' he said. 'I've recently spent a fortune on renovating it. But it's not a decision I have to make right now. I'll revisit in a year or so.'

How could she know for sure if that was his true reasoning? A business decision not a personal one? Was it a get-out clause? A back-up plan in case things didn't go according to plan? Over the last few days Allegra had been lulled into thinking he was developing feelings for her. The way he talked to her, listened to her, laughed with her.

The way he made love to her.

Yes, made love.

It didn't feel like 'just sex' to her. Not the way he worshipped her body, made it feel things it had never felt before, made her senses swoon and her heart lower its drawbridge.

She had fallen in love with him.

Not at first sight. Not since she was a teenager, but by degrees. Each time they made love the feelings would intensify. There was no denying them now.

She had fooled herself into thinking he would fall in love with her. Sooner. Later. Eventually. But how long was too long to wait? What if it never happened? What if he wasn't capable of being open emotionally?

'So, where will we go once we get back to London?' Allegra asked. 'Your place or mine?'

Draco slid his hand up between her shoulder blades and then under the curtain of her hair, cupping her nape. 'I have to fly to Glasgow for a meeting later that day. I got an email a few minutes ago about it. I won't be back for a couple of days so you'd be best to go to your place. I'll catch up with you mid-week.'

Allegra thought they'd be flying back together but now he was shooting off to Scotland. But she refused to show her disappointment. It was unreasonable of her to expect his career to take a back seat when she had her own professional commitments that couldn't be cancelled at short notice. It had been a logistical nightmare taking this week off as it was. But it worried her this would be an on-going pattern of their future relationship. How long before his 'catch ups' with her became not weekly, but monthly, or even less frequent? How long before he went from looking at her with those glinting 'I want you' eyes to avoiding her gaze altogether, as her father had to her mother when he'd come back from a new mistress's arms? 'Okay,' she said. 'Fine.'

Draco inched up her chin, his gaze searching. 'I know it's not ideal. I wish you could come with me to Scotland but I know how hard it was for you to get this week off. It was the same for me. There will be constant compromises as we juggle two demanding careers. But we'll figure it out as we go.'

Allegra stretched her mouth into a 'I'm cool with that' smile. 'That's what you get for marrying a career girl. You have to share her with her ambition.'

His thumb pad stroked over her beauty spot, his eyes still holding hers in a penetrating tether. 'I have a feeling you're not as ambitious as you make out.'

She forced herself not to shift her gaze but to hold his without wavering. How could he know how conflicted she felt about her career? She had barely acknowledged it to herself. She hadn't even talked about it to Emily. She'd played the 'career girl' card for years. Work had always been her top priority. But if she interrupted her career path with a baby what would happen to her place on the ladder?

And did she even care?

Allegra slipped out of his hold and held on to the

side of the yacht. 'I haven't even got time for a pet. I really don't know how women do it—have a family and keep their career on track.'

He put his hands on her shoulders from behind, his body brushing hers with its warm, hard temptation. 'These things have a way of working themselves out, *glykia mou*. Your circumstances might be completely different in a year or two.'

Yes, she would be divorced and single again.

Allegra turned around, her arms automatically going around his waist as if she had no will of her own to resist him. But then, she didn't. Not one little bit of willpower. She leaned her head against Draco's chest, his hand stroking the back of her head in a soothing motion. What if her body decided for her? She was on the pill but it was a low-dose one and she was woefully lax at taking it. They had made love numerous times now without a condom.

What if she was already pregnant with a honeymoon baby?

But, even if she was, it didn't change the fact Draco didn't love her. Not the way she wanted to be loved. Totally. Unconditionally. Bringing a baby into a marriage that wasn't based on love would not be the best start in life for a child. Didn't she see that every working day? Children traumatised by their parents' arguing, or worse, marked for life with the memories of their care-givers at bitter war with each other, sometimes even after the divorce.

Didn't she bear similar scars herself? Her parents hadn't fought overtly with each other, but she had seen the stone-walling and cold-shoulder treatment from her mother and the pay-backs with affairs and long absences from her father. Was it any wonder she had issues with trust? Big issues?

Draco brought up her chin, his gaze meshing with hers. 'We need to set sail soon if we're going to get back in time for our flights out of Athens this evening.' He pressed a soft kiss to her mouth and drew back to smile lopsidedly at her. 'Back to the real world, *ne*?'

I can hardly wait.

Emily followed Allegra into her office first thing on Monday morning. 'So, how was the honeymoon? Good? Bad? Sensational?'

Allegra put her tote bag and briefcase on the desk and gave her friend a prim look. 'Since when have I told you intimate details about my sex life?'

Emily's eyes twinkled like fairy lights. 'You haven't had one for the last year or more, so how could you? Did you do it with him?'

Allegra slipped off her jacket and hung it on the hook behind her door, hoping her hot cheeks weren't giving her away. Every time she thought of Draco and the intense pleasure he'd evoked in her over the last week it made her blush from head to foot. 'Isn't that what couples on their honeymoon do?'

Emily plonked herself on the corner of Allegra's desk, swinging her legs like an excited schoolgirl. 'So what happened to the marriage of convenience?'

Allegra gave her a self-deprecating look. 'It seems I have zero willpower when it comes to that man.'

Emily picked up a pen and examined it as though it were crucial evidence. 'Yes, well, I'm inclined to agree with you, given his best friend is enough to make a ninety-year-old nun think twice about staying celibate.'

Allegra angled her head. 'Don't tell me you…?'

Emily dropped the pen and jumped down from the desk, her arms crossing over her body. 'I don't know what came over me—I swear I don't. I've never had a one-night stand with a guy. Never, ever.'

Allegra looked at her friend in surprise. 'You *slept* with Loukas Kyprianos?'

Emily winced. 'Guilty, your honour.'

'So, are you seeing him? Dating him?'

Emily bit her lip, the earlier brightness of her expression fading. 'He didn't even ask me for my number.'

'Ouch.'

'Yeah, big ouchy-ouch. I have terrible taste in men. Why do I always pick men way out of my league? No. Don't say it. I know why. It's because I have this ridiculous life script where the only man I want is the one I can't have. I think my mum is right—I need therapy.'

I could do with some myself.

'But it's only been a week,' Allegra said. 'He might still get in contact with you. He could get your number easily enough through Draco or me.'

'I'm not holding my breath,' Emily said. 'I may have sabotaged my chances with him anyway.'

'How?'

She screwed up her mouth and nose in a bunny-rabbit twitch. 'I talked too much. It was like that third champagne did something to my tongue. No wonder they call it truth serum. My mum would say it's because I was subconsciously inviting rejection. You know how New Age-y she is.'

'But what did you say to him?'

'I told Loukas I wanted to get married before I turn thirty in March and I wanted four kids and an Irish retriever.'

'What was his reaction?'

Emily rolled her eyes. 'You would've thought I'd asked him to propose to me then and there. I might as well have put a gun to his head and said, "Marry me or I'll shoot". Although it pains me to admit it, my mother is right. I sabotaged what could have been a perfectly good relationship.'

'I don't know about that,' Allegra said. 'Draco told me Loukas isn't the marrying type. His parents went through a bitter divorce when he was a kid. He said Loukas would never get married. He made quite a point of it, actually.'

Emily's shoulders sagged. 'I sure can pick them. I thought I'd learned my lesson after my disastrous relationship with Daniel.' She sat down with a thump on the chair opposite Allegra's desk. 'Sorry. I shouldn't be dumping all my negative stuff on you. Tell me more about the honeymoon. Are you in love with Draco?'

Allegra avoided her friend's gaze and sat down opposite, making a business of straightening her desk as though she had full-blown OCD. 'It's that sort of marriage.'

'Like hell it isn't,' Emily said. 'You've been in love with him for years.'

'I had a crush on him, that's all—'

'Crush, schmush.' Emily's playful smile came back. 'You so do love him. Look at you. You're positively glowing with oxytocin.'

Allegra could feel her cheeks warming up like hot-plates on a cook-top. 'Yes, well, Draco certainly knows his way around a woman's body… Thing is, am I going to be enough for him? He doesn't love me. He *cares* about me.'

Emily did her cute little bunny twitch again. 'Oh…'

'Not exactly what a girl wants to hear on her honeymoon.'

'No, but words aren't everything,' Emily said. 'Actions are what counts and it looks like you two have had plenty of that over the last week.'

'He's keeping his own house in Hampstead.'

Emily blinked. 'So? Aren't you moving in with him?'

'Why should I?'

'Because that's what brides do. They move in with their husbands.'

'But I don't want to move out of my house,' Allegra said. 'It's my home and I don't see why I should give it up just because my husband wants to live somewhere else. Women are the ones who always make all the compromises. And in the end they lose out. Big time.'

'You've been working in this job way too long,' Emily said. 'Compromise is the key to a successful relationship. Not that I can talk, as I've not had one, personally. But I live in hope.'

Me too.

CHAPTER NINE

ALLEGRA GOT A phone call from Draco later that evening when she got home from work. She had been waiting on tenterhooks all day for his name to pop up on her screen, the little kick of excitement when it finally did making her realise how much she'd missed him in the last twenty-four hours. 'Hi. How was your day?'

'Don't ask.' His tone was flat and jaded. 'I've got to fly to Russia in an hour. I'm at the airport now. I probably won't be back until Friday. Sorry.'

'Oh…that's too bad. Is it something serious?'

'Just business stuff.'

'You can talk to me about it, you know,' Allegra said with more tartness than she would have liked. 'I'm not some nineteen-fifties housewife who has no idea of how the real world works.'

He gave a rough-edged sigh. 'My client is a Russian billionaire who wants some face-to-face time over a design we're working on for him.'

'Couldn't you have sent someone in your place? You do have other people working for you, don't you?' Now she was starting to sound like a nineteen-fifties housewife.

'He's a difficult client,' Draco said. 'But his business is too valuable to compromise. I won't be away long—three days, five at the max. But enough about my business. How was it back at work?'

'Oh, you know, the usual stuff.' Allegra paused and added, 'Have you spoken to Loukas lately?'

'Not since the wedding. Why?'

'Just asking.'

'Just asking…why?'

She chewed at her lip for a beat. 'He and Emily got it on after the wedding.'

Draco gave a deep chuckle. 'Yes, well, I did tell you he had a thing for English girls.'

'He didn't ask for her number.' Allegra said it as if it was a personality defect.

There was a small pause.

'Was that a problem for her?' he said.

'A bit, I think.'

'She liked him?'

'She slept with him, didn't she? She's not the sort of girl to put it out for just anyone. Although she did have a bit to drink.'

'Loukas wouldn't have taken advantage of her, if that's what you're suggesting.'

'I wasn't,' Allegra said. 'She was keen on him but over-played it out of nervousness or something.'

'Over-played it?'

'She mentioned the M word.'

'Bad move.'

'Yes, it was apparently quite a dampener. Poor Em. She's such a sweetheart but she always falls for the wrong men.'

'Do you want me to have a word with him?' Draco asked.

'God, no. I think it's best if we keep out of it. We have enough problems of our own to interfere in anyone else's.'

Another silence ticked past.

'I mean…we have to sort out stuff, you know?' Allegra said. 'The living situation, for instance.'

'I thought we discussed that.'

'But what are people going to say when they find out we're keeping two houses in London on the go?' Allegra said. 'It's hardly the behaviour of a normal couple.'

'Then move in with me. Problem solved.'

'Why don't you move in with me?'

'Mine is a much bigger house,' he said. 'It makes sense to move in with me. You can rent yours out if you're not keen to sell it.'

'Why do I have to be the one who compromises?'

'It isn't about compromising, Allegra. It's about doing what's sensible.' Draco sounded as if he were talking to a child who had failed to grasp the simplest information.

Allegra wished she were still wearing her heels so she could dig them into the carpet. 'So far, I've made all the sacrifices in this relationship. You simply get on with your life as if nothing's changed.'

'Look, I have to go,' he said. 'I'll call you tomorrow.'

Allegra put the phone down and sighed. It wasn't the most satisfying way to end a conversation. But so far the only satisfying thing about their relationship was the sex. And even that was out of the question now, with Draco travelling thousands of miles away for days on end. Maybe she was being silly about the house. It made sense to use the bigger of the two. It was a big step for her, but not as big as marrying him. How could she expect him to fall in love with her if she kept harping on about silly little issues that weren't worth worrying about?

You expect him to fall in love with you?

Allegra chewed her lip until the skin felt raw. Was it too much of a dream to hope he would?

Draco leaned his head back on the headrest once he'd boarded his plane and closed his eyes, wishing he could close off his thoughts as well. Truth was, he could have sent someone else to Russia, but he needed some distance to sort out of few things in his head.

Why was everything suddenly so complicated? He had a filthy headache and a gut full of worry over Yanni back at home, who was giving his staff merry hell over being under house arrest. Now he'd upset Allegra over real estate. Her house was nice but it was practically a doll's house compared to his. Besides, he didn't want to live on her territory. He was the one calling the shots in their relationship. If he moved in with her, she would have the power to ask him to leave. He wasn't giving her that power, no matter how good they were together in bed and out of it. He could pack his house up and rent it out, but why should he? She was being stubborn.

Like you.

Of course he was being stubborn. Being stubborn was how you got things done. How you set goals and saw things through to completion. Being stubborn was how you built up a business into a global empire that was worth millions. Being stubborn was how you rescued a drug-addicted kid of the street and got him clean so he could have a life.

It meant Draco's life was a little more stressful than he'd like it, but that was the way things were. Allegra would come round. It was early days and she was still getting used to sharing her life with someone. As was he. This short separation would hopefully help him get some perspective. He had never been this close to another person. Not just physically, but emotionally. He looked forward to being with her, and he dreamt about her when he wasn't.

He had to rein it in. Draco didn't want to turn back into that callow youth of nineteen who'd fancied himself in love only to find it was a mirage. A fantasy. A dream built on air. He wasn't in love. His heart was in a straitjacket, where it belonged. He would miss Allegra while he was in Russia, badly. But it didn't mean he was in love with her. It meant he cared about her.

It was a mild word, yes, but the way he felt about her was anything but mild.

But when Draco got back to his hotel, from his third and final difficult meeting with his client, he sat in his suite and thought about how lonely it was eating yet another meal on his own. He could have gone out to a restaurant but the thought of dining out alone held zero appeal. No one to sit opposite him, challenging him, debating with him, smiling at his jokes and giving him those sparkly-eyed looks that signalled the same desire he could feel burning in his loins.

He missed Allegra. More than he'd thought he would. This time away was meant to give him some breathing room but instead it was stifling him. There was no trace of her perfume in the hotel room, not even on his skin. When he turned over in bed, the place beside him was cold and empty. That had never bothered him before. An empty space beside him meant he was free of emotional entanglements, but now it made Draco feel…well…empty. He'd tried calling her a few times but the time difference and the long meetings he or she had been in hadn't always worked in his favour. He'd been left feeling strangely out of touch with Allegra. Wanting her with an almost violent ache. Needing to see her like he needed his next breath.

He wondered if she was missing him. Did she stare into space and daydream about their honeymoon the way he did? Did she get a shuddery shiver all over her body when she thought about how they had made love on deck under the star-studded sky? Did she reach for him in the middle of the night and get a sinking feeling in her stomach when she realised he wasn't lying beside her?

Maybe it wouldn't be such a bad idea to move in to one house when he got back. A little bit of compromise wouldn't go astray, especially when it got him what he wanted—Allegra.

Allegra got back from court the following day to find a beautiful bouquet of flowers on her desk. She picked up the card and read the message.

Miss you. Draco.

Her heart gave a leap and she pressed the card against her chest just as Emily buzzed her on the intercom.

'Allegra, your stepmother is here. Have you got time to see her?'

Allegra put the card down on her desk. *Elena was in London?* Why hadn't she mentioned it at the wedding? Or was it a spontaneous trip? But that didn't seem like Elena at all. She was a homebody through and through. She didn't really enjoy travelling all that much and had said only recently how content she was to stay at home with little Nico. 'Sure. I haven't got anyone till four, have I?'

'No, you're all good. I'll send her in.'

Elena came in pushing Nico in his pram. Her eyes were red-rimmed and her face puffy, as if she had been crying. 'Sorry to barge in on you…'

Allegra came up to her and took her hands. 'What's happened?' She glanced in the pram to make sure Nico was all right but he was sleeping soundly. She looked back at Elena. 'What are you doing in London? Is Dad with you? Why didn't you tell me you were—?'

Elena shook her head. 'He's in Paris.'

An ice-cold tap began to drip down Allegra's spine. 'Paris? What for?'

Elena's bottom lip quivered. 'He's got a mistress there. I only just found out about her. He's been seeing her since I got p-pregnant.' The tears started in earnest then, accompanied by hiccoughing sobs.

Allegra hugged her close and stroked her back in soothing circular motions. What was her father thinking? He had what he wanted, didn't he? He had a son and heir and a loving and attentive wife. What more did he want? The selfishness of it appalled her. The cruelty of it made her stomach churn with anger.

Once Elena got some of her composure back, she

eased out of Allegra's embrace. Her watery gaze went
to the bouquet of flowers on the desk. 'That's how I
found out.' She pointed to the flowers. 'The florist must
have got our names mixed up. I got this lovely bunch
of red roses, and when I looked at the card it said "To
Angelique, love always, Cosimo."'

'I'm so sorry.'

Elena turned a sharp eye on Allegra. 'Did you
know? Have you known all along?'

'No, of course not,' Allegra said, shocked and more
than a little hurt Elena would think it of her. 'Could it
be a mistake? Another Cosimo?' Even as she said it, it
sounded implausible.

'No, it's him,' Elena said. 'He didn't deny it when I
called him. He ordered the flowers online for me and
for her. He made some excuse about how he didn't want
to pressure me for sex while I was pregnant. And here
I was, thinking how kind and considerate he'd been
when I was having all that wretched morning sickness.
It makes me want to throw up all over again.'

Allegra wanted to throw up too. How could her father be so pathetic? 'What are you going to do?'

Elena's eyes streamed with tears and she brushed at
them with the back of her hand. 'I want to leave him,
but I've got little Nico to consider. If your father cuts
my allowance, how will I afford a good lawyer to represent me?'

'I'll act for you,' Allegra said, handing her a bunch
of tissues from the box on her desk. 'I know it's a little
unusual, given he's my father, but I would never allow
him to do you out of what's rightfully yours.'

'Oh, would you?' Elena asked, mopping at her eyes.
'Really?'

'Of course,' Allegra said, knowing it would be the end of her relationship with her father, but she no longer cared. Elena and Nico's welfare was a much higher priority.

Elena's situation was an unwelcome reminder of how much she herself had to lose. She was exactly like Elena—in love with a man who didn't love her back. He 'cared' for her. Like her father 'cared' for Elena. But at least Draco had had the decency to refrain from saying those three little words, unlike her father, who rattled them off all the time. And, unlike her father, he might be faithful to her for the duration of their marriage, but he planned to end it when it suited him.

He didn't love her.

That was the bottom line.

She would spend the next couple of years of her life—precious years she would never get back—waiting, hoping, praying he would fall in love with her. What if she had the baby she secretly longed for? She would be just like Elena, left holding it when he decided he wanted out. She didn't want to live like that. To be the sort of woman other women pitied. As she pitied Elena right now. If Draco couldn't say those words and mean them, then she had to make a choice.

'What are your immediate plans?' she asked Elena. 'Are you staying in London or flying home to Santorini?'

'I'm flying back to Athens to stay with my parents. I haven't told them yet. They'll be so disappointed but I have to leave him. I can't live with someone who doesn't love me enough to stay faithful. I just wanted to see you in person. I was worried you'd known about it.'

'I would never hide something like that,' Allegra

said. 'I'm appalled at Dad's behaviour. I'm shocked and sickened by it. I'm on your side in this. I'll get the paperwork drawn up and we'll take things from there.'

'I couldn't bear to lose Nico in a custody battle,' Elena said with a haunted look in her eyes. 'I'd rather die than face that.'

Allegra gave Elena another hug. 'I'm here for you every step of the way, okay? I can talk to Dad but I'm not sure it will do much.'

'No, please don't. This is my problem, not yours.' Elena took a calming breath and then gave a shaky smile that was a little off the mark. 'I'm sorry. I didn't even ask you how the honeymoon went. Did you have a good time?'

'It was lovely, thanks.'

'You're so lucky,' Elena said. 'Draco loves you. Anyone can see that.'

If only he did...

Allegra got home after a lengthy and arduous court hearing on Friday evening. She had only spoken to Draco a couple of times during the week, as he'd been in transit or busy with work commitments, or she had been in court and the time zones had made it even more difficult to connect. Besides, the conversation she intended to have with him was not one she wanted to have over the phone. She wanted to see him face to face. He'd arranged to meet her at her house. She had prepared a meal the night before and now she popped it in the oven to reheat before she showered and changed.

The doorbell rang as she was drying off her hair. The fact that he'd rung the doorbell was another reminder of how odd their relationship was. He didn't have a key to her house and she didn't have a key to his.

But then she didn't have the key to his heart, either.

Allegra's resolve took a punch when she opened the door to him. Draco looked as heart-stoppingly gorgeous as ever in an open-neck dark blue shirt and white chinos that showcased his olive complexion. 'Hi…'

He stepped over the threshold and took her in his arms, covering her mouth with his in a long, spine-melting kiss that made her resolve roll over and play dead. Her arms went around his waist, her hips flush against the potent heat gathering in his pelvis, her own body quaking with the need to get even closer. Draco pulled back to look down at her. 'That was a long week. Did you miss me?'

Allegra dropped her arms from his body and stepped back with a cool smile. 'I've been too busy to think about anything but work. How was your trip?'

His expression registered her response with a slight tightening around his mouth. 'Exhausting. I've crossed so many time zones in the last five days, I've got no idea what time to eat or sleep.'

'Come through.' She led the way to the sitting room where she had laid out drinks and some pre-dinner nibbles. 'Can I get you wine or beer or…?'

'What are you having?'

'White wine.'

'Half a glass will do.'

Allegra handed it to him with another impersonal smile. 'Here you go.'

He took the wine but put it straight back down on the coffee table. 'I have something for you.' He took out a package from his back pocket—a flattish square box wrapped in black tissue, tied with a gold ribbon.

She took it from him and carefully untied the ribbon and tissue to find a jeweller's box with a sapphire-and-diamond pendant inside. It was a delicate and elegant setting, almost simple in design, but the brilliant blue of the sapphire and the tiny sparkling diamonds that surrounded it made it one of the most beautiful pieces of jewellery she had ever seen. 'It's…gorgeous…' She glanced up at him. 'Thank you. It was very thoughtful of you.'

'Glad you like it,' Draco said with a smile. 'The sapphire reminded me of your eyes.' He took the box back from her. 'Here, let me put it on for you.'

Allegra turned around and lifted her hair out of the way while he looped the fine gold chain around her neck and fastened the clasp. The brush of his fingers against her skin made her whole body shiver in reaction. She turned back around to face him, her fingers absently playing with the sapphire. 'Thanks for the flowers, by the way.'

He placed his hands on her shoulders and meshed his gaze with hers. 'Why don't you tell me what's troubling you?'

Allegra pressed her lips together for a moment. 'I had a visit from Elena today.'

'Here? In London?'

She nodded. 'She flew over to talk to me face to face.'

'About…?'

'About my father's mistress in Paris.'

Draco's brows snapped together. 'He has a mistress? Already?'

Allegra slipped out of his hold and stood some distance from him with her arms crossed over her body, her hands cupping her elbows. 'Yes. Her name is Angelique. He sent flowers to her and Elena but the florist must have got the messages mixed up.'

He shook his head as if the situation was beyond belief. 'He's a fool. A damn fool. What's she going to do?'

'She's leaving him,' Allegra said, keeping her gaze steady on his. 'She says she can't live with a man who doesn't love her enough to stay faithful. I agree with her. You can't make someone love you—they either love you or they don't.'

There was a beat or two of pregnant silence.

'Allegra…' Her name came out on a heavy sigh that had 'don't do this' written all over it.

'I've been thinking this week while you've been away,' Allegra said, refusing to be daunted now she had made up her mind. 'This is how it's always going to be, isn't it? You don't love me. Not the way I want to be loved. The way most women want to be loved. The way Elena wants to be loved. I want love I can rely on, no matter what. Caring isn't enough for me, Draco. Flowers and expensive gifts and great sex aren't enough. I want you to love me. But, because you don't, our marriage has to end.'

He let out a harsh breath. 'Don't be ridiculous, *agape mou*. You're being—'

'You keep calling me your "love" but I'm not, am I?' she said. 'They're empty words. I want more than that. I deserve more than that.'

'Look, you're feeling let down about your father's behaviour and it's colouring your—'

'This has nothing to do with my father,' Allegra said. 'This is to do with us. But we're not an 'us', are we? Not in the true sense. We've married for all the wrong reasons and I can't be in a marriage like that. It will be like living my childhood all over again. Never feeling good enough. Never feeling enough, period.'

His brows came together over his eyes. 'You're not suggesting I'd carry on like your father? I told you I'd remain faithful. I promised you that.'

Allegra shook her head at him. 'Being faithful isn't enough. I can't be in a relationship that has a time limit. Every day that passes is a day closer to the one when you'll tell me you want out. That's not how a marriage should be. Even if you're not unfaithful, you could still fall in love with someone else, because without a solid commitment to me it leaves the door wide open for it.'

'I'm not going to fall in love with someone.'

'It's just as bad if you've ruled love out completely. I can't spend the next couple of years of my life hoping you will change. It's better to end it now. Before—'

'What about your father? The ink is barely dry on the deal.'

'You know something? Right now I don't give a fat fig if my father loses everything,' Allegra said. 'He deserves to lose everything, including his wife and son. I'm not going to be the sacrificial lamb for him. I've done it all my life. Papered over the cracks he made in my mother's and my life. I spent years compensating for his inadequacies but I'm sick of it. I'm reclaiming my life as of now, and it doesn't include you, because of the reasons I've stated.'

Draco showed no emotion. It was as if a curtain had

come down on the stage of his face. Allegra kept hoping he would say something…the words she so desperately wanted to hear…even though, if he did, she knew she would doubt their veracity. But why didn't he say them? What was so hard about saying 'I love you'?

'Is this about our living arrangements?' he said. 'If so, we can talk about a compromise. I was going to suggest it anyway, so…'

Allegra shook her head. 'Living together isn't going to solve this, Draco. Surely you can see that? We want completely different things out of life. Ultimately, you want your freedom and I want… I want a baby. A family.' There, she'd said it. Finally admitted the yearning that had been simmering inside her for the last few days. Maybe even longer…maybe since that night in London last December.

He flinched in shock. 'A baby? But you've always said you didn't want—'

'I know what I said but I've changed my mind.'

'Then let's have a baby,' he said, blowing out a breath as if everything was sorted. 'If that's the only issue, then it's easily solved. We'll have a baby and—'

'No,' Allegra said. 'I'm not having a baby to prop up a marriage that isn't working.'

'What do you mean it isn't working?' His gaze was forceful. Direct. 'Last time I looked, it was working just fine.'

'It's not working for me,' Allegra said. 'I'm not going to be second best, Draco. I want to come first. I deserve to be loved for who I am, not for what I can do. That was the script of my childhood; I don't want to follow it in adulthood.'

His expression returned to its inscrutable mask, all

except for a pulse at the base of his throat that seemed to be working a little overtime. 'Is this your final decision?'

Allegra set her chin at a determined height, even though everything in her was slumping, collapsing in despair. Why wasn't he saying it?

Tell me you love me. Tell me you don't want to lose me. Tell me. Tell me. Tell me.

'Yes.'

He gave a slow nod. 'We obviously can't get the marriage annulled.'

'No...'

'It will be embarrassing for both of us for a while,' he said. 'I won't speak to the press and I'd appreciate it if you didn't either.'

'Of course.' Why was he being so damn businesslike about it? So clinical and so composed, as if he wasn't ripping her heart out of her chest with his bare hands. Didn't that prove how little he cared? 'Erm...do you want this back?' Allegra touched the pendant around her neck. 'And the rings?'

'No. Keep them.' Draco's lips barely moved as he spoke, as if he resented the effort.

Allegra swallowed a puffer fish of sadness, but by some miracle she stopped herself from tearing up. Her eyes remained dry and focussed on his. 'I guess that's it, then.' She waved a hand towards the dining room. 'You could stay for dinner but I expect you'd—'

'No.'

'Right.'

There was another silence so acute Allegra was sure she could hear her heart beating. Boom. Boom. Boom.

'I'll see myself out.'

Allegra nodded, not sure she could take much more without showing the devastation she was feeling. Why wasn't he putting up more of a fight? Why wasn't he arguing his corner as he usually did? All he had to do was take her in his arms and show her what he found so difficult to say. Why was Draco walking away?

Because he doesn't love you.

CHAPTER TEN

DRACO WALKED OUT of Allegra's house as if he was on autopilot. His emotions were in lockdown. Emotions he hadn't known he had. He couldn't think past the thought of her pulling the plug on their marriage. He'd been blindsided. Again. What sort of fool was he to have fallen for it? He'd thought it was going so well. Why was she doing this? Why now, after that wonderful week away together?

All this talk of love… He hadn't said those words to anyone since he'd said them to his ex. He had sworn he would never say them in a subsequent relationship, and he had never needed to, much less wanted to. But Allegra hadn't said it, either. Somehow he had fooled himself into thinking she had, but then, he'd been wrong about that sort of thing before.

It was the same as all those years ago…

No. It was worse.

Much worse.

Back then, he'd been angry. Bitter. Furious.

Now all he felt was…*hurt*. Pain like he'd only ever experienced twice before, while staring at a coffin containing his mother and then later his father.

He had lost Allegra like he'd lost his parents. Without warning. Unexpectedly. They were there one minute and then they weren't.

Draco's chest was so tight it felt as if he was having a medical event. His throat was so raw it felt as though he'd drunk battery acid and swallowed the gear stick. Sideways. He walked to his car and got inside, gripping the steering wheel while he pulled himself together. But his thoughts keep running like a ticker tape in his pounding head.

Allegra wanted out.

She wanted him out of her life.

He was the one who was supposed to end things, not her. When he was good and ready. When it was time. She was supposed to be grateful he'd stepped in and saved her father's business and saved her from being blackmailed into bed by some sleazy creep.

Draco started the engine and backed out of the space. He had to get a handle on this. He couldn't allow someone to destroy him. Not like this. Not emotionally. He didn't do emotion. Or at least not emotion like this—the sort of emotion that pulled at every organ in his body until he couldn't draw a breath.

Fine.

He would get out of her life. What had he been thinking, trying to make a marriage between them work? Their relationship was doomed to fail and he was a fool for thinking he could pull it off.

All you had to do was say you loved her.

Draco braked on the thought. He didn't love Allegra. He hadn't fallen in love since he was nineteen and he wasn't going to do it now. He no longer had the 'falling in love' gene. Caring was his thing instead. He was damn good at it too. Look at the way Yanni was improving. Look at what he had done for Iona. Look at the way he provided for his staff all over the globe.

If Allegra couldn't settle for being cared about, then it was her problem, not his. So, he was alone again? He could deal with it. Would have to deal with it. He wasn't going to pay lip service to a concept he no longer believed in.

If he ever had.

Allegra wasn't sure how the press found out about her break-up with Draco but the newsfeeds were running hot by the end of the weekend. There was speculation on who was to blame for the split and she felt uncomfortable that most people assumed it was Draco. It seemed a little unfair although, given his 'playboy' track record and her quiet nun-like existence, it was an easy assumption to make. But it didn't sit well with her sense of justice.

Her father called and threatened to disinherit her for acting as lawyer to Elena but she'd simply hung up on him and blocked his number.

Emily called around to her house late on Sunday night with chocolates, wine and a shoulder to cry on. 'Are you sure you're doing the right thing, Allegra? I mean, it's only been a couple of weeks. Lots of marriages hit rough spots in the early days.'

'I had to leave him,' Allegra said. 'He doesn't love me. It's a deal breaker for me.'

'But some men are hopeless at admitting to loving someone,' Emily said. 'They literally can't say the words.'

Allegra sighed. 'I just can't bring myself to stay in a relationship that isn't equal. I love him. I think I probably always have. But he *cares* about me. That's not good enough. I want him to love me like I love him.'

Emily snapped off a big chunk of fruit and nut chocolate, ignoring the wine she had poured earlier. 'I don't know… I can't help feeling you're making a big mistake. But who am I to talk?'

'So, still no word from Loukas?'

Emily's shoulders drooped. 'Nope.' She eyed the chocolate in her hand for a moment then made a funny gurgling noise and dropped the chocolate to cover her mouth with her hand, her face draining of colour, as though someone had tapped the blood out of her body.

'Are you okay?'

Emily bolted out of the sitting room to the nearest bathroom. Allegra followed close behind and heard her being wretchedly sick. She pushed open the door and came over to where Emily was kneeling in front of the toilet. 'Oh, you poor darling.' She reached for a face cloth and rinsed it under the tap. 'You must have caught a bug or something.'

Emily buried her face in the cloth. 'Yeah, or something…' She came out from behind the face cloth and grimaced. 'You think you've got problems. Wait till you hear mine.'

Allegra frowned. 'You're not…?'

'I haven't done the test yet,' Emily said. 'I bought one—actually, I bought a couple—but I'm not game to do it. I keep hoping I'll get my period. I'm never late. I've never been even a day late. You could set Big Ben by me normally.' Her chin began to tremble. 'What if I'm pregnant? What am I going to do?'

'You'll have to tell Loukas. I assume he's the…?'

'Yes…'

'Are you going to keep—?'

'Yes.' Emily's expression had a look about it of a lioness protecting its cub. She even placed her hand over her flat abdomen. 'Of course I'm keeping it.'

'You'll have to tell Loukas.'

Emily scraped her hair back off her face. 'Yeah, really looking forward to that.' She gave a rueful twist of her mouth. 'You and I are a pair, aren't we?'

Tell me about it.

A few days later, Draco received a package in the post of Allegra's rings and the pendant he'd given her. There was a short handwritten note expressing her concern that he was getting the blame for their break-up.

But you are to blame.

He freeze-framed the thought. The last few days had been some of the most miserable of his existence. It was like reliving the grief of losing his mother and father. The unexpectedness of it. The blunt shock. The *how the hell do I cope with this*? The pointless 'what if?'s and '*what could I have done to prevent this from happening?*'.

Draco couldn't stay in his house with those gifts staring at him. They were the symbols of his failure. He walked out to the street but everywhere he looked he was reminded of what he had lost. Couples were walking hand in hand along the river. Families were picnicking on the lush grass, children playing and laughing in the summer sunshine. He saw a young father scoop a giggling toddler off the grass and hold her against him with a proud smile at her cuteness. His young pregnant wife came over and slipped her arm through her partner's, and beamed up at him with such affection it made Draco's chest tighten.

This was what Allegra wanted. Connection. Love. A family.

Didn't he want it too? Deep, deep inside was a locked compartment of his personality that secretly ached for what that young couple had. His parents had had it but it had been snatched away with his mother's early death. His father had done his best—more than his best—to provide a happy family life, but the threat of loss had hung over Draco and his father, until finally it delivered its felling blow.

Draco had shied away from loving people since because he always lost them. His mother, his father, his ex. Even his boss and mentor Josef had died soon after selling him the business. He had closed off his heart to protect himself from further loss, yet, by doing so, he had lost the person most important to him.

He had lost Allegra.

But, unlike with his mother and father, Draco could fix this.

He loved her.

Really loved her. Not just cared about her. But loved her with every cell of his being. Why else had he all but frogmarched her into marriage? He had married her before anyone else could because he loved her too much to see her suffer with a man who wouldn't respect and treasure her the way he would. His streak of protectiveness was a cover-up for love.

Everything he felt about her was real. Real love. Love that lived, breathed and blossomed for a lifetime. The sort of love he'd been too frightened to own because he didn't want to lose it. Like he had lost it when his gold-digger girlfriend had decided she wanted someone richer than him. But what he'd felt for that girl was nothing to what he felt for Allegra. He had blocked his feelings for so long, but they were seeping through the armour around his heart until it was all but bursting out of his chest.

It was time to fess up and win back the girl of his dreams. The love of his life.

Yes, that was exactly was what Allegra was—*his life*.

Allegra got home late after a mediation meeting ran over time and still the husband refused to settle. She thought longingly of that week, sailing around the Greek islands with Draco, when dirty divorces were the last thing on her mind. Not a minute went past without her thinking of him, wondering how soon he would find someone else once their marriage was formally over. She could have drawn up the papers herself, or got one of her colleagues to do it, but her heart wasn't in it. She would leave it to him to sort out. He was the one who'd wanted the marriage in the first place. It was his mess to undo.

She had only just got inside and slipped off her coat and heels when the doorbell rang. Something about how the bell rang made her pulse pick up its pace. Emily did a quick 'one-two' buzz. Her neighbour on the left held it down for three counts and the neighbour on the right used the brass door-knocker instead.

This sounded…urgent. Insistent. 'I'm not going away until you answer' insistent.

Allegra peered through the peephole and her heart did a backflip as good as any Olympic gymnast. She opened the door with a hand that felt more like an empty glove than a hand. 'Draco...'

'May I come in?'

She held open the door. 'Of course.' Allegra closed the door and turned to face him. 'Did you get the package with...? Oh, you've brought it with you.'

Draco placed the package on the hall table and turned to face her again. 'You didn't actually say you loved me the other day.'

Allegra licked her suddenly dry lips. 'I... No. I didn't see the point since—'

'Then let me be the first to say it.' He took her by the upper arms in a gentle grip, his dark, lustrous eyes meshing with hers. 'I love you.'

For a moment she just looked at him, completely stunned. She had longed to hear those words for so long and now she'd heard them she was too overcome with emotion to speak. She gazed into his eyes, her heart thumping so erratically, as if it was looking for an exit route out of her chest. 'You're not just saying it to get me to come back to you?'

His hands tightened as if he was worried she was going to slip out of his grasp. 'I'm saying it because it's true. I love you so much it, scared me to admit it. I've been a fool, Allegra. A stubborn, block-headed fool. Can you ever forgive me for putting you through the last few days? If you've felt even a quarter of the despair I've felt then I deserve to be horsewhipped.'

She touched his face, not sure if this was really happening.

He loved her. Draco loved her.

'I love you too. I think I may have done so since I was sixteen. But it's grown from a silly crush to love of such depth and intensity, I can hardly describe it. I just know I feel it and I can't imagine ever not feeling it.'

He smiled and hugged her close, rocking her against him as if he wanted them to be glued together. 'I'm sorry for the other night. I was blindsided by your decision to end things. I didn't see it coming because I was too proud to admit you had the raw end of the deal.' Draco eased back to look down at her. 'I've got a lot to learn about giving and taking in a relationship, but I hope you'll teach me. If you've got the patience, that is.'

Allegra pressed a kiss to his mouth, breathing in the familiar scent of him that thrilled her senses so much. 'Maybe you could teach me to be a little less insecure. I've been torturing myself with images of you taking up with someone else.'

'There is no one else for me, *agape mou*,' Draco said. 'I realised that during my epiphany earlier this evening. I made those promises when we got married because there could never be anyone else for me. My subconscious must have known it, even if I wasn't ready to admit it. I told myself I was marrying you to protect you, but what was motivating that protectiveness was love. You are my heart. My life. Can we start again? Stay married and live together for the rest of our lives, in a partnership others will envy and want to emulate?'

Allegra hugged him so tightly her arms ached. 'I can think of nothing I'd like better.'

'I wish I'd gone about this differently,' he said. 'It would have saved these last days of hell.'

'They were hell for me too,' she said. 'But that's all behind us now.'

A shadow passed through his gaze. 'I couldn't be in

my house after you sent back the gifts I'd given you. It was like coming back to the house after my parents' funerals. Even though they died years apart, the feelings were exactly the same. Seeing stuff sitting there but knowing they were never coming back to collect it. It's the worst feeling in the world. The sense of helplessness. Aloneness. Emptiness. That's when I realised I had blocked my feelings out of fear. I didn't want to lose you, like I'd lost everyone else I cared about, so I fooled myself into thinking I didn't love you. But then I realised why I was feeling so bad. Not out of pride or because of the business arrangement. But because my life is meaningless without you in it.'

Allegra stroked a fingertip around his mouth. 'I was so miserable after you left. I couldn't understand why you weren't fighting to keep our marriage. It sort of confirmed my doubts in a way. But now I realise how hard it must have been for you, with me springing it on you like that. I just couldn't go another day without knowing for sure how you felt.'

'I should have fought for you. But I guess I was feeling so raw I had to get away to process things. But it's not going to be how I solve conflict in the future.'

His eyes looked suspiciously watery. 'I saw a family today. A young family with a toddler, and the wife was expecting another baby. It made me realise what I was missing out on. I don't want to be surrounded by my wealth and possessions at the end of my life. I want to be surrounded by my family. *Our* family.'

She framed his face in her hands. 'You say you've been denying how you feel about me—well, I've been denying how I feel about having kids. I've suppressed my maternal longings for years as I worked to build my career. I don't want to get to the end of my life with a stack of legal documents for company. I want you. I want us to be family. And I want to live in Greece. It's my home. I want to set up a legal practice where I can help women like Iona and Elena. Iona might fancy a career change as a nanny. I'm going to ask her next time I see her. If ever there was a frustrated grandmother, she's one.'

His smile lit up his eyes, making them crinkle at the corners. 'That's been my mistake in the past—thinking "either, or" instead of both. We can both have what we want. It will take a bit of compromise on my part, but you're going to give me lessons, *ne*?'

Allegra gave him a teasing smile. 'When would you like me to start?'

He brought his mouth down to within a millimetre of hers. 'After I do this.' And he covered her mouth with his.

* * * * *

This one is for Bill.
Don't worry, you don't have t
Love M xx

THE
PLEASU
REVENG

ANDIE BROCK

CHAPTER ONE

'WE DON'T WANT any trouble, Kalanos.'

Lukas roughly shook off the hand on the sleeve of his dark suit, before turning to give its owner a bone-chilling stare.

'Trouble?' He let his eyes travel slowly over the sweating face of the middle-aged man who was trying but failing miserably to square up to him. 'Whatever makes you think I would bring any *trouble*, Yiannis?'

The man took a step away, glancing around for backup. 'Look, Kalanos, this is my father's funeral—that's all I'm saying. It's a time for respect.'

'Ah, yes, *respect*.' Lukas let the word slide through his teeth like a witch's curse. 'I'm so glad you reminded me. That must be why there are so many people here.' He swept a derisive stare over the sparsely populated graveside. 'So many people wanting to pay their "respects" to the great man.'

'It's a quiet family funeral. That's all.' Yiannis avoided his eye. 'And you are not wanted here, Lukas.'

'No?' Lukas ground out his reply. 'Well, you know what? That's too bad.'

In point of fact Lukas hadn't wanted to be there. Not yet. Lukas had been far from ready to bury this evil man. He'd had plans for him. The man who had killed his father as surely as if he had driven a blade through his heart. Whose evil machinations had seen Lukas thrown into prison for a crime he hadn't committed. Dark, unspeakable plans that would have seen him begging for mercy and, on realising there was none to be had, pleading for the oblivion of death.

Four and a half years. That was how long Lukas had been incarcerated in one of Athens's toughest jails, with only the dregs of society for company. Plenty of time to go over every detail of his betrayal, and worse—far worse—the betrayal of his father. Years of seething, boiling, melting rage that had solidified inside him until it had become all he was. No longer a man of flesh and blood but hard and cold, hewn from the lava of hatred.

Four and a half years to plot his revenge.

And all for nothing.

Because the object of his hatred, Aristotle Gianopoulous, had died on the very same day that Lukas had been released from prison. Almost as if he had timed it deliberately. Almost as if he had known.

Now Lukas watched the coffin being slowly lowered into the ground as the sonorous voice of the priest bestowing his final blessing filled the air. His cold eyes travelled round the circle of black-clad mourners, moving from one to the next. He let his gaze stay just long enough for his forbidding presence to register, to unsettle them, to shift their focus from the dead man to one who was very much alive. And who wanted them to know it.

Beside him Yiannis Gianopoulous fidgeted nervously, shooting him wary sidelong glances. The son of Aristotle from his second marriage, he was of no interest to Lukas. His brother Christos was here too, scowling at him from the relative safety of the other side of the open grave. There were a couple of old business associates, Aristotle's ancient lawyer, and one of his lady-friends, quietly dabbing at her eyes as if it was expected of her. Slightly to one side stood Petros and Dorcas, Aristotle's last remaining faithful employees, who had worked for him for longer than Lukas could remember. More fool them.

An assorted array of damaged and broken individuals, the detritus of Gianopoulous's life, all brought together under the punishing heat of the midday sun on this beautiful Greek island to bury the man who had doubtless managed to blight all their lives in one way or another. Lukas didn't give a damn about any of them.

All except for one.

Finally he let his eyes rest upon her. The slightly built young woman standing with her head bowed, clutching a single white lily tightly in her hand. Calista Gianopoulous. *Callie.* The offspring of Aristotle's third wife, his youngest child and only daughter. The one good thing Aristotle had produced. Or so Lukas had thought. Until she had betrayed him, too. Playing her part in his downfall in the most treacherous way possible.

Lukas allowed himself a moment to savour her discomfort. He had recognised her immediately, of course, the second he had burst onto this touching scene. Marching through the small graveyard, past the neglected resting place of his own father, he had stormed towards the freshly dug grave, enjoying the palpable wave of alarm that had rippled across the mourners.

And the look of panic that had gripped Calista. He had seen it, even though she was wearing a veil, had witnessed the flash of terror in those green eyes, registered the way her slender body swayed slightly before she had steadied herself and looked down.

Now he watched as she bowed her head still further, pulling at the black lace that covered her glorious red hair as if she could somehow disguise herself, hide from him. But there was no chance of that. No chance at all.

Look at me, Calista.

He found himself willing her to raise her eyes, to meet his searing gaze. He wanted to see her guilt for himself, to witness her shame, to feel it penetrate the solid wall of his contempt.

Or was some small, pathetic part of him still hoping that he'd got it wrong?

But Calista's eyes were firmly fixed on the grave before her, looking for all the world as if she would jump in with her deceased father if it meant she could get away from him. But, no. She would have no such escape. Aristotle might have died before Lukas could exact his revenge, but Calista was here before him—ready for the taking. It would be revenge of a very different kind, but none the less pleasurable for that.

Lukas stared at her through narrowed eyes. The young woman he thought he'd known. How wrong he had been. Over the years they had built up a friendship, or so he had thought, sharing their summers on the island of Thalassa, a private idyll bought jointly by their two fathers when G&K Shipping had made its first million. A symbol of their success and their enduring friendship.

So much for that.

Lukas, eight years Calista's senior, thought back to the lonely little kid whose parents had divorced before she'd barely been out of nappies. Her neurotic screwball of a mother had whisked her back to her homeland of England, but sent her alone to Thalassa for the school holidays. Cutting a forlorn figure, Calista had trailed after whichever half-sibling had happened to be in residence at the sumptuous Gianopoulous residence at the time, her fair skin turning pink in the hot Greek sun, freckles dotting her nose.

She had trailed after Lukas too, seeking him out on his family's side of the island, obstinately settling herself in his boat when he was off one of his fishing trips, or clambering over the rocks to watch him dive into the crystal-clear turquoise waters before pestering him to show her how it was done.

Later she had become Callie the awkward teenager. Motherless by then, she'd been packed off to boarding school, but had still came back to Thalassa for the long summer vacations. Hiding her mop of curly red hair beneath a floppy straw hat and her pretty face behind the fat pages of a blockbuster novel, she'd no longer had any interest in her brothers—nor, seemingly, in Lukas, except for the occasional giveaway glance from those amazing green eyes when she'd thought he wasn't looking, and blushing to the roots of her hair when he caught her out.

Callie, now Calista, who at eighteen, had somehow metamorphosed into the most stunning young woman. *And had tempted him into bed.* Although technically they had never actually made it as far as a bed. Caught up in the moment, the sofa in the living room had served them well enough.

Lukas had known it was wrong at the time—of course he had. But she had been just too alluring, too enticing to resist. He had been surprised, flattered—honoured, even—that she had made a play for him, chosen him to take her virginity. But most of all he had been duped.

And now he was going to make her pay.

Calista felt the ground sway beneath her feet, and the image of the coffin bearing her father blurred through the black lace of her veil.

Oh, please, no.

Not Lukas—not here, not now. But there was no mistaking the figure of the man who was glowering at her from the other side of the grave, or the power of his intensely dark stare as it bored into her. He was broader than she remembered him, and his muscled torso harder, stronger, more imposing, filling the well-cut dark suit like steel poured into a mould of the finest fabric. His sleeves tugged tight against the bulge of his biceps as he stood there with his arms folded across his chest, his feet firmly planted, clearly indicating that he was going nowhere.

All this Calista registered in a flash of panic before lowering her eyes to the grave.

This couldn't be happening.

Lukas Kalanos was in prison—everybody knew that. Serving a long sentence for his part in the disgraceful arms smuggling business that had been masterminded by his father, Stavros—her own father's business partner.

The sheer immorality of the venture had sickened Calista to the core—it still did. The fact that her father's shipping business had gone bust because of it, and her family had been financially ruined, was only of secondary concern. At the age of twenty-three she had already experienced great wealth and great hardship. And she knew which one she preferred.

Which was why five years ago she had walked away, determined to turn her back on her tainted Greek heritage. Away from the collapse of the multi-billion-dollar family business, from her brothers' bickering and back-stabbing. From her father's towering rages and black, alcohol-fuelled depressions.

But most of all she had walked away from Lukas Kalanos—the man whose dark eyes were tearing into her soul right now. The man who had taken her virginity and broken her heart. And who had left her with a very permanent reminder.

At the thought of her little daughter Calista felt her lip start to quiver. Effie was fine—she was safe at home in London, probably running rings around poor Magda, Calista's trusted friend and fellow student nurse, who was in charge until Calista could hurry back. She didn't want to spend any more time here than she had to—she was intending to stay a couple of days at most, to sort through her father's things with her brothers, sign whatever paperwork needed to be signed and then escape from this island for ever.

But suddenly getting away from Thalassa had taken on a new urgency. And getting away from the menacingly dark form of Lukas Kalanos more imperative still.

The burial ceremony was almost over. The priest was inviting them to join him in the last prayer before the mourners tossed flowers and soil onto the top of the coffin, the distinctive sound as they met the polished wood sending a shiver through Calista's slender frame.

'Not cold, surely?' A firm, possessive grip clasped her elbow. 'Or is this a touching display of grief?'

He spoke in faultless English, although Calista's Greek would have been more than good enough to understand his meaning. Using his grasp, he turned her so that now she couldn't escape the full force of him as he loomed over her, glowered down at her. 'If so, I'm sure I don't need to point out that it is seriously misplaced.'

'Lukas, please…' Calista braced herself to meet his searing gaze, her knees almost giving way at the sight of him.

The tangled dark curls had gone, in favour of a close-cropped style that hardened his handsome features, accentuating the uncompromising sweep of his jawline shadowed with designer stubble, the sharp-angled planes of his cheeks. But the eyes were the same—so dark a brown as to be almost black, breathtaking in their intensity.

'I am here to bury my father—not listen to your insults.'

'Oh, believe me, *agapi mou*, in terms of insults I wouldn't know where to start. It would take a lifetime and more to even scratch the surface of the depths of my revulsion for that man.'

Calista swallowed hard. Her father had had his faults—she had no doubt about that. A larger-than-life character, both in temperament and girth, he had treated her mother very badly, and had had a series of affairs that had broken her mother's spirit, albeit already fragile. In turn that had eventually led to her accidental overdose. Calista would never wholly forgive him for that.

But he'd still been her father—the only one she would ever have—and she had always known she would have to return to Thalassa one last time to lay him to rest. And maybe lay some of her demons to rest too.

Little had she known that the biggest demon of all would be present at the graveside, sliding his arm around her waist right now in a blatant show of possessiveness and control.

'I'll thank you not to speak of my father in that way.'

She was grateful to feel her hot-headed temper kicking in to rescue her, colouring her cheeks beneath the veil. Pointedly taking a step to the side to dislodge his hand from her elbow, she pushed back her shoulders and had to stifle a gasp as his arm slid around her waist, the ring of muscled steel burning through the thin fabric of her black dress.

'It is both disrespectful and deeply insulting.' Her voice shook alarmingly. 'Quite aside from which, *you* are hardly in a position to judge anyone.'

'Me, Calista?' Dark brows were raised fractionally in feigned surprise. 'Why would that be?'

'You know perfectly well why.'

'Ah, yes. The heinous crime I committed. That's something I want to talk to you about.'

'Well, I don't want to talk to *you*—about that or anything else.'

Particularly not anything else.

Cold fingers of dread tiptoed down her spine at the thought of what they might end up discussing. If Lukas were to find out that he had a daughter, heaven only knew how he would react. It was too terrifying an idea to contemplate.

Calista had never intended to keep Effie a secret from her father—at least not at first. She had been over five months pregnant before she had even realised it herself, convinced that stress was responsible for the nausea, her lack of periods, her fatigue. Because *no one* got pregnant the very first time they had sex, did they?

Certainly the stress she had been suffering would have felled the strongest spirit, even *before* she'd found out she was expecting Lukas's child. What with Stavros—her father's friend and business partner—dying so suddenly, and then the whole arms smuggling scandal coming out and the shipping business collapsing. And finally making the sickening discovery that Lukas was involved.

By the time she had seen a doctor Lukas had already been awaiting trial for his crime. And on the day she'd gone into labour, a full month earlier than expected, alone and frightened as she pushed her way through the agonising birth with only the midwife's hand to grip for support, Lukas had been in court, with the judge declaring him guilty and sentencing him to eight years in jail.

Effie's first screaming lungful of air had come at the exact moment when the judge had uttered the fateful words, 'Take him down.'

On that day—the day of her daughter's birth—Calista had resolved to wait to tell Lukas of Effie's existence until he was released from jail. Eight years had seemed a lifetime away. Time enough for her and Effie to build their own lives in the UK, to become a strong, independent unit. So the secret had been kept well hidden.

Calista had told no one—not even her father—for fear that if he knew the truth word would spread amongst her Greek family and find its way to Lukas. But if she was honest there was another reason she didn't want her father to know. She didn't want her precious Effie tainted by any association with him.

He would have tried to take control, Calista knew that—both of her and his granddaughter. He would have tried to manipulate them, bend them to his will, use them to his advantage. Calista had worked far too hard to build an independent life to let him do that. Simply not telling him about Effie had been the easiest solution all round.

Now Aristotle would never know he'd had a granddaughter. But Lukas… Calista moved inside the band of his arm, her heart thudding with frantic alarm and something else—something that felt dangerously like excitement. Lukas would have to know that he was a father. That was his right. But not yet. Not until Calista had had a chance to prepare herself—and Effie. Not until she had made sure all her defences were securely in place.

'Calista, people are leaving.' Beside her, but keeping a safe distance from Lukas, Yiannis tried to get her attention. 'They are waiting to speak to us before they go.'

'Leaving so soon?' Lukas gave a derisive sneer. 'Is there to be no wake? No toasting the life of the great man?'

'The boats are waiting to take everyone back to the mainland.' Yiannis wiped the sweat from his brow. 'You'll be on one of them, if you know what's good for you.'

Lukas gave a gruff laugh. 'Funny, I was just thinking the same thing about you.'

'You have brought ruination and disgrace to our family, Kalanos, but Thalassa is the one asset my father managed to protect. You may own half of it now, but not for much longer.'

'Is that right?'

'Yes. We intend to make a claim for your half of the island as compensation for the financial ruin you and your father caused us. Our lawyers are confident we will win the case.' Yiannis struggled to keep his voice firm.

'We?'

'My brother and I. And Calista, of course.'

At the mention of her name Lukas released his arm from her waist, turning to give Calista a stare of such revulsion that it churned her stomach. She had no idea what Yiannis was talking about. She had never agreed to instruct a lawyer to sue for compensation. She wanted nothing to do with Thalassa—even the small share she assumed she'd inherit now, on Aristotle's death. She certainly had no intention of fighting Lukas for his half.

'Well, good luck with that.' Narrowing his eyes, Lukas turned away, seemingly bored with the subject. 'Actually, no.' Turning back, he fixed Yiannis with a punishing stare. 'You might as well know—both of you. The island of Thalassa now belongs to me. *All* of it.'

'Yeah, right.' Christos had joined them, positioning himself between Yiannis and Lukas, sweating profusely. 'Do you take us for idiots, Kalanos?'

Lukas's pursed lips gave an almost imperceptible twitch.

'You are obviously lying.'

'I'm afraid not.' Lukas removed a tiny speck of dust from the sleeve of his immaculate suit. 'I'm only surprised your lawyers didn't tell you. I managed to acquire your father's half of the island some time ago.'

Christos's face turned puce, but it was Yiannis who spoke. 'That can't be true. Aristotle would never have sold to you.'

'He didn't need to. When he and my father bought the island they registered it in their wives' names. A touching gesture, don't you think? Or am I being naive? Perhaps it was simply a tax dodge? Either way, it has proved very convenient. *My* half, of course, came to me upon the death of my mother—God rest her soul. Acquiring *your* half was simply a matter of tracking down Aristotle's first wife and making her an offer she couldn't refuse. I can't tell you how grateful she was. Especially as she had no idea she owned it.'

'But you have been in prison for years. How could you possibly have done this?'

'You'd be surprised. It turns out that you can make some very useful contacts inside. Very useful indeed.' Lukas raised a dark brow. 'I now know just the man for any given job. And I do mean *any*.'

Yiannis visibly paled beneath his swarthy skin. In desperation he turned to Calista, but she only gave a small shrug. She didn't give a damn who owned the island. She just wanted to get off it as fast as she could.

Christos, meanwhile, always blessed with more brawn than brains, had raised his fists in a pathetic show of aggression. 'You don't scare me, Kalanos. I'll take you on any time you like.'

'Didn't I hear you say you had a boat to catch?' With a display of supreme indifference Lukas treated him to an icily withering look.

Christos took a step forward, but Yiannis grabbed hold of his arm, pulling him away to stop him from getting himself into real trouble. As he twisted sideways his feet got caught in the green tarpaulin covering the fresh earth around the grave and they both stumbled, lurching dangerously towards the grave itself, before righting themselves at the last moment.

Yiannis tugged at his brother's arm again, desperate to get him away from humiliation, or a punch on the nose, or both.

'You haven't heard the last of this, Kalanos!' Christos shouted over his shoulder as his brother hastily manoeuvred them away, weaving between the overgrown graves. 'You are going to pay for this.'

Calista watched in surprise as her half-brothers disappeared. Weren't they supposed to have been staying a couple of nights on the island to go through their father's papers and sort out his affairs? Clearly that was no longer happening. Neither did they seem bothered about leaving her behind to deal with Lukas. It was obviously every man for himself—or *her*self.

But it did mean that there was nothing to keep her there any more. Unless she counted the formidably dark figure that was still rooted ominously by her side.

Realising she was still clutching the single lily in her hand, she stepped towards the grave and let it drop, whispering a silent goodbye to her father. A lump lodged in her throat. Not just for her father—her relationship with him had always been too fraught, too blighted by anguish and tragedy for simple grief to sum it up—but because Calista knew she was not just saying goodbye to Aristotle but to Thalassa, her childhood, her Greek heritage. This was the end of an era.

She turned to go, immediately coming up against the solid wall of Lukas's chest. Adjusting the strap of her bag over her shoulder, she went to move past him. 'If you will excuse me I need to be going.'

'Going where, exactly?'

'I'm leaving the island with the others, of course. There is no point in me staying here any longer.'

'Oh, but there is.' With lightning speed Lukas closed his hand around her wrist, bringing her back up against his broad chest. 'You, *agape*, are going nowhere.'

Calista flinched, her whole body going into a kind of panicky meltdown that sent a flood of fear rippling down to her core. Bizarrely, it wasn't an entirely unpleasant sensation.

'What do you mean by that?'

'Just what I say. You and I have unfinished business. And you won't be leaving Thalassa until I say so.'

'So what do you intend to do? Hold me prisoner?'

'If necessary, yes.'

'Don't be ridiculous.'

She hardened her voice as best she could, determined that she would stand up to this new, frighteningly formidable Lukas. Pulling away, she looked pointedly at her wrist until he released it.

'Anyway, what *is* this unfinished business? As far as I'm concerned we have nothing to discuss.'

Her nails dug into her palms at the blatant lie. But he couldn't be talking about Effie. If he had found out about his daughter he would have blown her whole world apart by now.

'Don't tell me you have forgotten, Calista. Because I certainly haven't.'

Dark, dark eyes looked down on her, glittering with intent.

'Let's just say the image of you lying semi-naked on my sofa, your legs wrapped around my back, has stayed with me all these years. I've probably conjured it up more times than I should have. Prison has that effect on you. You have to take your pleasures where you can.'

Callie blushed to the roots of her hair, grateful for the black veil that still partially obscured her mortified face. That was until Lukas gently, almost reverentially, lifted the fine lace and arranged it back over her head. For one bizarre moment she thought he was going to kiss her, as if she were some sort of dark bride.

'There—that's better.'

He stared at her, drinking her in like a man with the fiercest thirst. She held her breath. Each testosterone-fuelled second seemed longer than the last. She shifted beneath his astonishingly powerful scrutiny, her skin prickling, her heart pounding in her ribcage.

'I had forgotten how beautiful you are, Calista.'

Her stifled breath came out as a gasp. She hadn't expected a compliment—not after all the bullying and the veiled threats. Except this was a compliment deliberately tinged with menace.

'I can't tell you how much I am looking forward to renewing our acquaintance. I've been looking forward to it for almost five long years.'

No! Calista choked back a silent cry.

Surely he didn't think she would repeat that catastrophic error? Panic and outrage stiffened her spine.

'If you imagine that I am going to go to bed with you again, Lukas, you are sorely mistaken.'

'Bed…sofa…up against the wall right here in front of your father's grave, if you like. It's all the same to me. I want you, Calista. And I should warn you, when I want something I go all out to make sure that I get it.'

CHAPTER TWO

LUKAS WATCHED THE alarm on Calista's face set her delicate features in stone.

He had been right to declare her beautiful—even if he *had* only meant to say it in his head. She was even more beautiful than he remembered. The intervening years had honed her heart-shaped face, the high cheekbones, the firmly pointed chin. But the small, straight nose was still speckled with a dusting of freckles and her mouth... That was just as he remembered it, wide and full-lipped and deliciously pink—even now, when it was pursed in an attempt at defiance.

How Aristotle had produced such an exquisite creature as this was almost beyond comprehension. Calista obviously took after her mother, Diana, the actress-cum-model whose beauty had ultimately been her downfall. They certainly shared the same colouring, but whereas Diana had been all leggy height and stunning bone structure, which the camera had loved, Calista was petite, with full breasts and a slim waist leading to curvaceous hips that begged to be traced with the flat of his palm. Lukas could feel that urge powering through him right now, and he responded by reaching for her hand, relishing the soft feel of it beneath his own.

'This way.' He started off across the graveyard, pulling Calista behind him, all too aware that he was behaving like some sort of caveman but not caring in the least.

'Lukas—stop this.'

No way. Her feeble protestation only made him all the more determined that she was going to come with him—back to his villa and back to his bed. He had waited far too long for this moment to allow any second thoughts to creep in, or even to let common decency stand in his way. Certainly not her breathless objections.

'Lukas, stop—let me go!'

They had reached the small copse behind the ancient chapel, where he had left his motorbike. Positioning Calista between it and him, Lukas finally let go of her hand.

Calista snatched it back, her eyes flashing with fire. 'Just what the hell do you think you are playing at?'

'Oh, I'm not playing, Calista. This is no game.'

'What, then? What are you trying to prove? Why are you behaving like such a…a horrible bully?'

'Perhaps that's what I've become.' He gave her a casually brutal stare. 'Perhaps that's what four and a half years in prison does to a man.'

Calista's expression tightened. 'I don't even understand why you aren't still there. You were sentenced to *eight* years.'

'Time off for good behaviour.' His eyes glittered coldly. 'You see, I was a very good boy whilst I was in there—as far as the authorities were concerned, that is. Now I intend to make up for it.'

He watched her swallow.

'I do hope my early release hasn't inconvenienced you?'

'It hasn't. I couldn't care less where you are…what you do.'

'Good. Then get on the bike. We are going to Villa Helene.'

'No, we are *not*.' Her hand flew to her chest. 'I'm not going anywhere with you.'

'And there I was, hoping we wouldn't have to do this the hard way.'

Easily spanning her waist with his broad hands, Lukas lifted her off her feet and planted her unceremoniously on the pillion seat of the bike. The thin fabric of her skirt rode up over her thighs, pulling seductively taut, while her breasts heaved with indignation.

Lukas fought down the kick of lust.

'If you don't get me off this thing right now I am going to scream.'

'Feel free.' He smiled darkly. 'It won't make any difference. Your dear brothers, along with the other brokenhearted mourners, are already on their way back to the mainland. No one will hear you.'

He saw the flicker of fear in her eyes but she didn't move. Her pride refused to give him the satisfaction. And for some reason that only increased his admiration—and his arousal. Perched on the leather seat of his bike, she looked like some sort of erotic goddess, her back arched in defiance, her glorious Titian hair tumbling over her shoulders. The mourning veil, he noticed, had fallen to the dry ground at his feet.

'There's Petros…and Dorcas. They're still on the island. Villa Melina is still their home.'

He gave her a telling look. That was something for *him* to decide—not her. Clearly she was forgetting who called the shots around here.

'Look…' She suddenly changed tack, trying for a conciliatory tone. 'What's this all about, anyway?'

'You used to love this bike, Callie, don't you remember?' He deliberately used her shortened name, taking them back to the long hot summers of their shared past. 'You were forever pestering me for a ride.'

They had both loved this motorbike—the sleek black beast that had been Lukas's sixteenth birthday present to himself. He'd had other bikes since, and sports cars, luxury yachts, a helicopter—all the extravagant modes of transport that great wealth could afford. But nothing had surpassed the feeling of straddling this powerful beauty all those years ago, made even better by the feel of Callie's skinny arms clinging to his waist as they had roared off, the sound of her excited squeals in his ear.

Coming across it in the garage this morning, just where he had left it, he had felt as if he were meeting an old friend. One old friend, at least, that hadn't let him down. She had obediently started first time after he had charged the battery.

'I think we've both grown up since then.' Calista tossed back her flame-red hair, all sharp-angled defiance and dignified posturing. 'Or at least *I* have.'

'Indeed…I wouldn't dispute that.' Lukas gave a derisive laugh. 'I seem to remember we engaged in some *very* grown-up activity last time we met.'

Again she flushed, as if she found the memory of what they had done intensely shameful. As well she might.

'Well, that's not something that is going to be repeated, I can assure you. Despite your earlier threats.'

'Not threats, Calista. Think of it more as a promise.'

'You are such an arrogant piece of work, Lukas, you know that?' Emerald eyes flashed with fire. 'I promise you this: what happened between us will *never* happen again.'

'No? You're sure about that, are you?'

'Quite sure.'

'Then coming back to my villa for a couple of hours

won't hurt, will it? Unless you don't trust yourself, of course?'

'I trust myself, Lukas. It's *you* I don't trust.'

'Ah, yes, of course. I keep forgetting that *I'm* the villain of the piece here.'

'Yes, you are!' Calista immediately fired back at him.

He had to hand it to her—her acting skills had improved significantly over the years.

'In that case let me reassure you that nothing will happen between us unless you want it to.'

Was that true? It should be. His well-rehearsed plan had always been to trick her into wanting him, just the way she had him. But if she carried on looking at him the way she was now he wasn't sure he'd be able to hang on to his control.

He studied her from beneath lowered lashes, lazily, slowing himself down. Unless he was very much mistaken there was something else in that fiery look of hers. For all her prim deportment, her expression of outrage, her feisty comebacks, *something* simmered beneath the surface. Something that looked remarkably like sexual arousal. *Yes.* He would have her screaming his name with pleasure before the day was through. And then revenge would be his.

Swinging his leg over the bike, he turned the key in the ignition, gripping the handlebars and feeling the mechanical vibrations rumble through him.

'I'd hang on if I were you.' Speaking over his shoulder he twisted the throttle and the engine roared in reply. 'Let's let this old girl off the leash and see what she can do.'

And with a sudden jolt and a screech they were off.

Calista had no choice but to wrap her arms around Lukas's waist as they sped away from the cemetery, leaving its occupants in blissful peace as Lukas navigated the bike onto the coastal road that wound its way round the island. She leant her body into his, the wind whipping her hair back from her face, drying the breath in her throat as she clung on for dear life.

He was driving deliberately fast, she knew that, trying to frighten her, make her squeal. Well, she wasn't nine years old any more, and she certainly wasn't going to give him the satisfaction of behaving as if she was. In fact as soon as they got to the villa she would show him that she didn't intend to take any more of his bullying ways.

The stunning Greek scenery flashed past, the dramatic coastline with its towering cliffs and secluded coves stretching before them. Screwing up her eyes against the glare of the sun sparkling on the sea, Calista knew it wasn't fear she was feeling anyway. It was exhilaration. She felt alive, invigorated, realising how good it was to be back on Thalassa. More than that, realising how much she had missed it.

She adjusted her position slightly and felt Lukas's body respond, the broad width of his back heating against the crush of her breasts, the muscles of his waist shifting beneath the grip of her hands. A dangerous shudder of pleasure went through her. The island wasn't the only thing she had missed. And she was going to have to be very careful about that.

The twisty road took them past the turning for Villa Melina, *her* family villa, and continued east across the top of the island in the direction of Villa Helene—home to Lukas and his father, Stavros, now deceased.

It was a road Calista knew well—probably a distance of six miles or so. She had cycled it many times as a child, frequently seeking out the company of Lukas and his kindly father in preference to her own curmudgeonly father and boring half-brothers, with whom she'd had absolutely noth-

ing in common. But she'd never paid much attention to
the names of the two villas before—Melina, the name of
Aristotle's first wife and Helene, Lukas's mother. She
hadn't known either woman, but it was obvious now she
thought about it that the villas had been named after them.

What she *hadn't* known—what no one had known by
the look of it—was that Thalassa had actually belonged
to them. No one except Lukas, of course, who had used
that information to buy the entire island—presumably as
a way of getting back at her family. She had no idea what
had happened to the Lukas she had once known. What
had become of him...

Turning off the coastal road, Lukas bumped the bike
up the dirt track that lead to Villa Helene and pulled up in
front of the entrance in a spray of dry dust.

Quickly dismounting, he held out his hand to her, but
there was nothing gentlemanly about the gesture. It was
done with an aggressively urgent air. Shepherding her before him, he unlocked the front door—an action that surprised Calista in itself. *No one* bothered to lock their doors
on the island of Thalassa.

Inside, the villa was just as she remembered it. Even
the smell was familiar—somehow both comforting and
unsettling. She followed Lukas down the cool hallway
until they reached the large living room that ran the entire width of the villa. It was still and dark in there, until
Lukas strode over to the bi-fold doors, unlocked them and
pushed them wide open, undoing the shutters so that the
light streamed in.

Calista blinked. The stunning panoramic view of the
Aegean Sea appeared before them, but Calista's focus was
solely on the room she now saw so clearly. Or, more spe-
cifically, on the sofa in the room. The one she had so recklessly fallen onto with Lukas that evening, in a tangle of

fervid, scorching, pumping desire. The one where Effie had been conceived.

'Drink?' Lukas grabbed a couple of glasses from the sideboard and reached for a decanter of whisky.

'No, thank you.' Calista dragged her burning eyes away from the scene of their complete madness.

'Mind if I do?' Pouring himself a generous slug, he knocked it back in one gulp, then poured another.

Clearly he wasn't waiting for her consent.

Averting her eyes from the sheer brutal beauty of him, Calista quickly scanned the rest of the familiar room; the white walls displaying colourful local artwork, the rustic wooden furniture and the travertine marble flooring. She had always loved this villa. More so than her own family's, in fact, which Aristotle had massively extended over the years as a succession of different women had needed to be impressed and the urge to display his wealth had become ever more important.

Villa Helene was more modest, more traditionally Greek, with towering walls affording much needed shade and the exterior woodwork painted that particular Mediterranean blue. Not that it lacked any modern comforts, with its large stainless steel kitchen, a beautiful infinity pool that glistened invitingly through the open doors, five bedrooms, a gymnasium and a library. There was even a helipad where, out of the corner of her eye, Calista had noticed a gleaming helicopter, heating up in the sun as they had walked in. So *that* was how he had got here...

'So, what is this unfinished business?' She decided to take the lead rather than wait for Lukas like a fly in his web. She watched as he set down his glass, swallowing hard as he started towards where she stood in the middle of the room. 'What is it you want to talk about?'

'The talking can wait.' He stopped before her, towering

over her as he gazed down her flushed face. 'Right now I am more interested in action.'

With no warning he reached forward, sliding a hand around the back of her neck, lifting the weight of her hair for a second, before dropping it so that it rippled down her back. 'Right now I want you to kiss me the way you kissed me the last time we were here, *agapi mou*. Do you remember?'

Calista felt herself sway. His hand was branding the back of her neck…his hot, whisky-tinged breath was shooting sharp waves of longing throughout her body. Of course she remembered. She remembered every minuscule, heart-stopping, life-changing detail. She had been living it for the past five years.

It had been her eighteenth birthday party—a gloriously warm June evening. Calista had finished her exams and finally left the boarding school that she had disliked so much, and she'd been intending to soak up a few weeks of Greek sunshine before returning to the UK to start university.

She had been looking forward to the party—not so much to the actual event, the guest list for which had mostly comprised her father's business cronies and their families, rather than her friends, although that had partly been *her* decision. Aristotle had told her to invite as many people as she wanted, offering to pay for their flights from the UK and to put them up at the villa, 'So they can see the sort of wealth you come from.' But she hadn't had that many friends—she'd always been the outsider at school, a motherless red-haired creature with a Greek name—and she hadn't intended to scare off the couple of friends she *had* had by subjecting them to the full force of her father.

Because far from wanting to show off Aristotle's wealth she had been embarrassed by it—or, more precisely, embarrassed by Aristotle. Over the years he had become ever more boorish, more overbearing, and the large quantities of alcohol he'd consumed, along with the banquet-type meals that he demanded every night, had not helped his general health or his temper. It had seemed the larger he'd got, the more obnoxious he'd become.

But there had been one person Calista *had* wanted to see—Lukas. He had promised her that he would be there, and that alone had been enough to see her struggling to straighten her unruly tumble of red hair, carefully applying some lipstick and eyeliner and easing herself into a short emerald-green silk dress that had hugged her youthful curves in just the right places. Donning a pair of strappy gold sandals, complete with killer heels, she had been ready to go—or, more importantly, ready for Lukas.

Except he hadn't showed up.

The disappointment had been crushing. Calista's fragile hopes had been dashed every time another group of guests had appeared and he hadn't been amongst them. It had seemed as if more and more people had come, spilling out onto the terrace, laughing, drinking, dancing...

Finally Lukas's father Stavros had arrived, bursting onto the terrace in a highly agitated state, seeking out Aristotle and demanding that he go inside with him so that they could talk in private. Calista hadn't even had a chance to ask him where Lukas was.

In the end she had decided to take matters into her own hands. Suddenly she had no longer just wanted to *see* Lukas. Being with him had become an all-consuming compulsion, taking on a frightening urgency that would have seen her do almost anything to achieve her aim.

Which had turned out to be stealing a car. Or rather 'borrowing it' from Stavros, who had left the keys of his SUV in the ignition. Calista had only had a handful of driving lessons—she had certainly never passed her driving test—but such had been her determination to see Lukas that she hadn't been about to let a little thing like that stand in her way.

Somehow she had managed to negotiate the twisty coastal road without tumbling the car off the cliff and then, armed with a bottle of champagne and what she hoped was a winning smile, she had burst into Villa Helene and found Lukas anxiously pacing the floor.

He had looked astonished to see her. 'Callie! What on earth are you doing here?'

'I've come to find you, of course. It's my birthday, in case you've forgotten.'

'No, I've not forgotten. Happy Birthday.'

He'd said the requisite words but there had been none of his usual warmth, no kiss on the cheek or birthday hug.

Instead he had looked distractedly over her shoulder. 'Have you seen my father?'

'Yes, he's at my birthday party. Which is where *you* should be. You promised, Lukas.'

'Did he seem okay?'

'Yes—why?'

'It's just that he left here in a hell of a hurry and refused to tell me what was going on.'

'Well, he seemed fine to me.' It had only been a small lie. Calista could have had no idea of the consequences. 'He was chatting with Papa. He told me to come and get you.'

'He gave you the keys to his car?' Clearly puzzled, Lukas had obviously tried to work out what was going on. But Calista hadn't gone there to talk about Stavros. Right up until that moment she hadn't been entirely sure why she *was* there, but suddenly she had known with an all-consuming certainty.

She wanted Lukas to make love to her.

She still remembered his look of surprise as she had

moved towards him, the way he had finally smiled when she had flung her arms around his neck, the bottle of champagne still in her hand, clunking heavily against his back. He had laughed, telling her to stop being silly, that she must have had too much to drink, but when he had pulled back to look into her eyes he had seen the truth.

That she wasn't a child any more. That she knew what she was doing. *That she wanted him.*

Even so, he had resisted. But as she had shamelessly pressed her body up against his, chucking the bottle of champagne onto a chair so that she could thread her fingers through his dark curls to pull him closer, she had felt him weaken. And when she had finally claimed his lips, when the first split second of panic and insecurity on her part and complete shock on his had vanished, rapidly melting into desire and then into a burning passion that had seen them stumble backwards onto the sofa, there had been no turning back.

And now they were here again—in the exact same spot. And Calista was horrified to find that the pull of his attraction was just as strong…that she still wanted him every bit as much as she had that June night, even knowing what he had done, even having seen the man he had become.

For Lukas was no longer the warm, funny, laid-back guy she had originally fallen in love with. Along with the dark curls, the mischievous twinkle in his eyes had gone, to be replaced by a cruel stare and a grim determination that sent a shiver down her spine.

And yet still she wanted him.

Her whole body thrummed, all but begging to be his. He was too close—far too close—his head bent so that there was no escaping the searing intensity of his eyes.

'Of course I remember.' She dragged up the words from

somewhere, fighting to find some control. 'But, believe me, I won't be making the same mistake again.'

'So it was a *mistake*, was it? That's an interesting choice of word.'

'Yes…yes, it was.' Heat flared in her cheeks.

'Because, you see, *I* don't think it was a mistake at all.' He lowered his head until their lips were only a fraction apart. 'I think it was all very carefully planned.'

'What do you mean?' she whispered hoarsely against the seduction of his mouth.

'And now it's time for my plan to be put into place. My turn to seduce you.'

'No, Lukas, don't be ridiculous!' She tried to pull back but he held her firm.

'And you know what? I have to say I am *very* much looking forward to it.'

Suddenly his mouth was on hers, his hand pushing up through her hair, grasping the back of her head and holding her to him. She was powerless to escape. Even if she had wanted to. Even if she had somehow managed to harness the will-power that had scattered in all directions at the very first touch of his mouth.

His tongue had easily parted her lips and he continued his relentless assault, kissing her with a force driven by need, by hunger and by the dark greed that had clearly overtaken him. It was totally uncompromising, ruthless in its pressure, devastating in its delivery. And impossible to resist.

Because despite everything—despite the whole damned mess of their lives—Calista felt herself melt, dissolve. Molten heat slid through her, unerringly finding its way to her core, where it settled, pulsing hot and deep and hard and relentless. As Lukas continued his skilful assault she found herself leaning in to him, shuddering with pleasure when his hand lowered to the swell of her bottom, tantalisingly skimming over her buttocks before clenching tight in a blatant display of dominance and possession.

She moaned softly, but it was swallowed by Lukas's mouth as he changed the angle of his head so that he could plunder her mouth more deeply, take her completely. His hand flattened, searing into her, pressing her against the thick swell of him. If she had had any resistance before it vanished completely at the shockingly real evidence of his arousal and the deeply carnal response that ricocheted through her body.

He was moving them now, propelling her eager body backwards, one hand still holding her bottom, the other pressed into the small of her back so that he could steer her where he wanted her to go. Together they stumbled as one entwined unit, until Calista felt the wall behind her and realised she had nowhere else to go. Nowhere else she *wanted* to go. Nowhere except into the drugging dark oblivion of Lukas's power.

For a second their eyes met, and Calista felt her breath stall at the darkly savage look that shadowed his handsome face. But then his mouth was on hers again, and she was lost in the rush of sensual need and the burning hunger that shook her entire body.

She felt his hand move to her thigh, lifting her leg over his hip. She wrapped it around him to steady herself, to expose herself more to the pulsing throb of him. She heard his low growl of approval—or maybe it was victory…she didn't have the capacity to tell. His hand pushed up her skirt, his impatient fingers tugging aside the flimsy fabric of her panties so that he could feel her, slide against her, letting out a grunt, a mirthless sort of half-laugh, as he felt her buck against his touch, her shudder of pleasure immediately starting to build and grow.

Quickly pulling away, he released her from his grasp, letting her leg drop to the ground. Feeling in the pocket of his jacket, he took out a condom, ripping open the packet with his teeth at the same time as shrugging off the jacket and unbuttoning his trousers so they fell to the ground. His boxer shorts went next, before he rolled the condom onto himself with one deft movement.

Then he was all hers again, picking up her arms and moving them around his neck, so that when she clung on, holding him as tightly as he knew she would, he was able to lift her off her feet and wait for her legs to wrap around his waist, as he knew they would, her shoes clattering to the floor.

With his free hand he tugged her panties aside again. Only this time it wasn't his finger that nudged against her, it was the head of his arousal—hot and hard and silky and perfectly positioned to sink into her.

It felt like the most erotically glorious promise in the world.

And a second later that promise was delivered.

Suddenly he was inside her, smooth and hard and deep, filling her body and soul, and her every heightened emotion tuned in to nothing except this one incredible moment. Her mew of pleasure turned into a shriek of need, wordlessly commanding him not to stop, to keep going, faster, deeper, to take her to that place she had feared she would never find again.

Which was exactly what he did. Their bodies banged heedlessly against the wall behind them, until Calista could hang on no longer and, screaming out his name, found her shuddering, hollowing release. She felt Lukas stiffen, his body go into a rigid spasm, before he too gave in to the inevitable and roared his surrender into the tangle of her hair.

CHAPTER THREE

PUSHING HIMSELF AWAY from the wall with the palms of his hands, Lukas caged Calista between his locked arms. He wasn't going to give her any more space—not yet. Not while his breath was still heaving in his lungs, his heart hammering in his chest. He stared down at the top of her head, registering the way her slight figure shook, even though she had returned both feet to the floor, rearranging the skirt of her dress as if to pretend nothing had happened.

Well, it had. He had exacted his revenge.

All the hours he had spent plotting and scheming had finally come to fruition. Exactly as he had planned. Exactly on his terms. All done in the name of retribution.

At least that was what he had told himself. But, in truth, lying awake at night and reliving that fateful evening they had spent together had become something of an obsession. And conjuring up Calista's image had not been purely about revenge—far from it. It had become his guilty pleasure. The soft swell of her breasts, the silky touch of her pale skin, her fresh scent, her sweet breath… The memory had transported him from the dismal walls of his cell to a very different place indeed.

He had lost count of the number of times he had travelled the length of her body in his mind, leaving no part of her soft curves untouched by his attentions, and his own body had responded in the most carnal way as he'd listened to the dry snoring of his cellmate in the bunk above him and cursed to hell the situation he had found himself in.

But now he was free. Now he had achieved his goal.

So why wasn't he feeling it? Why wasn't he getting the satisfaction he so badly craved? Why wasn't it enough?

The sex itself had more than lived up to its promise. Just like the first time, there had been something about the connection between them—the chemistry, the fit—that had taken it beyond just sex to another level, as if they had been created solely for the gratification of each other. Not in an easy, comfortable way—not in the way of friends or gentle lovers—but with a wild, dramatic energy.

Like asteroids colliding in the vastness of space, their paths predetermined by a higher being, they had exploded against one another, set each other alight. And ultimately they had blown each other apart.

He could take her again—right here and now—he felt himself harden at the thought of it. In fact he could take her over and over again—keep her here in his villa until he had got her out of his system once and for all. After all, didn't she deserve it after the way she had treated him?

He was halfway to crazily convincing himself it was a good idea when he stopped, looking down at himself. A thirty-one-year-old man, standing there with his pants around his ankles. A man whose desire for the woman in front of him was dangerously close to being out of control.

Perhaps he needed to take a step back to examine his motives. And fast.

Dropping his arms, he wrenched off the condom and quickly disposed of it, then saw to his pants and trousers, buttoning the waistband as he turned away.

'Do you want that drink now?' He spoke over his shoulder, not wanting to look at Calista for fear of what he might see in her eyes. He needed another drink before he could do that.

'Lukas…?'

She whispered his name like a baffled question. The way she might speak to a person she had come across after a very long time—someone who had changed so irrevocably, so much for the worse, that she couldn't be sure it was him. Well, this was him now. And she had better get used to it.

With two glasses of whisky in his hand he turned, bracing himself for what he would see. But still she got to him, those green eyes of hers instantly finding their target, making the glasses clink together in his hand. It was a look of turmoil—of confusion and hurt and something Lukas refused to acknowledge, let alone try to analyse.

He had made her feel bad. But hadn't that been his intention? He refused to let his conscience prick him now.

Striding towards her, he handed her a glass, noticing the way her hand shook as she reached for it, immediately raising it to her lips to take a sip. The whisky seemed to restore her, and the flush of colour in her cheeks lessened from feverish red to a gentle pink.

'Yes, Calista?' He returned her question with the mocking sarcasm built up over five bitter years. He saw her flinch.

'Whatever has happened to you?'

'Let me see…' He pretended to consider. 'Lies, betrayal, deceit, the death of my father, and…oh, yes, four and a half years rotting in an Athens jail.'

He watched as she shook her head. 'I have no idea who you are any more, Lukas. Do you know that?'

'No? Well, maybe that makes two of us.' He took a deep slug of whisky. 'And yet *still* you let me push you up against a wall and have my way with you. Why is that, do you suppose?'

'I…I don't know.'

'*Still* you come apart at the very first touch of my hands, urging me on as if you can't get enough of me, screaming my name as you take what you so badly need from me.'

This felt better—dishing out the punishment he knew she deserved.

'And you are still dressed in black, your dear, departed father scarcely cold in his grave. It's hardly becoming, is it, Calista? It's hardly fitting behaviour for a grieving daughter.'

'No, it's not. It should never have happened. And, believe me, I regret it now.'

'Oh, I'm sure you do. But that doesn't mean it won't happen again.' He closed the space between them with one menacing step. 'Because you and I both know, Calista, that I can have you any time I want, any place I want.'

He watched the way his words inflicted pain, sawed away at her just the way he'd intended them to. But with the pain came adrenalin, swiftly followed by that glorious flash of temper.

'So *that's* what all this is about, is it?' She threw back her shoulders, her hair rippling down her back. 'You have lured me here to prove that you can have sex with me in some sort of pathetic attempt to get your own back?'

'Something like that.'

She opened her mouth, but for a second words failed her. 'You are a despicable, vile creature—do you know that? A lousy piece of—'

'Yeah, yeah.' He shut her down with a bored flick of his wrist. 'I'm sure I'm all that and more. You can call me all the names you want, if it makes you feel better, but it won't change the facts. And do you know what the worst of it is?'

He let his eyes drift lazily over her outraged face.

'You didn't even put up a fight. I had been looking forward to the challenge, the thrill of the chase, to working out how I was going to win you over. But in the end it was so easy it was almost pathetic.'

It was as if he'd punched her. The shock of his words made her fold at the stomach, reach for the back of a chair beside her to stop herself from falling. Raking in a breath, she pulled herself upright. Then, shooting him one last look of utter revulsion, she turned to go.

With lightning speed Lukas reached the doorway before her, easily barring her way. 'Not so fast.'

'I would like you to move, please.' Her voice was brittle with anger and hurt.

'Uh-uh. You will leave when *I* say so.'

'Is this part of your master plan?' She put her hands on her hips, as if to try and anchor herself. 'To hold me against my will? Keep me here as your prisoner so that you can prove just what a detestable macho bully you have become?'

'And supposing I did?' Lukas arrowed her a lethal look. 'You and I both know what would happen. You would be all over me, Calista. Oh, you might pretend to be outraged…put up a display of resistance in the name of decorum. But in truth I would only have to click my fingers and you would be mine. Writhing beneath me, on top of me, down on me, begging for my attentions and then screaming for more. Look how you behaved just now. It's pitiful, really. I should feel sorry for you.'

Slap.

The weight of Calista's palm connected with the side of his jaw with an impressive crack.

He had seen it coming. He could have stopped it. Spending time amongst some of Greece's most notorious criminals had honed his instincts, taught him to read the situation before it happened. Lukas had always had fast reactions—now they were razor-sharp. But for some reason he had let it happen. For some reason he had wanted to feel it—that burn, that most primitive connection—to show that he was alive. To show that he could get to her. And the sting from her palm *had* set his heart racing.

Calista Gianopoulous—the young woman he hadn't been able to get out of his mind, whose betrayal had consumed him so obsessively that it had become part of the fabric of who he was. Now he had her where he wanted her. Now her humiliation was in his grasp. And he could squeeze as tightly as he wished.

He studied her intently, standing there with her chin held high, her breasts heaving seductively beneath the demure black dress, pulling the fabric tight with every gasping, defiant breath. Her eyes flashed with a green so intense, so wild, it was as if she had been stripped of her sanity.

He should be feeling vindicated, triumphant. But he didn't feel either of those things. Instead he was simply consumed with the overwhelming need to possess her body again. His only conscious thought was how utterly magnificent she looked.

He let a second of silence pass and tried to pull himself together, waiting to see what she would do next—almost willing her to strike him again so that this time he could intercept it, grasp her wrist and feel that physical connection between them again, see where it might lead. But instead she let her hand drop by her side, lowering the tawny sweep of her lashes. The pink pout of her lower lip, he noticed, had started to quiver.

'Resorting to violence, Calista?' He gave a derisive laugh. 'I would never have thought it of you.'

'It's no more than you deserve.'

'No? Maybe not. But if we're dishing out home truths, perhaps it's time that you took a look at yourself.'

Her head came up and there was fear in her eyes. 'What do you mean by that?'

'Oh, come on, Calista, let's drop the pretence. You see, I *know*.'

'Kn…know what?'

If Lukas had had any doubt about her part in his downfall it was well and truly dispelled now. Guilt was written all over her pretty face—not just written, but spelled out in big, bold capitals. She positively shook with it, her hands trembling as she raised them to her mouth, her legs looking as if they wouldn't be able to hold her up much longer.

He let out a grim laugh. 'Do you *really* need me to spell it out for you?'

'Lukas…I…'

'Because I will if you want.'

Taking a couple of steps away he then turned, his eyes pinning her to the spot, as if they were in a courtroom.

'Let me take you back to the night of your eighteenth birthday party. The night my father discovered that the police had boarded one of the ships and found it was loaded with arms. While Stavros was over at Villa Melina, trying to find out what the hell was going on, *your* father dispatched you to "entertain" me. And you did a magnificent job—I have to say that.'

He paused, his whole body brittle with seething contempt.

'Aristotle must have been very proud of you. While my father was suffering a heart attack you were in full seduction mode…while people were mobilising a helicopter to get him to the mainland we were in the throes of passion. And by the time they got him there it was too late.'

'*No*, Lukas.' Calista bit down hard on her quivering lip. 'It wasn't like that.'

'Oh, but it *was*, Calista. It was *exactly* like that. Before my father had the chance to confront yours, to defend himself, he conveniently had a heart attack and died. I bet Aristotle couldn't believe his luck.'

'That's…that's an awful thing to say.'

'It was an *awful* deed.' He mocked her use of the totally inadequate word. 'Not only was he profiting from his vile trade in arms, but when he got caught out he set up *my* father to take the blame. He betrayed his oldest friend. It doesn't get much more *awful* than that.'

'No! I don't believe you!' Calista let out a cry of anguish. 'My father had nothing to do with the arms-smuggling. And he would never have betrayed Stavros.'

'And I don't suppose he was responsible for getting me arrested and banged up in jail for four and a half years either?' Lukas gave a harsh laugh.

'No! I don't believe that either. How would that even have been possible?'

'Remarkably easily, as it turned out. It seems your father had villainous friends in remarkably high places. Or should I say *low* places?'

'No! You're making all this up.'

'Don't insult my intelligence by pretending you didn't know.' Lukas ran a hand over his close-cropped hair. 'No doubt you have tried to dress it up over the years—reshape your traitorous actions to ease your conscience, help you sleep at night. But the fact is you betrayed me in the same way your father betrayed *my* father. You traded your innocence for my guilt. I just hope it was a price worth paying.'

Calista turned away from him, stumbling across the room towards the open doors of the terrace. She clearly couldn't face him—well, that was hardly surprising. He stared at her silhouette, dark against the azure blue of the sea meeting the sky. He could feel the thrum of his pulse in his ears, a tightness in his chest that had yet to be released.

He wasn't done with her yet.

'So you see, *agape mou*, this is my little payback. My turn to let you see what it's like to be used. To be taken advantage of. To have your body violated by someone for their own gain.'

Closing the gap between them, he placed a hand on her shoulder, turning her so that she couldn't avoid the hard, dark glitter of his eyes.

'So tell me, Calista. How does it feel?'

Calista tried to swallow past the shock that was blocking her throat. Her heart was thudding wildly in her chest, her palm still stinging from where it had connected with Lukas's jaw. But her brain had gone into slow motion, struggling to process all the terrible things he had said.

Her father had been responsible for the arms-smuggling scandal? He had somehow pinned the blame on Stavros, and then Lukas? And Lukas thought she was part of the conspiracy plot.

It was all too much. She suddenly felt dizzy, clammy. But at least he didn't know about Effie...

Dragging in a breath, Calista made herself focus on the one small speck of relief amid these horrendous revelations.

For one heart-stopping moment she had thought she'd got it wrong—that he had known all along. She had been on the brink of blurting it out—getting in first before he could use it as some sort of weapon against her. Because that was undoubtedly what he wanted to do—hurt her. But hadn't he already done that a thousand times without even trying?

But, no, it wasn't Effie he was talking about. It was all about *her*—how she had betrayed him, used him, somehow been responsible for his downfall. It seemed he had brought her here solely to humiliate her. Setting a trap to lure her into having sex with him as some sort of payback. And she had leapt right in.

The shame of it shuddered through her, right down to her core, which still throbbed where he had been, where she had let him possess her. No, not *let* him—encouraged him, urged, pleaded, begged… She could hear her breathless entreaties as he had taken her, devoured her, driving into her with a raging desire that had consumed them both, obliterating all reason.

Now her reckless words scraped across her skin like sandpaper. It was bad enough that she had fallen so wantonly into his arms. But for it all to have been a trap…? A wave of sickness engulfed her.

She ran a shaky hand over her forehead, pushing back the hair that was sticking to her forehead. She had to get away from here—back to Villa Melina, where she had left her overnight bag, and then across to the mainland so she could catch a flight back to the UK.

She stepped out onto the terrace, squinting against the light, not knowing whether Lukas would try and stop her, no longer having any idea what he was capable of. She could feel his cruel eyes boring into her, following her every movement.

'Nothing to say, Calista?' he called mockingly after her.

'Only that I'm leaving.' She hurled the words over her shoulder.

'No grovelling apology, then? No promises that you will somehow make it up to me?'

'*I* have nothing to apologise for.' She turned on her heel, determined to fire one last parting shot. '*You* are the one who needs to take responsibility for what you did.'

'Have you not understood a word I said?' He was right behind her now, his dark shadow engulfing her. 'Or are the lies so deeply ingrained that you have started to believe them yourself? I had nothing to do with the arms-smuggling. My father had nothing to do with the arms-smuggling. The only person responsible for the whole deadly disgrace was your father—Aristotle Gianopoulous.'

'No!' Calista spun around, focussing on channelling her outrage rather than having to face the awful prospect of letting herself believe it. Because there *was* that niggle of doubt…that worm of suspicion crawling up her spine.

'*Yes*, Calista.'

'But the court case…' Her voice began to crack. 'Stavros was proved to be guilty… You were proved to be implicated.'

'I've told you—it was all a set-up. A couple of corrupt lawyers, someone high up in the police department, a good forger and a few fake witnesses. You'd be amazed what money can buy if you offer enough of it. And at the time Aristotle was positively awash with it—his hands stained red with the blood money that had passed through them. He'd never get away with it now, of course.' He paused for effect. 'Now I too know the right people, and I am fully conversant with the way these things work. But at the time I was naïve enough to think that justice would prevail.'

Calista covered her face with her hands. She desperately didn't want it to be true, desperately wanted to be able to defend her father. But something about the steady look in Lukas's eyes, the flat, leaden tone of his voice, made it impossible not to believe him.

Suddenly the truth of it struck her like a blow to the chest.

'A pretty performance.' Like a big cat stalking its prey, Lukas held himself very still, as if ready to strike with the killer pounce. 'Are you trying to tell me you didn't know?'

'No, Lukas, I didn't know.' Her voice was barely more than a whisper from behind her hands.

'Sadly the evidence doesn't support your claim.' He inched closer. 'What brought you to Villa Helene that night, if not orders to keep me out of the way?'

'I wanted to see you—that's all.' She let her hands fall from her face, looking down at her feet to avoid Lukas's punishing stare.

'Hmm… I'm afraid you're going to have to do better than that. Much better. Because you were a girl on a mission that night, dressed to kill, and I was your unwitting prey. That whole seduction routine was totally out of character. Why exactly *was* that, Calista, unless you were following your father's orders?'

'I'm telling you—my father knew nothing about it. It was my birthday, and I wanted to spend it with you.'

'But *why*, Calista?'

A beat of silence passed before Calista dragged in a breath. She might as well say it. What did it matter any more? What did *any* of it matter?

'Because I was in love with you, of course.' She uttered the words with a quiet, despondent clarity. 'I'd been in love with you ever since I turned thirteen—before that, even.'

Reaching for her chin, Lukas tipped up her face so that he could see into her eyes, searching for the truth. 'But you were just a kid.'

'And that's exactly what I was trying to do.' She blinked against his stare. 'Prove that I wasn't a kid any more.'

She saw his jaw clench as he assimilated this information, his brows lowering into a considering scowl.

'And you expect me to *believe* that?' When he finally spoke his voice was as dark as the night. 'You expect me to believe that it is pure coincidence that you offered yourself to me at the exact same time as my father was confronting Aristotle? In an exchange so heated, so monumental, that the stress of it took my father's life?'

'Do you know what, Lukas?' Calista let out a jagged breath. 'I really don't care what you believe.'

All she could think about was getting away while her legs still had the ability to carry her. Somehow she had to process the shock of her father's guilt, but she couldn't do that here—not on top of the shame of what had just happened with Lukas, not with him standing over her like this, all dark, menacing force.

Turning away, she set off across the terrace, intending to go around the side of the villa and make her way up to the road so she could find her way back to Villa Melina. If she was lucky she might come across Petros in his battered old car. If not she would walk. Anything would be better than staying here to be verbally abused by Lukas.

But she had taken no more than a couple of steps before Lukas had headed her off, blocking her way with the powerful wall of his honed physique.

'Not so fast.' His hair shone blue-black in the sunshine, sharp shadows highlighting the stark angles of his cheeks and jaw. 'I'm not done with you yet.'

'Well, I'm done with *you*. Get out of my way.'

'You didn't really think I would fall for that pathetic *"but I loved you, Lukas"* routine, did you?'

Calista flinched, her body hollowed out by the cruelty of his words. '*Loved,* Lukas. Firmly in the past tense. Now I loathe your guts.'

'Ah, that's more like it. Now we're getting to the truth. And, for the record, I know exactly why you're so desperate to get away, to run back to the cosy little world you have created for yourself in England. *Guilt*, Calista. No matter what you say, how you try and wriggle out of it, your guilt is written all over your face.'

He was right, of course. Calista knew—the guilt he was talking about—she could feel it gripping the muscles of her face, clenching her abdomen. But it wasn't the kind of guilt Lukas thought it was. It had nothing to do with luring him to have sex with her. It was about Effie, and the very real consequences of that fateful night. The fact that Lukas had a daughter he knew nothing about. She knew she would have to tell him. Just not here—not now. Right now she didn't have the strength.

'Perhaps you're mistaking the look on my face.' Still she fought to stand her ground. Because fighting for survival was what she did. What she had always done. 'It's not guilt I feel—it's shame.'

'Guilt, shame—call it whatever you like.' He moved closer, as if scenting a kill. 'Either way I am pleased to see you accepting responsibility for your actions.'

'Oh, I do. I can't ignore what just happened between us—much as I would like to. Because that's the shame I'm talking about, Lukas—the shame I feel for having let you touch me, violate me.'

'Ha!' He let out a cruel laugh. 'So I *violated* you, did I? Was that before or after you wrapped yourself around me, screaming my name in pleasure?'

'I *hate* you, Lukas!'

'Yeah, yeah—so you keep saying. Who are you trying to convince? Me or you? Because you should know that I don't give a damn.'

His eyes narrowed dangerously, glinting as some new idea occurred to him. Calista felt a fresh wave of alarm.

'Or is there another reason you're so desperate to get away, to pin the blame on me?' His voice was as sharp as the edge of a blade. 'Are you seeing someone? Is that it? Do you have a boyfriend, a lover?'

Suddenly the air stilled. The sun that was beating down on them was stiflingly hot. The force of his question felt like a hand around her throat.

'If I did it would be none of your business.' Calista twisted her head as if to dislodge the imaginary grasp, clinging on to her defiance like a shield to protect herself.

'Is *that* why you can't look me in the eye, Calista?' His voice became ever more urgent, more demanding. 'Is *that* why you're so desperate to apportion blame, to make me out to be the bad guy?'

'No. That has nothing to do with it.'

'Then tell me it's not true.'

Clasping hold of her wrist, Lukas held it in his grasp.

'Very well.' She indignantly tried to snatch back her hand, but Lukas held on. 'I do not have a lover, Lukas.'

'A boyfriend, then? A partner of some description?'

'No, none of those things. Now, kindly let me go.'

'What, then? Tell me. Because I can *see* it, Calista. I can see it in your eyes.'

Calista hesitated. She could feel the moment closing in on her, weighing down on her with leaden pressure. Suddenly there was no escape.

'I do not have a lover, Lukas.' She summoned the words from deep inside her, where the truth had lain dormant for so long. 'But I *do* have a child.'

'A child?' He dropped her arm as if it were made of molten metal. 'You have a *child*?'

'Yes.' She watched as the shock that had contorted his handsome features settled into a brutal grimace of stone. 'I have a four-and-a-half-year-old daughter.'

She paused, sucking in a breath as if it might be her last. *This was it.*

'And so, Lukas, do you.'

CHAPTER FOUR

Lukas stared at Calista in frozen, abject horror. No, it couldn't be true. He couldn't *possibly* have fathered a child.

But of course he could. They had had sex—unprotected sex, he recalled with blistering clarity. At the time he had been too astonished, too blown away by the turn of events, even to think about taking precautions. And since that evening he had never given it another thought.

He reined in the emotions that were ricocheting around his head like gunfire and forced himself to think logically. Calista was a scheming, manipulative piece of work—he already knew that. So what was to say she wasn't making this up? Perhaps there was no daughter, or if there were the child wasn't his?

But, much as he wanted to believe either of those versions as fact—any version that meant this was all a pack of lies—the contortion of Calista's face said it all. She looked sick, visibly paling beneath her creamy white skin. She looked as if she wanted to stuff the reckless words back down her throat.

She looked horrified that she had just revealed a deeply hidden truth.

'Sit down.' He pulled out a metal chair, physically lowering her into it before she collapsed in front of him or toppled into the pool, which was only a few feet away.

'So, let me get this straight. You are telling me that I have fathered a child?'

'Yes.'

He saw her painful swallow.

'And you have only just seen fit to tell me about this?'

'You have been in prison, Lukas.'

'Don't you think I *know* that?' Fury roared in his voice…his hands clenched into fists. Calista flinched. 'But that was no reason not to tell me that I was a father.'

'I thought it best to wait…until you were released.'

'Did you, indeed?' Sarcasm ripped through his voice. 'Best for whom, exactly?'

Calista lowered her head.

'So who else knows? Your family? Aristotle? I'm sure he must have enjoyed being a doting grandfather to my child.'

'No, I didn't tell him. I've told no one.'

Lukas hoped this was true—for Calista's sake.

'So what's her name, this daughter of mine?'

'Effie.'

'Effie?' He snarled the name.

'Short for Euphemia.'

'And where is she now?'

'At home in England.'

'Does she know about me?'

He fired the questions at her as they came into his head, not caring in the least about the way they were making Calista wince, shrink into herself.

'I've told her that you live in a different country. Too far away to visit.'

'Well, we will just have to put that right, won't we?'

Raking a hand through his hair, Lukas let his eyes travel over the smooth turquoise water of the pool before swinging them back to Calista's lowered head. His decision was made.

'I want to see her. As soon as possible. I want my daughter brought over here right away—right now.'

'What?' She looked aghast.

'I will have the jet put on standby.' He checked his watch. 'She could be here by this evening.'

'This evening?' Calista gaped. 'You're not seriously expecting me to fly to the UK, pick up Effie and then fly back with her, just like that?'

'No.'

'Well, thank God for that.' Her shoulders dropped.

'*You* are going nowhere. I am keeping you here until I have seen for myself that my orders have been obeyed and the child has been safely delivered to me.'

'Don't be ridiculous!' she shrieked with alarm. 'Effie is four years old. You can't put her on a plane by herself.'

'My staff will take care of her.'

'No, she would be terrified! I won't allow it!'

'I'm not asking for your permission, Calista.' His voice roared around them. 'Your shameful deceit means that I have already missed four and a half years of my daughter's life. I don't intend to miss any more.'

'Well, think of Effie, then.' Real panic clawed at her throat. 'Please! She's never even been on a plane. She would be completely traumatised by having to travel on her own with a group of strangers. You don't know what she's like…how sensitive she is.'

'You are right.' He saw the flicker of relief on her face, savouring the moment before he twisted the knife still further. 'I *don't* know what she's like.' The look of relief vanished as she realised where he was going with this. 'And whose fault is that?'

She lowered her eyes, then suddenly sat up straight

as a thought occurred to her. 'Anyway, Effie can't travel abroad—she doesn't have a passport.'

'Is this another of your lies, Calista? Because if it is...'

'No, it's the truth.'

'Very well.' The synapses in his brain were firing wildly as they adjusted to every new piece of information. 'You and I will fly to England together. That way you can introduce me to my daughter personally.' He met Calista's horrified gaze full-on. 'I will tell my pilot to have the jet ready within the hour.'

Despite his best efforts, by the time they finally pulled up outside Calista's London home dawn was breaking on a new day. The journey had been frustratingly slow. Whisking Calista from Thalassa to the mainland by helicopter hadn't been a problem, but his private jet had had to undergo a series of safety checks before it had been fit to fly.

Apart from a brief period when it had been impounded by the police, before being found legally to belong to Lukas, it had been languishing for years in a hangar at Athens airport, with no one thinking to service it. Lukas had not taken this news well. Now he was out of prison things were going to change—*that* was for sure.

Pulling up outside Calista's house in the car he'd hired from the airport, he craned his neck to take a look. It seemed reasonable enough—a three-storey Victorian terrace on a quiet narrow street.

Beside him Calista was fumbling in her bag for her keys. She had barely spoken to him on the journey here, nor during their long wait at the airport in Athens, or the night flight to London. Not that he cared. He had needed the space to get his head around this astonishing development. To try and work out how to proceed.

Calista had eventually agreed to his suggestion to use

the bedroom on the plane, but by the look of her she hadn't had much sleep. Dark circles shadowed her eyes.

'We need to go in quietly. Effie will still be asleep. And Magda.'

Magda, he had managed to ascertain, was some friend of Calista's who shared the house and helped look after Effie. He would be checking *her* out too, making sure she was a suitable person to be around his daughter. Although it was probably a bit late for that. Bitterness had him clenching his fists.

Calista let them into a hallway that was cluttered with bicycles, a child's scooter and a pile of unwanted post.

'Follow me—we're on the top floor.'

'You don't own the whole house?'

'I don't *own* any of it, Lukas,' she hissed over her shoulder as she climbed the stairs. 'I rent the flat. And I can only afford to do that because I share the cost with Magda.'

Lukas remained silent, straining for the sound of imaginary violins. If she imagined he was going to feel sorry for her she had another thought coming. Besides, he was annoyingly distracted by the sight of her bottom as she climbed the stairs ahead of him. Firm and rounded, it moved seductively beneath the tight jeans that she had changed into when she had collected her stuff from Villa Melina.

'Here we are.'

Inserting the key in the lock, Calista pushed open the door and switched on the light in the narrow corridor. She led him into a kitchen. For a second they stood, staring at each other. Lukas felt too big—out of place in this small but tidy space.

'Cal?' A muffled voice came from down the corridor. 'Is that you?'

'Yes,' Calista answered in a hushed whisper, then turned to Lukas. 'I'm going to speak to Magda. Do you want to make yourself some coffee or something?'

She opened a cupboard and quickly took out a bag of ground coffee, thrusting it into his hands and pointing to the cafetière next to the kettle.

'Do it quietly.'

Lukas filled the kettle, looking out over the London rooftops at the pigeons as he waited for it to boil. Twenty-four hours ago there had been no way he would have expected to find himself here.

'Hello.'

A small but very clear voice had him spinning his head around. A young girl with tousled dark curls and sleepy green eyes was standing in the doorway staring at him.

His daughter.

'Who are you?' She looked at him curiously.

'Lukas. Lukas Kalanos.' Lukas stepped forward with his hand outstretched, then dropped it again, feeling inordinately foolish.

'I'm Effie.'

'Um…yes, I know.'

'That is actually short for Euphemia.' Deciding that this man was clearly no match for her social skills, Effie took the initiative. 'I'm four and a half. How old are you?'

'I'm…er…thirty-one.'

Effie stared at him, as if considering such a great age. 'Mummy is twenty-three and Magda is twenty-three too. But Magda is older than Mummy because her birthday comes first.'

'Right. Um…do you want to go and get your mummy?'

'I can't do that, silly. Mummy has gone to Greece to say goodbye to my grandpa. I've never met him. He's dead. D'you want some juice?'

Dragging over a chair, she climbed up to open the fridge door. She was peering inside when Calista reappeared.

'Effie?'

'*Mummy!*' Slamming the fridge door closed, she launched herself at her mother, winding her skinny legs around Calista's waist and hugging her tight. 'You're back! I've missed you *so* much!'

'I've missed you too, my darling.'

'I have actually been brave, though. You can ask Magda.'

'I'm sure you have.'

Kissing the top of her head, Calista extricated herself from the arms and legs and set her down on the floor, holding on to her hand very tightly.

'I see you've met Lukas.'

'Yes. He's thirty-one.'

'Yes.' Calista shot him a glance. 'I expect you're wondering what he's doing here.'

'Maybe he's lost?' Effie offered helpfully.

'No, Effie, he's not lost. He's come here to meet you.'

'Oh!' Effie looked at him with renewed interest.

'The thing is, Effie…we have something to tell you. Why don't you come here and sit on my lap?'

Scraping back a chair, Calista sat down, bringing Effie with her. Lukas was struck by how close they were—not just physically, although with Effie's arm hooked around her mother's neck and her little pyjama-clad body pressed right up against her a whisper couldn't have got between them—but emotionally. They seemed bonded together, like a single unit.

Under different circumstances it would have been a delight to behold. Now it just made Lukas feel even more of an outsider. Even more incensed by the situation.

'The reason Lukas has come here is because we want to tell you...'

Effie's big green eyes looked from one to the other.

'The thing is... Well, the fact is, what we have to tell you is...'

'I am your father, Euphemia.'

Lukas's voice boomed around the small room, sounding far louder, far more aggressive than he had meant it to. He watched Effie's eyes widen with astonishment before Calista pulled her close, her own eyes blazing with anger.

'*Lukas!*'

'What?' Pushing himself away from the worktop, he drew himself up to his full height. 'The child needs to know.'

In his determination to take control of the situation, not to be painted as the bad guy, it seemed he had managed to do just that. With Effie hugged against her chest Calista started to rock slightly, as if trying and take away the pain. But Effie was struggling to be freed and, finally extricating herself, she stared at him, tucking her hair behind her ear in a gesture that so mimicked Calista it took his breath away.

'Is he telling the truth, Mummy?' Clearly she didn't trust him any more than her mother did.

'Yes—yes, he is, darling. I wish we had broken it to you a little more gently, but Lukas *is* your daddy.'

Sitting up straighter now, Effie reached for the comfort of Calista's hair, twiddling a curl between her fingers. 'Will he be coming to live here with us and Magda?'

'*No!*' Calista and Lukas chorused together.

'Lukas lives in Greece—where I have just been.'

'With my dead grandpa?'

'Well, sort of...'

'Was he very sad that Grandpa died too?'

'Um…tell you what—why don't you run along and get some clothes on? Then we can all have breakfast together and we'll talk about everything. How about that?'

Effie had barely left the room before Calista rounded on Lukas, eyes blazing. 'What the *hell* do you think you were doing?' She snarled under her breath. 'We agreed we were going to break it to her gently and then you go and blurt it out without any warning.'

'*You* agreed. Besides, you were taking too long about it.'

'Too long! I'd barely had two minutes with her!'

'Well, it's done now. She seems fine with it.'

'And you'd *know*, would you?'

'I know she needs to be told the truth. You have deceived her for long enough.'

'It wasn't deceiving her—I was protecting her.'

'Don't give me that. The only person you were protecting was yourself. It's time the child learnt some decent values that don't involve a web of lies.'

'How *dare* you criticise the way I have raised my daughter?'

'*My* daughter too, Calista. Just remember that.'

'Here I am!'

Effie reappeared in the doorway. She was wearing a stripy tee shirt, some sort of skirt made from pink netting and red wellington boots.

'Well done, darling.' Calista turned to smile at her. 'What would you like for breakfast?'

'I've got a better idea.'

Suddenly Lukas was desperate to get out of the stifling atmosphere of this cramped flat.

'Why don't I take us all out for breakfast?'

'Ooh!' Effie's eyes shone with surprise. 'Can I have a doughnut?'

'You certainly can. As many doughnuts as you like.'

Effie looked from him to her mother and back again, not able to believe her luck. When Calista remained silent a huge smile spread across her face.

Lukas puffed out his chest. Round one to him and the doughnut. It might only be a small victory, but it felt good.

'Faster! Faster!'

Calista looked across the small park to where Lukas was pushing Effie on the roundabout. Her daughter had her head thrown back and her eyes closed, her dark curls streaming out behind her. To the casual observer they might look like any father and daughter, enjoying some time together in the sunshine, but Calista could see the hitch in Lukas's shoulders, the tightness in his jaw as he whirled the roundabout round with one strong hand, the other thrust deep into the pocket of trousers.

Breakfast had been taken at the outside seating area of a café in Hyde Park. Effie's choice, as it was close to a children's playground and the boating lake—two of her favourite things. Effie had valiantly fought her way through two and a half doughnuts and Lukas had watched in smug silence, presumably waiting for Calista to react—which she had refused to do.

She wasn't going to get involved in petty point-scoring. Not when there were so many much bigger issues at stake. And besides, if he carried on whizzing Effie round at that speed there was a good chance that nature would score the point for her—preferably all over his immaculate designer suit.

She took another sip of her third cup of coffee. This was so bizarre—it simply didn't feel real. The three of them, here in a London park, with Lukas knowing about Effie and Effie having finally met her father. This enormous guilty secret had been in the back of her mind for so long, gnawing away at her, that it felt like a living part of her.

She had always known that at some point she was going to have to tell them both the truth. It was one of the many things that could keep her awake on those nights when her troubles seemed to pile in and sleep refused to come.

Now it had happened. But as she gazed across at the two of them Calista could feel no sense of relief, no lifting of the burden she had carried for so long. Instead a dark thread of dread wound its way through her, pulling ever tighter as she studied the two of them together.

Lukas had changed so much from the funny, easy-going, generous young man she had fallen in love with. He was a different person now. Cold, calculating, ruthless. A man who would stop at nothing to get what he wanted.

The roundabout slowed to allow a young boy to get on, and Calista saw the boy's mother—or nanny, maybe—eyeing Lukas, moving closer to say something, giving a little laugh and tossing back her head.

She heard Effie's bossy little voice taking command of the situation as the boy scrambled on. 'You will have to hold tight. My daddy's a fast pusher.'

My daddy. Was it really possible that Effie had accepted Lukas just like that? And, if so, why did that only increase Calista's sense of deep unease?

A few minutes later Effie came running back towards her, her eyes shining, the little boy close behind her.

'Can I go on the slide with Noah, please?'

'Yes, that's fine. I'll watch from here.'

The two of them scampered off and Calista raised her eyes to see the woman with Noah looking at her with disappointment. They smiled politely at one another as Lukas came to sit beside her and the woman turned to follow the children.

'More coffee?' Lukas looked round to call the waitress over.

'No, thanks. In fact we should probably be thinking about leaving.'

'Have plans for the day, do you?' He smiled at the waitress as she took his order for another espresso, making her blush prettily. But his words were weighted with sarcasm.

'And what if I do?' Calista leapt to the challenge. 'Effie and I *do* have a life, you know. A good one, in fact. I have made sure of that. I have done everything in my power to ensure that she is happy and secure, that she wants for nothing.'

'Apart from a father, of course.' Lukas stirred sugar into his coffee and raised the cup to his lips.

Calista scowled.

'Luckily I am in a position to be able to rectify that now.'

'Well, that's as may be.' Calista pursed her lips. 'But don't start thinking you can come storming in and take over our lives. Effie is settled—happy. The last thing she needs is a lot of disruption.'

Slowly replacing his cup on the saucer, Lukas raised heavy-lidded eyes. 'The sooner you start to realise who calls the shots around here, the better it will be for all of us.'

'*I* call the shots.' She could feel a flush creeping up her neck—indignation mixed with righteousness and something horribly like panic. 'Where Effie is concerned, *I* make the decisions.'

'Uh-uh. Not any more, *thespinis mou*.'

With her heart thumping painfully in her chest, Calista turned to see Effie waving madly at them from the top of the slide. She waved back and then Effie pointed at Lukas.

'She wants you to wave.' She forced the words through gritted teeth.

Lukas raised a hand and a purposeful Effie launched herself down the slide.

'So what is it, this life you are so determined to protect?' Lukas's all-seeing gaze swung back in her direction.

'I've told you—it's just a normal life, me and Effie.'

'Tell me about it. Do you work? Does Effie go to school?'

'Effie has just finished pre-school. And I'm about to graduate, as a matter of fact.'

'Graduate in what subject?'

'I've been training to be a nurse for the past three years.'

'A *nurse*?' Clearly this had taken him by surprise.

'Yes.' On safer ground now, Calista pushed back her shoulders. She was proud of her achievement. 'It's been hard, trying to fit it around Effie, but luckily I met Magda. She's on the same course as me and she's been such a huge help. I couldn't have done it without her.'

'So you work where? In a hospital?'

'Not yet. I have to wait for my certificate to come through before I can apply for jobs. I'm going to try and co-ordinate it so that I start work in September, when Effie begins full-time school.'

This information was met with narrowed eyes, absorbed, processed and filed away.

'And Greece? Thalassa? You say Effie has never even been there?'

'No.'

'Why *is* that?'

'Because there has been no need. Greece is no longer a part of my life. I would never have gone back myself if it hadn't been for my father's funeral.'

'And yet you gave our daughter a Greek name?'

'Well, yes.' Calista wasn't sure herself why she had done that. Somehow it had just felt right. 'But that's only because it's a pretty name.'

'Nonsense. You are half-Greek… Euphemia is three-quarters Greek. You both have Greek blood running through your veins, pumping in your heart—it makes you who you are. Do you *really* believe you can dismiss it as easily as that?'

'Well, no, but—'

'Greece will always be a part of your life, whether you want it to be or not. And it will certainly be a part of Effie's. *I* intend to see to that.'

A chilling calm settled over his handsome features, pulling the skin taut against his cheekbones, holding his handsome head high.

A trickle of dread seeped into Calista's veins. 'What do you mean by that?'

'I mean that I have no intention of missing any more of my daughter's life. I am going to take Effie back to Thalassa with me.'

'No! No, Lukas, you *can't*…'

'Yes, Calista, I can. Either she comes on her own or you accompany her. The choice is yours. But either way my daughter *will* return to Thalassa with me.'

CHAPTER FIVE

AS THE HELICOPTER blades whirled to a stop Calista watched Lukas flick off the controls and unbuckle his seatbelt. Less than twenty-four hours had passed and they were back at Villa Helene, just as he had decreed.

He had won.

There was no way she would have let Effie travel to Thalassa without her—the idea was unthinkable. So instead she had tried to reason with him, suggesting they paid a visit at a later date, or that perhaps Lukas could stay in London for a while and get to know his daughter slowly. But Lukas had had none of it. Even Calista's trump card—that Effie didn't have a passport—had been swept aside, and a visit to the passport office had been arranged and completed with scary efficiency.

So there had been nothing for it. Calista had had to agree.

She looked down at Effie, who was sound asleep in her arms. The journey to Thalassa was a long and tiring one when you were only four, and Effie's huge excitement had finally given way to sleep on the final leg of their journey. She had been nestling into her mother's lap and closing her eyes before the helicopter had even left the mainland.

Now Lukas turned to face them, his expression closed, businesslike.

'I have instructed Petros and Dorcas to make the villa

ready for us. I imagine Effie will want to be put straight to bed?'

Calista nodded. 'Yes, she's exhausted.'

Petros and Dorcas. They were working for Lukas now? How had that happened? And what on earth would they make of the fact that she and Lukas had a child together? A child that she had failed to mention when she had been reunited with them on the day of her father's funeral.

Calista had known this lovely couple for ever, Dorcas had served as a surrogate mother for her during the long hot summers on the island, doing a much better job than her own mother had when she was alive and providing a much-needed pair of loving arms after Diana had died.

They had been the only constant members of staff at Villa Melina. Aristotle's irascible nature had meant that over the years employees would come and go with depressing regularity. And latterly it had been just them, his reduced circumstances meaning that Aristotle hadn't been able to afford any more staff even if he had managed to find any. It occurred to Calista that he probably hadn't even been paying them.

But Thalassa was their home—they had moved here at the same time as Aristotle and Stavros. Calista had worried what would happen to them now that Lukas owned Villa Melina, the island…everything. She wouldn't have been surprised to find he had sacked them on the spot, banished them from Thalassa. He was certainly ruthless enough. But it seemed that not only were they still here on the island, they were working for their former enemy.

She extricated herself from the seatbelt that was wrapped around her and Effie, trying not to wake Effie up as Lukas opened the helicopter door on their side.

'Here—hand her down to me.'

Strong arms reached out to take Effie from her, and reluctantly Calista passed her daughter over before clambering down herself. She noticed the trusting way Effie clung onto her father, nuzzling into him in her sleep as he strode purposefully towards the illuminated villa.

The front door opened and there was Dorcas, silhouetted against the light, her hands clasped to her chest at the sight of Lukas with Effie in his arms.

'Come in, come in—you must all be so tired after your long journey.'

'*Kalispera*, Dorcas.' Calista felt decidedly awkward, embarrassed to be turning up like this with a child no one had known about—not even Aristotle, Effie's grandfather.

But as Dorcas flung her arms around her in the warmest of hugs she felt her anxiety evaporate.

'You are a *bad* girl.' Speaking in English, Dorcas repeatedly kissed her cheeks, clearly delighted. 'You never tell me you have a beautiful daughter. And you and Lukas! Whoever would have thought such a thing?'

Ushering them into the villa, she fussed about, issuing instructions to her husband, who was shaking hands with Lukas, peering curiously at the sleeping bundle in his arms. But when Petros turned to Calista she could see that he too had a broad grin on his face.

'We have made one bedroom into a nursery for little Effie. Petros has painted the walls pink for her—haven't you, Petros?—so that she will love it.'

Petros nodded proudly. But Calista felt an increasing unease. *A nursery?* This was all starting to sound alarmingly permanent.

'Well, thank you, Petros.' Squashing down her fear, Calista reached to take Effie from Lukas's arms. 'If you show me which room it is, I'll put her straight to bed.'

'Of course. Follow me.'

Bustling ahead, Dorcas led the way, opening the door

into a room that stopped Calista in her tracks. It had been transformed from what she remembered as a relatively spartan guest room into a pretty nursery, with white-painted furniture, pink and white striped curtains, a child-sized bed, even pictures on the walls of fairies and Disney princesses.

'You like it?' Dorcas whispered expectantly.

'It's lovely, Dorcas. But how did you get it all done so quickly?'

'Lukas say there is no time to waste. It must be done by the time you arrive. So Petros engage a small team of decorators from the mainland. Lukas want everything to be perfect for his daughter.'

Did he indeed?

Her unease was rapidly turning into something more like alarm.

Together she and Dorcas undressed Effie and gently lowered her into the pristine bed, pulling the covers over her and tucking her beloved teddy in beside her. All the time Dorcas was exclaiming in hushed whispers, saying what a beautiful little girl she was, as pretty as her mummy but with her daddy's dark curls. Closing the shutters, Calista almost had to pull her out of the darkened room, leaving the door slightly ajar behind them.

'So are you working *here* now, Dorcas? You and Petros?' Calista was still having trouble figuring this out. She wanted to know what the arrangement was before they rejoined the men.

'Yes. Lukas say he would like us to work for him now.'

'And you are okay with that? I mean after everything that has happened?'

'More than okay, *agapite mou*. Petros and I, we have known Lukas for a very long time, ever since he was a baby. We never believed him to be guilty of such a crime.'

'Really?' Calista stared into the time worn face of kindly woman. 'Then my father... does that mean... did you have suspicions about him, about his involvement?'

'It is not our place to have suspicions, my dear. Now that the Lord has taken the judgement is in His hands.'

Calista swallowed the lump in her throat. 'So, are you living here now? At Villa Helene?'

'No—this is the wonderful thing. Lukas say we can stay at Villa Melina for as long as we want. For ever, even.' The relief was obvious in her voice. 'He say the place is ours.' She turned to look at Calista, suddenly upset. 'I am sorry, Calista—this is your home I talk about. I say to Lukas, *Are you sure you don't want to make Villa Melina your family home?* But he say no—that you will live here, in Villa Helene.'

Now the blood in her veins turned to ice. 'He said *what*, Dorcas? *Who* will live in Villa Helene?'

'All of you—you, Lukas, and dear little Effie, of course. Petros and I couldn't be happier for you. To have a family here on Thalassa again—not just any family, but a Kalanos and a Gianopoulous, joined together like this. Well, it is a dream come true, it really is. To think that Effie will be growing up...'

But Calista could no longer hear Dorcas over the roaring of blood in her ears. A wave of sickness was threatening to knock her legs from under her.

This wasn't just a visit for her and Effie—a few days' stay on Thalassa, even the couple of weeks that Calista had just about been prepared to agree to. Lukas intended that they should stay here *for ever*. No, not *they*—Effie. He had made it quite clear that Calista could do whatever she liked. That she was of no interest to him. It was Effie he wanted. He had as good as kidnapped her.

Well, they would see about that.

Marching back into the living room, Calista squared her shoulders, ready for a fight.

But Lukas met her fierce gaze with infuriating calm. 'Everything all right?'

'No.' Calista spat the word at him. 'Everything is most certainly *not* all right.'

Behind Lukas, Petros was laying the table in front of the window. He looked up with the cutlery in his hand. 'Excuse me? You do not like the room?'

'No—yes. Petros, it's not that. I *love* the room.'

'Your little girl? She no like it?'

'Effie is sound asleep. But I'm sure she will love it when she wakes in the morning.'

'That is good.' Petros went back to laying the table.

'I think what Calista is *trying* to say, Petros, is thank you very much—to you and Dorcas—for doing such a fantastic job in such a short time.'

All relaxed reasonableness, Lukas quirked a dark brow at Calista.

Calista could have hit him—could have cheerfully wiped that smug, supercilious smirk off his face with a hard slap. Except, of course, she had already tried that and it had achieved absolutely nothing. Apart from exposing her lack of control and somehow reinforcing *his* control.

'It was our pleasure, wasn't it, Petros?' Dorcas came bustling through from the kitchen with a casserole dish in her hands. 'Now, come and sit down, both of you. I'm sure you must be very hungry.'

Calista looked from Dorcas to Lukas and back again, suddenly panicky at the idea of being left alone with him. 'Are you and Petros not joining us?'

'Me and Petros? Goodness, no! Whatever are you thinking, Miss Calista?' Dorcas laughed at her. 'I make this especially for you and Lukas. Your first meal here together as a couple…a family.'

'Thank you, Dorcas. I'm sure it will be delicious.' Lukas interjected smoothly. 'Now, you and Petros must go—you have already done far too much for us. Calista and I will be fine from now on. Won't we, Calista?'

'Fine.' Calista spoke the word through clenched teeth. But the door had hardly closed behind them before she launched into her attack. 'Would you like to tell me what the *hell* is going on?'

Pulling the cork from a bottle of wine, Lukas glanced at her briefly before casually pouring two glasses and handing one to her.

'Going on…?' Now he was serving up the meal—dolloping moussaka onto two plates and placing one before her. 'I wasn't aware that anything was "going on". Please—do sit down.'

Calista thumped into her seat. 'Why do Dorcas and Petros seem to think we will all be living here, as a family? What have you said to them?'

He took a forkful of moussaka, chewing and then swallowing before deigning to reply. 'I suppose Dorcas may have got ahead of herself. She has a rather excitable nature.'

'I'll say she has. You need to put her straight, Lukas. Tell her that Effie and I are only here for a short holiday. That we're returning to the UK.'

'I was actually referring more to our situation—me and you. It would seem that Dorcas has got it into her head that we are a couple. An understandable mistake, I suppose, especially for an old romantic like her.'

'Well, yes—obviously she's got that wrong as well.'

'Aren't you going to eat anything?' Lukas waved at her plate with his fork. 'It's really very good. I can see now how your father got so fat, with Dorcas cooking for him.'

Sticks and stones. Calista refused to rise to the bait.

'So are you going to tell her or shall I? That we're not staying, I mean.'

'You can tell her what you like, Calista. You can *do* what you like. Neither thing is of any interest to me. But Effie will be staying here, with me. For as long as I say.'

'No!'

'Yes, Calista.'

'But that's not what we said. It was to be a short holiday—a fortnight at the most. You agreed.'

'Did I?' Lukas continued to eat his supper, totally unperturbed. 'Perhaps that was a small deception. And don't bother to look so surprised. You are hardly a stranger to deceit yourself.'

'That's not fair!'

'None of this is *fair*, Calista. Having my father die from a heart attack wasn't fair, being thrown into prison for four and a half years wasn't fair, and not being told I have a daughter wasn't fair. But now I intend to redress the balance. From now on things are going to be done *my* way. Starting with Effie staying here on Thalassa with me.'

'No! You can't take your grudge against me and my father out on Effie.'

'I have no intention of taking *anything* out on Effie. Quite the reverse. I look forward to building a relationship with her, being a part of her life.'

'But you can't just *keep* her here!'

'I think you will find that I can. Oh, we can do it the hard way, if you like—lawyers, courts, injunctions—but I would advise against it if I were you. Because I *will* win. I can assure you of that. I'm sure I don't need to remind you that we are on Greek soil and Effie is three-quarters Greek.'

'And *I'm* sure I don't need to remind *you* that you have been in prison for arms-smuggling!'

Calista regretted the words before they had left her mouth. The look of thunderous fury on Lukas's face curdled the contents of her stomach.

'No, Calista.' His voice was a low, mean drawl. 'You do *not* need to remind me. And, believe me, I intend to clear my name. But in the meantime I have money and I have contacts. To try and fight me would be very foolish indeed. I am confident the Greek authorities would look favourably on my custody application.'

'Custody application?' Calista thought she might pass out. 'You intend to fight for *custody* of Effie?'

'Maybe… I'm not sure yet.' Lukas picked up his glass and swilled the wine around. 'That all depends.'

'On what?' She could hear the panic in her voice, strangling her vocal cords.

'On you. On how you behave. If you persist in being difficult, obstructing me, fighting me every step of the way, then you will leave me no alternative.'

'So what do you expect me to do? Hand over my daughter to you? Agree to all your terms and conditions without question? Roll over and let you do whatever you want?'

'Well…' The air between them suddenly thickened like syrup. 'If you're offering…'

'I am not offering *anything*.'

'No?' A lazy smile curved his lips. 'That's a shame. Because if you were to roll over and let me do whatever I wanted, I guarantee you would enjoy it.'

'Stop this, Lukas.'

'As would I, of course. Because despite everything you've done, despite who you are, I find that I still want you.'

'Well, I don't want *you*.' She threw the words back at him far too fast, and with far too much passion. And they elicited totally the wrong response—a low, primal groan of amusement.

'No? Of course you don't.' His arrogant smirk belied his words.

Calista looked away, refusing to dignify his facetious comment by attempting to challenge it. Besides, there was a danger she would only dig herself a deeper hole.

'So, you see, how we proceed is up to you. You allow Effie to stay here, accept that she has just as much right to be with me as she does with you, and we can keep everything amicable. No court cases, no custody battles—at least for the time being. Just a civilised arrangement between the two of us.'

Calista bit down on her trembling lip. She felt anything *but* civilised. She felt like a wild, raging beast. One that would do anything to protect its young. But she also knew that to try and fight Lukas on this would be extremely dangerous. She had no doubt that he would carry out his threat to take her to court for custody of Effie. And that he would most likely win.

'It seems that I have no choice.' Her heart thumped heavily in her chest.

Lukas shrugged.

'But I'm not leaving Effie here on her own. If she stays, I stay too.'

'As you wish.'

'Very well.' She sucked in a breath. 'I will agree to Effie remaining here, to us both remaining here, at least for the time being. But this is not for ever, Lukas. Effie starts school in September. Obviously we need to be back in the UK by then.'

'I'm very glad that you have decided to see sense.'

Lukas's eyes slowly travelled over her heated face, down her throat and across her chest, lingering on the swell of her breasts beneath the pale blue tee shirt. Instantly Calista felt her nipples harden, and she folded her arms to cover them up. Lukas responded with the quirk of a dark eyebrow.

'And who knows?' he drawled idly. 'Maybe it doesn't have to be so bad. Maybe we can find some interesting ways to keep each other entertained.'

'I am here strictly for Effie. That's all. Do I make myself clear?'

'Crystal-clear. But, unfortunately for you, like crystal I can see right through you.' His lips twitched with a deadly smile. 'And do you know what I see? A woman fighting her sexual desires. A woman who already knows it's a losing battle because deep down she wants me. Much more that she will ever admit.'

'You are *wrong*, Lukas Kalanos. You are nothing but conceited, arrogant and delusional.'

'Am I, indeed?' Lukas put his head on one side, his eyes glittering as dark as the night. 'Well, it takes one to know one.'

Lukas watched his fiery companion through narrowed eyes. She might be fooling herself, he thought complacently, but she wasn't fooling him. Despite the hot-headed rant, her determination to take him to task, the abject denial that he meant anything to her, Calista's body had given her away. And what was more she knew it. The way those rounded breasts had hitched beneath the tight tee shirt, her nipples hardening at his provocative words, had infuriated her as much as it had delighted him.

Lukas had never had any trouble attracting women. The combination of his dark good looks and easy charm had made him a magnet for members of the female sex ever since he'd hit puberty. Even during his time in prison the few women who had worked there had been putty in his hands—the social workers, the prison librarian, the cooks.

It had been well known that the Kalanos charm bought special privileges, and rather than complain about it the wiser inmates had kept in with him in the hope of picking up the scraps.

But something about Calista's obvious arousal was special. Maybe it was because of the way she tried to deny it, or because it showed he had some power over her.

Or maybe it was just because it was her.

He had always known that she would never leave Effie alone with him. They came as a pair—that much was obvious. Telling Calista that he didn't care whether she stayed or not had been a bluff he'd been sure of winning. Because he *did* care. He was beginning to realise that he cared too much. He felt a creeping sort of awareness that she was somehow invading his thought processes, influencing his judgement.

It did nothing to improve his temper, and at the same time sent his libido soaring off the scale.

He picked up the wine bottle, gesturing towards Calista's glass but only refilling his own when she shook her head. His eyes travelled to the wall behind them—the scene of their crazed lovemaking session only a couple of days before. No, they hadn't made love—they had had sex. Fast, furious, frantic sex.

At the time he had been too riddled with lust to examine what he was doing, but afterwards he hadn't experienced any of the sense of satisfaction he had expected to feel. Instead he'd been left with a vague feeling of distaste.

Not for Calista, or for what they had done—never that. Far from regretting their coupling it had just made him want more…much more. Far from dulling the hunger that clawed inside him, it had turned it into a dangerously powerful craving. The distaste was for the way he had behaved. His motives, his twisted reasoning…

Lukas took a gulp of wine, searching his brain to try and find some justification for this unwanted attack of conscience. All those years without a woman in his bed was bound to have messed with his head. Especially when he considered the lifestyle he had enjoyed prior to walking into Ms Gianopoulous's trap.

As a young man in his twenties he had enjoyed himself, making the most of his looks, his wealth and his power. He'd loved woman, and women had loved him—as the string of beauties who had graced his bed would be able to testify. He fully intended to pick up where he left off... make up for lost time. But first he had to get this infuriating woman out of his system.

Plus there was the fact that he was now a father. Perhaps bedding a succession of women was no longer appropriate. Perhaps it was time to be more responsible. He certainly wouldn't want his daughter faced with a variety of different lovers over the breakfast table. Not that that had *ever* been his way. He had always preferred the anonymity of a hotel room—valued the freedom of being able to close the door and walk away. He'd believed in keeping his private life private.

Unlike Aristotle, of course.

Lukas looked across at Calista, who was pushing her food around her plate, her cheeks still flaming with resentment. Aristotle had had no qualms about parading his latest conquests around in front of his daughter—or anyone else, for that matter.

That was if you could call the succession of increasingly greedy and desperate women that he'd taken to his bed 'conquests'. The older he'd got, the more obese he'd become—and the more obvious it had been what those women were after. And it certainly hadn't been his body. Or his bonhomie or his grace.

He had never been faithful to any of his three wives. Each marriage had ended in misery or, in the case of Calista's mother, tragedy. And Calista had grown up with that. A different woman in residence every time she returned to Thalassa for the holidays…sometimes more than one. She had witnessed the terrible destruction Aristotle had wreaked on her own mother, ending in her death. And yet still she had been prepared to do his bidding—prepared to debase herself and betray Lukas. Still she had stood by Aristotle's grave with a single lily in her hand, the dutiful daughter to the end.

Frowning, Lukas put down his fork. None of it made any sense to him. Unless, of course, Calista was telling the truth about that fateful night. Unless it really *had* been pure coincidence that she had come to him—not to trap him but because she'd wanted him to make love to her.

No. He refused to be fooled. No doubt the old adage was true—blood was thicker than water. Look at how he felt about Effie. Three days ago he hadn't even known he had a daughter. Now she was already shaping his life, changing his future. There was certainly no way he would allow *her* to be treated the way Aristotle had treated Calista. No way would he let Effie be subjected to such cruel indignity. The very thought of emulating Aristotle Gianopoulous in any way turned his stomach.

Because little Effie had already won his heart.

With a stab of surprise Lukas realised there was nothing, absolutely nothing he wouldn't do for her—to protect her, to keep her safe. He intended to be a very permanent fixture in her life.

The question was, what the hell was he going to do about her mother?

CHAPTER SIX

'WAKE UP, SLEEPYHEAD.'

Calista opened her eyes to see her daughter clambering into bed beside her. She was clutching a half-eaten *koulouri* in her hand—a ring-shaped bread roll, covered in sesame seeds that were now being scattered liberally over the bedclothes.

'You need to get up.'

Calista drew Effie towards her, breathing in her gorgeous little girl smell.

'Good morning, my darling. Did you sleep well?'

'Yes.' Effie squirmed impatiently in her arms. 'But you need to hurry up. We've got a busy day.'

Calista propped herself up on one elbow, pushing the hair out of her eyes. Checking her watch, she was surprised to see how long she had slept—a deep, drugging sort of sleep that had left her brain feeling slow to catch up. But the harsh reality of where she was kicked in soon enough.

She had spent the night in the largest bedroom in the villa, Dorcas having obviously decided to allocate it to the happy couple, filling it with fresh flowers and scented candles. She had even scattered rose petals over the bed—something which had produced a sardonic smile from Lukas when he had opened the door and ushered her in, suggesting she might like to make this room her own before turning to disappear down the corridor. She could still see some of the crumpled petals caught in the bedding.

Now she was faced with the reality of what she had agreed to—staying here on Thalassa with Effie, at least for the foreseeable future. But what choice did she have? She had no money, no contacts. She didn't doubt that Lukas had plenty of both, and the memory of the smug, self-satisfied way he had informed her of that still managed to send her blood pressure skywards.

But then *everything* about Lukas Kalanos sent her blood pressure rocketing skywards. And not just her blood pressure either. Her common sense, her self-control, her temper and her sanity all seemed to cut loose from their moorings when she was around him—not to mention her libido. Just the sight of his lean, muscular body, the athletic way he moved, the tilt of his head or the quirk of his dark brow was enough to see her fighting to hang on to her composure, to counter the extraordinary effect he had on her.

'Come on, Mummy. We are going on my daddy's boat.'

Closing her eyes against an inward groan, Calista opened them again to see her daughter's excited face.

A day on Lukas's boat—that was all she needed. Sailing was Lukas's passion—something he had skilfully turned from an indulgent hobby to an extremely successful business by investing in a fleet of luxury yachts and renting them out. Most of his business was conducted from the mainland, but at any one time there had always been a few of his magnificent, sleek vessels anchored off the coast of Thalassa. As a youngster Calista had loved to watch them glittering in the sunshine, gently rocking on the azure sea.

She had loved to watch Lukas too, who had never been happier than when he was clambering barefoot over the deck of a boat or sailing into the wind, his dark curls blowing madly in the breeze and the spray of the sea on his face. She knew that he preferred sailing the smaller, more intimate yachts in favour of the floating gin palaces—remembered him telling her that it made him feel more at one with the sea, more alive.

'Quickly, Mummy. Get dressed!'

Taking in a deep breath, Calista pushed back the covers and swung her legs over the edge of the bed—but there she stopped. The image of Lukas, smiling and relaxed, his eyes dancing with the exhilaration of a day's hard sailing, had lodged in her mind and refused to be shifted. He had had such a zest for life back then—had been so spirited. So free.

And that freedom had been taken away from him.

She stretched her arms out to her sides to steady herself, bunching the sheets in her hands. For the first time she thought about what it must have been like for him—*really* thought. For Lukas, of all people, to have been deprived of the outside world, the sun and the sea, the rolling waves and the whistling wind. To lose his freedom for four and a half years…

It must have been torture for him—pure torture. Which would have been bad enough if he'd been guilty. But what if he *had* been wrongly convicted? What if all this time he had been innocent…?

Calista put her fist in her mouth, biting down on her knuckles. Ever since her world had exploded so dramatically she had been using Lukas's 'crime' as a shield to protect herself, to keep her strong. She couldn't help it that she had fallen in love with him. Fallen into a deeply painful, fathomless love that could never be cured. But Lukas was not the man she'd thought he was. He had been convicted of a heinous offence, as an accomplice in a shockingly immoral crime.

Finding out she was pregnant with his child might have

all but finished her—felled her on the spot—especially
as she had been so young, so alone. But it hadn't. She
had pulled through—more than pulled though. She had
done a great job of raising her daughter single-handedly,
as well as completing her nursing training and making
sure there was always enough money to keep them both
fed and clothed. Somehow she had drawn strength from
Lukas's disgrace. From the knowledge that she was on her
own. That she was totally responsible for both her own life
and her daughter's.

And during her darkest hours—those miserable lonely
nights when she had thought the dawn would never come—
she had forced herself to remember what Lukas had done,
the man he really was. Used his terrible crime as a prop
to keep her upright.

But now that prop had gone—had been kicked away
from under her. Now she was left sprawling on the floor
by the shockingly painful truth. *Lukas was innocent.* She
knew it in her heart—maybe she had always known it.

Which meant that her own father had been as guilty
as sin.

'Mummy!' Effie slipped her hand into hers, attempting
to tug her to her feet. 'Daddy is waiting for us.'

Heading to the bathroom, Calista felt as if her legs were
made of lead. She would have to talk to Lukas—face up
to the truth, no matter how painful it was. If nothing else,
she owed him that.

Shading her eyes from the glare of the sun, Calista watched
her daughter splashing about in the turquoise sea. Effie and
Lukas were some distance from the boat, but instinctively
Calista trusted Lukas to keep her safe. Effie couldn't yet
swim—it was one of the things Calista had been meaning to teach her, but the thought of London's municipal

swimming pools hadn't held much appeal. Now a couple of brightly coloured water wings were keeping her afloat as Lukas patiently explained to her how to kick her legs, holding her under the tummy and getting showered in the process.

'Well done—nearly there.' His voice carried clearly across the water. 'Now, see if you can swim across to me.'

Taking a few strokes away, he turned and waited for her to splash towards him, her little legs kicking wildly behind her.

'Yay, you did it!' Catching her up in his arms, he held her aloft to squeals of merriment, before safely tucking her beside him to swim back to the boat.

Calista quickly returned to her book.

'Did you see that, Mummy?'

The boat started to rock as first Effie and then Lukas climbed aboard.

'I was swimming all by myself.'

'That's brilliant, darling.' Calista made a show of closing her book and putting it down beside her, to prove that she was now in charge. She rose to her feet. 'Now, come on—let's get you dry.'

Moving in for a hug, Effie pressed her chilly wet body against Calista's sun-warmed skin, sending a rash of goosebumps skittering all over her. She felt Lukas's merciless gaze travelling over every bare inch of her. Concentrating on pulling the water wings off Effie's skinny arms, she took hold of her hand and made her way towards the cabin.

But Lukas was in the way.

'Excuse me.' She tried to squeeze past him but still he refused to move, meaning she had no alternative but to raise her eyes to the magnificence of his body, to take in all his masculine glory. Just as he had planned she would.

Wearing an extremely snug pair of black trunks that

left little to the imagination, he stood before her, the epitome of glorious manhood, tall and bronzed, with sculpted muscles in all the right places. Droplets of water glittered on his skin and in his tightly curled chest hair, running in rivulets down his long, shapely legs and pooling at his feet on the varnished wood of the deck.

Calista swallowed. She had already sneaked a look at him when he had taken a graceful dive into the sea, before swimming round to the steps at the back of the boat to help Effie into the water. That had been more than enough to get her pulse racing. This blatant display of rampant masculinity was in danger of sending it into overdrive.

Mustering what little will-power she had left, she stepped deliberately round him, chin in the air, and led Effie down into the relative cool of the cabin.

'Next time I'm going to do it without the water wings.' Teeth chattering, Effie let herself be towelled dry. 'Daddy says I'm a fast learner.'

'I'm sure you are.' Rubbing at the dark curls, Calista kissed her daughter lightly on the nose. 'But you don't have to call him Daddy, you know. Not if you don't want to…not if it seems too soon. It's quite all right to call him Lukas.

'That's okay, I like calling him Daddy. He says that the Greek children call their daddies Bampas. That's funny, isn't it?' She wrinkled her little nose happily. 'Is that what you called *your* daddy?'

No, Calista thought silently. She had never called Aristotle anything other than the formal word—Pateras. The more affectionate Bampas had seemed wrong when addressing the short-tempered, irascible, rather frightening figure that her father had been.

'And the word for yes is *nai*.' Effie was still chattering on as Calista tugged dry clothes onto her. 'That's funny too. Daddy said I must learn how to speak *all* the Greek words—then I can talk to anyone.'

'Well, we'll see.' Calista tried to disguise the tension in her voice. 'You won't need to speak Greek when we go back to London, will you?'

'S'pose not. I like it *here*, though.' Giving a yawn, Effie twisted a damp curl around her finger.

'Yes. Holidays are fun, aren't they?' Calista persisted. 'But going home will be good too. I bet Magda is missing us.'

'Hmm…' Effie nodded thoughtfully. 'P'raps she could come here too?'

'No, I don't think so darling. Now, d'you want to have a little nap?'

To her surprise Effie nodded and, lifting her arms, let Calista carry her through to one of the cabins, where she gently laid her down on the bed. Her eyes closed almost immediately.

Calista looked around her, tempted to stay down there rather than go back on deck and have to face Lukas again. But that would be cowardly—and she was not a coward. Reluctantly she climbed up into the sunshine.

Lukas had his back to her, squatting on the bow of the boat, doing something with some ropes.

Hearing her approach he turned. 'Effie okay?'

'Yes, she's fine. She's having a sleep. Must be all this fresh air.' She attempted a light-hearted laugh.

'A child can never have too much fresh air.'

Calista pursed her lips. So he was the expert now, was he? She watched with feigned indifference as he lithely rose to his feet and came towards her.

'Can I get you anything?' He bent to open the cool box that held the remains of their picnic. 'More food? A beer?'

'No, thanks.' She was already regretting the glass of

chilled white wine she had had earlier. What with that and the sun, her head was starting to swim a little. 'I think I'll just sit under the canopy here and read my book.'

'As you wish.'

Arranging herself on the comfortable cushions in the shade, Calista opened her novel. She heard the hiss of gas as Lukas took the cap off a bottle of beer, and raised her eyes to see him moving about with the bottle in one hand, checking on the winches of the rolled up sails, swinging under the beam to get to the back of the boat. The sea slapped gently on the sides. A seagull squawked overhead. She closed her eyes…

Lukas eased his tall frame onto the cushions beside Calista. She was sleeping peacefully, and a strand of red hair was caught on her slightly open lips, moving as she breathed. He let his eyes travel slowly over her body, lingering on the swell of her breasts under the small emerald-green triangles of her bikini top. Two strips of bare skin were just visible beneath, peeking out from where she had shifted and dislodged the fit of the bikini.

Lukas's throat moved. The temptation to run his finger over the exposed pale flesh was almost too much to resist. Or to run his tongue over it…then release the string ties around her neck and push the fabric away, so that his mouth could give her warm, full breasts the attention that they so blatantly deserved… He felt himself harden painfully beneath his trunks.

Tearing his eyes away, he looked out to sea to the hazy horizon way in the distance. He knew if he put his mind to it he could have pretty much any woman he wanted. So why was he torturing himself by lusting after this one? How had Calista got to him like this, so that his whole body thrummed for her…ached for her? Why was it that suddenly no other woman held the slightest interest for him?

He had been her first lover, of course. Could that explain this ludicrous obsession? He would never forget the moment they had both realised that there was no going back. That first exquisite moment of penetration when Calista had gasped for air, holding herself rigid as he had eased himself so carefully into her. The way she had clung to him, urging him in further, deeper, until she had taken all of him.

She had been so passionate, so aroused, so totally convincing. Over the years he had told himself that it must have been an act. But now… Now he wasn't so sure. Now when he looked into those remarkable green eyes of hers he saw lots of things—anger, hurt, fear, defiance. But not betrayal. And when he had laid bare Aristotle's guilt before her she had looked genuinely devastated. Broken.

Lukas raked a hand through his damp hair, narrowing his eyes as he watched the white sails of the boats in the distance. He wanted to move on, to stop agonising over the past and concentrate on the future. A future that would now most definitely involve his daughter.

Because Effie was the one truly miraculous thing to have come out of this mess. He still found it hard to believe that he had fathered a daughter. And one as undoubtedly special as Effie. He got a buzz every time he looked at her…every time he thought about her.

But there was something far less agreeable he was struggling to come to terms with. Something that had grown from an annoying niggle into a monster that refused to go away. He might have been Calista's first partner, but how many lovers had she had since? Five years had passed—ample time for her to have taken up with any number of suitors.

The very thought of her with another man—any man—boiled the blood in his veins, made his hands shake with impotent fury.

At least there didn't appear to be anyone on the scene at the moment. He'd had a quiet word with Effie, casually mentioning Mummy and her boyfriend in the same sentence, and had been mightily relieved when she had just looked at him in puzzlement.

That didn't mean there wasn't someone in the background, of course, but the way Calista had given herself to him on the day of the funeral—with such need, such greed, even, like a starving woman—suggested that there wasn't. Or if there had been he was now history. Or he damned soon would be. Because Calista was going to be his and his alone for as long as he deemed fit. To do with as he deemed fit.

Had he always intended this? Lukas wasn't sure. But the decision was made now. He wanted Calista. Not just once—clearly that had done nothing to slake his thirst—and not even for the occasional casual sex, albeit amazing. He wanted her in his bed every single night. And, more than that, he was going to make sure that she wanted *him*.

Hearing her stir, he turned back to look at her, watching as she moistened her lips with the tip of her tongue, moved back against the cushions. Leaning forward, he picked up the book that was resting on her stomach, the open pages sticking slightly to the suntan lotion on her skin. He had watched her applying it earlier on, rubbing it onto shoulders dusted with freckles, then her chest, down her arms and the flat of her stomach. He had been itching to take over, to smooth the lotion over her himself, to push aside the scraps of fabric and let his hot fingers slide across her breasts, her buttocks, to the places that were hidden from the sun…

But too late—or maybe just in time—she had finished. Snapping the cap of the bottle shut and shooting him a look of such haughty disdain it had made him smile despite himself.

Now she opened sleepy green eyes. He was close enough to see a split-second swirl of desire before alarm and then indignation took over.

'Lukas!' She scrabbled to push herself upright, sweeping her hair away from her face. 'You made me jump.'

'Guilty conscience?'

'No.' Immediately she was on the defensive. 'What are you doing, anyway? Why are you watching me?'

'Just admiring the view.'

'Well, don't.'

Calista didn't know which Lukas she found the more intimidating—the fiercely brutal and vengeful one she had been met with at her father's funeral, or the arrogantly sarcastic one who was deliberately letting his gaze rake over her now.

Neither of them represented the Lukas she had once known. The one she had fallen in love with. And yet she *had* caught a glimpse of that man. She had seen it in the way he was with Effie—so gentle, so patient. She had even seen it earlier on today, when he had been at the helm of the yacht, shooting her an unexpected smile as they had tacked fast into the wind, the pleasure of doing something he so clearly loved making him forget himself for a minute. Forget how much he hated her.

Calista felt her body begin to tingle beneath his scrutiny, the thrum of desire starting its traitorous beat. She needed to put a stop to it.

'Is there any water in the cool box?'

'Sure.'

Pushing himself to stand with one lithe movement, Lukas retrieved a bottle of mineral water and passed it to her. Calista took several deep gulps and looked down at herself. Even in the shade her skin was starting to turn pink—she burnt so easily it was ridiculous. She was glad that Effie wasn't going to have the same problem. She had inherited her father's colouring, albeit several shades lighter.

Feeling restored by the water, she started to get to her feet. 'I'm just going to check on Effie.'

'No need. I just did. She's still asleep.'

'Oh, right.' Calista sat back down.

There had been a cold inflexibility in Lukas's voice—as if he expected her to challenge him, or as if he was waiting for something. His eyes held hers for a couple of seconds before he stretched himself out on the cushions beside her, lying on his side with one arm under his head to prop him up.

He looked magnificent, even from the quick sideways glance that was all she would allow herself. She refused to give him the satisfaction of ogling that beautiful body, those tanned, honed muscles that screamed to be admired, to be touched. Because that was what he wanted. For some reason he seemed determined to taunt her with his perfect physique.

Calista pulled up her knees and hugged them to her chest. The more blatant his display, the more she was determined to cover herself up.

A couple of highly charged seconds ticked by, Lukas owned the silence by doing absolutely nothing. Calista drew in a breath. There was one sure way to counter the sexual tension that he was deliberately stoking between them. Much as she hated to fling herself into the pit of misery that had been caused by her father, she knew that she had to.

She cleared her throat. 'Lukas, I've been thinking.'

She shifted nervously on the sun lounger, forcing herself to meet his gaze. Lukas quirked a dark brow in response.

'What you were saying about my father…it's true, isn't it? He *was* responsible for the arms-smuggling.'

'Yes, Calista. It's true.' He stared at her, scanning her face with an intensity that stripped her bare—as if he could read her mind, see her more clearly than she could see herself.

'And Stavros, he had no part in it, did he?'

'None whatsoever.'

'And neither did you.'

With a very slight tilt of the head, his reply was given in the glittering blackness of his eyes.

An agonising second ticked by. The yacht rocked gently from the wake of a fishing boat heading out to sea. Calista wished that she was on it. That she could leap aboard and be chugged further and further away from this awful situation.

Instead she wrapped her arms around her knees more tightly, letting her hair fall over her face to cover her shame as she stared down at her painted toenails.

'I'm so sorry, Lukas.' It came out as barely more than a whisper.

'Sorry?' Lukas repeated the word, rolling it around his mouth as if it were made of stone. 'I hardly think "sorry" makes up for what happened.'

'Well, no, but…'

'Makes up for taking away my freedom, blackening my name, ruining my life.'

'No. I mean obviously nothing will make up for that.'

'For killing my father.'

That brought Calista's head up.

'That's not fair.' She lifted her hair from the nape of her

neck to try and cool herself down. 'Stavros had a weak heart—it said so in the autopsy report. He could have died at any time.'

'And yet he died after a furious row with Aristotle.'

'Even so…'

'Still defending him, Calista? That monster of a father of yours?'

'No—'

'Because if so I suggest you open your eyes and take a long, hard look at the man who sired you.'

'I don't want to. I don't need to.'

'Because if you did you would see exactly the sort of vile creature he was.'

'I know he did a terrible thing, Lukas.'

Close to tears, Calista covered her face with shaking hands. Admitting her father's guilt was excruciatingly painful but she knew she had to face up to it before she could move on. Face up to Lukas too, who shimmered quietly beside her like some sculpted bronze Greek god. But she wasn't responsible for Aristotle's crime. Despite what Lukas thought, *she* had done nothing wrong. She had to make him see that.

Taking a deep breath, she removed her hands from her face to see Lukas staring at her, his expression inscrutable. 'I swear to you, I had no idea what he was involved in. You *have* to believe me.'

'Okay.' There was a beat of silence before Lukas gave a small shrug. 'I believe you.'

'Good.' Calista felt her shoulders drop. 'Then you accept that I played no part in the conspiracy?'

'If you say so.'

'I do.' On a firmer footing now, Calista straightened up, pushing back her shoulders. This was the point when some sort of small apology from him might be called for.

Clearly that wasn't happening. 'Much as I regret what happened, I am not guilty of my father's crimes.'

'No.'

Lukas lifted the arm that was resting over his waist. For a moment Calista thought he was going to touch her, make some sort of conciliatory gesture, but instead he rubbed his hand around the back of his neck.

'But you are still guilty of betraying me.'

'No, I've told you—'

Lukas raised his hand to silence her.

'You accepted your father's version of events without question. You were prepared to believe that I was capable of such a heinous crime without even speaking to me. *That's* the betrayal I'm talking about.'

'I was wrong—I know that now.' She bit down on her lip. 'I'm so sorry I didn't trust you.'

'I don't want your wretched apologies!' Suddenly his voice was harsh, bitter. 'I don't give a damn what you think about me now.' He shifted the length of his body fractionally, his eyes boring into her. 'You still don't get it, do you?'

Calista stared back at him.

'Your father may have been responsible for getting me locked up, but in believing his lies you denied me the knowledge that I was a father. You stole from me the first four and a half years of Effie's life.' He shook his head in disgust. 'And if we hadn't met at the funeral—if I hadn't dragged it out of you—I still wouldn't know of her existence.'

'No, I *would* have told you. I was *going* to tell you.'

'Really? When, exactly? When she was eighteen? Twenty-one?'

'I had to think of Effie. To put her first...do what was best for her.'

'And what was "best for her" was to deprive her of her father?' His voice leached scorn. 'Thanks for that, Calista.'

Calsita cast about, desperately looking for a way to counter his contempt. 'For your information, life these past few years hasn't exactly been easy for me, you know.'

'Is that so?' He stared at her with obvious distaste. 'Have *you* been sharing a cell with an armed robber who would slit your throat for an ounce of tobacco?'

'Well, no, but…'

'Spent the one hour a day that you're allowed outside marching round a prison courtyard? Had your every movement recorded by security cameras?'

'No, of course I haven't.'

'Then don't you *dare* start telling me you have had it tough.'

'I can't undo the past, Lukas!' she cried out, her voice heavy with the weight of shame. 'I don't know what else I can say.'

'Nothing—there is *nothing* you can say.' There was a long beat of silence. 'But maybe there is something you can *do*.'

Reaching forward, he trailed a finger along her jawline, running it over her lips.

Calista felt her heart stutter, her eyes widening as his head lowered until his mouth was barely a centimetre from her own, his breath a whisper of soft promise.

'Maybe there is a way you can start making it up to me…'

And with one lithe movement he swung his magnificent body over hers.

CHAPTER SEVEN

His body hovered above her, braced by locked arms and toes that were pushed firmly into the padded lounger. Calista held herself very still, achingly aware of the corded muscles of his biceps, the hard-packed torso that was only inches away from her trembling body. She could feel the heat radiating off him, prickling over her, finding its way unerringly to her inner core. His breath fanned over her face, making her eyelashes flutter close until his lips touched hers and the familiar bolt of electricity made them shoot open again. One touch—that was all it took. One graze of his lips for her to shake with need. For her to fall apart.

Bending his elbows, Lukas lowered his body, adjusting the angle of his head very slightly until he deemed it just right and increased the pressure of his lips. It was a coaxing, persuasive kiss, gloriously sensual but leaving her in no doubt as to who was in control here—who had all the power.

For a split second Calista tried to fight against it, holding her facial muscles taut, her lips tight. But it was hopeless—and they both knew it. With a giddy rush of surrender she parted her mouth and immediately Lukas was there, giving a low growl of approval as his tongue found hers, tangling and stroking, hot and hard and heavy as he devoured her, stoking the familiar madness that gripped them both.

Calista thrust her hands into his hair, spreading her fingers so that she could hold him to her, seal them together. Sliding one arm under her back, Lukas flipped them so that she was on top of him, their mouths still fused by that burning, bruising kiss. The skin of their near naked bodies was erotically sealed all the way down—and then Lukas peeled them apart, his hand spanning her hips and moving her down until he had her where he wanted her: pressed firmly into his groin, where the length of his arousal welcomed her with its might and its power and its mind-numbing promise.

Calista heard herself moan, the wondrous feel of him shooting through every cell of her body, making her want him inside her so badly she had to stop herself from begging for it, right there and then. Instead she rocked against him, increasing the pressure, heightening the gloriously erotic sensation.

Lukas growled his approval.

The thin fabric of their swimwear was in danger of melding to their skin with the blistering heat they were generating. Raising herself up on one arm, Calista slid a hand between them, running it down the rippling muscles of his chest until she found the straining fabric of Lukas's trunks, where she traced the steel length of him. Lukas gave a primal shudder and suddenly his hands were all over her, pulling at the ties of her bikini behind her back and around her hips, the scraps of fabric falling apart in his hurry to possess her, his animal craving every bit as desperate as her own.

'God, Calista...' He ground the words into her shoulder. 'Look what you do to me.'

His mouth was on hers again, his hands skimming over

the warm skin of her naked buttocks, dipping into the valley between, his fingers sliding down to where she wanted him most.

'I can't get enough of you.' He groaned through the kiss. 'I will *never* get enough of you.'

Was that a threat or a promise? Calista didn't know—she didn't care. Her only conscious thought was that she wanted him so badly she feared she might explode with it.

But they had to find some control. Effie was asleep in the cabin below. They had to act responsibly.

As if Calista had somehow willed it to happen they both heard the sound at the same time. A sort of scuffling noise beneath them and then a clear little voice calling out.

'Mummeee!'

Hurriedly pushing herself away from Lukas's body, Calista looked down at herself—at the bikini top that hung loose around her neck, the bottoms that were just a scrap of fabric between her legs.

'I'm coming, darling. Just hang on one minute.'

After fumbling to retie all the fiddly strings she hastily adjusted the triangles of her bikini top to cover nipples stiff with longing, breasts still heavy with desire. Only then did she raise her eyes to Lukas, to see that he had been watching her every move. She caught the intensely dark gleam in his eyes—almost fierce, but with a hint of vulnerability—before he moved away, searching for a pair of board shorts to cover his considerable arousal.

And only just in time. A second later a tousled-haired head appeared at the top of the cabin steps, blinking into the sunshine.

'Here you are.' Effie looked curiously from one to the other, as if they were both being quietly assessed and found to be guilty. 'I didn't know where I was when I woke up.'

'Didn't you, darling?' Calista went to give her daughter a hug. 'It's okay. We're still on the boat.'

'I know that *now*!' She rolled her eyes before a broad grin spread across her pretty face. 'Can I go swimming again?'

'Um…yes, I don't see why not. I think I'll go in with you this time.' The idea of cooling water was suddenly very appealing.

'Yay! And Daddy too?'

'Maybe in a bit.' Lukas moved so that he was standing behind Calista, laying a hand on her shoulder and dipping his head so that he could whisper in her ear. 'To be continued, Ms Gianopoulous.' His breath fanned softly against her hair.

Calista swallowed. But with Effie tugging on her hand she was mercifully spared having to come up with any sort of reply.

Leaning back in his chair, Lukas stretched his arms behind his head. He had been working in his office all afternoon and he needed a break, but picking up the reins after being away for so long meant a lot of hard work and commitment.

His luxury yachting business, Blue Sky Charters, had been ticking over nicely in his absence. His staff had stayed loyal to him and, even though it hadn't grown the way it would have done had he been there in person to oversee it, it was a very thriving concern. He had been lucky, he supposed—though 'lucky' was hardly a word he would use—that the authorities had made no claim on his personal business. There was no connection between that and G&K Shipping, which had been decimated by the scandal.

But Lukas fully intended to see *that* concern succeed

again too, in honour of his father. He had already managed to buy back seven super-tankers. Nothing like the fleet of eighty they had had before Aristotle Gianapoulous had seen fit to blow the business sky-high, but it was a start. He also intended to clear his name—and, far more importantly, his father's name. He wanted the world to know just who had really been responsible for the vile trade in arms. Who the *real* guilty party had been.

Leaning forward, he closed the lid of his laptop. The villa was very quiet and still in the early evening sunshine. Too quiet, he realised. It was over a week since the three of them had arrived at Villa Helene, and Lukas had become used to having Calista and Effie around—to hearing the patter of Effie's feet running along the marble-tiled floors, her shrill little laugh echoing through the open-plan rooms. Even when he should have been relishing his solitude he found himself listening out for them. Just as he was doing now—waiting for sounds to indicate that they had returned from their trip to the beach.

Calista had stuck her head around the door after lunch, to announce that she was taking Effie down to the small sandy cove that was only a few hundred yards from the villa, approached by some rickety old wooden steps. By the tone of her voice it had been quite plain that he wasn't invited. Not that that would have stopped Lukas if he'd wanted to join them, but he had work to do. Besides, it appeared he and Calista were playing some sort of game. Over the past week she had seemed determined to hold him at arm's length, going out of her way to put distance between them whenever she could and finding excuses never to let them be alone together for any length of time.

Lukas had deliberately gone along with it, refusing to react. Being unreasonably reasonable just to wind her up. He'd decided he was prepared to play the long game. Well, long*ish*. In point of fact, watching that pertly rebellious body moving around the villa was driving him crazy—killing him. But in a perverse sort of way he was enjoying it. And knowing with increasing certainty that she was faking her casual indifference only added to the sexual tension that hummed steadily between them.

Lukas looked at his watch. Gone six o'clock. He had thought they would be back by now—although he knew that Effie always pleaded to stay longer when she was told it was time to leave the beach.

Seeing how much Effie obviously adored being here on Thalassa was a source of great satisfaction to Lukas—not least because of the way it made her mother squirm. On the one hand Calista was obviously happy that her daughter was having such a great time, but she also felt she had to keep reminding her—and him—that this was nothing more than a holiday, that they would shortly be returning to London.

Well, they would see about that. Lukas hadn't fully formulated his plans yet, but when he had he would be making quite sure that Calista abided by them. One thing was certain: now he had discovered Effie he had no intention of letting her go again.

Because he adored everything about this little girl. She had stolen his heart from the very first moment he had laid eyes on her, back in the kitchen of Calista's flat. She was a complete delight—the most unexpected joy to have come out of such terrible circumstances. Lukas would do anything to keep her close. And that included taming her flame haired mother.

Although 'taming' wasn't the right word. Lukas didn't want Calista tamed. He loved that wild, fiery streak of hers. The green eyes that flashed with fire as she glared at him, the way her hair whipped around her face, the nostrils that flared with contempt and the obstinate defiance that held her chin high. She was as maddening as hell, but somehow he kept coming back for more punishment.

And it *did* feel like punishment, the way she had got to him. Like a burr against his skin, she was impossible to ignore, to dismiss. For the sake of his own sanity Lukas had decided he would concentrate only on the sexual attraction between them. That was more understandable. And infinitely more pleasurable.

He would concentrate on the free spirit behind that feisty façade, the vibration between them whenever he took her in his arms, the abandoned, almost feral way she responded. As if overtaken by the force of nature. As if there was nothing she wouldn't do for him or let him do for her. That was what he would focus on. Because Lukas had never experienced a high like it before. No other sexual experience had come even close.

Not that he had been able to put his erotic theories into practice—not yet. They had only made love twice, with a four-and-a-half-year gap in between, and neither time had been perfect. The first time—thrilling though it had been—he had been too shocked, too caught up in the preciousness of the moment to make it last the way he should have. And the second time... Pushing Calista up against the wall and taking her like that had hardly been his finest hour—far from it. No matter how she had responded... how good it had felt.

No, the next time he and Calista made love—because there *was* going to be a next time, and soon—he was going to make sure the conditions were just right. He was going to see just what he and Calista could do together, just what intense sexual magic they were capable of.

Which was why he had spent some time carefully formulating a plan.

This morning a small batch of post had arrived for Calista—presumably forwarded on by the woman she shared her flat with. Petros had picked it up from the mainland and delivered it to the villa, along with a large flaxen-haired doll in a presentation box that he had proudly given to Effie as a gift from him and Dorcas. Effie had thanked him most politely, even though Lukas had seen her looking at it slightly askance. After he had gone she had set about divesting the doll of her fussy dress whilst Lukas had watched Calista flicking through the letters, only bothering to open one, reading it quickly and then stuffing it back in the envelope.

'Anything interesting?' Something about the pinched look on her face had begged the question.

'Not really.' Calista had taken a sip of her coffee. 'It's from my father's lawyer. They're reading the will on the twenty-eighth.'

'As in tomorrow?'

Looking at her phone, she'd checked the date. 'Um... yes.'

'Will you be going?'

'No. The office is in Athens. Besides, I want nothing to do with my father's legacy—not now I know the truth.'

Lukas had watched as she lowered her eyes, picking nervously at the corner of the embossed envelope. It had surprised him that he felt no sense of satisfaction that she had finally accepted the truth. Instead her obvious pain had arrowed to his heart.

'My half-brothers can share whatever meagre spoils there may be between them.'

'Not without you being there to sign them over, they can't.' Lukas had briskly switched to business mode. 'I suggest you go to Athens and take this opportunity to legally tie up the loose ends. Then perhaps you can move on.'

'And *I* suggest you drop the amateur psychology and mind your own business.'

Lukas had waited for the anger to kick in. Normally he didn't take kindly to being spoken to like that. Normally he would have made the perpetrator pay. But Calista's backlash had simply served to show him she still had plenty of fight left in her. It was almost a relief.

'Touched a nerve, have I?'

'No. I just don't need you to tell me what I should and shouldn't be doing, thank you very much.'

'Very well. But perhaps you might allow me to make a small suggestion. I also have business in Athens. We could go there tomorrow...maybe stay overnight in my apartment.'

'No,' Calista had replied firmly. 'It would be too disruptive for Effie.'

'Then perhaps Effie could stay here?' He had kept his voice deliberately light. 'I'm sure Dorcas and Petros would be happy to look after her.'

'Oh, *please*, Mummy.' Never one to miss a trick, Effie had looked up from where she had been walking the semiclad doll across the table, turning her big green eyes on her mother. 'Can I stay with Dorcas and Petros? *Please?*'

'I don't know...' Calista had hurried to find an excuse. 'I mean, they might not want the bother of looking after you overnight.'

'Oh, they will. And, anyway, I won't be any bother. I can help Dorcas make some *kouloulou* biscuits.'

'*Koulourakia,*' Calista had prompted, repeating the name of the buttery biscuits that Effie loved so much.

'Yes, those. So *can* I, Mummy?'

'Well, maybe. We'll talk about it later.'

At which point Lukas had allowed himself a secret

smile. Thanks to his brilliantly wonderful daughter, step one of his plan had been successfully implemented.

Now he walked through the empty villa and out onto the terrace, shading his eyes against the glare of the swimming pool. In the distance he could hear the faint chatter of a small voice, coming closer, and then mother and daughter appeared at the top of the steps to his left. They both looked warm and windswept. Calista was wearing a sarong tied low around her hips and was weighed down by a beach bag and a cool box. Effie was struggling with an inflatable crocodile that was nearly twice her size, the breeze flapping it against her small body.

As Lukas started towards them he realised with a jolt of surprise just how pleased he was to see them.

'What the hell is *he* doing here?'

Calista's two half-brothers jumped to their feet as she and Lukas entered the lawyer's office. Behind her, Calista felt Lukas stiffen.

'He has no business being here.' Christos directed his venom at her. 'Get him out, Calista.'

'Sit down, Christos.' With a calm she didn't feel, Calista took a seat across the desk from the aged lawyer. 'Lukas is merely accompanying me.'

'To survey the damage he has caused, most likely.' Christos's eyes bulged in his head. 'To check that he has decimated our inheritance as much as he has his own. The cheating, lousy, lowlife—'

'Why would you want him here, Calista?' Yiannis cut across his brother when the sound of Lukas's intake of breath was enough tell him that Christos was in danger of getting himself into serious trouble.

Calista hadn't actually wanted Lukas to join them, but somehow she had ended up being cleverly outmanoeuvred by him. First he had insisted on delivering her to the revolving door of the office block, then on accompanying her in the lift to the correct floor, and before she had known it he had followed her right in.

'Why don't we all sit down?' From the other side of the desk Mr Petrides, the Gianopoulous family lawyer, who had to be at least eighty years old, showed that he had no time for family squabbles. 'The reading of the will shouldn't take too long. For Calista's benefit I will speak in English, if that is agreeable to you all?'

'Just get on with it.'

Christos returned to his seat, followed by Yiannis. Lukas drew up a chair to sit on the other side of Calista.

Clearing his throat, Mr Petrides began slowly reading through the legal jargon. Calista tried to concentrate, but it was difficult with Lukas beside her, sitting perfectly still but radiating enough suppressed hostility towards the Gianopoulous brothers to decimate a small country. Was he planning some sort of showdown? Was that why he was here? For the first time she wondered if she had been tricked into bringing them all together. But if so, did it matter?

Time ticked by. The office was cramped and stuffy, and before long Calista found her mind wandering. She hoped Effie was okay, although she didn't really have any doubt that she would be. Dorcas and Petros had been absolutely delighted by the idea of babysitting for twenty-four hours, and all three had waved them off gleefully. The couple were staying overnight at Villa Helene—presumably Lukas still didn't want his daughter anywhere near Aristotle's Villa Melina.

She, of course, had somehow found herself agreeing to stay the night at Lukas's Athens apartment. She had never been there before. As a teenager she had tried not to think about it, imagining all the women Lukas might have taken back there, picturing some sort of wild bachelor pad with black satin sheets and handcuffs hanging off the bedhead. Not that Lukas had ever given her reason to think that. He had been notoriously discreet about his private life. But that didn't mean he hadn't had one.

One thing was for sure: tonight she was going to have to be careful not to slip between those black satin sheets herself. All week long, ever since *that* kiss on the boat, she had been fighting the crippling effect he had on her. The seductive power that made her speech stilted, made her steps stumbling, made her insides turn to jelly.

So she had deliberately distanced herself from him, avoiding potentially intimate situations by ensuring that Effie was with her at all times. And in the evenings, after she'd had no alternative but to put Effie to bed, by burying her head in a book or deciding on an early night.

And, surprisingly, Lukas had put no pressure on her at all. In fact he had behaved like the perfect gentleman. Far from trying to persuade her to stay for a nightcap on the terrace, or go for a stroll under the starlit sky, he had seemed perfectly happy to see her disappear, politely wishing her goodnight before returning to his laptop and burying himself in work.

Calista had told herself that was a relief. He had obviously forgotten his whispered promise on the boat. He had decided to drop the whole seduction routine and give her some space. But as the days had gone on somehow her relief had turned to frustration and then doubt. His gentlemanly conduct had started to seem more like uninterest than respect. And despite herself Calista had found that she was lingering a few seconds longer than strictly necessary when she said goodnight, holding his dark hooded gaze when she should have looked away, threading her fingers through her hair in what might have been construed as a suggestive manner.

Not that it had made any difference. In return Lukas had simply given her one of his infuriating half-smiles, leaving her feeling flustered and stupid before heading for the safety of her room.

'So basically you are telling us that there is absolutely *nothing*!'

Christos's furious voice jolted her back to the present.

Mr Petrides surveyed him over the top of his glasses. 'I am saying that the small amount of assets your father had will need to be divided between his remaining creditors.'

'And Thalassa?' Yiannis leant forward. 'That has gone too?'

'There is no mention of the island of Thalassa.' Mr Petrides looked down at the papers before him. 'My understanding is that it was the property of your father's first wife and has recently been sold. To Mr Kalanos.'

'Why, you—'

Christos was on his feet again, but Yiannis intercepted, roughly shoving him back in his seat.

'So it is true?' Yiannis turned to Lukas, defeat etched into his face.

'Just as I said,' Lukas replied with icy calm, his fingers steepled beneath his chin, his gaze steady.

'So why the hell are we here?' Christos turned on Mr Petrides. 'Just to be humiliated? So that this man can gloat over the despicable way he has tricked us?'

'No, Christos.' The old man suddenly seemed to age before their eyes. 'The reason I have gathered you here today is because I have something to tell you. I believe it is time you learned the truth about your father.' He sat back, a shudder racking his body. 'These past few years I have kept quiet. At the time I thought it was out of loyalty to your father, but now I see it was just cowardice. However, now the situation has changed. I have been diagnosed with a terminal illness. And I feel the need to unburden myself before I die.'

'Oh, I am *so* sorry, Mr Petrides.' Calista reached forward to take hold of his hand, but he withdrew it, placing it in his lap.

'I don't deserve your sympathy, Calista. You see, I have been concealing information—from you and from the police. I am very sorry to have to tell you this…' He cast rheumy eyes over the three Gianopoulous siblings. 'But I am of the opinion that your father was responsible for the arms-smuggling. Not Stravros Kalanos.'

'*No!* You are lying.' Christos was on his feet again, spittle flying from his mouth. 'He's paying you to say that, isn't he?' He waved a finger at Lukas. 'This is all a filthy conspiracy.'

The old man sadly shook his head. 'I wasn't privy to the details of your father's dealings, but I have had my suspicions for some time. Suspicions that I should have mentioned to the authorities. That I now intend to share with them. Lukas…' He struggled to his feet. 'It is indeed fortuitous that you are here today, so that I can offer my apologies to you in person.' He beckoned Lukas closer. 'I won't ask for your forgiveness, because I know I don't deserve it, but I want to express my deepest regret for not coming forward before now. For the miscarriage of justice you have suffered and for the ruination of your father's name.'

Lukas stood up, his tall frame rigid with control. The air in the office was suddenly stiflingly hot. Mr Petrides held out a shaky hand, and for a second Lukas hesitated, before finally reaching to take it in his. Mr Petrides grasped it firmly, patting it with his other hand.

'Thank you, my son. That is more than I deserve. Rest assured I will do the right thing now—'

'Wait a minute,' Yiannis interrupted. 'You are only talking about *suspicions* here, Petrides. You need to think very carefully before making accusations you can't substantiate.'

'No one will believe the old fool, anyway.' Christos snarled.

'It's the truth.' Calista's voice rang out clearly. 'You need to know—both of you. Our father was the guilty party. Not Stavros, and not Lukas.'

'And *you'd* know, would you?'

'Yes, Lukas has told me everything and I believe him.'

'Well, more fool you.' Christos turned on her. 'We all know you've been simpering around your precious Lukas ever since you could walk. He could tell you black was white and you'd believe him.'

'That's enough.' Moving to stand beside Calista, Lukas rested his arm along the back of her chair. 'You need to learn some respect for your sister. Both of you.'

'Respect?' Christos sneered. 'D'you really think I'd respect *that*?' He waved a finger at Calista. 'That pathetic ginger creature who has never been anything but a worthless parasite.'

Calista felt Lukas go terrifyingly still.

'What did you just say?'

'Even her own mother didn't want her. Packing her off to Thalassa every summer before she eventually went and killed herself. Calista needs to watch out—that sort of madness is probably in the blood.'

'Christos!' Yiannis tugged at his brother's arm to pull him away.

But Lukas was already there, hauling Christos up by the scruff of the neck, his menacing face only inches from his sweating victim. For a second he held him there. Christos's legs kicked helplessly beneath him, and a look of blind panic came into his eyes as Calista shrieked Lukas's name and Yiannis stepped forward, wildly flapping his hands and tugging at his brother's jacket to try and release him.

'Leave him, Lukas!' Fearing for Christos's very life, Calista tried to get between them. 'He's not worth it.'

Lukas hesitated, letting out a low, savage snarl that curdled Calista's blood. But finally, slowly, he lowered Christos to the ground. Calista could see the effort it took for him to control his fury flaring in his nostrils, throbbing in the veins of his neck.

Hooking his fingers under the knot of Christos's tie, he held him at arm's length, giving him a look of utter disgust. 'Don't you ever, *ever* speak of Calista that way again.'

Christos attempted a grunt.

'Now, apologise.' Releasing his throat, Lukas took hold of his shoulders, roughly turning him to face Calista.

'It's okay. I don't care—'

'It is very much *not* okay!' Lukas's voice roared around the office. 'This creep is going to apologise, right now.'

'I'm sorry, okay?' Christos looked down at his feet.

'Not good enough. Look your sister in the eye, take back your filthy remarks and apologise properly.'

'I shouldn't have said those things.' Under Lukas's punishing gaze Christos did as he was told. 'I apologise.'

'Sit down.' Throwing him back into his chair, Lukas turned to Yiannis. 'You too.'

Yiannis did as he was told.

'It's time you two learnt a few home truths. Firstly, your father was an immoral, scheming villain who lied his way out of trouble by betraying my father and framing me. Secondly, if I ever hear either of you bad-mouthing

Calista again I won't be responsible for my actions. Do I make myself clear?'

The brothers nodded.

'Out of respect for Calista I won't pursue this any further. But that doesn't mean I don't want to.' He fixed Christos with a terrifying glare. 'Because, believe me, taking you outside would give me the greatest pleasure. You don't deserve a sister like Calista. She is brave and strong and honourable and she has more brains than you two idiots put together. Which brings me to my third point.' He paused, shooting a look at Calista. 'You might as well know: I am proud to say that Calista is also the mother of my child.'

Yiannis and Christos gaped in unison, rendered mute by this astonishing revelation.

'Yes, we have a daughter. And one day she will inherit my fortune, carry on my legacy. One day she will preside over the great Kalanos shipping empire. And believe me...' He levelled cold eyes at them. 'This time I intend to make sure that nothing and no one will ever have the power to bring us down.'

CHAPTER EIGHT

'NIGHTCAP?'

Lukas moved over the sideboard and picked up a bottle of brandy.

'Um…yes, why not?'

Calista accepted the glass from him and, taking a sip, felt the comforting burn slide down her throat.

They had returned from an evening meal at a small family-run restaurant, hidden in one of the many cobbled backstreets of this beautiful city. Sitting outside, sharing a table so small that their knees had touched and Lukas had been forced to stretch his long legs out to the side, she had felt blissfully relaxed after the drama of Mr Petrides's office.

The food had been delicious too and, combined with the warm night air, filled with the scent of jasmine and orange blossom, and the indigo sky dotted with stars overhead, she had found herself forgetting her problems for a while and just enjoying Lukas's company. Which was easy when he was being like this: charming, attentive, funny. The old Lukas. Neither of them had even mentioned the hateful scene earlier on—Mr Petrides's confession and the shocking behaviour of her brothers.

Now, however, Calista suspected that was about to change. Swilling the brandy around in her glass she looked about her, trying to delay the inevitable. 'Your apartment is beautiful.'

'Thank you.' Lukas came and stood by her side. 'Though I could do without the note of surprise.'

'Sorry!' Calista laughed. 'It's just not how I imagined it.'

'Dare I ask how that was?'

'No, probably best not to.'

'Let me guess—all black leather sofas and widescreen televisions?'

'Something like that.'

'And maybe a waterbed with satin sheets? A drawer full of sex toys.'

Calista felt herself flush. Could he read her mind? Or was she just guilty of dreadful stereotyping?

'You mean I've got that wrong too?' She tried to bat back a flippant quip to cover her embarrassment.

'Play your cards right and later on you might find out.'

Calista swallowed. She had walked right into that one.

She moved away from him into the centre of the open-plan room. 'I love all the artwork. Is that an original?' She pointed to a colourful portrait on the wall.

'It is indeed. Modern art is an interest of mine. It's a good investment too. But nothing in my collection really compares to this.' He pressed a switch and the curtains swished to one side and a wall of windows appeared. 'There. What do you think?'

Calista gasped. Before them twinkled the lights of the city of Athens, and in the distance, high above the city, was the Acropolis, glowing proudly against the night sky. 'That's incredible!'

'Even better from out here.' Crossing the room, Lukas took hold of her hand and, opening the glass doors, ushered her out onto the balcony. 'Quite something, isn't it?'

It certainly was. It was magical. Tipping back her head,

Calista let the soft night wrap itself around her, drinking in the majesty of the scene. It put life into perspective somehow, thinking about the thousands of years the ancient citadel had been standing there, watching over them, about generations of people gazing up at it, just as she did now, caught up in their own totally absorbing but all too fleeting worlds.

A small movement beside her made her turn. Lukas was studying her, his head on one side, as if she was some sort of fascinating puzzle. Boldly Calista returned his stare, and immediately the flame between them ignited. His dark, raw, intensely primal presence shuddered through her body, making her stomach contract and a heavy beat pulse in her core. Lukas raised his eyebrows fractionally... a small but infinitely telling gesture that weakened her knees.

God, she wanted him so much. She positively ached with it. If he were to kiss her now she knew exactly where it would lead.

But he didn't. Pulling his eyes away from hers, he gestured to a pair of stylish metal chairs. 'Shall we sit down?'

'Oh, yes—why not?' Desperate to hide her disappointment, Calista quickly did as she was told, all chirpy enthusiasm.

'So...' Lukas turned the dark force of his eyes back on her. 'It would seem that your dear brothers finally know the truth about your father.'

Calista pulled a face. 'They are not my "dear" brothers. I never want to see either of them ever again.'

'Well, that makes two of us.'

He stilled, eyes narrowed, suddenly deadly serious. 'If Christos ever dares to speak about you like that again, I swear I won't be answerable for my actions.'

Calista saw his fists clench.

'I'm still not sure how I stopped myself from killing him there and then.'

'You showed great restraint.' She risked a quick smile.

'I would cheerfully serve a life sentence for that.'

'No, you wouldn't.' Her smile immediately faded. 'He's not worth it.'

Lukas grunted. 'That's true.'

'Thanks for sticking up for me, by the way.' Calista hurried to move the conversation away from the toxic subject of prison sentences.

'That's okay.' His gaze sharpened. 'I meant what I said.'

'Well, thank you. I appreciate it.' Suddenly vulnerable, she looked away, searching for more solid ground. 'What you said about Effie inheriting the shipping business, though... Don't you think that was a bit premature?'

Lukas shrugged. 'No harm in letting them see that the Kalanos dynasty is set to thrive.'

'Hmm...' Calista was far from comfortable with that, but decided not to break the fragile ceasefire by challenging him now.

'I must admit I had always assumed that pair of clowns *knew* the truth about Aristotle,' Lukas continued. 'But judging by the look on their faces today I'm not so sure.'

'I think we were all taken in by our father's lies.' Calista gave him an anxious glance. 'I'm so sorry, Lukas.'

Lukas shook his head wearily. 'Let's call a truce—for tonight at least.'

She nodded. That was fine by her. Given the choice, she would never talk about it again. She would bury the whole wretched business so deep that it would take a nuclear explosion to bring it to light. But it wasn't as simple as that. Lukas had vowed to clear his name and his father's name. Presumably, thanks to Mr Petrides, he was now going to have the evidence to do it.

Aristotle would be exposed for the villain he had been. Which was only right. But that didn't mean the idea didn't fill her with dread. He had still been her father—Effie's grandfather.

Reluctantly she braced herself to ask the dreaded question. 'Can I ask you what you intend to do now?' She placed her glass down on the table between them. 'When will you go public about Aristotle?'

'When I am good and ready. What is it they say? Revenge is a dish best served cold?'

Calista shivered.

'Well, I would be grateful if you could give me some warning before you do…'

'Trying to cover your back, Calista?'

'No!' Indignation saw her temper flare, and she tossed back her head so her hair rippled over her shoulders. 'I'm just saying that if you give me some warning I can prepare myself and make sure Effie is shielded from any press intrusion.'

'Let me assure you that I will have Effie's best interests at heart at all times.'

'Oh, well…thanks…' Her voice tailed off. She had no idea what he meant by that—knew only that the statement held a dark possessiveness that thickened the blood in her veins.

'Speaking of Effie, there is something I have neglected to say to you.'

Now her heart leapt into her throat. If he was going to start talking about applying for custody again she was ready to fight. And fight she would. Tooth and nail and with any other body part she had.

'Yes?' Her green eyes flashed a powerful warning. 'And what's that?'

Lukas deliberately let a second pass. Far from being intimidated by her reaction, he seemed to be rather enjoying it. He picked up his glass and took a sip of brandy, clearly in no hurry to put her out of her misery.

'Just that I realise I have not given you the credit you deserve.'

'Credit for what?' Wrong-footed, Calista frowned back at him.

'For the excellent way you have raised our daughter.'

'Oh.' She finally let out a breath.

'Effie is obviously a happy, well-balanced and frankly exceptional child. You have done a great job.'

'Well, thank you.' Stupidly Calista felt herself flush.

'I can see she is highly intelligent too.' The smile in his voice raised her eyes again. 'Though I suspect she gets that from me.'

'Of course.' Calista played along. 'Along with her humility and modesty.'

Their eyes locked and the tension between them melted away—only to be replaced with something far more dangerous.

'Let's drink to that, then.' Lukas's glittering gaze held hers. 'To Effie, our very special little girl.'

They clinked glasses, and Calista swallowed down the lump in her throat with the swig of brandy. She could feel tears pricking the backs of her eyes, but she had no idea why.

'And to the future, of course.' Missing nothing, Lukas continued to hold her captive. 'Whatever it may hold.'

What, indeed? Trapped by the power of his eyes, Calista had lost the ability to think straight. She needed to get away. *Fast.*

'Well…' She gave an exaggerated stretch. 'It's getting late. I think I'll go to bed.'

She waited for Lukas to say something, to do something. In truth she was waiting for him to stop her. Instead he remained motionless, those mesmerising eyes still fixed on hers, burning into her, managing to awaken every cell in her body. She watched, tingling with anticipation, as he silently took another sip of brandy, his eyes never moving from her heated face.

'I'll say goodnight, then.' Rising to her feet, she made as if to go, but somehow her feet didn't get the message her brain was trying to transmit and she ended up in a sort of frozen pose, twisted away from him but not moving.

From behind her she heard Lukas laugh—a softly arrogant laugh that had her turning her head, ready to challenge him.

Except that didn't happen. Because suddenly Lukas was there, towering over her. His hands were everywhere—skimming across her shoulderblades, down her back, tracing the curve of her waist, cupping her bottom, pulling her against him. And finally plunging into her hair so that he could hold her steady for his kiss.

And what a kiss.

Hungry, possessive, masterful, it sent a white bolt of craving through Calista, pulsing deep, deep down inside her, throbbing hard and insistent with illicit need. Without a second thought she responded, moulding herself against his body, her mouth greedily crushing his as her lips parted to allow more of this gloriously forbidden pleasure. Her tongue sought his, tasting the hint of brandy on his breath, revelling in the raw, damp heat that mingled between them, tightening her breasts, weighting her core. Rendering her helpless with longing.

'Did you mention bed?'

Sweeping her up in his arms, Lukas moved them both inside, marching through the living area with her clinging to his neck until they were in his bedroom, where he laid her down almost reverentially on his enormous bed.

'Stay like that.'

His throatily sexy command shuddered through her, but the words were superfluous. Calista had no intention of going anywhere. She held her breath as he started to tear off his clothes, undoing a few top buttons of his shirt before giving up and impatiently tugging it over his head, leaving his hair deliciously ruffled. Next came his jeans and boxers and then he was naked before her. Gloriously, proudly naked. His magnificent body gleamed in the dim light of the room...the muscles of his chest were shadowed, hard and unyielding. Calista let her eyes travel south, feeling her mouth go dry as she took in the sculpted V-shape of his pelvis, the line of curling dark hair and then...the mighty swell of his arousal.

But she had no time to feast her eyes. Lukas was on the bed in a flash, kneeing astride her, his hands pushing the straps of her dress over her shoulders, his fingers feverishly working the zipper down her back as she arched up to allow him access. She raised her arms and together they pulled the dress over her head, Calista felt the hard swell of her breasts tugged upwards. Reaching behind her back, she undid her bra, and the hunger in Lukas's stare at the sight of her swollen breasts tightened her nipples to peaks of stone.

They crashed back down onto the bed together again, Lukas straddling her with the length of his body now, their mouths fused with blistering, scorching passion. She moved her hands to grip his jaw, trying to hold him steady so that she could drag in a breath, but he only allowed her one gasp of air before he commandeered her mouth again, continuing his wickedly relentless assault on her senses. Meanwhile his hands had found her panties, pushing them to one side so that he could find her swollen core.

Calista groaned against his mouth, throwing back her

head and writhing beneath his touch. *It felt so good. Too good.* It was ridiculous the way he could transport her to the realms of ecstasy just by the touch of his fingers. But she had no defences against this man. This was Lukas— the only man she had ever wanted. The only man she had ever loved.

She was teetering deliciously on the very edge when Lukas stopped, pushing himself back on his heels so that he could pull down her panties and discard them. Calista reached out her arms, desperate to bring him back to her, the small space between them feeling like a yawning chasm. But Lukas had other ideas. Moving her legs apart, he positioned himself between them, shooting Calista a look of dangerously dark promise. Then he lowered his head.

'Lukas...'

She didn't know what she had been going to say and it didn't matter anyway, because as soon as his tongue started to work its magic she was paralysed by the grip of some unknown euphoria. Shooting sensations spread out from her core, fanning through her body, reaching every nerve-ending and pinching them tight. Then tighter still.

'Nice?' Lukas looked up, a wickedly smug expression on his face.

Her only reply was to reach for his head, grasping his hair to push him back down on her again. He couldn't stop *now*.

'I'll take that as a yes.'

His words were muffled against her as he started his glorious assault again. Licking, tasting, nudging just the right spot, over and over again, somehow unerringly altering the pressure to her exact need until he finally quickened the pace and the pressure and she felt herself start to fall. Over and over an edge that wasn't there. To a place that didn't exist.

* * *

Moving his position, Lukas gazed down at Calista. She was lying on her back, sated, still reeling from the after-effects. Pride surged through him. *He had done that to her.* She looked so beautiful lying there, her eyes closed, her skin creamy white in the dim half-light of the room. Her hair rippled across the pillow in a tangle of gold. He wanted Calista with a possessiveness that shocked him with its power.

Leaning forward, he kissed her gently on the lips, watching as heavy eyelids slowly opened. Stretching out beside her, he slipped one arm under her body, pulling her on to his chest, catching the look in her eyes as they sparkled, stealing the breath from his lungs with their gloriously erotic promise.

Positioning her so that she was exactly where he wanted her—no, *needed* her—so that he could finally do the thing that seemed more imperative than life itself, Lukas thrust into her, and her ecstatic gasp of pleasure rang like music in his ears. Picking up speed, he felt her match his rhythm, thrust for thrust, taking him—all of him—and giving all of herself in return.

Her obvious confidence filled Lukas with inexplicable pride as she arched her body to take him deeper, her head thrown back so that the wild red curls tumbled down almost to her waist. With a few final delirious strokes they were there, both shattering into pieces, each screaming the other's name.

CHAPTER NINE

As THE ISLAND of Thalassa came into view Calista felt her spirits soar. She couldn't wait to see Effie again. Even though they had only been apart for twenty-four hours she had missed her like mad. But it was more than that. Despite everything, Thalassa still held a special place in her heart.

That place had been well and truly buried the last time she had arrived here—for her father's funeral, less than two weeks ago. Then she had vowed that she would never return, that she would say goodbye to the island for ever. But things had changed. *Everything* had changed.

Lukas had happened.

The previous night had been just incredible. Never in her wildest dreams, her craziest fantasies, had she ever imagined a night like that. The intensity of their lovemaking, the blazing passion between them, had gone way beyond anything she had thought possible. It had been as if all the time they had been apart, all that had happened—the hurt, the anger and the secrets—had been distilled into pure, unadulterated desire. And that had been all it took for them to fall headlong into the madness that had consumed them both.

She had finally woken this morning to see Lukas staring down at her, his ebony eyes deeply serious. Then he had blinked the expression away, leaning forward to touch her lips with a gentle kiss and announcing that they really ought to get up.

But she had seen it—that closed, inscrutable look—and it had been then that it had struck her just how completely she had given herself to Lukas, how recklessly she had laid herself bare. And not just in the physical, earthly sense. By surrendering to such wild abandonment she had exposed her heart and her soul, her most fragile, deeply held emotions. Emotions that she knew Lukas would never share.

And that, she had realised with a stab of sorrow, had been a dangerously foolish thing to do.

They had gone to a small local café for breakfast. Over bowls of yogurt and honey topped with figs and walnuts Lukas had told her he had business to attend to in Athens that would take several days to complete, and had suggested she stay and keep him company. He had left her in no doubt as to what sort of 'company' he meant, and the look he had given her had arrowed straight to her loins, just as he had meant it to do.

With super-human effort she had declined. She had to get back for Effie. She wouldn't have felt comfortable being apart from her for another night, even though her daughter was most probably having the time of her life with Dorcas and Petros. And besides, she had already given far too much of herself to this man.

So Lukas had arranged for one of his charter yachts to take her back to Thalassa—one thing he was never short of was boats. It was crewed by a couple of young Greek gods—or at least that was what they thought they were. Bronzed and athletic, Nico and Tavi leapt about the yacht, winding in ropes and adjusting sails, all with rather more exhibitionism than Calista suspected was strictly necessary. Not that she minded. Even though they were probably about the same age as her, to Calista they seemed like boys. They couldn't hold a candle to Lukas. But that didn't mean she didn't enjoy their attentions. She felt young. She felt sexy. Right now she felt she could do anything.

'Miss Gianopoulous—over there!' Nico called down from his position halfway up a mast. 'Dolphins! And they are coming our way.'

Calista looked to where he was pointing and sure enough there was a large pod of dolphins, swimming towards them. Suddenly they were alongside the boat, all around them, joyfully leaping out of the water and rolling over in the wake behind them. It was such a wonderful sight, and strangely emotional too—as if the dolphins were escorting her home.

Fighting back the tears, Calista told herself to stop being stupid and get a grip. Thalassa was *not* her home. Nor would it ever be. She had to remember that. Last night had been completely wonderful, but in terms of their future nothing had changed between her and Lukas.

What was it he had said? *Let's call a truce—for tonight at least.* They were telling words. She would be very foolish indeed to ignore them.

Back at Villa Helene, just as Calista suspected, Effie had been having a wonderful time, being thoroughly spoiled by Dorcas and Petros. She was delighted to have her mother back, of course, but after her initial rapturous welcome seemed overly focussed on where Lukas was.

'So when *is* Daddy coming back?'

They were seated outside, at a long wooden table shaded by vines that were trained overhead to provide shade. Dorcas had prepared a delicious late lunch for them all—including Nico and Tavi, who ate with ravenous appetites. There was lots of chatter and laughter, but clearly Effie was missing her father.

'I told you, darling, he'll be back in a few days.'

'How many, *exactly*?' Effie's turned her huge green eyes on her mother, her forkful of food momentarily forgotten.

'I don't know exactly. Maybe a week.'

Effie stuck out her bottom lip.

'Ah, see how she misses her *baba*.' Nico leant across and ruffled Effie's hair, managing to extract a smile from her. 'I tell you what, little one, Tavi and I—we take you out on the boat and show you the dolphins. You like that?'

Effie nodded vigorously.

'That's settled, then. We are here for two more days. We have some fun.'

He shot Calista a cheeky glance which she pointedly ignored. Now they were on dry land the flirty banter she had enjoyed on the boat seemed misplaced. She certainly didn't want to give these young Adonises the wrong idea. But on the other hand they were only having a bit of harmless fun. What was wrong with spending a bit of time enjoying their company? Why did she always have to be so buttoned up?

Back in England, Calista's friends had despaired of her. Try as they might, they had never been able to prise her out for a night of revelry—seldom even persuaded her to join them for a girly night out. Student nurses knew how to party—that was a given—and Calista was letting the side down by refusing to join in. Sure, she had Effie to consider, but that didn't excuse her total inability to let her hair down at any time.

It also didn't excuse the way she rebuffed the advances of some of the teaching hospital's most attractive and eligible junior doctors. The ones who would have had many a young nurse vying for their bedside manner. But Calista seemed impervious to their charms. She had tried to explain that it was different for her—she had responsibilities. But in truth that was only part of the reason. A very small part. The real reason she had no interest in any other man could be summed up in one name: Lukas Kalanos.

But that didn't mean she couldn't enjoy a few Lukas-free days of relaxation on this beautiful island. She ought to make the most of the fact that his darkly dominating presence wasn't everywhere she looked. That she was being spared the penetrating hooded gaze that seemed to see right through her.

As the euphoria of the night before started wear off, and reality crept in, Calista knew it was time to bring herself down to earth. And keep herself there. So if Nico and Tavi wanted to entertain her and Effie over the next couple of days, why not?

'How many more days now?'

Calista glanced up from her phone, where she'd been looking at nursing jobs on the internet. She would need to start applying soon if she wanted to have a job lined up for September.

'How many days till what, darling?' She didn't really need to ask. She knew perfectly well what her daughter was talking about. She should too—she'd been fielding the same question for well over a week now.

'Till Daddy comes back.' Effie spelled out the question with impatient clarity.

'Um…I'm not sure.'

Calista looked down at her phone again, flipping from email to text. Nothing. That was nine days of silence from Lukas now…and counting… She tossed the phone onto the sofa beside her.

'Still, we're having a nice time here without him, aren't we?' Her voice sounded hollow even to her own ears. And it clearly didn't convince Effie, who wrinkled her small nose in reply.

'I suppose so. But it would be even nicer if Daddy was here.'

Calista drew in a breath. She was trying so hard to put on a brave face for Effie, but underneath she was a churning cauldron of hurt and anger. Two or three days—that was what Lukas had said when she had left him in Athens. Some business he had to attend to. It was unforgivable that he should abandon them like this, with no word of when he planned to return. *He* was the one who had insisted that she and Effie came to Thalassa and now he was ignoring them, leaving their lives suspended until such time as he deigned to honour them with his presence again.

With each day that crawled past, bringing still no word from him, Calista made up her mind that she and Effie should just go—pack up their stuff and return to London. But somehow she couldn't do it. One look at Effie's expectant little face and her resolve crumbled. She longed to see her daddy again. Somehow, in such a short space of time, Lukas had woven his magic spell around her and she adored him. To whisk her away now, with no real reason, would be just plain cruel. She couldn't punish her daughter for her own desperate heartache.

Because that was what it was. Her heart ached as if someone had reached in and crushed it, squeezing and squeezing with an unrelenting grip that would never loosen. And the worst thing was it was all her own fault. Despite denying it, even to herself, she had secretly taken the one night she and Lukas had shared and turned it into something it wasn't—and never would be. The start of a meaningful relationship. And she hated herself, *and* her wretched stupid heart, for being so utterly, blindly foolish.

Because this was *Lukas* they were talking about here.

The new Lukas. Cold and calculating and ruthless in the extreme. And how had she gone about protecting herself from this man? By falling into his arms, that was how. By urging him to make love to her, whispering his name against his skin and screaming it out as he brought her to orgasm. By betraying her feelings for him in the most obvious was possible.

Thinking back, she could see how he had manipulated her. The way he had drawn her in, let her come to him, waited like a wolf in his lair as she had come closer and closer. Only pouncing when he had been sure that she was his for the taking. Heat scorched her cheeks at the thought of how she had been used, how wantonly she had given herself to him. And now presumably she was being punished. By maintaining this silence Lukas was exerting his control, showing how little regard he had for her. How neatly she had fallen into his trap.

Well, she could nothing about what had happened that night, but at least she could pull her defences back into place now. And that meant not contacting him—treating his radio silence with the contempt it deserved. On the face of it at least.

She bitterly regretted the one text she had sent him, written on the boat when she'd been coming back to Thalassa, still glowing from the thrill of what they had shared. She had thanked him for a wonderful night. Actually *thanked* him. And there had been kisses. And a smiley face emoji. The thought of which now turned her stomach, even though the message had long since been deleted.

Somehow she had to put her stupidity behind her and move on. She needed to be strong now—banish all thoughts of a happy-ever-after and behave like the sensible adult she'd used to be. Before Lukas had decimated her heart. She would *not* run away. She would face up to him when he finally returned and do her best to convince him that what had happened between them had meant nothing to her. Clearly it hadn't to him.

'It's time for bed, my love.' Pulling Effie to her, Calista wrapped her arms around her daughter in a tight hug.

'Aw…not yet.' But her protestations were muffled by a big yawn. All the fresh air and sunshine of another day spent on the beach meant that sleep was not far away. 'I hope Daddy comes back tomorrow, then I can show him my shell collection.'

'Yes, well, I'm sure he'd love to see it. But Daddy is very busy, you know. He has a lot of work to do.'

'I know…he told me.' Effie yawned again. 'He's buy-ing lots of big ships. *Really* big ships that cross the oceans full of things for other people.'

Was he? This was news to Calista. She'd had no idea that he was building up the shipping empire again. Not that she was surprised. She could see that restoring the family business—*his* family business, at least—would be a priority for Lukas. And at heart he was an entrepreneur, a highly successful businessman.

'Did he say anything else?' Calista asked the question lightly. She knew she shouldn't be grilling her daughter for information, but curiosity had got the better of her.

'Um…yes.' Effie snuggled into her side and tipped up her chin to meet her mother's eyes. 'But it's sort of a se-cret.'

'Oh. Well, in that case perhaps you had better not say.' Calista stroked Effie's hair, deliberately leaving a pause. In common with most four-year-olds, keeping secrets was not one of Effie's strong points. Calista knew she just had to wait.

'If I tell you, you must promise not to tell anyone else.'

'I promise.'

'Well…' Effie struggled to sit up so she could face her mother full-on, excitement shining in her eyes. 'The next big ship that Daddy buys—he's going to call it after *me*!'

'Really?'

'Yes. He's going to call it *Euphemia*. My proper name—not Effie.'

'Well, that is *very* exciting.'

'I know.' Effie felt for a lock of her mother's hair, twisting it around her fingers. 'I expect it must be hard to buy a big ship. That's why he's been away such a long time.'

'Maybe.' Calista pulled her close again for another hug. 'Come on then, you—bedtime.'

She carried Effie through to her bedroom, setting her down and sending her into the bathroom to brush her teeth. While she waited she sat down on the bed and a small cardboard box on Effie's bedside table caught her eye. She had never noticed it before. Picking it up, she lifted the lid and what she saw inside gave her a jolt.

'What's this, Effie?' She raised her voice over the running water and Effie's vigorous toothpaste-spitting.

Effie dutifully appeared in doorway, toothbrush in hand. 'Oh, that. It's a little bit of Daddy's hair.'

Calista stilled, a creeping feeling of unease spreading over her as she looked down at the small lock of hair. 'Why have you got a bit of Daddy's hair?'

'We did a swap. He cut a bit of *his* hair off to give to me, and I cut off a bit of mine to give to him. Daddy helped me because the scissors were sharp.'

Effie returned to the bathroom and replaced her toothbrush in the glass with a clatter.

'Oops!' Calista saw her troubled face reflected in the mirror. 'I've just remembered that was a secret too.'

'That's okay, darling.' Somehow Calista managed to keep her voice steady as Effie re-joined her. But a tremor was starting to ripple through her body, already making her hands shake as the realisation of what Lukas was up to took hold.

'Don't look so worried, Mummy.' Climbing into bed, Effie stopped to give her mother a reassuring kiss on the cheek.

Calista hastily tried to rearrange her frozen features.

'It was only a little bit of hair. I've got lots more.'

'Of course you have.'

Returning the kiss, Calista tucked her daughter up in bed, moved to close the shutters and then silently left the room, pulling the door almost closed behind her.

Walking through to the living room, she seated herself on the sofa and picked up one of the cushions, holding it against her mouth. Only then did she allow herself a muffled scream.

Lukas adjusted the microphone on his headset as he waited for clearance for take-off. He was certainly in no mood to be kept waiting today. As he flicked the switches on the dashboard clearance finally came through and, grasping the controls, he took the helicopter up into the air.

It had proved to be an exhausting couple of weeks. But now he was heading back to Thalassa with his plans for the future finally in place. Plans that would see Calista abiding by his rules. Rules that he would control meticulously, ruthlessly, but above all with his brain—not his traitorous body.

The night that he had spent with her…those hours of wild, uninhibited, mind-blowing sex…now seemed a lifetime ago. As if it had happened to a different man. Which in a way it had. Because Lukas was no longer the deranged lover who had reached repeatedly for Calista's soft body, murmuring her name into the darkness, crying it out on the wave of his release. Actions that had seen him laid dangerously bare.

He had wised up.

Not that he wouldn't still have to be on his guard at all times. Because where Calista was concerned his madness was never far away. Look at the way she had managed to get his granite heart pumping again, firing it with something dangerously close to feeling. *Almost*. And she was addictive, too. He had even asked her to stay on in Athens because he'd wanted more, had been greedy for another night of passion. And then another. But Calista had, of course, declined. Presumably she felt she had done enough already. Enough to bring him to heel.

He had been in a meeting the following day when the worm of doubt about her motives had crept in. Deep in negotiations to buy a multi-million-dollar freighter, he had been enjoying the bargaining, the high-powered cut and thrust. This vessel was another of the fleet that G&K Shipping had owned before their downfall and that Lukas was gradually buying back. And it was going to be named after his daughter. *Euphemia*.

When his phone had beeped with a text from Calista he had scanned it quickly, allowing himself a smile. He would phone later. When he could pass on the good news to Effie that he had her ship.

The deal had been successfully concluded and he'd been shaking hands with the CEO of the rival shipping company when the turn of their conversation had brought him up short.

'So it's true, then?' Georgios Papadakis had given him a quizzical look. 'You're intent on buying back the old fleet?'

Lukas had nodded his assent. He wasn't surprised that Papadakis knew the truth—that the secret was out. At this level the shipping industry was a small and tight-knit group of astute capitalists who made it their business to know everything.

'It is.'

'Well, I admire your tenacity, young man. But buying back the fleet is one thing—finding traders who have any confidence in the Kalanos name will be quite another. That was some scandal you and your father embroiled yourselves in.'

'For your information…' Lukas had fought to control the rage in his voice '…my father and I were entirely innocent of all charges. Aristotle Gianopolous was responsible for the arms-smuggling. Something I will prove to the world very shortly.'

'Is that so?' Lukas had noted that Papadakis didn't look entirely surprised. 'And just how do you intend to do that?'

'I have my ways. New evidence is coming to light all the time.'

That was certainly true. Apart from the old lawyer's testimony, that very morning a new line of enquiry had been opened up. A large South American drugs cartel had recently been busted, and during the police investigations it had come to light that *they* had been the intended recipients of the arms that had been illegally stowed on the G&K freight ship. The last fateful deal that Aristotle had struck.

Lukas was intending to fly to Bolivia that very afternoon to find out as much as he could. He didn't know how long it would take—only that he wouldn't be leaving until he had accomplished his mission. Until he finally had the evidence to expose Aristotle for the man he really was. For all the world to see.

'Interesting…' Papadakis had steepled his fingers. 'And taking up with the Gianopolous girl? Is that somehow part of the plan?'

'I have *not* taken up with Calista Gianopolous!'

'No? Well, that's not what I've heard,' Papadakis had replied. 'I must admit I was surprised. I would have thought she'd be a dangerous bedfellow—especially in view of what you've just told me. Keeping your enemies close. Is that what this is all about, Kalanos? Or is it something else?' The older man's eyes had twinkled mischievously. 'Have you fallen victim to her feminine charms?'

'No!'

'You wouldn't be the first to be taken in by such a siren, that's for sure. And the girl *is* a beauty—I'll give you that. But I would advise you to be careful. Trust any member of the Gianopolous family at your peril. If you are about to expose her father I dare say Calista is keen to save her own skin—and she won't much care how she goes about it.'

'I don't need your warnings, Papadakis.' Lukas's voice had been too loud, carried too much force. 'I've told you—there is nothing between me and Calista.'

'Except the small matter of a child, of course.'

Lukas stilled. So he knew about Effie too.

'Euphemia?' Papadakis indicated the paperwork on the desk between them, which showed the new name that Lukas had registered for his latest purchase. 'It doesn't take a genius to figure out the connection. So the Gianopoulous-Kalanos dynasty is set to rise from the ashes?'

'No.' Lukas's growl had echoed round the room. 'The Gianopoulous family will have no part in this. This will be a new dynasty, solely bearing the Kalanos name.'

Papadakis had given Lukas a knowing look. 'And yet you have just admitted that the child is Gianopoulous's granddaughter?'

'But she is *my* daughter!' Jumping to his feet, Lukas had glared down at the older man. 'That means she is a

Kalanos. That is all you need to know. That is all *anyone* needs to know.'

'If you say so.' Standing up, Papadakis had given him a friendly slap on the back. 'My advice to you would be to make sure you have everything legally tied up. And I mean *everything*. In my experience mixing business with pleasure can be a lethal combination.'

Lukas knew he was right. He had to stake his claim for the Kalanos family. And, although he hadn't fully known it until that moment, stake his claim for Effie as well.

Suddenly Calista's recent behaviour had come into sharp focus. Those subtle little references to Aristotle being Effie's grandfather. About lessening the impact of the truth on Effie. Well, Stavros Kalanos was Effie's grandfather too. Something Calista seemed to have conveniently forgotten. Had she been trying to manipulate him all this time to get him to keep quiet about her father's atrocities? Carry on taking the blame for them himself? Was that what their night together had been all about?

If so, she was going to be sorely disappointed. He might have wanted her in his bed that night—wanted her in his bed every night, come to that—but that was just sex. A basic physical attraction. She might have thought she could wheedle her way into his head, appeal to his better nature, but Lukas had news for her.

He didn't have a better nature. Only a darker, blacker version of himself that had been honed to lethal perfection by his spell in prison.

He had looked back down at the text she had sent him, suddenly filled with rage. All that thanking him for a wonderful night, the kisses, the smiley face emoji. What kind of fool did she take him for? He'd have had more respect for her if she'd begged.

Deleting the message there and then, he had felt in

his pocket for the small plastic bag containing a lock of Effie's hair, possessively closing his hand around it. If there had been any doubt before about what he was going to do, if he had felt any guilt, it had been washed away on a tide of cold realisation.

And, should he have needed any *more* convincing of Calista's betrayal, then this morning's distasteful little incident had thoughtfully provided it.

After an arduous ten days in Bolivia, Lukas had returned to Athens earlier today, having successfully secured all the information he needed. Before heading back to Thalassa he had decided to pay a quick, unannounced visit to Blue Sky Charters. He had been about to enter the office when voices from inside had jerked him to a halt.

'You don't stand a chance, man. A babe like Calista Gianopoulous wouldn't look at you twice.'

Lukas's hand had all but fused to the door handle.

'Oh, you think so, do you? I'm telling you—that day on the boat she was definitely giving me the come-on.'

'In your dreams!'

'Don't underestimate the Tavi charm, my friend. It never fails.'

'Yeah, right. If anything it was *me* she fancied. All that "Can you show me how to tie some knots?". I suspect it was more than my rope skills she was interested in.'

'Then perhaps we should settle this with a wager, Nico. First one to get a kiss out of Calista scoops the prize.'

Shaking with fury, Lukas had flung open the office door, crashing it against the wall. Nico and Tavi had scrambled to their feet, and Lukas had waited a beat for the red mist to settle, watching as they'd tried to arrange themselves before him, flushed-faced and sweating. Only then had he delivered his pronouncement—clearly and unequivocally.

'You're fired! Both of you! Get out!'

Now, as he flew the helicopter over the vivid blue Aegean Sea and the island of Thalassa came into view, Lukas could still feel that anger, that all-consuming rage. He could still taste its venom. But it had changed its form, had settled into solid, impenetrable rock that only served to strengthen his resolve.

Calista Gianopoulous had shown her true colours and the scales had fallen from his eyes. Now everything was in place. And she was about to find out the kind of the man he really was.

CHAPTER TEN

AT THE SOUND of the helicopter landing Calista felt her heart lurch. *He was back.* Putting down her book, she leapt to her feet, positioning herself in the middle of the room with her hands on her hips. But as the seconds dragged by and he still hadn't appeared she started to pace up and down, smoothing the fabric of her sundress with shaky hands, her blood pressure rising with every step.

'Kalispera.' Eventually he appeared, throwing her a casual glance before going into the kitchen and returning with a glass of water. 'Where's Effie?' He looked around him.

'She's not here.' Calista ground out her reply.

'I can see that.' Placing his glass down on a low table, he came and stood before her. 'Where is she?'

'It doesn't matter where she is. What's more to the point is where the hell have *you* been?'

'Missed me, have you?' He angled his broad shoulders in a deliberately casual pose. But the look in his eye was anything but casual. It was hard, ruthless, calculating.

'You flatter yourself, Lukas.' Calista averted her gaze from his face and took a couple of steps to the side. He was far too close. 'But it might have been nice if you had told us when you intended to return. Just out of common decency.'

'Common decency has never really been my thing.'

'No.' She met his eyes again, flashing an emerald-green warning. 'I should have realised that.'

He returned an infuriating smile, as if he was enjoying himself, playing with her. 'Well, I can see you are delighted to have me back now.' He looked around him. 'Where did you say Effie was?'

'I didn't.' Calista could feel her colour rising, staining the column of her neck. 'But, since you ask, she is over at Villa Melina. Dorcas is going to give her some tea and then Petros will bring her back.'

'Interesting…' Lukas closed the space between them with a single stride, looking down at her with heated, possessive intent. 'So we are alone.'

'We are. Which is just as well.'

'Even more interesting.' Reaching forward, he took hold of a curl of red hair, twisting it seductively around his finger, his eyes dancing over her face. 'What do you have in mind for us, Calista?'

'I'll tell you what I have in mind.' With a violent toss of her head Calista freed herself. 'Let's start by talking about what you have been doing for the last couple of weeks.'

'What I do with my time is none of your business, *agape*.'

'No? So nothing you have done is any of my business?'

'That's what I said.'

'Then you are a liar, Lukas Kalanos!'

'I beg your pardon?' Lukas's nostrils flared, the chill of his words freezing the air. 'What did you just call me?'

'A liar.' Fear stuttered in Calista's heart but she carried on regardless. She had gone too far to stop now. 'Because that's what you are.'

'I would take that back if I were you, Calista. You are treading on very dangerous ground.'

'No. I won't take it back.' She was riding the wave now, trying to ignore the crash that would inevitably follow.

'Then perhaps I need to put you straight about a few things.' Lukas fixed her with a brutally punishing stare. 'That you of all people should call me a liar is almost beyond belief. You, who have done nothing but deceive me by failing to tell me that I had a daughter for over four years, who would most likely never have told me if I hadn't forced the truth out of you. For you to have the bare-faced nerve to challenge my honesty is staggeringly hypocritical.'

'Not telling you about Effie is completely different. There is no comparison.'

'You lied by omission, Calista. And that is every bit as bad as lying to my face. Worse, in fact. It is even more cowardly. So don't even *think* about trying to defend yourself.'

'I am not interested in defending myself.'

'And, since we are on the subject of liars, why don't we talk about your father? The most heinous liar of all.'

'This is not about me or my father!' she hurled back, hitching her shoulders, wild-eyed with fury. 'This is about *you* sneaking behind my back and taking a sample of Effie's hair to be DNA-tested.'

Lukas remained silent, his eyes narrowing to lethal thick-lashed slits.

'Yes, you see, I know.' Triumphant now, Calista continued. 'So don't bother to deny it.'

'Why would I try and deny it?' Lukas folded his arms across his chest.

'So you admit it, then?'

'It is true that I have had a DNA test done to establish the paternity of my daughter. That's not an admission. It's a statement of fact.'

'A *fact* that you just happened to fail to tell me about?'

He shrugged his indifference.

'Lying by omission.' Calista threw his phrase back at him. 'I believe that was your expression.'

Lukas gave a low growl. 'Taking steps to establish a legal footing for my relationship with my own daughter hardly compares to the atrocities your family have inflicted on mine.'

'A legal footing?' Calista spat the words back at him. 'And what exactly does *that* mean? You weren't sure that she was yours—is that it?'

She fired the accusation at him like a missile, but deep down she hoped she was right. Because, insulting though that would be, it was far better than the alternative. The nightmare that had been tormenting her ever since she had discovered he'd taken a sample of Effie's hair.

'On the contrary.' Lukas's voice was as smooth as glass. 'I have never had any doubt that Effie is my daughter.'

Panic made her legs tremble, stealing the breath from her chest. 'So what, then? Why do a DNA test if you already knew the answer?'

A small but deadly smile touched Lukas's lips. 'You're a bright girl, Calista. I'm sure you can work it out. But if you want me to spell it out for you, I will. In order to have any legal control over my daughter I have to be able to prove paternity. Step one is to get my name on her birth certificate.'

Calista felt something shrivel inside her. She could have pointed out that she had hardly been in a position to ask him to sit beside her in the register office and put his name on the birth certificate, but that would only have strengthened his case. And besides, her terrified focus was elsewhere.

'And step two?' She tried to sound rational, but her heart was pounding at a terrifying rate.

'Step two?' Lukas ran a hand over his jaw, as if considering. 'Well, you might as well know. Step two is to apply for full custody of my daughter.'

'No!' The full horror enveloped her like a black shroud. Fists flying, she threw herself at Lukas, pounding at his chest. *'Never!'* The word was twisted into a strangled scream as she thrashed about, lashing out with wild but increasingly futile blows to the solid wall of his chest.

Lukas did absolutely nothing to stop her, taking the assault with a contemptuous calm that only made her more frantic, more desperate. With her hair flying around her face she raised her hand, ready to strike, but with lightning speed Lukas caught it, and along with the other one brought it down so that they were both trapped between them.

'Oh, no, you don't,' he growled. 'You have slapped my face once. You won't be doing that again.'

'Get off me! Let me go!' Calista tried to buck away but that only made Lukas tighten his hold. He looked down at her for a second, before pulling her towards him, releasing her wrists only to wrap his arms around her in a powerful embrace from which there was no escape.

Lowering his head, he whispered in her ear. 'I'll let you go when I am good and ready.'

Calista held herself rigid, her heart raging in her chest, the blood roaring in her ears. And there it was again—that febrile connection pulsing between them, hot and hard and impossible to ignore. *Desire.* Although that was too delicate a name for what she and Lukas felt for each other. It was hunger, craving, infatuation, a greedy obsession that tore at her soul, weakened her, at the same time as giving Lukas all the strength, all the power.

She could feel it now, rampaging through her as Lukas held her tightly against him. Feel the way it sapped her energy, melted her bones to liquid. She let out a breath, giving herself a moment, her body sagging with the sheer exhaustion of trying to fight this physical attraction. This all-consuming madness.

Above her, around her, almost a part of her, Lukas overpowered her—body and soul. Not by his physical strength, although that was undeniably a part of him, but simply by being the man he was. She swallowed against the pain of unshed tears blocking her throat as the reality of the terrible situation hit home.

She loved Lukas.

And right now that felt like the cruellest fate of all.

Loosening his hold, Lukas angled his head so that he could see her face, moving aside the thick twist of hair, the back of his hand brushing her cheek as he did so. Calista closed her eyes. She sensed his head coming closer, felt the soft whisper of his breath on her lips, felt them part slightly, provocatively, inviting his kiss.

With superhuman effort she controlled herself, rearing up and pushing him away. 'You may think you have all the power, Lukas—the wealth and the contacts to gain custody of Effie.' She brushed away the hair that was stuck to her lips. 'But you are wrong. I will never let you take my daughter away from me. *Never.*' Her voice cracked with all the pain inside her, all the sadness and anger, the bitterness and regret. 'I would sooner die than give up my child.'

Taking several steps away, she glared at him, giving him the full force of her temper, fury glittering in her eyes. But inside she had never felt more scared, more vulnerable.

'Aren't we being a little melodramatic?'

Closing the gap, Lukas went to put a hand on her shoulder, but she ducked beneath his arm, turning on her heel and marching from the room. She heard him following her down the corridor as she headed for her bedroom, but she refused to acknowledge the way he propped himself against the doorframe, watching her every move. Tugging open drawers, she dumped the contents on the bed before opening the wardrobe and pulling all the clothes off their hangers. Then, retrieving a suitcase, she unzipped the lid and started to stuff everything inside.

'Can I ask what you think you are doing?'

'Work it out for yourself, Lukas, you're a bright man.' She threw his words back at him before disappearing into the bathroom, collecting up an armful of toiletries and coming back to chuck them into the suitcase. 'I should have thought it was pretty obvious. I'm leaving.'

'Leaving?' Shouldering himself away from the doorframe, Lukas advanced towards her. 'Or running away?'

'Call it what you like.' Pointedly stepping past him, Calista headed for the adjoining room—Effie's bedroom—and began a repeat performance with her belongings. She couldn't stop to think—not now, not with Lukas hovering ever closer, his tall frame right beside her as she stuffed Effie's clothes into her little tiger-shaped suitcase. Glancing at her row of possessions on the windowsill—the collection of seashells, the doll that Dorcas and Petros had given her, the finely modelled sailing boat—a present from her father, which Effie adored—she made a split-second decision and snatched up the doll. The boat could stay there.

'Just in case you should be in any doubt, I am taking Effie with me.'

She had no idea what her plans were other than that she had to get away, right now, whilst her anger still had the capacity to propel her forward. Before real misery rendered her incapable of anything.

'Running away solves nothing, Calista. I would have thought you had learned that by now.'

'On the contrary.'

Brushing past him, she exited the room, pulling the tiger suitcase behind her, swinging the doll from her free hand. Back in her bedroom, she threw it on top of her own suitcase before attempting to zip up the lid. Her chaotic packing meant it refused to close. Opening it again, she saw the doll staring at her with glassy-eyed reproach before Callie turned her over, pressing her down firmly into the muddle of clothes.

'It gets me and Effie away from *you*. And there is nothing more important than that right now.'

'Really? And why do you suppose that is, Calista?'

He was beside her again, leaning over her, barring her way.

'Why are you so desperate to get away from me?'

'Because you are a deceitful, scheming bully—that's why. Because you are plotting to take my daughter away from me. Because—'

Her breathless tirade was silenced by Lukas taking hold of her chin, tipping her face so that she couldn't avoid the inky-black stare of his cruelly beautiful eyes. She felt her skin flare in response, her body straining with tension, but her darting gaze was steady as it was caught in his thrall.

'Because what, Calista? Go on—say it.'

'Because...because I *hate* you!' The words came out in a blind rush of emotion.

Calista took in a deep breath. She had said it before, of course, and it had always felt as if the only person she was punishing was herself. But at least she had come down on the right side of the dangerously thin line that separated the two most extreme of emotions. For she knew she could easily have fallen the other way—knew that as far as Lukas was concerned love and hate were inextricably linked in her neural pathways and always would be. Something he must never find out.

'Hate is a strong word, *agape*.'

Lukas ran a finger over her lips, resting it there as if to silence her. It was only a light pressure but it burned like fire, searing into her until she had to prise open her mouth to free herself from the sensation and take a gasp of air. Immediately Lukas's head lowered, until his mouth hovered over hers, just a hair's breadth away from possessing her with his kiss. A split second away from crashing through her defences...

'Hello!'

At the sound of their daughter's voice Calista sprang away, fleeing the bedroom as fast as her sandaled feet would take her. Lukas was left staring after her, exasperation, raging lust and impotent fury all surging through him in the cacophony of insanity that he had come to accept was part and parcel of his relationship with Calista. If you could call it a relationship.

'Hello, sweetheart.' He could hear her talking to Effie, her voice unnaturally high, false. 'Have you had a lovely afternoon?'

'Is Daddy here?' Effie cut to the chase. 'The helicopter's outside.'

'Well, yes, he is. But the thing is...'

'*Yassou*, Effie.' Lukas strode into the living room, spreading out his arms in time to catch his daughter as she launched herself at him.

'Yay! You're back.' Throwing her arms around his neck, she snuggled against him as Lukas settled her onto his hip. 'Why were you away so long?'

'I had a lot of work to do.'

'Did you buy my ship?'

'I did.'

'Cool. When can I see it?'

'Well, the thing is, darling—' Calista cut in.

'I'll see if I can arrange a visit very soon.'

'But it won't be that soon.'

Taking control, Calista advanced towards him, reaching out to take Effie from his arms then setting her on her feet and clasping her hand.

'Because there has been a change of plan, Effie. We are going back to England.'

'Aw…' Effie's expressive little face was furrowed with disappointment. 'Why?'

'Because we need to go home.'

'But *why*? I like it here.'

'I'm sure you do. But holidays can't last for ever.'

Effie stuck out her bottom lip. 'Will Daddy be coming with us?'

'No, he won't.'

Big green eyes gazed up at him and Lukas felt something twist inside him. 'Why not?'

'Because Daddy lives here, as you well know.' Calista looked down at her daughter, the patient reasoning in her voice starting to crack. 'Now, I've already packed our suitcases, so if Petros would be kind enough to give us a lift to the harbour…'

'I bet *Daddy* doesn't want us to go—do you, Daddy?'

Two pairs of green eyes swung in his direction, one beseeching, the other glistening with tension and anger and most of all warning.

'You must do as your mother says.' He had been silently watching the exchange between mother and daughter, but now Lukas gave his pronouncement with the full weight of his authority.

He saw the flash of surprise in Calista's eyes before she let out an audible breath.

He had to fight his every instinct, but Lukas knew this

was the right thing to do. The clever thing. He had no intention of getting into a slanging match with Calista now—not in front of Effie. If there was any moral high ground to be had he was going to take it. If Calista wanted to pack her bags and leave he wouldn't try and stop her. He could wait—at least a short while longer. And this was just the sort of unreasonable, unpredictable behaviour that would help him in the custody case. A case *he* was going to win.

Yes, very soon he would hold all the cards, and then he would see Calista come crawling back to him. It was an idea that already tightened the muscles of his groin. Once he held all the power he would have Calista just where he wanted her. And that, he knew with blinding certainty, was in his bed.

'Come on, now, little one.' Seeing Effie's bottom lip start to tremble, Lukas picked her up again and held her close. 'There's no need to be sad. I will be seeing you again very soon.'

'Promise?' The word was muffled against his chest.

'I promise. You must go with your mother now, but we'll be together again in no time.'

He put her down, giving her a little pat on the back to send her towards Calista, and their eyes clashed again. Sparks of fear and fight flew at him. She looked like a cornered animal, protecting her young. Which he supposed she was.

He chose to respond with nothing more than the faint quirk of a brow. 'Would you like me to take you back to the mainland in the helicopter?'

The more agitated he felt, the more reasonable he made himself sound. Whether he was trying to convince Calista or himself, or just limit Effie's distress, he wasn't sure. But he did know that the twisting pain in his gut had to be controlled at all costs.

'No, thank you.' Calista's brittle reply snapped between them. 'I am perfectly capable of sorting out my own travel arrangements.'

'As you wish.' But nevertheless he turned to address Petros, who stood in the doorway awaiting instructions, a worried look on his face. 'Petros, please see to it that there is a boat to transport Calista and my daughter back to the mainland.'

'Yes, sir.' Petros nodded solemnly.

'Come on, then, Effie.' With an arm around Effie's shoulder, Calista began to herd her out of the villa. 'Oh, the cases…' She looked behind her.

'Allow me.' Striding back into Calista's bedroom, Lukas picked up the two suitcases and followed them out to Petros's car, where he stowed the cases in the boot. He waited as Calista secured Effie's seatbelt, then leant to give his daughter another hug.

'Don't forget, *paidi mou*, I'll be seeing you again very soon.'

Effie nodded tearfully and, straightening up, Lukas turned to Calista who stood beside him, steadfastly avoiding his eye as she waited to close the car door.

'Calista.' He pronounced her name as a farewell.

'Goodbye, Lukas.' Proud and defiant, Calista returned his valediction.

For a moment they stared at one another, tension radiating between them like a palpable force.

'Until we meet again.' Leaning forward, Lukas spoke quietly against her ear. To a casual observer it might have looked like an affectionate gesture of parting, but it was far from that. The intent in his voice left no room for sentiment or ambiguity. 'I will be in touch very shortly to discuss arrangements.'

'Then you will be wasting your time.' Calista tossed

back her head, the rich red curls gleaming in the sunshine. 'There will be no arrangements. Effie is my daughter and she is staying with me.'

Moving past him, she went round to the other side of the car and opened the door.

Lukas was beside her in a flash, barring her way. 'Then you had better get yourself a good lawyer, Calista. You're going to need one.'

Calista glared back at him, eyes ablaze as she waited for him to get out of her way. Lukas watched as she seated herself inside the car, tugging her short dress down over her thighs before reaching across to take hold of Effie's hand.

'Oh, just so you know...' He ducked his head inside for one last parting shot. 'I will shortly be going public about your father. You might want to mention *that* to your lawyer as well.'

And with that he closed the door and banged on the roof as a signal for Petros to leave.

Standing with his hands on his hips, Lukas watched as the car took off, throwing up a cloud of dust as it bumped over the dry single-track road. He was staring at the rear window, at the back of Calista's head, when Effie's little face appeared. With her fingertips pressed to her lips she blew him a series of quick kisses before Calista's arm reached out to her to face the front again.

Walking back into the villa, Lukas closed the door behind him and looked around. Strangely enough, he had never felt more alone in his life.

CHAPTER ELEVEN

'PUT IT ON, Mummy.' Effie pointed to the mortarboard resting on Calista's lap.

They were on their way to her graduation ceremony in the grand university hall—something that Effie was looking forward to far more than her. Calista hesitated.

'Go on,' Effie prompted. 'Then everyone can see that this is your special day.'

'Okay!' Giving her daughter a smile, Calista did as she was told and positioned the silly hat on her head, waggling the tassel at her. 'There. Happy now?'

Effie nodded and turned to look out of the taxi window again. Calista stared at her profile. Effie being happy meant more to her than anything else in the world, and it tore at her heart to see how much quieter she had been these past few weeks, how withdrawn. She would have worn a clown outfit to the graduation ceremony if she'd thought it would cheer her up, complete with flappy shoes and red nose. But she knew there was only one thing that would light up Effie's life again, and that was to be reunited with her father.

It had been three weeks since they had returned to London, and Effie's persistent pestering about when she was going to see her daddy again had eventually settled into a gloomy acceptance that she wasn't. And that had only made Calista feel worse.

But she had fought against it—adopting a relentlessly upbeat and positive attitude, determined that she was going to make up for Lukas's absence. They'd had trips to the zoo and the park, picnics and ice creams. Effie had even been allowed to stay up long past her bedtime, snuggled against her on the sofa. Although in truth this last had been more for her own benefit. Because anything was better than being alone…being left to stare at the whole hideous mess of her life.

Every day she expected it to happen—she would hear on the news that her father's heinous acts had been exposed or a solicitor's letter would come saying that Lukas had filed for custody of Effie. Or both. Every morning she woke with the sick dread of what the day might bring, only to find that it brought nothing. No word from Lukas at all. And, far from finding any sense of relief, all she felt was pain. A tangible, physical pain—as if someone had reached in and ripped out her heart. Because that was what loving Lukas did to her. It tortured her.

The sudden screech of brakes brought her back to the present, followed by the thud of an impact that jerked them both forward against their seat belts.

'What's happened, Mummy?'

'I'm not sure, darling.' Calista looked anxiously at her daughter. 'Are you okay?'

'Yes, I'm fine.' Effie peered out of the taxi window. 'But I think that man is dead.'

Following her gaze, Calista saw a young man sprawled across the road. Quickly she unbuckled her seatbelt. She could deal with this. She was, after all, a qualified nurse.

'I'm sure he's not dead. You stay here, Effie, I'm going to see what I can do to help him.'

Effie nodded obediently and Calista leapt out of the cab to where the casualty lay. He was unconscious, still wearing a crash helmet, and his head was twisted sideways. Blood poured from a serious wound to his leg. A few feet away was the mangled wreck of his motorbike. She knelt down beside him to feel for the pulse in his neck. It was scarily weak.

'I didn't see him!' Beside her the taxi driver was choking with panic. 'He came out of nowhere. I couldn't have avoided him.'

'Call an ambulance!' Calista said firmly. This was not the time for apportioning blame.

A small group of onlookers had started to gather around them—pedestrians and people getting out of their cars as the traffic backed up behind them, horns tooting impatiently already.

'Does anyone here have any first aid experience?' There was an ominous silence.

'You.' She pointed to an intelligent-looking young man on the edge of the crowd. 'Come and help me.'

He obediently stepped forward. 'Are…are you some sort of doctor, miss?'

Standing upright, she realised she must look a bit odd, dressed in her flowing black and red graduation gown, complete with mortarboard.

'I'm a nurse.' Tossing the mortarboard to one side, she took off the gown and thrust it at the young man. 'Rip this up. We need to make a tourniquet to stop the blood.'

She bent over the casualty again, just in time to see his eyes roll back in his head. *No!* She wouldn't allow him to die. She simply wouldn't.

Grabbing the strip of fabric offered by her helper, she tied it tightly around the casualty's thigh and then, unzipping his leather jacket, started CPR, pumping at his chest with her linked hands as hard as she could, totally focussed on what she had to do.

Minutes passed and still she worked, blotting everything else out, refusing to give up no matter how much her arms ached, how heavily her breath rasped in her throat. She could hear the wail of an ambulance siren in the distance, coming closer. *Hurry up, hurry up.* She could do this. She was going to keep this young man alive.

Lukas held his finger against the buzzer for Calista's flat. Irritation clenched his jaw. She was either ignoring him or she was out. Or, worse still—he felt the irritation turn to something much darker—she and Effie had upped sticks and left.

He should have told them he was coming, of course. That would have been the sensible thing to do. But all sense went out of the window as far as Calista was concerned. Besides, he was looking forward to surprising Effie. And her mother too—but in a very different way.

He had spent the intervening weeks in Athens, working all hours, pushing himself harder and harder to achieve his goals. And he had succeeded, leaving the staff of Kalanos Shipping reeling from the full force of his formidable demands and expectations. As for Blue Sky Charters—the sacking of Nico and Tavi had sent shock waves through that company. The sheer ruthlessness of their boss meant they were now all on high alert to make sure the same thing didn't happen to them.

Aside from business, Lukas had instructed his lawyers to start custody proceedings for his daughter and had collated more than enough information to expose Aristotle Gianopoulous for the monstrous villain that he was.

He should have been feeling pleased with himself, satisfied with all he had accomplished. Instead he just felt knotted up with tension. Far from feeling any sort of triumph, he couldn't shake off the feeling that he had somehow overstepped the boundaries—mistreated Calista right from the start. *Somehow she had made him feel bad.* And that was despite everything he knew, all that she had done. It didn't make any sense.

He missed Effie, of course. Villa Helene felt horribly empty without her there, without her cheery little face opposite him at the breakfast table, without hearing her asking him what they were going to do that day. He had hoped that relocating to his apartment in Athens would improve his frame of mind, but he had found no relief from his gloom there either. Quite the reverse.

Throwing himself into his work had only darkened his mood, made him more irritable, more unreasonable. And the fleeting thought that maybe he should go out, seek some entertainment in one of Athens's many exclusive clubs, had been so repugnant that he'd wondered if he was ill—if there was something physically wrong with him.

But he wasn't ill—at least not in the accepted sense of the word. Deep down he knew all too well where the source of his malaise came from. *Calista Gianopoulous,* that was where. She had crept under his skin, peeled back the protective layers, made him question everything about himself—his motives and his morals. *She had got to him.* His hollow yearning for something undefined had gradually given shape to the certainty that he had to have her in his life. Permanently.

It was a deeply shocking realisation.

And he didn't just mean in his bed at night—although the recollection of what they had done still mercilessly ripped into him. The image of Calista…beautiful Calista… her hair wildly cascading down her back, was seared onto his retina, appearing without his permission whenever he tried to close his eyes. The memory of the way she had looked when he had brought her to orgasm, the way she had felt, tasted, smelled, filled his mind, blocked his sleep and stole his sanity. Try as he might, he simply couldn't get her out of his head.

Which was why last night he had finally given up and made the decision to come to London and sort out this infuriating state of affairs once and for all. How he was going to do it, Lukas no longer had any idea.

But first he had to find her.

The front door opened and Magda appeared.

'I'm looking for Calista. Is she in? Is my daughter here?'

'No. She and Effie have already left.'

'Left?' The word struck fear into his heart and mentally he was already tracking them down, bringing them back, doing whatever it took to return them to where they belonged. With him.

'Yes, for our graduation ceremony.'

Magda held up the gown that Lukas had failed to notice was draped over her arm. Then she pointed over at a taxi idling on the other side of the road.

'That's my taxi, there. Calista went ahead of me because she wanted to—'

'It doesn't matter why.' Rudely interrupting, he ushered Magda towards the waiting taxi and all but bundled her in, following behind her and slamming the door. Leaning forward, he went to speak the taxi driver before realising he had no idea where they were going. 'Wherever *she* says.' He indicated the astonished Magda. 'And make it fast.'

But it wasn't fast. They had been travelling for less than ten minutes when the traffic ground to a halt. There was a queue of vehicles backed up as far as the eye could see.

'There's been an accident, mate.' The taxi driver slid back the glass partition to speak them. 'You might find it quicker to go on foot.'

Hell and damnation. Thrusting some money at him, Lukas took hold of Magda's hand and pulled her out after him.

'You know the way?' He raised his voice over the sound of the ambulance that was fighting its way through the traffic on the other side of the road.

'I should do.' Magda straightened her skirt. 'I've studied there for three years.'

'Then what are we waiting for? Lead the way.'

'How is he, Dr Lorton?' Calista leapt up as the A&E doctor came towards her.

'Out of danger.' The doctor put an arm around her shoulders. 'You did a great job, Nurse Gianopoulous.'

'And the leg?'

'They've taken him up for surgery now. Mr Dewsnap is pretty certain he can save it.'

'Oh, thank God for that.'

'Seriously, though, Calista, I mean it. You saved that young man's life. Your mummy…' he bent down to speak to Effie, who was busy colouring in some complicated anatomical drawings that someone had found to keep her occupied '…is a proper hero!'

Effie beamed back at him.

'Shame you had to miss your graduation ceremony, though.' Straightening up, Dr Lorton eyed Calista.

'Oh, I'm not bothered about that. At least the gown was put to good use!'

'And this was far more exciting.' Effie joined in the conversation. 'I had a ride in the front of an ambulance and everything.'

'So I heard!'

Calista scooped up her daughter and gave her a big hug. She hoped this incident hadn't been too traumatic for her.

The ambulance that had arrived at the scene had come from the hospital where she'd done her nursing practice and she'd known the paramedics on board. Reluctant to leave her patient, she had accepted their suggestion that she accompany them back to the hospital. There was no way she could have gone on to the ceremony looking as she did anyway—all wild and bloodied. Plus the fact that in all the confusion she'd left her handbag in the taxi, which meant that as well as missing her purse and her phone she didn't have the keys to get into her flat.

She'd called the taxi firm, who had promised to return her bag to the hospital, but in the meanwhile she'd had a shower and found a change of clothes in her locker while various members of staff had fussed over Effie. Judging by the look on her face, Effie had had the time of her life.

'I think I'm going to be a nurse when I grow up.' Wriggling to be put down, Effie went back to her colouring. 'Either that or a shipping *magnet* person.'

'Wow!' Dr Lorton gave Calista an astonished grin.

Calista tried to smile back but her lips had frozen on her face.

'Just like my daddy.'

Lukas's patience was wearing dangerously thin. It felt as if he had been here for hours, seated at the back of this echoing hall of hallowed learning, watching an endless parade of students filing onto the stage to collect their scrolls of achievement, shaking hands, smiling, moving on. What was worse was that there was no sign of Calista. Now he could see Magda, lining up at the bottom of the steps, waiting to be called. This had to be Calista's class. Where the hell *was* she?

'Calista Gianopoulous!'

Suddenly her name echoed around the hall, only to be

met with silence, followed by whisperings and some shuffling of papers before they moved on to the next student.

Lukas rose to his feet and moved to the edge of the hall, then made his way towards the front, waiting in the wings. Had Calista found out that he was here? Was that why she had done a disappearing act?

He looked around him, scanning the assembled audience as if half expecting her to have donned some disguise or to be hiding under a seat. Though he had no idea why. Calista never shied away from confrontation. If she were here now she'd be more likely to be laying into him, eyes flashing, breasts heaving, that wild red hair being tossed around her heart-shaped face. Lukas sucked in a breath. God, how he had missed her.

'Magda Jedynak.'

He positioned himself at the bottom of the steps as Magda descended, deftly ushering her to one side as the applause rang out for the next student.

'Where is she, Magda?'

'I don't know!' Moving them into a small chamber off the main hall, Magda looked at him with genuine concern. 'I can't understand it. She and Effie left well before me... us, I mean. I've tried texting her—but nothing.'

'Then try again.' He omitted to say that he himself had already left countless unanswered messages on her phone.

Fumbling beneath her robe, Magda produced her phone and flicked on the screen. 'One message, but it's not from Calista.'

Lukas scowled. He had no intention of standing there watching her read a message from her boyfriend.

'Oh, it *is* Cal—she's using someone else's phone. There's been an accident...she and Effie are at the hospital.'

'Which hospital?' A wave of black panic washed over

him, consumed him, and his words sounded as if they'd been spoken by someone else.

'Um… St George's. But she says not to worry. They are both—'

Before Magda had the chance to finish her sentence Lukas was gone, his footsteps thundering down the central aisle between the rows of seats, every head turning in his direction as he wrenched open the ancient wooden doors and flung himself out into the street.

'How much longer do we have to stay here?'

'Not long. As soon as the taxi company bring my bag we can go. Now, come away from the doors.'

Clearly the novelty of being at the hospital had worn off for Effie, and she was entertaining herself by activating the automatic doors at Reception. Calista threw the well-thumbed magazine back down on the table in front of her and yawned. All she wanted to do was to go home.

'He's here!'

Looking up at Effie's yelp of pleasure, Calista saw her jumping up and down, waving madly.

'All right, calm down!' A taxi had pulled up outside, but it hardly merited Effie's ecstatic welcome. She was obviously emotionally overwrought.

'Look, look. It's Daddy! He's *here*!'

Calista felt the world do a giddy spin. *Lukas?* No, he couldn't be! But suddenly there he was, powering through the doors towards them, so commanding, so strikingly handsome that all eyes were on him.

As if watching in slow motion Calista saw him scoop up an overjoyed Effie, quickly casting his eyes over her, and saw the look of grim determination on his face soften as he bent to kiss her on the forehead. Then he turned and straightened up, and suddenly the full force of his attention was on her.

Calista swallowed. Eyes as black as midnight tore into her, immediately shredding the paper-thin patches she had tried to put in place to protect her heart. It was as if he could destroy her with just one look. Tear her apart. This man could control the pumping of her heart, the breath in her chest, the blood in her veins.

He was everything to her, and the more she tried to fight it the more entangled she became. Like a fish caught in a net, the more she thrashed about trying to escape, the worse it was for her.

'Calista.' He was right in front of her now, swallowing her space, with Effie clamped to his side like a limpet. 'What's happened? Are you okay?'

Calista realised that she was standing up, one hand gripping the back of the seat. *No!* she wanted to scream at him. *I am not okay. Every fibre of my being yearns for you… every molecule aches because of you. Loving you has undone me, destroyed me. And I will never, ever recover.*

But none of those words could be said. So, straightening her spine, she pulled in a breath. 'Yes, I'm fine.'

'And Effie?'

'She's fine too. We are both…fine.'

'Then what are you doing here?' Setting Effie down on her feet, he bore down on Calista, placing possessive hands on her shoulders.

'I could ask *you* the same question.'

'For God's sake, Calista.' He frantically searched her face. 'What's going on? Magda said there had been some kind of accident.'

'A man on a motorbike,' Effie helpfully chipped in. 'Mummy saved his life.'

'But neither of you was injured?'

Calista shook her head.

'Thank God!' Lukas's shoulders visibly dropped.

'We were in the taxi that hit him, that's all. Did you say you'd seen Magda?' Calista furrowed her brow, struggling to understand.

'Yes. At the graduation ceremony.'

'You've been to Magda's graduation ceremony?' Her brain seemed to have turned to pulp, like a ball of newspaper left out in the rain. Nothing was making any sense.

'No—well, yes…'

'What were you doing there?'

'I went looking for *you*, of course.'

'Right…' Calista made herself breathe through the fog. There was something about his phrase—*looking for you*—that sent a chill down her stiffened spine. He hadn't come to *see* her, He had come to *find* her. And that had a very different connotation.

She stared into his face, so beautiful but so brutally punishing. A rogue muscle twitched in his cheek and she knew she had read him right.

'Can I ask why?' Her voice held a thread of steel but as she waited the dread of his reply wound around her, tightening its grip. She held her head very still, as if afraid it might part company from the rest of her body.

Silence fell between them. The voices of the people around them were reduced to a soft babble. Lukas shifted his weight from one leg to the other, staring at her with a dark intensity that seemed to be searching her soul.

Or was it his own soul?

For the first time Calista caught the flash of vulnerability in his eyes. Could it be that he was actually battling with himself? Fighting some internal conflict?

His eyes never leaving her face, he took the black

leather document case from under his arm and after a moment's pause chucked it onto a nearby seat.

'To do this.'

With a rapid movement he wrapped his arms around her, pressing her against him, one hand moving to the small of her back, where it branded her with its possessive heat.

'And then this.'

Lifting her chin, he took a second to gaze at her startled face before lowering his head and claiming her lips in a blisteringly passionate kiss.

And Calista surrendered to it, melting against him, because there had never been any question of her doing anything else.

She was dimly aware of a ripple of applause, a whistle of appreciation. And then the gleefully shocked voice of her daughter, saying, 'Ew, *yuck*!'

CHAPTER TWELVE

'SHE'S ALREADY SOUND ASLEEP.' Coming through from Effie's bedroom, Calista accepted the glass of champagne that Lukas proffered and sank down onto the sofa. 'She was obviously worn out.'

'I'm not surprised.' Magda came and sat beside her. 'From the sound of it she has had quite a day!'

Calista laughed. Effie had certainly made the most of the day's events, explaining them first to Lukas and then to Magda, and then to the florist who had delivered an enormous bouquet of flowers sent by the patient's family. She had gone into graphic detail over just how her mummy had saved this man's life because he had actually been totally, properly dead, and how she was the biggest hero ever because everybody said so.

'Mmm...yum.' Magda took a sip from her glass. 'Thank you for this, Lukas.' She looked up at him with a mixture of curiosity and blatant admiration.

'My pleasure.'

Calista followed her gaze. Standing with his back to the window, Lukas stood tall and imposing, owning the space even though this was supposed to be *her* domain. She tried to look at him dispassionately—the way Magda would see him. But that only set her heart racing, the way it always did. The way it always would.

Wearing dark grey suit trousers and a fine pinstriped grey and white shirt with the sleeves rolled up, he epitomised the billionaire businessman at ease. Except there was something tense about the set of his shoulders, the angle of his lightly stubbled jaw. His hair had grown since that day she had glimpsed him on the other side of her father's grave—the day that had so dramatically impacted on her life. The severe style he had worn in prison was now softened by loose dark curls at the nape of his neck and starting to fall over his forehead before they were raked back by his impatient hand.

But if his hairstyle was softer it was the only thing about him that was. As she stared at him now, still exuding that chillingly austere authority, Calista felt a knife plunge into her soul. Because she knew why he was here. Despite the urbane courteousness, despite the very public kiss they had shared in the hospital, he was here to try and take Effie from her. It was written all over his treacherous face.

'I would like to propose a toast.' His rich, dark voice resonated around the small room.

'Oh, yes—good idea.' Magda sat upright, her glass raised.

'To the two newly qualified nurses. May you both have long and distinguished careers.'

'Thank you. I'll drink to that.' Magda smiled and Lukas stepped forward so that the three of them could clink glasses.

'And, of course, to Calista.'

'Yay! Callie! Our very own hero!'

They clinked glasses again, and Magda leant in to give Calista a big hug. But as Magda pulled away she caught the look on Lukas's face, saw the way his eyes had settled on Calista and she gave a little cough.

'You know what?' She tugged theatrically at the neck of her blouse. 'I think I might make myself scarce.'

'No, don't do that.' Calista reached for her hand, clutching at it in desperation.

'Actually, Magda,' Lukas cut in, 'I want to ask you a favour. Would you mind babysitting this evening, so that I can take Calista out for a meal?'

'Of course.' Magda grinned helpfully. 'Gladly. You go.'

'Oh, no, Magda.' Calista looked at her friend with beseeching eyes. 'I'm sure you must have plans of your own for this evening.'

'No, no plans at all—other than polishing off the rest of that bottle of champagne. You go. And don't hurry back.'

Calista looked daggers at her. Was Magda doing this deliberately? Wasn't she making it perfectly obvious that the thought of being left alone with Lukas filled her with a sickening dread?

'Good, that's settled, then.' Putting his glass down on the table, Lukas picked up his jacket and hooked it over his shoulder with one finger. 'I have a couple of things to do, so I'll pick you up in an hour. Oh…'

He turned, and Calista saw the hard light glittering in his eyes. 'You might want to dress up. After all, this evening is something of a celebration.'

Lukas's dark brows drew together as he watched Calista's mouth close around her forkful of lobster mousse, seeing her swallow, licking her lips with the tip of her tongue to savour the last morsel. They were seated in an exclusive French restaurant in the heart of Mayfair, chosen by Lukas in the hope that the intimate atmosphere would be conducive to conversation. To them starting to sort out their differences. But there had been precious little of that so far.

Polite on the surface, Calista seemed to be paying great attention to her meal. But her body language was stiff, bordering on hostile, as if she was poised, ready to strike back at anything he might say. He, in turn, was still wrestling with the internal struggle that had been plaguing him ever since he had arrived in London, so intent on achieving his aims.

Aims that now floated dead in the water.

The custody case would be dropped. He could never take Effie away from Calista. The idea was preposterous—it always had been. He had been fooling himself from the start. He had been so angry, so hell-bent on making Calista pay for the past, on making up for the years he had lost with his daughter that he had allowed a red mist to cloud his vision, bitterness and vitriol to twist his logic.

Seeing them together in the hospital had forcibly changed his mind. The fact that they were safe, unharmed, had brought such a massive rush of relief it had left him winded, unbalanced. How else could he explain what he'd done—kissing Calista like that, in front of everyone?

No, he could never separate them. Calista and Effie came as a package—a warm, loving, funny, devoted package. He didn't want to tear them apart. He wanted them both. With *him*. Permanently. The question was, just how did he achieve that?

Lukas looked down, fighting to try and order his thoughts. It was hellishly difficult. Seeing Calista again in the flesh, that beautiful porcelain-pale flesh so smooth and warm and incredibly inviting, messed with his head to the point where he thought it might explode. It messed with other parts of his body too.

Suggesting that she dress up this evening had not been such a clever idea. The short gold-coloured cocktail dress shimmered over her curves, catching the light as she turned. With a fitted bust, square neckline and wide shoulder straps it was not particularly revealing—more classy and sexy, a little bit quirky...just like Calista herself. She had swept her hair up into a loose bun at the nape of her neck, the stray curls of hair falling softly around her face giving her a Renaissance, ethereal look.

She looked enchanting, eminently tempting, but most of all *deadly*.

Because Calista was like a drug to him—dangerous and addictive. She made him act in ways that were totally out of character. Firstly his brutish behaviour on the day of her father's funeral—something that he now looked back on with shame—and, even worse than that, the way she was making him feel right now. Raw, hollow, vulnerable. Like no other woman ever had made him feel. Not even close. Hungry with something that wasn't just lust.

Lukas had always known that he craved Calista's body. After all, hadn't he spent years in his prison cell plotting how he would claim her, repeat the sexual experience they had shared, only this time on *his* terms? It had been one of his few pleasures in that echoing temple of misery— something to keep him sane.

Oh, he had dressed it up as revenge, or maybe some sort of sexual infatuation that he needed to get out of his system, but now he knew it was neither of those things. It wasn't just sexual possession he craved—he wanted all of her…body and soul. This wasn't an animal urge. This went deeper—much deeper. To a dark and unknown place where feelings lurked that he didn't want to acknowledge, where emotions that had lain dormant had suddenly started to shift, to rise up, become real. Sentiments that had no part in his life.

The word *love* floated unbidden into his mind, refusing to be batted away. Was it possible that he was in love with Calista? It was an idea so alien, so ridiculous, that he refused to give it countenance. Instead he turned it around to make it more palatable. He wanted Calista to love *him*—

that was what it was. The way she said she once had. *That* he could deal with.

He picked up his glass and took a swallow of red wine.

'Well, you have certainly made our daughter proud today.'

'Yes.' Calista allowed herself a small smile. 'But I hope seeing all that drama hasn't been too much for her—you know, gives her nightmares or something.' She glanced at the watch on her wrist. 'I probably shouldn't be too late back.'

'Effie will be just fine.' He spoke firmly, taking control. He wasn't going to let her slip away from him like that. 'First there are things we need to discuss.'

'Very well.' She sat back as the waiter cleared away their plates, folding her arms across her chest. 'Say whatever it is you have to say. But I warn you, Lukas, if it's about taking Effie away from me—'

'It's not.'

His words brought her up short and he saw the look of hope in her eyes as she raised her hand to her mouth in a gesture so charming, so beguiling, that it twisted something inside him. For all her bravado he could see she was afraid of what he might do to her. Once he would have gained satisfaction from that—now it just made him feel like a heel.

'I have decided not to file for custody of Effie.'

'You have?' Relief lit up her eyes and she leant forward to clasp his hand. But almost immediately doubt set in and she let go again, tightly linking her hands in front of her. 'What made you change your mind?'

'I have come up with a better solution.' He concentrated on making his voice even, as flat and smooth as a becalmed sea. 'You and Effie will come and live with me in Greece.'

Calista's shoulders sagged, her eyes clouding over for

a moment before her head went back and the fire returned with a vengeance. 'No, Lukas!'

'I think Athens would be the preferred location.'

Lukas continued as if she hadn't spoken. If he stopped to consider her insulting automatic refusal he feared his self-restraint, already tested to the limit, might well shatter completely.

'Though I am prepared to consider other areas, as long as they are not too far from Thalassa.'

'You are not listening to me. Effie and I are going nowhere. We are staying here—in the UK.'

'You may choose the property—more than one, if you so wish, as large and as grand as you like. We will find the very best school for Effie.'

Still he persevered, ignoring the roaring in his ears, his nails digging into his palms as he fought to control the frustration that was surging inside him. The overwhelming urge to sling her over his shoulder and carry her off to his cave there and then.

'I said no.'

'You will want for nothing.' He made one last almighty effort.

A current of electricity crackled between them, waiting to be touched, to do its harm.

'Nothing except my freedom.'

Calista reached for it, whispering the words under her breath.

For a long moment they stared at one another, bitterness and anger holding them both taut, silent. And something else—always that something else that neither of them could control, try as they might.

'I hardly think *you* are in a position to talk about loss of freedom.' The words trickled out insidiously, like a ribbon of poison.

'No. And you are never, *ever* going to let me forget it, are you?' Calista snatched up her napkin, balling it in her fist. 'That's what all this is really about, isn't it, Lukas? You are still trying to make me pay for the sins of my father by threatening to take Effie away from me.'

'Dammit, Calista!' His raised voice turned the heads of other diners and he took a moment, forcing himself to find some control. 'This is nothing to do with your wretched father. This is about Effie being a part of my life. *My life.*' He almost hissed the words at her. 'Not just yours—no matter how much you would like it to be that way. Can't you see? I'm *trying* to find a workable solution!'

'By insisting that we move to Greece?' Still she pushed. 'By putting me and Effie in a golden cage and throwing away the key?'

'Did I *say* it would be like that?'

'No?' She tossed back her head. 'Then tell me what it *would* be like.'

Lukas dragged in a breath, searching for the very last shreds of his patience. 'You would have your own life, your own friends. If you wanted to pursue your nursing career I wouldn't have a problem with that.'

'Oh, how very gracious of you.'

Lukas ground down hard on his jaw. She was really pushing him now.

Reaching forward, he covered her fidgeting hands with his own and fixed her with a merciless stare. 'If I were you, *agapi mou*, I would drop the attitude.'

'Or what?' She fired the shot back at him.

What, indeed? *Or I will make you pay.* The words remained unspoken in his head. Along with the image of how he would do it. With her naked beneath him, on top of him, in front of him. With her screaming his name in ecstasy, begging for more. He could have happily taken her right there and then—swept aside the silver cutlery, the fine china plates and crystal glasses and really given the other diners something to stare at. So strong were his feelings for her. Such was the power she had over him.

He let his eyes close for a second, reining in the crazy madness that was threatening to drag him under.

'Or you may regret it.'

It was a poor substitute for what he wanted to say, what he wanted to do, but as the waiter arrived with their next course he let go of her hands and sat back.

Minutes passed. Lukas began eating his steak. Calista nudged her sea bass with her fork.

'So, how would you see it working?' Her voice was quiet, brittle.

'Working?'

'Well…' She pushed her plate away from her. 'You say that I would have my own friends. Would that be *men* friends?'

Instantly every muscle in Lukas's body tightened, the veins in his neck throbbing with suppressed rage at the very thought.

'No, I thought as much.' Calista gave a hollow laugh of victory. 'Whereas *you*, presumably, would be free to see who you wanted, whenever you wanted. A pretty parade of women on your arm, in your bed.'

'And that would bother you?' He tried to cover his body's betrayal with a deliberately flippant reply.

Calista twitched. 'It wouldn't bother *me*.' She was lying through her pretty white teeth. 'But it would be very damaging for Effie.'

'And if I were to promise that there would be no women?'

'Don't make promises you can't keep, Lukas.'

'Oh, believe me, I don't.' He paused, choosing his words

with care. 'If we live together there will be no women in my bed.'

'Yeah, right.'

'Other than you, of course.'

'Me?' Pure shock flushed her cheeks.

'Yes—you, Calista. I have every confidence that you will be enough to satisfy my sexual needs.'

'Then your arrogance has taken over your senses.' Green eyes flashed back at him, twists of flame-coloured curls dancing around her heated face. 'Whatever makes you think that I would agree to share your bed?'

'Because I have seen the way you come apart in my arms, felt your nails clawing my back, heard your voice scream my name.' He was going to spare her no mercy. 'You can deny it all you want—do the whole ice maiden routine if it makes you feel better. But you and I both know the truth. You want me every bit as much as I want you. The attraction between us is mutual. And, more than that, it is beyond our control.'

'You flatter yourself. I can control it any time I like.'

'The way you did after your father's funeral? In my apartment in Athens? Even at the hospital today when I kissed you? If that is your definition of control I look forward to being there when you lose it.'

'You know what, Lukas?' Throwing down her napkin, Calista started to get up from the table. 'I'm leaving.'

'No, you are not.'

The booming power of his voice saw Calista glance around her, then sit down again. Picking up his glass, Lukas took a deep swallow of wine, taking a moment to steady himself.

'You can leave when you've heard what I have to say.'

'I've heard enough, thank you.'

'No, you haven't.' He looked down at his wine glass,

twisting the stem between his fingers, rotating it once, twice. 'Not so long ago you told me that you once loved me.'

'So?'

'That has led me to a surprising conclusion.' He raised his eyes, deliberately spearing her with their lethal intensity.

Calista stared back at him. Her brow was furrowed but there was a softness there, a tenderness that clutched at his chest.

'I put it to you, Calista Gianopoulous…' he swallowed firmly '…that you still do.'

CHAPTER THIRTEEN

CALISTA FELT HER face crumple, her cheeks burn with humiliation. Stupid woman that she was. *Stupid, stupid woman.* Instinctively she raised her hands to try and cover her mortified expression, but it was too late. He had seen it. She had caught his complacent look before she had shamefully lowered her eyes to the floor.

He knew.

She might has well have had the words pinned to her back on a piece of paper, the way children did in the school playground. *Calista loves Lukas. Spread it.*

She had spent so long trying to cover it up—from him, from herself, from the whole damned world—that now, when it came to the crunch, when she really should have had her defences shored up, Lukas had brought them crashing down with a simple, elegant theory. But worse than that—far worse…and she could hardly believe her own idiocy here…for one moment of pathetic lunacy she had thought he was going to tell her that *he* loved *her.*

She was obviously losing it. The balance of her mind was clearly disturbed. She was ill.

Reaching down, she felt for her bag. She really was leaving now, and nothing Lukas could say or do would stop her. Scraping back her chair, she pushed herself shakily to her feet and automatically Lukas did the same. She could feel his eyes all over her, spreading goosebumps across her skin as if he had reached out to stop her. But he didn't.

She started to move, weaving her way between the tables and past the *maître d'* at the entrance, convinced that at any moment she would feel Lukas's strong grasp on her arm, bringing her to a halt. But, no. Now she was through the main door and outside, racing up the steps and onto the pavement. She paused for a split second, unsure which way to go, listening to her heart thudding in her chest.

A soft rain was falling, dampening the London streets, picked out by the orange glow of the streetlights. Calista turned right, with no clear idea of where she was going other than that it had to be far away from Lukas. She had embarrassed herself enough for one evening. Now she wanted to hide away and lick her wounds. She walked at a brisk pace, dodging past other pedestrians: laughing groups of young people dressed in their glad rags, foreign tourists putting up their umbrellas, a few late-night shoppers.

Every now and then she glanced over her shoulder to see if Lukas was following her. Her relief was tinged with absurd disappointment when she realised he was not. She strode on through St James's Park, where people were walking their dogs, lovers strolling arm in arm, until she reached the Embankment, where finally she slowed to a stop, leaning against the wall and dragging in a painful breath.

The River Thames flowed lazily before her, lights dancing on the black water, illuminated pleasure boats gliding by, smaller craft going about their business. All totally oblivious to her misery.

Lukas watched her from his position against a tree, twenty or so yards away. She had been easy enough to follow,

her red hair bobbing up and down as she had marched
through the streets, that golden dress of hers shimmering beneath the streetlights before disappearing again
into the shadows.

No matter how dark it was, how much she tried to blend
in with the crowd, he could always have picked her out.
Even blindfolded, with a hood tied over his head. Because
Calista shone like a bright light for him. And like a moth
he was drawn to her, hypnotised by her. He was under
her spell…

Calista shivered, the fine rain settling on her bare skin,
running in rivulets between her breasts. She should hail
a taxi and go home.

For the first time it occurred to her that maybe that was
where Lukas had gone. Why would he chase through the
streets of London after her when he could simply park his
elegant self down on her shabby couch and wait for her to
return? Or maybe he had done neither of these things but
returned to the executive suite of his exclusive hotel to
gloat over his victory—the fact that he had won her heart.

'Calista?'

With a gasp of shock she spun around, straight into
the solid wall of Lukas's body. Strong arms encircled her,
pressing her against him. He felt so good. So right.

'You are soaking wet.' Moving them apart, Lukas
shrugged off his jacket and wrapped it around her shoulders, pulling the lapels together under her chin. Then, taking hold of her face, he gazed into her eyes.

'Why are you following me?' She made a weak attempt
to confront him, but in truth she was tired of fighting. So
very tired.

Lukas gave a short laugh. 'You didn't think I would
let you go, did you?' Releasing one hand, he smoothed it

over the damp curls of her hair, tucking the stray locks behind her ear. 'I will *never* let you go.' His voice was terrifyingly calm.

Calista stared back at him. Like a deadly promise his words permeated her skin and her bones, squeezing past her internal organs until they found her very core, where they pulsed low and hard and unforgiving.

'And I have no say in the matter?'

'None whatsoever.' He lowered his head, and his breath was a warm caress against her face before his lips brushed hers with a soft, feather-light touch. 'From now on you do as I say.'

'Oh, you think so, do you?' Calista whispered hoarsely.

'Yes, I do.' He pulled back a fraction. 'Firstly I want a proper answer to the question that saw you bolt from the restaurant.' Ebony-black eyes searched her face. '*Do* you love me, Calista?'

Calista waited a beat before finally giving in. 'Yes.'

One hushed word said it all.

'Then say it.' It seemed he was determined to torture her.

'I love you, Lukas.' There was no point in denying it now. She was already stripped bare. 'I wish I didn't, but I do.'

'Hmm…I'm liking the first part of that confession. The second part less so.' He traced his fingertip across her mouth as if to erase it.

'This isn't funny, Lukas.'

'I'm not laughing. In fact when it comes to you and me I have never been more serious about anything in my life.'

'There *is* no "you and me".'

'Oh, but there is.' His eyes shone black. 'I must admit I was afraid that there might never be. I knew I had the power to force you to share custody of Effie, to come and live with me in Greece or the UK or wherever. That didn't really matter. But the one thing I couldn't do was force you to love me.'

'You didn't need to force me.'

'I know that now. And I thank the gods that have intervened on my behalf to make this happen.'

'Lukas…'

'No, hear me out, Calista. There is nothing standing in our way now. We can be a couple—a *real* couple, in every sense of the word. In fact…' He paused, suddenly deadly serious. 'I want us to be man and wife.'

With a gasp Calista freed herself from him arms. 'You're asking me to *marry* you?'

'Is that so shocking?'

'Yes!' She wobbled on her feet as if she had stepped off the highest rung of a ladder. 'Shocking and impossible. It can *never* happen.'

'Why? You have admitted that you love me. We both love Effie. What is there to stop us?'

Calista looked down, unshed tears blocking her throat. 'To make a relationship work…a marriage work…both parties need to love each other.' Her voice was very small. 'Not just one.'

Lukas let his eyes travel slowly over her dejected but still defiant figure. Her head was bent, her torso swamped by the jacket that hung over her shoulders. Raindrops sparkled in her hair and as he reached for her, bringing her close and tipping her head, he could see the glitter of tears in her eyes.

And the shackles of his pride fell away.

Suddenly, miraculously, he was able to say what he thought—accept what he had always known. He was free to face up to the truth and express the one thing that mattered—the only thing that mattered. He was in love with

Calista. He had never said it before, even to himself, but it was a simple incontrovertible fact.

He sounded out the words in his head. *I love you, Calista.* They seemed surprisingly natural—as if they had always been there waiting to be spoken. But there was also a strange sense of loss. Because by giving his heart to Calista he was losing a part of himself. The bitter and resentful part...the hostile, vengeful part. It had been with him so long, knew him so well, that he had thought it made up the man he was.

But now he knew differently. Without even trying, without even knowing it, Calista had slain that vicious monster and set him free. Free to love her.

And yet she had no idea what she had done.

Taking her face in his hands, he turned it towards him and caught the pain in her eyes, the hurt. He wanted to take it away with a blistering kiss. He longed to show his love for her, right there and then, and not by using mere words. But that would have to come later. Right now words would have to do. If only he could find them.

'If love is the issue then there is no impediment to our marriage.'

Calista stared back at him, uncomprehending. Which wasn't surprising, considering he'd sounded like a jumped-up lawyer or a jerk—or both.

'What I'm trying to say is...' He rubbed the pads of his thumbs along her jaw. 'What I'm trying to tell you...'

'Yes?'

Oh, for God's sake, man.

'Calista.' He pulled in a breath. 'You are the most obstinate, infuriating, maddeningly wonderful woman that I have ever had the good fortune to come across.' Calista blinked back at him. 'And I love you with all my heart.'

There was a stunned silence.

'No.' Calista pulled away. 'You can't.'

'Yes, Calista, I do.'

'You're just saying that.' She cast about as if looking for an answer, her eyes following the inky-black river. 'This is just some plan you have come up with to try and trick me. Or you think it's what I want to hear. Or maybe it's some sort of aberration.'

'You mean I would have to be suffering some sort of mental illness to be in love with you?' The corner of his mouth quirked.

'Yes—no. I don't know.' Looking back at him, she frowned solemnly. 'Maybe...'

'Then I am indeed afflicted.'

He smiled at her now...an open, guileless smile that was rewarded with a small twitch of her lips. But that wasn't enough—he wanted much more. So he waited, his head on one side, his eyebrows raised, his eyes holding hers. And finally he was rewarded with a real smile, so dazzling, so heartfelt that it threatened to undo him completely.

He pulled her back into his arms, burying his face in her wet hair, inhaling her uniquely wonderful scent mixed with the dampness of a London night.

'I love you, Calista. Whether you believe it or not. Whether you want me to or not. If that makes me crazy in the head...' he pulled back to look into her face again '... Then I'm guilty as charged.'

'Oh, Lukas!'

'And I want to marry you more than anything in the world.' Dropping down onto one knee, Lukas took hold of her hands and clasped them to his chest. 'Calista Gianopoulous, would you do me the greatest honour of becoming my wife?'

Calista looked down at him, her eyes shining with love and tears and with what Lukas desperately hoped was the most important 'yes' of his life. From somewhere behind them Big Ben began pealing the hour. He counted three, four, five agonising chimes before Calista finally spoke.

'Yes, Lukas Kalanos.' Her voice cracked and tears started to run down her cheeks. Hysteria was not far away. 'My answer is yes. I *will* marry you!'

Relief and elation and pure, fathomless love sprang Lukas to his feet and he held out his arms for Calista to fall into, wrapping her in a crushing embrace.

Big Ben's final toll rang out unheard. Because as their eyes closed and their lips met for this most precious, tender kiss time for Calista and Lukas stood perfectly still.

'Does this look okay?' Calista stood before Lukas wearing one of his pristine shirts over the gold cocktail dress, artfully tied around her waist, sleeves rolled up. 'I don't want to go back looking like a dirty stop-out.'

'But that's exactly what you are, *agape*.' Lukas pulled her towards him, linking his arms around her waist. 'And a very sexy one at that.'

Pressed so closely against him, Calista felt the stirrings of his arousal.

'How about we ring Magda and say we will be another hour or so?'

'No!' With a laugh she pushed him away.

Having spent the night at Lukas's hotel, they had only just managed to get themselves up and showered and dressed—all of those things repeatedly interrupted by more carnal matters. And this after a night of such passion, such intense emotional and physical joy, that it didn't seem possible that they could still crave more of one another. But of course they did. And always would.

'We can't impose on Magda any more.' She gave him

a quick kiss. 'And, besides, Effie will be waiting for us. I can't wait to tell her we're getting married!'

'You think she will be pleased?'

'Pleased? She'll be *ecstatic*! She adores you, Lukas, surely you know that? Just like her mother does.' Her eyes shone with love. 'Plus, of course, she'll get to be bridesmaid.'

'Whatever did I do to deserve you two?' Suddenly serious, Lukas pulled back to look into her eyes. 'I've been such a fool, Calista—such an idiot, trying to control you rather than letting myself love you, mistaking the intensity of my feelings for anger and revenge when all the time I was just madly in love with you.'

'You had every right to be filled with fury after what my father did to you. What *I* did.'

'No, not you, Calista. You were completely blameless. I concocted that story because I couldn't believe you'd come to me that night simply because you wanted me.'

'Not just wanted you, Lukas—*loved* you. Even then. But I couldn't tell you. I let my pride get in the way of admitting the truth.'

'I love your pride. And your smile and your scowl and your temper and your big heart. Especially your big heart.' He gave her a lopsided smile. 'Even when it means I end up having to reinstate members of my own staff.'

Calista grinned. 'Thanks for agreeing to do that. I'm sure Nico and Tavi have learnt their lesson, and you said yourself they're good workers. It was just a bit of silly chest-beating, you know that.'

'I do now.'

For a second they gazed at one another in silence. Then Calista bit down on her lip.

'Come on—spill.' Lukas searched her face. 'What's troubling you now?'

'I was just thinking about my father.'

'Ah.' The hollow sound rang with bitterness. 'I'd rather not think about him.'

'But we have to.' Calista felt the familiar feeling of torture start to seep into her happiness. 'I'm assuming you still intend to expose what he did?'

Lukas shook his head and, reaching for her hands, held them against his chest. 'No, not now. Not knowing how it would impact on you.'

He moved over to the table and pulled a sheaf of papers from the document case Calista remembered he had been holding when he had arrived at the hospital.

'Here. These are for you.'

'What are they?' Nervously she reached to take them from his outstretched hand.

'Evidence of Aristotle's involvement in the arms-smuggling. How he wrongly implicated my father and me. It's all in there.'

'Oh, God…' Calista's free hand flew to cover her mouth. 'I'm so sorry, Lukas.'

'No more apologies, Calista. Please. Let's put the past behind us. I don't care about any of it any more. You can chuck it on the fire, shred it—do whatever you want with it. The future is all that matters now. You, me and Effie. The most wonderful future I could ever wish for.'

Calista looked down at the hateful papers in her hand. There was nothing she would like to do more than destroy them. But she knew with depressing certainty that she couldn't. Destroying evidence didn't destroy the past. Her father's evil deeds couldn't be eradicated. And the damage he had inflicted along the way to Stavros and to Lukas…

No, she couldn't keep the burden of that secret. She wouldn't be able to live with herself.

'I'm going to take these to the police.' She held up the papers with a shaky hand.

Lukas stared at her in alarm. 'No, Calista, you don't have to.'

'Yes—yes, I do.'

'Please think very carefully before you do anything rash. The fall-out could be pretty nasty.'

'I know that. But you and your father have taken the blame for Aristotle's crimes for far too long. It's time the truth came out.'

'And you're sure about this?'

'Yes, quite sure. My loyalties are to *you* now—you and Stavros, the Kalanos family. Very soon I will bear the Kalanos name, and Effie too, once the paperwork is sorted. I will no longer be a Gianopoulous and neither will she. Maybe when the truth is out I will be able to move on, put my traitorous bloodline behind me. Free myself of the ties of my father.'

'Calista Kalanos. I can't tell you how good that sounds.'

'Mmm…for me too.'

They kissed again.

'You are extraordinarily brave, Calista—you know that, don't you?'

'Not brave. Just doing what has to be done.'

'Then I will be right there beside you to support you. No one will lay any blame at *your* door. I will make sure of that. If they try they will have me to answer to.'

'You and me against the world, eh?'

'No, not against it. Owning it—making it ours. You and Effie are my world. All I could ever want and all I could ever ask for. Except maybe…'

'Yes, go on—what?'

'Maybe a little brother or sister for Effie. Or both. Or a couple of each… In fact maybe we should start now.'

Laughing, Calista pushed herself back from his embrace to gaze into his midnight eyes. 'I love you, Lukas. So, *so* much.'

'I love you too, Calista, more than words can say. And I can't wait to spend the rest of my life with you.'

'Me too, Lukas,' Calista whispered softly against his lips. 'Me too.'

* * * * *

LET'S TALK
Romance

For exclusive extracts, competitions
and special offers, find us online:

f facebook.com/millsandboon

🐦 @MillsandBoon

📷 @MillsandBoonUK

Get in touch on 01413 063232

For all the latest titles coming soon, visit
millsandboon.co.uk/nextmonth

MILLS & BOON

THE HEART OF ROMANCE

A ROMANCE FOR EVERY KIND OF READER

MODERN

Prepare to be swept off your feet by sophisticated, sexy and seductive heroes, in some of the world's most glamourous and romantic locations, where power and passion collide.
8 stories per month.

HISTORICAL

Escape with historical heroes from time gone by. Whether your passion is for wicked Regency Rakes, muscled Vikings or rugged Highlanders, awaken the romance of the past.
6 stories per month.

MEDICAL

Set your pulse racing with dedicated, delectable doctors in the high-pressure world of medicine, where emotions run high and passion, comfort and love are the best medicine.
6 stories per month.

True Love

Celebrate true love with tender stories of heartfelt romance, from the rush of falling in love to the joy a new baby can bring, and a focus on the emotional heart of a relationship.
8 stories per month.

Desire

Indulge in secrets and scandal, intense drama and plenty of sizzling hot action with powerful and passionate heroes who have it all: wealth, status, good looks…everything but the right woman.
6 stories per month.

HEROES

Experience all the excitement of a gripping thriller, with an intense romance at its heart. Resourceful, true-to-life women and strong, fearless men face danger and desire - a killer combination!
8 stories per month.

DARE

Sensual love stories featuring smart, sassy heroines you'd want as a best friend, and compelling intense heroes who are worthy of them.
4 stories per month.

To see which titles are coming soon, please visit

millsandboon.co.uk/nextmonth

JOIN US ON SOCIAL MEDIA!

Stay up to date with our latest releases, author news and gossip, special offers and discounts, and all the behind-the-scenes action from Mills & Boon...

 millsandboon

 millsandboonuk

 millsandboon

t might just be true love...